Stanley Brambles and the Lost City

Stanley Brambles and the Lost City

Owen Spendlove

STANLEY BRAMBLES AND THE LOST CITY

iUniverse books may be ordered through booksellers or by contacting:

iUniverse
1663 Liberty Drive
Bloomington, IN 47403
www.iuniverse.com
1-800-Authors (1-800-288-4677)

ISBN: 978-1-4917-7866-1 (sc)
ISBN: 978-1-4917-7865-4 (e)

Library of Congress Control Number: 2015917293

Print information available on the last page.

iUniverse rev. date: 11/04/2015

PROLOGUE

DREAMING

The boy tosses and turns in his sleep. His eyelids flutter as the eyes behind them move rapidly. He murmurs something incoherent, then makes a mournful moaning sound.

The boy is dreaming.

Suddenly, he stops moving. He rolls over onto his back, and his eyes snap open. He stares up into the darkness of his bedroom, at the faint light creeping in through his curtained window. Dawn is coming.

But the boy does not see the dim light of the approaching dawn. His eyes are glazed. He is not awake.

He is still dreaming.

But now he is in a new dream. He lies there for a time, very still, staring up at the ceiling with unseeing eyes … and then he starts to tremble.

He trembles only slightly at first, but soon his bed starts to shake.

He is trembling with fear.

His breath comes in short gasps, and his face is contorted, as if he is being forced to look at something loathsome. His breath quickens further, the expression on his face intensifying into one of unmistakable terror. He opens his mouth as if to scream …

And then, with a loud gasp, he awakens. His eyes come into focus, and he blinks repeatedly. He is still shivering violently, but it quickly passes, and his breathing slows. He glances about, as if to assure himself that he is still safe in bed. He can hear the birds outside starting to sing, starting their day while he and his family are still in bed. He sighs and closes his eyes, returning to sleep for a few more hours.

When he wakes up soon after eight o'clock, he will not remember his horrid nightmare. He will remember his other dreams—one, in particular about a great blue crystal rising out of a vast jungle—but he will not remember this one.

He will not remember the colossal darkness that surrounded him. He will not remember the small sphere of light in his hand, the one that kept getting dimmer and dimmer … he will not remember the horrifying impression of something vast and infinitely dark crouched just beyond the light of the small sphere, or the great, gleaming red eyes which peered at him from out of that shapeless darkness. He will not remember the hellish voice that spoke to him, nor the words themselves, spoken in some strange, alien tongue:

Rhu hond ine eom zhun …

Nor will he remember that he has had this same nightmare before—almost every night for the past few months, and always in the quiet time just before dawn.

Which, I suppose, is just as well.

Let's let him sleep now, though. Growing boys need plenty of rest, and there are still a few hours before he has to get up.

CHAPTER 1

THE FIRST DAY OF SCHOOL

The red numbers on the digital clock radio proclaimed the time to be 8:14 A.M. Dark blue curtains covered the smallish window, preventing all but the most stubborn and clever rays of sunlight from sneaking into the room. In the twin bed beneath the window and to the left lay Stanley Brambles, fast asleep.

For another 30 seconds, that is.

30 … 20 … 10 …

5 … 4 … 3 … 2 … 1 …

"WHOOOOOAAAHHHHYEEEAAAAAAGHHH!"

Stanley sat bolt upright in bed as his alarm clock radio turned on, obliterating the peaceful quiet of the morning with the last few bars of an extra loud rock & roll anthem.

"AND THAT WAS *THE AZTECS* WITH THEIR LATEST HIT SINGLE, '*WARLORD LOVER*'! I'M STYLIN' STEVE SMITH, AND YOU'RE LISTENING TO ONE-OH-ONE-POINT-SIX, *THE STOAT,* EAST STODGERTON'S NUMBER ONE ROCK ALTERNATIVE. NOW, ON WITH THE ROCK COUNTDOWN!"

Before 'Stylin' Steve Smith' could bombard him with any more loud music, Stanley switched off his radio and flung the curtains wide. The morning sun came pouring in, and he sat on his bed for a moment, rubbing his eyes tiredly. He glanced up at the calendar on the wall, and groaned when he realized what day it was:

It was the first day of school. The summer holidays were officially over.

"That explains why I set my alarm," Stanley said to himself, hunching forward and leaning on the windowsill. It also seemed to explain why he felt so gloomy as he looked out at Bubbletree Lane, the most boring street in the most boring neighbourhood of the most boring town in the whole entire world. No, the first day of school is never easy, and can come as a rather miserable (if not unexpected) shock after a long summer of fun and leisure.

Stanley didn't hate school, but he didn't love it, either. A car drove by, past the corner of Bubbletree Lane, heading up Butter Street. The car was towing a huge motorboat, and Stanley was reminded of the Ogopogo, his great uncle Jack's sturdy little ship. It seemed like an age had passed since he'd set off on a fantastic (and somewhat dangerous) voyage aboard that ship, with Uncle Jack, Benjamin Stone, Pericles the parrot, and his best friends in the world, Alabaster and Nell. In reality, it had only been a couple of months. Stanley sighed. Going back to school was going to be a horrendous bore compared to an adventure on the high seas. He supposed a voyage like that was what some would call a *'once in a lifetime experience'*.

There came a knock at the door.

"Stanley, dear," said Mrs. Brambles from the other side, "are you up?"

"Yes, Mom," said Stanley, turning away from the window.

"Well, don't dawdle," said Mrs. Brambles, "you don't want to be late."

"No, that'd be *awful*," Stanley muttered to himself.

"Oh, and don't forget," said Mrs. Brambles, now opening the door a crack, "you should wear that nice new shirt I bought you."

"Mo-om!" said Stanley, "You're not supposed to just open the door! I could've been naked in here!"

"Stanley dear, you were *born* naked," said Mrs. Brambles, sounding both annoyed and amused. She closed the door, just the same, though.

Stanley rolled his eyes. It seemed that over the past little while, his parents had suddenly made it their personal mission to annoy and embarrass him every chance they got. His mother was always fussing about his appearance, even in public! She would always try to fix his hair, or wipe a spot of dirt off his face after licking her thumb. These had both happened at least thrice, at the mall, while people he knew from school were around.

His father was just as bad, always making loud, ridiculous jokes for no reason, or pointing out funny-looking people on the street.

Many times, Stanley had wondered if it was possible to die from embarrassment.

Shaking his head, he opened the second drawer of his dresser and drew out the shirt his mother had suggested he wear. It was a light blue button-up with long sleeves and a collar, and if that weren't bad enough, the collar had a stupid little extra button on the back of it. Stanley had recently begun to hate wearing button-up shirts. If you asked him why, he probably wouldn't be able to give you a straight answer, aside from, 'they look stupid.' The fact that his mother had picked it out for him, probably had something to do with it, though.

Stanley sighed and tossed the shirt onto his bed, shifting his gaze to the small oval mirror on the wall above his dresser. Not so long ago, he would have had to stand on tiptoe to be able to face himself full-on in this mirror, but now he could stand flat-footed and see his entire visage reflected therein. He had definitely grown during the summer. The face that gazed back at him from the depths of the glass was thin but pleasant, with features that, someday, would probably be called 'strong' and 'chiseled', but were, for the moment, becoming perhaps a tad awkward as Stanley began to morph into a teenager. For his part, Stanley thought he looked a bit goofy, with a big nose and long chin, but more than a few of the girls at his school would have strongly disagreed.

Just before he closed the drawer, he noticed a small, square wooden box in the corner, half-hidden under a shirt. He took the box out and smiled to himself as he opened it. Inside was the small blue moonstone that Uncle Jack had given him earlier on in the summer. It was about the size of a golf ball, and glowed softly with its own light.

As he gazed at the moonstone, something flashed into his mind ... something from a dream he'd had recently ...

An image of a towering blue crystal rising out of a vast jungle ... yes, that was what he had dreamed about last night. Had he dreamed about it before?

His thoughts were interrupted as his mother knocked again on his door.

"Stanley, it's almost 8:30."

"I know, I know," said Stanley, putting the moonstone away. He finished getting dressed, grabbed his backpack, and went downstairs. In the kitchen, he was surprised to see his father seated at the table, reading the newspaper and finishing off what appeared to be a nice, leisurely breakfast.

"Morning, Stanley," said Mr. Brambles brightly, as Stanley joined him at the table.

"Morning, Dad," said Stanley, helping himself to some Rice Krispies, "Uh … you're up early."

"Quite so!" said Mr. Brambles, taking a relaxed sip of orange juice. "I've been up since eight! I'm turning over a new leaf. No more rushing around in the morning. From now on, I'm getting up at eight o'clock, on the dot."

"Great," said Stanley.

Mr. Brambles finished his bran muffin, took another sip of orange juice, and consulted his watch. "Well, I suppose I'd better be getting ready to go. All I have to do now is go upstairs and brush my teeth!" He drained the last of his juice, and, looking thoroughly pleased with himself, left the room.

Ten minutes later, Stanley had finished his own breakfast, and was just about to get ready to leave, himself, when Mrs. Brambles appeared at the front door, looking and sounding annoyed.

"Stanley dear," she said, "are you going upstairs?"

"Yup," said Stanley.

"In that case, could you please go and find out what your father is up to? We're already running late."

"Sure, Mom," said Stanley. He went upstairs, and had just peeked into the bathroom, when he heard a loud snort coming from his parents' room. Looking in, he couldn't help but laugh out loud. Sprawled on the bed in his best suit and tie, was Mr. Brambles. He was fast asleep and snoring loudly, with a small trickle of drool issuing from his mouth.

"Robert?" came Mrs. Brambles' voice from downstairs, "Stanley? What's going on up there? What's your father doing?"

"He's asleep, Mom," said Stanley, before he could stop himself.

"Asleep?" said Mrs. Brambles, sounding shocked. She then repeated, "*Asleep?*" in a much more savage tone, before storming up the stairs and into the bedroom, where she roared, "ROBERT! WE!

ARE! LATE!" at the top of her lungs. A loud *thump* suggested that she had tipped Mr. Brambles out of the bed.

"Um? What?" came Mr. Brambles' bewildered voice.

"*You impossible man!*" shrieked Mrs. Brambles, "*I left you eating breakfast in the kitchen, and fifteen minutes later I find you back in bed, drooling all over your best suit!*"

"Oh!" said Mr. Brambles, "I must have fallen asleep!"

"OUT!" roared Mrs. Brambles, "GET OUT! MOVE! NO, YOU DON'T HAVE TIME TO CHANGE! MOVE!"

Stanley stood back as Mrs. Brambles stormed out, carrying a protesting Mr. Brambles under her arm.

Seconds later, the front door slammed shut. Stanley went to the bedroom window and looked out to see Mrs. Brambles stuff Mr. Brambles unceremoniously into the family car. Mrs. Brambles then leapt into the driver's seat, and the engine roared to life. Stanley watched as the car sped off down the street and turned the corner on two wheels.

"Just another morning on Bubbletree Lane," Stanley said to Bruno, the family dog, who was looking sulky at having been woken up.

Minutes later, Stanley was out the door and down the street, waiting for his best friend, Alabaster Lancaster.

"Hey Stanley," said Alabaster, as he came sauntering up soon after. Like Stanley, pale, dark-haired Alabaster had grown during the summer; always long and lanky, he now looked even more so, making his hunched gait seem even more ludicrous, his long arms swinging like a pair of five-fingered pendulums. "All ready for the first day of school?"

"As ready as I *can* be, I guess," said Stanley. "You?"

"Rrready and rrrarin'," said Alabaster, as they started to walk down Butter Street. "It's always sort of exciting, the first day back! There's a whole school year ahead of us! Who knows *what'll* happen?"

Stanley assumed that what Alabaster really meant was, *who know what kind of shenanigans we'll get up to?*

To be fair, Alabaster wasn't the sort to go looking for trouble, but he *was* the sort to go walking blindly into it.

"Plus, we'll finally get to see Nell again!" Alabaster added brightly.

Stanley felt his insides jump a bit. Nell, the only girl Stanley had ever been friends with, was supposed to have moved to East

Stodgerton towards the end of the summer. Stanley and Alabaster, however, hadn't seen her since the end of June. She had written Stanley three letters, all of which were safely stowed in his drawer at home. Getting a letter from someone and seeing them face to face, however, are two completely different things.

Before they knew it, the boys were standing before the doors of Babblebrook Public School. It was to be a momentous year—they were going into grade eight, which meant that next year, they were off to high school. Alabaster sniffed loudly.

"I just … just can't believe this is our … our last y-year at dear, dear Babblebrook!" he said loudly, pretending to be overcome with emotion.

Stanley laughed, as did a few girls who were standing by the door, talking. Alabaster looked surprised at having someone besides Stanley laugh at his jokes, and did an unintentionally funny double-take. The girls laughed again, and one of them said,

"Hi, Alabaster!"

Alabaster stared for as second, then said, "Uh, h-hi, Debbie," after being elbowed by Stanley. Debbie smiled and the whole group of girls started giggling and chattering. Stanley and Alabaster went inside, Alabaster looking more than a little confused.

The front hall was swarming with students. The class lists were posted on the wall by the office, and everyone was jostling and nudging everyone else, trying to get close enough to see who would be teaching them this year. Alabaster slithered into the crowd, looking for the 'L' list, while Stanley sidled over to where the 'B's were gathered. Stanley wasn't particularly tall for his age (his mother kept saying that he just hadn't had his growth spurt yet), but as he was now a grade eight, he was one of the bigger kids in the crowd. Several smaller children looked up at him nervously as he made his way forward. They got out of his way as he drew near, but he smiled kindly at them and waved them ahead, saying,

"That's okay, you guys were here first."

Suddenly, something like a big, flabby ham collided with Stanley's shoulder, and he stumbled sideways into a cluster of grade five boys.

"Outta the way, dorks," said a deep, ape-ish voice, as a big, tall, heavy-set boy shouldered and shoved his way through the crowd. The small children whom Stanley had let go ahead of him were pushed aside as well by the boy, as he went to check the list.

"Hey!" said Stanley, as the grade five boys helped him up. The large boy turned around. He had a pudgy, pig-like face and short, dark hair. His beady little eyes were barely visible beneath his thick, shaggy eyebrows. He didn't look happy as he said,

"Who said that?"

The crowd parted immediately, leaving Stanley in plain view.

"It was him!" said one of the grade five boys, pointing at Stanley.

Stanley shot the boy an incredulous look, then turned back towards the big, dark-haired oaf, who was pushing his way back through the crowd towards him.

"So that was you?" he said, towering over Stanley.

"Yeah," Stanley said bravely, looking up into those beady, piggish eyes. He could see that this guy was going to be trouble, but he had certainly seen things much more frightening than him.

"You got some kinda problem?" said the boy, shoving Stanley roughly in the shoulder.

"Hey, stop it!" Stanley shouted, after stumbling backwards. He was getting angry, and he shoved back. The bully was almost a head taller than Stanley, and much heavier, so it was a surprise to everyone (Stanley included) when the oaf was sent sprawling backwards. He sat there on the ground for a moment, looking as surprised as Stanley.

Stanley, himself, was suddenly feeling lightheaded. He blinked a few times, and then noticed that the fat boy had picked himself up and was stalking towards him, looking furious. He raised a clenched fist, clearly meaning to punch Stanley then and there. The boy leaned in, and Stanley raised his hands defensively.

Before Stanley knew what was happening, the bully had backed off, holding a hand over his nose. It seems that in raising his hands so suddenly, Stanley had accidentally hit his foe in the nose. The boy took his hand away from his face. A tiny trickle of blood could be seen just below his left nostril, and he regarded the minute red drops on his hand with a furious look in his beady eyes.

"You're dead now, nerd," he growled. He came at Stanley again, but someone suddenly cried,

"*Nooooo!*"

And the next thing he knew, the fat boy had been set upon by tall, lanky Alabaster, who had leaped out of the crowd like a jaguar, and was trying futilely to drag him to the ground. Just then, a loud voice rang out through the hall.

"*Stop that at once!*"

Everyone obeyed. A tall bald man with hollow cheeks and pale skin had appeared in the crowd. Silence descended on the hall as combatants and audience alike recognized Mr. Grimm, the school principal.

"Everyone to your classes. *Now!*" he commanded sternly. There was much scuttling as the crowd dissipated.

"Not you three," he said, rounding on Stanley, Alabaster and the bully. "I've spoken with *you* before, Daniel," he said, nodding to the fat boy, "but I don't believe I've met you two. May I have your names, please?" He looked squarely at Alabaster.

"Uh, Alacaster Langbaster," said Alabaster, who was clearly nervous. "Uh, I mean—"

"Ahh, so *you're* Alabaster Lancaster," said Mr. Grimm. "It is good to finally have a face to go along with the reputation." Before Alabaster could say anything else, Mr. Grimm turned to Stanley. "And you are?"

"Stanley Brambles," said Stanley quickly, adding a "sir" for good measure.

Mr. Grimm simply nodded at him. "Gentlemen," he said, addressing the three of them, "I will be blunt. Fighting is not permitted on school grounds. You should all three be suspended from school without delay, but as it is the first day of school and I am in a forgiving mood, I will reduce your sentences to a mere detention. Today. After school. I am also under the assumption that this will never happen again."

"He started it," said Daniel, pointing at Stanley.

"I did not!" said Stanley.

"Yeah, he did not!" said Alabaster.

"Enough," said Mr. Grimm, not loudly, but in a slicing tone that made the boys shut up instantly. "I do not *care* who started it. I did not *see* who started it. What I care about, is that it ends, *now*. Do I make myself clear? I will now escort the three of you to your class. You are all in room 137, I believe." He motioned for the three boys to follow him, and led them down one hallway and up another.

"Ah, here we are."

Alabaster and Daniel went in.

"Mr. Brambles," said Mr. Grimm, "A moment, if you please."

Stanley waited.

"There is no doubt in my mind," said Mr. Grimm, "that Daniel was the instigator of that confrontation. Please understand, though, that if I had punished him and let you go free, things would have been the worse for you."

Stanley thought that one over for a moment. "I think I understand, sir," he said at last.

"Good," said Mr. Grimm. "Well then, your class awaits. When next we meet, may it be under happier circumstances."

Stanley nodded, and went into his classroom. He stopped short, though, because he had apparently walked into the wrong room. Seated behind the teacher's desk was the one person who could have made this day worse than it already was:

Mrs. Drabdale.

"Well well," she said, looking up from the attendance sheet and grinning like a hyena, "If it isn't Stanley Brambles. So nice of you to grace us with your presence, Stanley."

"Whoops!" said Stanley, doing a quick about-turn and heading for the door.

"*And where do you think you're going?*" roared Mrs. Drabdale, getting up from her desk.

"My, uh, class," said Stanley, turning to face her. "I'm in the wrong room ..." But he knew he wasn't. There was Alabaster, sitting in the front row, looking horrified.

"*Save yourself, Stanley!*" he cried. Several people laughed, but Mrs. Drabdale did not.

"Silence, Lancaster!" she spat, without even looking at him. "No, Stanley," she said, advancing on Stanley like some predatory cat, "you're in the right room. Your seat is right up there beside your cheeky sidekick!" She pointed at an empty desk beside Alabaster's.

"N-no!" said Stanley, backing towards the door. This had to be some kind of trick, a sick joke ... or maybe a nightmare. "You can't be teaching us this year! You taught grade *seven* last year!"

"And grade six before that!" wailed Alabaster. A few more people laughed.

Mrs. Drabdale bared her teeth at him. "One more word out of you, Lancaster, and you'll have detentions for a month!"

Silently, Alabaster screwed up his face in an expression of agonized horror, and clapped his hands to his cheeks in an admirable impersonation of Edvard Munch's *The Scream*, then crumpled into a ball and flopped out of his chair onto the floor.

Debbie Greene, the girl who had said *hi* to Alabaster outside, giggled loudly. Her friend, Bonnie Wart, who was one of Mrs. Drabdale's *'helpers'* (or, if you prefer, *teacher's pets*), hit Debbie on the arm as if to tell her to stop being such an idiot.

Mrs. Drabdale glared down at Alabaster, then rolled her eyes and shook her head, muttering something about retirement as she lumbered back to her desk. "Take a seat, Stanley," she growled.

Stanley shuffled over to his own desk and sat down. He was stunned. He couldn't believe what was happening. He'd gotten into a fight, earned himself a detention, and now it turned out that he had to endure Mrs. Drabdale for yet another year!

"And all on the first day of school," he muttered to himself.

"Silence!" barked Mrs. Drabdale. "As I was saying before we were so rudely interrupted …" she glared at Stanley. "I would like to welcome each and every one of you to another year at Babblebrook Public School."

A hand shot up.

"Yes, Bonnie?" said Mrs. Drabdale.

Stanley *hmphed*. If *he* had raised his hand just then, Mrs. Drabdale probably would have bitten it off.

"Mrs. Drabdale," said Bonnie Wart in a sickeningly sweet voice, "On behalf of everyone here, I would just like to say what a *pleasure* it is to be in your class once again."

Mrs. Drabdale's 'helpers' all clapped, even Debbie Greene, though not nearly as enthusiastically as the others.

"Thank you, Bonnie, and thank you all," said Mrs. Drabdale, as though the whole class had broken into applause. "Moving on," she said, glancing at the attendance sheet, "I see many familiar names here on my list, but I'm afraid there's one I've never seen before. Is there a Prunella Hawthorne present?"

Stanley exchanged a quick glance with Alabaster, then joined everyone else in looking around for the owner of the 'new' name.

A hand slowly rose into the air.

"Here," said a voice from the back of the classroom. Stanley recognized the voice immediately. It certainly was good to hear it again.

Stanley's deep blue eyes finally met a pair of vividly green ones several rows over, near the back of the room. The eyes widened and their owner smiled brightly upon meeting Stanley's gaze, scrunching up some of the freckles that lightly dusted the tops of her cheeks and nose.

"Ah, there you are," said Mrs. Drabdale, using her most simpering tone. "Why don't you come up front and introduce yourself? Don't be shy, dear."

Mrs. Drabdale always went through this routine whenever someone new joined her class. She did it to decide if she wanted the new person as a 'helper' or not.

Nell looked reluctant as she got up and made her way to the front of the class. She turned and faced everyone, then waved at Stanley and Alabaster. Stanley waved back, but didn't look to see if Alabaster did.

"Oh, that's enough of that," said Mrs. Drabdale, doing her best to sound as if she wasn't bothered by the fact that this potential 'helper' was friends with Stanley Brambles and Alabaster Lancaster. Nell looked at Mrs. Drabdale, who said,

"Why don't you tell us a bit about yourself, Prunella?"

"Er, okay," said Nell, "Um … well, I prefer to be called Nell—"

"Nonsense!" said Mrs. Drabdale, smiling ghoulishly, "Prunella is a lovely name!"

Nell ignored this. "I like reading, and drawing … I like carpentry, and mechanics, and I'm into martial arts …"

"Whoa!" said one of the boys in the back row.

"Oh," said Mrs. Drabdale, her smile faltering. "Well, er, those are some, er … interesting hobbies …"

"Thank you," said Nell.

"Show us some moves!" someone called.

Mrs. Drabdale looked more than a little disappointed. "Well, ah, thank you, Prunella, that was most … er, informative."

Nell said, "You're welcome," and returned to her seat.

Stanley noticed that some of the boys were staring at her. What was with them? Had they never seen a girl who liked carpentry and mechanics and martial arts before?

Alabaster leaned towards him. "I didn't know she did martial arts!"

"Me neither," Stanley whispered back. He glanced back at Nell, who caught his eye, and gave him another little wave. He smiled and waved back. She looked a bit different than she had earlier on in the summer. She was certainly a bit taller, and her chestnut hair was shorter, and tied back in a ponytail, instead of the elaborate plait she'd sported before. Stanley noticed Daniel Briggs looking at her approvingly.

"What're *you* looking at, you ugly baboon?" he muttered under his breath.

"*What was that?*" snapped Mrs. Drabdale.

"Nothing," said Stanley.

"Good," said Mrs. Drabdale. "Now then, open your textbooks to page one hundred and two …"

★ ★ ★

Stanley and Alabaster wanted to talk to Nell at lunch, but she seemed to have vanished without a trace. It wasn't until after the three o'clock dismissal bell that they were able to meet up with her, and even then they couldn't talk long because they had to go up to room 302 for their detention with Mr. Grimm. Nell looked disappointed.

"Oh, I was hoping I could walk home with you guys," she said, once Stanley had explained himself.

"Frightfully sorry about that," said Alabaster, putting on his best cockney accent.

"Well, I'm going to be at my dad's garage for a while," said Nell. "Why don't you stop by there when you're done? It's just on the corner of Butter Street and Faultline Road."

"Sure," said Stanley, to which Nell smiled and said,

"Great, see you there—it's called *Hawthorne's Auto Repair*, of course."

And then she was gone, and Stanley and Alabaster were left to trudge upstairs to their destiny.

★ ★ ★

At long last, the school day was over for Stanley and Alabaster. Stanley couldn't remember a worse first day of school, not even back in kindergarten, when he'd thrown up all over the teacher.

The two boys made their way down Butter Street, discussing the day's events, as well as the sure-to-be-arduous year ahead of them. Soon they arrived at a long, low building made of yellow-painted brick. A big sign above the door read:

HAWTHORNE'S AUTO REPAIR

There were four gleaming white garage doors along the front of the building, one of which was open.

"Should we just go in?" said Stanley.

"Sure," said Alabaster, "the door's open."

They went through the door and found themselves in a large repair bay. The bay was long and rectangular, with pieces of machinery and car parts lying all over the place. There were two huge hydraulic hoists, neither of which was being used at the moment, and two mechanics were at work on two separate cars. One of the mechanics looked to be somewhere around Stanley's age, but the other was a great hulk of a man with a mostly-bald head and a big, bushy brown beard. He looked up from his work, and, noticing Stanley and Alabaster, he shouted,

"*Hey, what're you doin' in here?*"

Stanley and Alabaster both jumped at the man's loud voice. "Uh, we're supposed to meet Nell here," said Stanley.

"'Zat so?" said the man, tromping towards them and eyeing them suspiciously.

"Um … yes," said Stanley, after a moment of awkward silence.

"And just *what* are your intentions with my daughter?"

"Wh-what?" Stanley stammered.

"What are your intentions with my daughter?" the man repeated. "What, d'you want to *marry* her? Hm? *Date* her? *Hmm?* Tell me why I should let you court my daughter, little man!"

"Uh!" said Stanley, feeling his face burning, "I, uh, don't … I don't actually want to—"

"*Don't want to?*" boomed the man, "So she's not *good* enough for you, is that it?"

Stanley was staring wide-eyed at the big, rude man, not knowing what to say, not knowing what in the world Nell had gotten him into.

Suddenly, a familiar voice cried, "*Daddy*!" and the other mechanic came running over. Stanley was surprised and relieved to discover that the other mechanic was actually Nell, though she looked different in a set of grimy coveralls, and with her hair tucked up under a ball cap.

"Stop it!" she said to the big man, "You're scaring them!"

"Scarin' them?" The big man looked at Nell, then back at Stanley and Alabaster. He squinted fiercely at them for a moment, then grinned hugely and stood up straight, letting out a booming roar of laughter. "Aah, I was just kiddin' with 'em," said Nell's father, clapping Stanley on the back so that his legs buckled. "Just a bit of fun, eh lads?"

"Heh, yeah, fun," Stanley said weakly.

"Sorry about that," Nell said, looking uncertainly at Alabaster, who was staring at her father with wide eyes. "Daddy thinks it's funny to scare my friends half to death." She shot Mr. Hawthorne a reproving look, and he turned a bit pink.

"Heh," said Mr. Hawthorne, "sorry, 'bout that, my lads, sorry. Here, allow me to introduce myself: Hawthorne's the name, Hubert Hawthorne." He reached out with a large, grimy, calloused hand, and shook hands with Stanley.

"Uh, I'm Stanley, Stanley Brambles," said Stanley.

"Pleased to finally meet you, Stanley, Stanley Brambles," said Mr. Hawthorne. "We've certainly been hearin' enough about *you*, past little while."

Nell turned bright pink at this, but Mr. Hawthorne had already moved on to Alabaster.

"So that means *you* must be the annoying one who talks too much?"

Nell looked mortified at this, but Alabaster, who had by now re-composed himself, said, cheerfully, "No sir, I'm actually Alabaster Lancaster."

"Uh … right," said Mr. Hawthorne, but he was smiling. "Well, I've got loads o' work to do here yet, but you can head home whenever you want, pumpkin."

Clearly, he was referring to Nell, whose complexion darkened from pink to red. "Okay, thanks Daddy," she said, nudging Stanley and Alabaster over to the other side of the garage, before her father could call her 'pumpkin' again.

"So, pumpkin—I mean, Nell," said Alabaster as they made their way past the hydraulic hoists, "do you … y'know, *work here* in addition to going to school five days a week?"

Nell gave him a look that promised a sound thrashing if he ever called her 'pumpkin' again, then said, "No, I'm just helping out. My mom and dad have been going crazy these past couple weeks, trying to get the garage open for business. We've had some customers already, but Daddy hasn't hired any new mechanics, so ..."

"You were really going to town on that car, from what I could see," said Stanley, for lack of anything better to add to the conversation.

"Oh, I was just changing a spark plug," Nell said offhandedly. "So? What have you two been up to for the past few weeks? We sort of lost touch in August, sorry about that ..."

"That's okay," Stanley said quickly. "We knew you were busy with moving, and stuff."

Nell smiled. "So? Come on, what have you been doing?"

Alabaster clasped his hands together. "Oh, the *things* we've been doing, Nell, I just don't know where to begin! You wouldn't *believe* the things we've been doing! Such things! Such *exciting* things! Things so incredibly exciting and amazing—"

Nell pushed Alabaster playfully to shut him up, but she was laughing.

Stanley was trying furiously to come up with something blisteringly witty to say, when he felt something grab onto his leg. Looking down, he was more than a bit surprised to see what looked like a big metal bug latched onto his ankle.

"AAARGH!" he cried, leaping backwards and dragging the metal bug with him, "*It's got me!*"

"Whoa!" said Alabaster.

"Stop jumping around, Stanley!" said Nell, diving to his rescue. Stanley obeyed, and seconds later, the metal bug was off his leg and in Nell's arms. It was about the size of a toy poodle.

"There's no reason to flip out," said Nell, "It wasn't going to hurt you."

"S-sorry," said Stanley embarrassedly. "What the heck *is* it, though?"

"It's a robot," said Nell, holding it up so Stanley could see. The mechanical bug had wires all over it, and seemed to have been made from a bunch of small metal bars. It had six moving, jointed legs, and a pair of claws for forelimbs, with which it had grabbed Stanley. It looked like a scorpion, only without the tail. The robot raised a claw as Stanley leaned in for a closer look.

"That's awesome!" said Alabaster, also taking a closer look, "Where'd you get it, Nell? I want one!"

"I built it," said Nell.

"You built *that*?" said Stanley, "You built a *robot?"*

"First a plane, now this!" exclaimed Alabaster. "Did you buy a kit, or something? '*Build your own robo-thing in twelve easy steps* ..."

"No," said Nell, "I just put it together from spare parts lying around ..."

Stanley couldn't believe it. Nell had built a robot bug—from scratch! Could she *be* any cooler?

Alabaster was clutching his head in his hands. "Nell, what *are* you? Some kind of mechanical *genius?"*

"No," said Nell, turning pink again, "it's just a hobby ..." She set the robot down and it scurried away.

"Is there a remote control?" asked Stanley, trying to discern how Nell was making the robot move.

"No," said Nell, "it just wanders around wherever it wants—as long as it's got batteries."

"Oh," said Stanley, "Well ... why did it grab me?"

Nell looked at him with bright, smiling eyes. "It likes you," she said simply.

* * *

As it was now getting close to five o'clock, the three of them decided it was time to head home. As they walked down Butter Street, their talk turned back to what Nell had said in front of the class. The boys knew about her interest in carpentry and mechanics, but they demanded to know just what type of martial arts she was in to. It turned out that she had her red belt in Karate, which was the second last belt before black.

Stanley, who was feeling particularly blown away by this point, was barely able to stammer, "B-but ... we've never seen you do any ... any ..."

"But we *have!"* said Alabaster, snapping his fingers, "Of course, it all makes sense! Remember the *kraken*?"

Stanley shuddered at the memory of the kraken attack on board the Ogopogo. "Yeah ... what's that got to do with—"

"Didn't you see Nell fighting off those tentacles with an oar? She was spinning and hitting, and jabbing, and parrying ... It was amazing! Do they teach you how to fight with oars in Karate, Nell?"

"No—staves," said Nell, not quite sure if Alabaster was joking or not. "The oars were pretty close, though."

"Wish I knew Karate," Stanley said, half to himself. "Then I could use it on that jerk, Danny Briggs."

"Well, hopefully he'll leave you alone if you leave *him* alone," Nell said sagely. "Just don't go starting anything with him."

"I won't," said Stanley.

By now they'd reached Nell's street, Cracker Crumb Drive. She bid the boys goodnight, and headed for her house. Five minutes later, as Stanley made his way towards the big red brick house on Bubbletree Lane, he gazed briefly at the sun setting behind the houses. It was the end of the worst first day of school he could remember. Not for the first time, he found himself wishing that he wasn't in East Stodgerton, but back aboard the Ogopogo, sailing across the ocean towards who-knows-what kinds of incredible adventures.

The voyage back in June was still frequently on his mind these days, but it seemed strangely distant lately, almost like a movie, or a dream. Sometimes he wondered briefly if it had really happened, but yes, of course it had happened, and that was a good feeling—to know that it had been real, that every word he had written on the pages hidden in his drawer upstairs, was true.

It just seemed such a terrible shame, a waste, to go back to this mundane life after such an adventure. Stanley sighed heavily and climbed up the front steps, preparing to tell his parents just how his first day of school had gone. It seemed to him that his days of adventure were over for good.

How wrong he was.

CHAPTER 2

SCHOOL DAZE

Mrs. Drabdale's behaviour became worse as the year wore on. She was never nice to any student that wasn't a 'helper', but to Stanley and Alabaster, she was particularly vicious. She was sarcastic, loud, and just plain rude with them, never missing a chance to criticize or belittle them, and woe betide them if they ever answered a question wrong.

She was particularly adept at dishing out detentions for no reason. She had even tried to punish Stanley because the pages of his essay on *Lord of the Flies* were slightly out of order. Fortunately, Mr. Grimm had gotten wind of this, and had set Stanley free, while Mrs. Drabdale spluttered and protested.

Many of the other teachers at Babblebrook Public School didn't approve of Mrs. Drabdale's methods any more than the students did, though they never said as much. Mr. Steele, the Phys Ed teacher, in particular, was often ready to stick up for Stanley, especially on the frequent occasions when Mrs. Drabdale tried to give him detentions for being too sweaty after gym class. Mr. Steele was also duly impressed with Stanley's performance in gym, and asked him frequently if he was sure he hadn't been training like mad all summer.

One of Stanley's worst confrontations with Mrs. Drabdale actually happened fairly early on in the year, in the second week of October. The class had been instructed to 'think back a few months' and write a five paragraph essay explaining why their summer holidays had been a complete waste of time. The 'correct' thesis statement, of course, was something like this:

My summer holidays were a complete waste of time because I was not furthering my education.

No one seemed to enjoy this assignment, Stanley, in particular. But, as he sat there at his desk, staring out the window, a thought came to him. His summer holidays *hadn't* been a waste of time—he'd had the best holiday ever, aboard Uncle Jack's ship! He decided that he would throw caution to wind, and write about his adventure.

Soon the essays were handed in, marked, and ready to be returned. Mrs. Drabdale had the obnoxious habit of reading everyone's mark as she returned each paper.

"Bonnie Wart, 'A+', very well done, indeed," she said, a hideous smile on her face.

"Thank you, Mrs. Drabdale," Bonnie gushed, taking back her essay and sticking her tongue out at Alabaster for no reason.

"Hillary Stroug," said Mrs. Drabdale, "'A', well done. Sarah Steward, 'A' … Debbie Greene, 'A' …"

Debbie accepted her essay, but seemed to be making a point not to look at Alabaster.

"Prunella Hawthorne, 'B+'" Mrs. Drabdale said coolly, handing Nell her paper.

Many more names and marks were called out. Stanley was wondering when his would come up.

"Marcus Welsh, 'C'. I expect better next time, Marcus. Olivia Schmidt …" Mrs. Drabdale had never liked Olivia, who had once called her something rather rude in front of the whole class. "'C-'. Daniel Briggs … 'D'. Complete and utter bilge, Mr. Briggs, I thought you might have learned to read and write over the summer."

Stanley glanced over at Danny Briggs, who was muttering something to his doltish friend, Bobby Traski. He noticed Stanley looking at him and made a very rude gesture with one of his fingers.

"Robert Traski … 'D'. I suppose you let Daniel copy your essay, hm? … Alabaster Lancaster—"

Debbie Greene let out an involuntary squeak. Bonnie Wart slapped her on the arm.

"'C+'. Utter tripe, of course, but a notable improvement on the trash you usually hand in. Keep this up and you might get a 'B' one of these days."

Alabaster accepted his paper with a ridiculous smile on his face. He turned to the rest of the class, held the essay aloft, and yelled "VICTORY!" as loud as he could.

Almost everyone laughed, especially Debbie Greene, who received another slap on the arm from Bonnie Wart.

"*Silence!*" cawed Mrs. Drabdale. "I have one last essay to hand back, but before I do, I would like to say a few words over it ..."

Stanley didn't need to be the only one who hadn't gotten his essay back, to know whose paper Mrs. Drabdale was holding.

"I have saved this essay till last," said Mrs. Drabdale, brandishing the paper, "not because it received an abysmal mark—"

Stanley felt a faint surge of hope.

"—but because it was too outrageous, too ridiculous, too monumentally *foolish* to merit any kind of mark at all!" The hand holding the essay had begun to shake so much that the paper itself became a white blur. "Allow me to read the first few sentences of this dungheap of an essay. And I quote:

"*My summer holidays were not a complete waste of time. I spent them at sea, with my great uncle Jack, and my two best friends. My uncle Jack is a pirate, and, with his friend Benjamin and his talking parrot, Pericles, we sailed all over the ocean, looking for buried treasure ...*"

Several people laughed, including Bonnie Wart, who had tears in her eyes as she shrieked with mirth, and Danny Briggs, who guffawed stupidly as he high-fived Bobby Traski.

Alabaster glanced at Stanley and gave him an encouraging 'thumbs up'. Nell gave him a look that he couldn't decipher. Was it sadness? Or pity?

Mrs. Drabdale held up her hand for silence, but waited a long time for Bonnie Wart's forced laughter to stop.

"Of course, this goes on and on," said Mrs. Drabdale, her eyes skimming wickedly over the typed words, "but I won't bore you with any more of it. I will, however, remind the author of this 'essay'," she glared at Stanley, "That this is *not* a children's fantasy workshop, but a *classroom*, and my assignments will be taken *seriously!* I will not, under any circumstances, accept childish bedtime stories in place of actual, viable work!"

She flung the essay down on Stanley's desk and stomped over to the blackboard to write the day's assignment. Stanley stared down at his rumpled essay. A few words had been scrawled across the title page in red ink:

Terrible. A vast disappointment, even for you.

He stared at the words, and felt tears building up in his lower eyelids. It wasn't the words, though. It was the fact that Mrs. Drabdale had called his adventure a childish bedtime story. It was the fact that he had had to put up with this kind of thing for the past four years. Constant put-downs, endless sarcasm, ceaseless snide remarks. And he'd just taken it, all this time.

No more, though. This was his last year at Babblebrook, and he wasn't going to let her ruin it like she had the others—and he certainly wasn't going to let her call his adventure with Uncle Jack a childish bedtime story. Blinking back his tears, he raised his head and glared fiercely at Mrs. Drabdale.

"It really happened," he said tonelessly.

The class fell silent. Mrs. Drabdale paused in her writing. Turning her head slightly to the side, she said, quite calmly,

"Who said that?"

As if she didn't know. Stanley hammered his fists onto his desk and sprang to his feet, knocking over his chair with a crash.

"*I did!*" he said loudly, causing several of the girls (and Alabaster) to gasp.

Mrs. Drabdale wheeled around, a ferocious grimace on her face. "*Stanley Brambles!*" she seethed, "*Sit down and shut up, you ridiculous child!*"

"I'm not a child!" Stanley shot back. He was angry, and he wasn't going to back down. "And this," he said, snatching up his essay, "is *not* a childish bedtime story! It really happened, every word of it is true! I almost got eaten by a fish, and a squid, and a siren, and a sea serpent! It's all true!"

"Sit down, Stanley Brambles!" spat Bonnie Wart.

"Yeah, siddown, dork," said fat Danny Briggs.

"SHUT UP!" Stanley roared.

Suddenly, the lights flickered and began to dim. Most of the people in the room didn't notice this, though—they were too absorbed in the battle raging before them.

"Yeah, shut up!" yelled Alabaster, jumping to his feet beside Stanley. "It really did happen, I was there, too!"

"Oh, be silent, Lancaster," bellowed Mrs. Drabdale, flecks of spittle flying from her mouth, "You are just a stupid, immature, foolish—"

"He's not stupid!"

"Debbie!" said Mrs. Drabdale, looking shocked.

Debbie Greene had indeed spoken, and was now standing, as well, looking both nervous and elated. Bonnie Wart tried to pull her back to hear seat, but Debbie swatted her away. Mrs. Drabdale was looking positively murderous. A large vein had popped out on her forehead.

"*You … you …*"

"No, he's not stupid, and how dare you say that to one of your students!" Nell was now on her feet, her eyes blazing. "And … and Stanley *is* telling the truth! I was there, too!"

Mrs. Drabdale was temporarily unable to speak, though her mouth kept opening and closing while her forehead vein pulsed angrily. Her face was redder than a tomato when she was finally able to scream,

"YOU ARE ALL EXPELLED! GET OUT! GET OUT OF MY CLASS! GET OUT OF MY SCHOOL! *GET OUT!"*

But no one moved. Stanley took grim satisfaction in that. He felt his heart hammering in his chest. His hands were shaking. It seemed to be getting dark in the classroom. Had a heavy cloud bank obscured the sun outside? … No matter.

"NO!" Stanley bellowed, "*YOU'RE* EXPELLED! YOU'RE THE MOST HORRIBLE TEACHER IN THE WORLD! *YOU* GET OUT!"

Mrs. Drabdale simply stared for a moment, then clenched up her fists and let loose an earth-shaking roar that would have put a dinosaur to shame. She then made for the door, and tore it right off its hinges before thundering out into the hall.

She was gone.

Silence descended on the classroom, broken only by Stanley's heavy breathing.

"Alright Stanley!" someone called from the back of the room, and the whole class erupted into applause. The whole class, that is, except for Bonnie Wart, Hillary Stroug, and Sarah Steward, who raced out of the room hot on Mrs. Drabdale's heels. Debbie Greene did not go with them.

As the lights came back on and the sun came shining back in through the windows, Stanley picked up his chair and sat down heavily. He felt inexplicably tired, but he didn't care. He was only half aware of the laughing and whooping and the loud chatter which filled the room. Alabaster patted him on the back, but was one of the few people who said nothing. He simply smiled proudly at Stanley and sat down, looking very much at peace with the world. Nell came over as well. She gave him a quick hug and said,

"You could have handled that better," but Stanley could see that she was smiling at him, just like Alabaster. Well, maybe not *just* like Alabaster.

Soon the chatter died down, and people started to wonder what was going to happen for the rest of the period. Was Mrs. Drabdale coming back? Had she fled the school? Bobby Traski swore he'd seen her running away across the back field. Suddenly, a voice came over the loudspeaker:

"*Stanley Brambles, please report to the main office. Stanley Brambles to the main office, please.*"

Everyone went silent. Stanley looked around at his classmates, most of whom were looking at him as if he'd just been summoned to the gallows.

"Hah! Dead man walkin'!" said Bobby Traski.

"Nice knowin' ya, Stan-the-man-dorkface!" Danny Briggs gurgled.

"Shut up, you ignorant jackasses!" said Nell, and they did.

Stanley got up slowly and headed for the door. He felt numb. It was all up, and now he really was going to get expelled …

"Stanley, wait!" said Alabaster, "I'll come with you!"

"No!" said Stanley, although truthfully, he would have dearly liked to have had his best friend by his side as he went to his fate. "You stay here," he said to Alabaster, as well as to Nell, who had opened her mouth to protest. "I'll be fine." He took one last look at Nell, who gazed back at him with a helpless expression in her bright green eyes (they sure were green. Had they always been that green?), and left the room.

⋆ ⋆ ⋆

Stanley arrived at the principal's office feeling lower than the mark he'd gotten on his paper … which was nothing. He now deeply regretted losing his temper and yelling at Mrs. Drabdale. Now he was in for it. All that remained was to find out what punishment awaited him beyond the door marked *W. Grimm – Principal.* He passed by Bonnie Wart, Hillary Stroug, and Sarah Steward, who were flanking Mr. Grimm's door. They gave him some extremely venomous looks as he went in.

Mrs. Drabdale was there, seated in front of Mr. Grimm's desk. She didn't look up as Stanley entered the room.

"Take a seat," said Mr. Grimm, gesturing to an empty chair beside Mrs. Drabdale. Stanley sat. "Mrs. Drabdale tells me you said some rather … impolite things to her. Is this true?"

Stanley had no idea what Mrs. Drabdale had told the principal, but he answered "yeah," all the same.

Mr. Grimm put his hands together and nodded shortly. "Can you tell me why you called her the most horrible teacher in the world and ordered her out of her own classroom?"

Stanley searched for the most appropriate answer, fighting the urge to say 'because she *is*'.

"She said … um … rude things about my essay, and … made fun of me in front of the class."

Mrs. Drabdale made a small, angry noise, but Mr. Grimm held up a hand for silence.

"I see," he said calmly.

Pressing his advantage, Stanley added, "Just like she's been doing since grade five—"

"That will do, Mr. Brambles," said Mr. Grimm. He sat in thought for a moment. "Has this ever happened before, Rowena?"

"Er … why, no," said Mrs. Drabdale.

"Hmm,' said Mr. Grimm.

"But he's quite and impossible child, Waldemar, I assure you—"

Mr. Grimm held up his hand again. "Rowena, please." He sat in thought for another moment. "May I see the essay in question, please?"

Stanley looked down at his right hand, and noticed for the first time that he was still clutching his paper. He handed it to Mr. Grimm, who began to read.

"This is a fascinating tale," he said at last, lowering the paper. "Rowena, why did you write *'terrible'* on it?"

"Well … I … it—" Mrs. Drabdale spluttered, "It doesn't adhere to the specifications I laid out for the assignment!"

"It's very creative."

"But I told him to write about his summer vacation, not some juvenile fairytale!"

"It's not a fairytale!" said Stanley loudly, "It really happened!"

"It did not!"

"It did!"

"*Enough!*" snapped Mr. Grimm.

"It really *did* happen," said Alabaster, popping up from behind the wastepaper basket and making them all jump with surprise.

"Great scott!" exclaimed Mr. Grimm, nearly falling out of his chair, "How in blazes did *you* get in here?"

"Followed Stanley," said Alabaster.

"Please leave," said Mr. Grimm, pointing at the door. Looking a bit put out, Alabaster left the office. Mr. Grimm blinked a few times, shook his head, and said, "What were we talking about?"

"The essay,' said Stanley and Mrs. Drabdale in unison.

"Ah, yes," said Mr. Grimm. He glanced again at Stanley's paper. "Rowena … what does it matter if it's true or not?"

Mrs. Drabdale stared. "Well, I … it's … er …"

"I don't think it matters at all," said Mr. Grimm, interrupting her spluttering. "What I see here is a well-written, imaginative, and dare I say *exciting* piece of literature. Since when is truth a criterion for creative writing?"

"But it's not what I—"

"It's a grade eight writing assignment, Rowena," said Mr. Grimm. "And it deserves an 'A'." He took a red pen out of his desk and scrawled a big letter A over Mrs. Drabdale's note. "As for you, Mr. Brambles," he said, handing the essay back to Stanley, "In the future, please keep your opinions about my teaching staff to yourself."

Stanley nodded. "Yes, sir."

"Excellent," said Mr. Grimm. "Now, if the two of you could make an effort to treat each other civilly from here on in, I think the year should proceed much more smoothly, don't you?"

Stanley and Mrs. Drabdale murmured their assent.

"Good," said Mr. Grimm, "I'm glad that's settled." He stood up and waved them towards the door. "Dismissed."

Chapter 3

DANNY BRIGGS GETS HURT

Stanley and Mrs. Drabdale seemed to have reached an uneasy truce. There were no more violent verbal outbursts, and the vein in Mrs. Drabdale's forehead seemed to have gone into hibernation. There was also a significant reduction in scathing remarks written on Stanley's tests and essays. It could be said that the two old enemies had adopted a policy of 'live and let live', and that suited Stanley just fine.

Meanwhile, however, Stanley had become something of a legend among the student body at Babblebrook Public School. Where before he had not been particularly popular, he was now being acknowledged and praised everywhere he went. Never in recent memory had anyone ever stood up to Mrs. Drabdale the way he had. People he didn't even know were saying 'hi' to him in the halls. People whom he would have barely called acquaintances were now acting like they were some of his oldest friends. Girls had even begun to come up and talk to him, which was positively unheard of.

Stanley took all this attention with a grain of salt, of course, and ignored it as much as he could. He just wasn't the type to bask in public adoration.

Also, he had enough to worry about, without dealing with people who suddenly wanted to talk to him. For one thing, Danny Briggs became more and more of a pain as the school year wore on. For whatever reason, he was not pleased that 'that Brambles nerd' had won the respect and adoration of the entire school. And while he wasn't clever enough to spread subtle discord in an attempt to discredit

Stanley, he *was* big enough, dumb enough, and mean enough to push him around every chance he got.

Stanley was wise enough to suspect that his 'friendship' with some of his fellow students was only skin deep, and his suspicions were confirmed by the way they all scattered the first time Danny came looking for him after the 'Drabdale Incident'.

Only Alabaster and Nell had stood by him that time, and it was an unlucky thing for Danny that Nell was there. Before he could get within punching range of Stanley, she'd leapt forward, grabbed Danny's round, pudgy head, took a half step backward, and flung him to the ground in what's called a 'head winding throw (do not attempt)'.

"Why don't you pick on someone your own size?" Nell had enquired of Danny, as he struggled to his feet, eyes wide.

Danny had simply snorted, trying to hide his surprise and humiliation. "I'll get you later, when your girlfriend's not around, Stan-the-man," he said, before loping away. Several people who had been watching cheered, and Stanley said an awkward 'thanks' to Nell. It was strangely embarrassing to have been saved by her, even if she *was* a red belt in karate.

★ ★ ★

Time wore on, and the Danny Briggs problem only got worse. Stanley did his best to avoid the oaf, but once in a while, Danny caught him off guard. The first time, Stanley had come away with a bloody lip. Nell had then shown him how to guard his head in a fight, and a stance that enabled quicker movement, and left less of one's body exposed to the enemy. She'd also shown him a few simple punches and deflections, which came in handy with a bit of practice.

Some time later, Danny had come after Stanley again and received a bloody nose for his trouble. Danny was beyond furious at this, but by that point the situation had been brought to the attention of the staff, as well as Stanley's and Danny's parents. There were a few conferences in Mr. Grimm's office, and things got better from then on.

"I'm proud of you for standing up for yourself, Stanley, dear—" Mrs. Brambles had said, after the situation had been resolved to everyone's satisfaction.

"Quite proud," Mr. Brambles had added. "Well done, son!"

"—but from now on, try to stay away from that Briggs boy."

"Or just knock him out cold."

"*Robert!*"

"Sorry, dear."

Things were fine after that, all the way up until the end of March. Then one day, something unsettling happened.

Everyone in Mrs. Drabdale's class had received a notice regarding an upcoming field trip. Stanley usually liked field trips, but he groaned when he realized that they were going to

"*The East Stodgerton Museum of Natural History?*" he said with dismay as he read the notice.

"What's wrong with that?" Nell asked, as they made their way along the chain link fence that encircled the school grounds.

What was wrong, was that Stanley's father was the curator of the museum, and, as such, Stanley had been there at least three hundred times.

"Oh," said Nell when Stanley told her this.

"At least we get out of school," said Alabaster, trying to lift his spirits.

"Yeah, I guess," said Stanley, before being hit on the side of the head by a huge gob of mud. "*Bleeargh!*" he said, shaking his head and trying to wipe the smelly stuff out of his hair. "What the—"

"Down, Stanley!" cried Alabaster, pushing Stanley out of the way, and taking the second gob of mud full in the face.

Stanley cast around for the culprit, and found him standing not far beyond the fence. Danny Briggs was there, and Bobby Traski was beside him. Both were guffawing with infuriatingly stupid looks on their faces.

An angry flame sprang to life in Stanley's chest, and he was about to yell something, but Nell beat him to it.

"Oh, Briggs and Traski playing in the mud together, what a surprise," she yelled, before dodging another flying lump of mud.

"Hey, Stan-the-man," hollered Danny, "looks like your *girlfriend's* still fighting your battles for you, eh?" He and Bobby both guffawed. "You'd better shut that (and here he called Nell something very rude) up, or I'll do it for ya!"

The angry flame in Stanley's chest erupted into an inferno. No one talked about his friends that way.

"SHUT YOUR FAT FACE, YOU HALF-WIT PIECE OF GORILLA CRAP!" he bellowed (he'd learnt the term 'half-wit' from Nell).

"What did you just call me?" said Danny, but he sounded genuinely confused.

"He called you a stupid piece of monkey poo," said Alabaster, wiping mud off his face.

Danny looked angry. And stupid. "I'll get you for that," he said, shuffling towards the fence. "I'm gonna deck all three of ya!"

Stanley was so angry his hands were shaking. "*What's your problem, Briggs?*" he yelled, as Danny started to climb over the fence. "*Why do you always want to fight? You jerk! Just leave us alone!*"

"SHUT UP!" roared Danny, before falling off the fence. No one laughed. "I'm gonna teach all three of you a lesson!" he said, picking himself up and stalking towards them like an ogre.

"*Yeah, you're really tough, picking on someone who's half your size,*" yelled Nell as Danny drew closer. "You coward."

Danny's face went beet red, and he ran at Nell, teeth bared and beady eyes popping. Before he could reach her, though, Stanley darted forward and …

And it isn't exactly clear what happened next. Stanley leaped into Danny's path, reached out to grab his arm for some reason, and the next thing he knew, he was being eased down into a sitting position by Nell and Alabaster. He was feeling dizzy and disoriented, and thought he could hear someone screaming and crying close by.

"What … what happened?" he asked, as Nell and Alabaster sat him down on the pavement. Neither of them answered, but stared uncertainly at him. Then he caught sight of who was screaming and crying. Danny Briggs was on the ground, wailing like a baby (a very big baby) as he cradled his right arm, which was soaked in blood.

"Ohmigosh!" breathed Stanley, the dizziness fading enough for him to lurch to his feet. Even though Danny had been trying to beat him up, he still felt a strange surge of pity and compassion for him. "Danny," he said, approaching the wounded bully, "what happened?"

"GET AWAY FROM ME!" Danny bellowed, trying to crawl away from Stanley. "HELP! HELP ME!"

Danny seemed terrified of him, but why, Stanley couldn't figure out. Suddenly, Nell was at his side.

"Stanley," she said, "go find a teacher, Danny might need an ambulance." Stanley just stood there, too shocked to understand at first. "*Go!*" Nell shouted at him.

"Uh! Right!" said Stanley, and he ran around to the other side of the school. He saw Mr. Steele walking towards the football field. "*Mr. Steele!*" he yelled.

Stanley told Mr. Steele as much as he could. Mr. Steele then ducked inside, and returned seconds later with a first aid kit. "Go to the office and tell them to call an ambulance!" he barked at Marcus Welsh, who had just shown up for football practice.

"Right, coach," said Marcus, and he ran back inside.

"Okay, show me where he is, Stan," said Mr. Steele. They ran back to where Danny was lying on the pavement. Nell had pinned Danny to the ground, ripped off his left sleeve, and instructed him to hold the material over his wound. Mr. Steele screeched to a halt and knelt down beside them.

"Okay, pal," he said bracingly, "you're gonna be just fine, let's see that arm …" he pulled on a pair of latex gloves and gingerly removed the blood-soaked sleeve from Danny's arm. He and Stanley both winced at what they saw.

Danny's forearm had been scored by four deep cuts. It looked as if he'd been clawed by a wild animal. He screamed and wailed as Mr. Steele took bandages from the first aid kit and began to dress his arm.

"Okay, champ," said Mr. Steele once he had finished, "you're fixed up for now, but you're gonna need stitches."

"*Stitches?*" Danny shrieked.

As much as he hated Danny, Stanley couldn't help but feel bad for him.

"How the heck did this happen?" demanded Mr. Steele.

"*HIM!*" said Danny, pointing at Stanley.

"Stanley cut you?" Mr. Steele said skeptically, "Four times?"

Danny just stared at Stanley and repeated, "*HIM!*"

"He's going into shock," said Mr. Steele.

Just then, an ambulance pulled up. A pair of paramedics came running up with a stretcher. Mr. Grimm had joined them.

"What happened here?" said the principal as the paramedics knelt down beside Danny. Mr. Steele glanced over at Bobby Traski, who was climbing over the fence. He tumbled off, ripping his jacket in the process, then got up and came running over.

"I think I know," said Mr. Steele. "I'd say Dan was climbing over the fence, but he fell off and cut himself on the way down."

Mr. Grimm scratched his head, looked over at the fence, then at Danny. "Hmm," he said.

"We're always telling kids not to go climbing around on that thing," said Mr. Steele. He turned to Stanley and the others. "Did you guys see what happened?"

"No, we didn't," said Nell.

"Nope," said Alabaster.

Stanley stared at them. They were lying! They'd seen Danny fall off the fence, and he certainly hadn't cut himself doing it.

"But—" said Stanley, but Nell looked fiercely at him and shook her head.

"Well, I hope you've learned a lesson today," Mr. Grimm told Danny as the paramedics lifted him up on the stretcher. "You go get healed up now, and no more foolish antics."

The ambulance pulled away, and Mr. Grimm returned to the school, leaving a bewildered Stanley staring after him. Before he could ask what in the world was going on, Bobby Traski wheeled him around and said,

"What did you do, Brambles?" He looked both angry and afraid.

"I … I don't … what do you mean?" said Stanley.

"He didn't cut himself on that fence," Bobby said darkly. "You did something to him. D'you have a knife? Just tell me, I won't rat on you."

"I *don't* have a *knife*," said Stanley, feeling slightly annoyed.

Bobby looked at him searchingly for a moment, before saying, "Whatever. Just stay away from me, Brambles. Danny, too." And he shuffled away.

"Gladly," Stanley said half under his breath. He turned to Nell and Alabaster. "What was *that* all about? Why did you guys say you didn't see what happened? You lied—"

"We had to," said Nell looking at him with haunted eyes.

"*What?*" cried Stanley, "Why?"

"I'm not sure how to say this, Stanley," said Alabaster, putting a hand on his shoulder, "but—"

Nell finished for him. "*You're* the one who hurt Danny Briggs."

Chapter 4

THE MUSEUM

"Tell me what's going on!" Stanley shouted. Nell and Alabaster were leading him down into the ravine beyond the school property, and were refusing to answer his questions.

"Stanley, just shut up for a second," snapped Nell. "We'll tell you, but we want to make sure no one overhears." She and Alabaster led Stanley further into the damp, shadowy ravine, stopping at the old culvert through which Stanley and Alabaster had escaped Mrs. Drabdale's wrath back in June. They each sat down on a large rock. Stanley looked at Alabaster, then at Nell. They both had strange looks on their faces.

"Well?" he said impatiently.

"Uh," said Alabaster.

"Danny didn't cut himself on that fence," said Stanley, "and you just said *I* was the one who did it. C'mon, what happened?'

"We're not even really sure ourselves," said Alabaster.

"But—" said Stanley.

"What do you remember?" Nell asked abruptly.

Stanley thought. "Uh, let me see … I remember Danny climbed over the fence … he fell down, then he ran towards you, I jumped in front of him …"

Nell and Alabaster leaned forward expectantly.

"…and next thing I knew, I was sitting on the ground," Stanley finished. "I thought Danny might have brained me or something."

Nell and Alabaster exchanged a quick glance.

"What?" said Stanley. "You're trying to tell me I did something to Danny, so what did I do?"

"You … clawed him," said Alabaster. At first, Stanley thought he was joking.

"*Clawed* him? Yeah, right—"

"*You clawed him,*" Nell said loudly.

"What are you talking about?" said Stanley, matching her volume. "With *these?*" He held up his hands, displaying his short, recently-trimmed fingernails.

"Not so much," said Alabaster. "Um, it looked like your hand sort of … changed for like one second …"

"It was like your hand suddenly turned into a big black claw," said Nell. "But I didn't see it change—one second it was normal, the next second it was a claw, and the second after that it was normal again, and you were falling backwards. You really don't remember any of this?"

"No!" Stanley said vehemently.

"I thought I'd imagined it," said Nell, "but then Alabaster told me he'd seen it, too."

Stanley could not believe it. Alabaster and Nell were telling the truth, or at least they thought they were. What had really happened? What did it mean? And why could he not remember it?

… But he could. It was slowly coming back to him, the memory of the moment just after he'd stepped in front of Danny, and just before he found himself sitting on the ground. He remembered being very angry … and meaning to hurt Danny if he got anywhere near Nell. Suddenly, some instinct had told him to grab Danny's arm … but he hadn't grabbed, he'd taken a swipe at him with … with …

With a black, clawed hand. For barely a moment, his hand had not been a hand, but a monstrous paw, or talon, with sharp claws … and with it, he'd wounded Danny.

"What … what in the world happened to me?" Stanley asked aloud.

Nell leaped up off her rock and threw her arms around him. "I don't know," she said to his shoulder, "but don't let it happen again."

"I won't," said Stanley, secretly hoping that he was telling the truth.

★ ★ ★

That night, Stanley tossed and turned in his sleep. His dreams were full of dark jungles, and shadowy creatures with long, black claws …

and always in the distance, he could see, rising high above the trees, a towering blue crystal pointing towards the heavens. He knew he had to get to that crystal, but despite his burning desire to do so, he never seemed to be getting any closer to it.

Towards dawn, he had another dream, a dream that he'd had many times since the end of June, but would not remember when he woke up in the morning.

Rhu hond ine eom zhun ...

★ ★ ★

Stanley woke up the next morning feeling much better. It's true that things often look better in the morning, and as he thought about yesterday's events, he started to think that maybe what he'd thought had happened, really hadn't. Sometimes the imagination runs a bit wild, making people see things, when in fact, there is a perfectly logical explanation for whatever happened, no matter how odd or unsettling. Like yesterday's episode, for instance. The whole thing seemed rather silly—Stanley, wounding Danny with a claw that was there one minute and gone the next? It was ridiculous, really. Obviously Danny had cut himself on the fence. The whole thing was *so* ridiculous, in fact, that there really seemed no reason to bring it up to Alabaster and Nell, especially not on the way to school, or ever again.

When he met up with his friends soon after, he was pleased to discover that they were clearly thinking along the same lines as him, because neither of them said a word about the events of the day before. He would have been less pleased had he noticed the look the two of them exchanged as he turned and led the way down Butter Street.

★ ★ ★

The week went by quickly, and soon it was Friday, the day of the class field trip to the East Stodgerton Museum of Natural History. Stanley, Alabaster, and Nell arrived at school that morning at five to nine, and joined a line of their classmates that had formed beside a big yellow school bus out front. Danny Briggs was standing close to the front of the line, looking morose. His injured arm was bandaged and in a sling, and he seemed to be making every effort not to notice that Stanley had arrived. It was the first day that Danny had been back at school since his injury, and Stanley, feeling that it was the decent thing to do, went over to apologize to him. After all, he'd had a good three days in which to convince himself that nothing weird had happened on Monday, and he couldn't help but feel partly responsible for Danny's condition.

Danny looked a bit fearful as Stanley approached him, but he stood his ground.

"Danny," said Stanley, "I just wanted to say I'm sorry about what happened the other day."

Danny looked at him sourly. "Don't worry about it," he muttered, refusing to make eye contact with Stanley. "It wasn't *your* fault …"

Stanley nodded, then got back in line in front of Nell.

"Well, at least *that's* cleared up," she said, when Stanley told her what Danny had said, though she didn't sound very sure of herself.

Mr. Steele and Mrs. Drabdale came striding across the pavement. "Okay, everyone," said Mr. Steele, "all aboard, we're shipping out."

They all climbed aboard the bus, which was being driven by a hefty-looking woman with frizzy blonde hair. Stanley sat down beside Alabaster, and Nell reluctantly took the seat across from them, which was already half occupied by Debbie Greene, who kept glancing fixedly at Alabaster, as if mentally willing him to switch seats with Nell.

Mrs. Drabdale stood up before the company and said, "No more than two to a seat. There will be no standing, no yelling, no screaming, no eating, no drinking, no switching seats. You will sit still until we reach our destination, and if anyone does *anything* they aren't supposed to be doing, they will be given a detention. Is that clear?"

"No," said someone towards the back of the bus, but as she couldn't tell who it was, Mrs. Drabdale just growled savagely and sat down heavily beside Mr. Steele.

About ten minutes later, the bus pulled up in front of the East Stodgerton Museum of Natural History. It was a vast building, and looked a bit like a castle.

"Nobody is to wander off," said Mrs. Drabdale, as they all made their way up the front steps. "Everyone is to stay with the group, and any trouble-makers will be dealt with *severely*." She glared at Stanley and Alabaster.

Mr. Steele sighed. He looked a bit unhappy, and Stanley didn't blame him. Mrs. Drabdale could take the fun out of any situation.

In the museum's lobby, there hung from the ceiling a huge skeleton of a Pteranodon. Several people pointed and whispered upon seeing it. It was an impressive display, but Stanley barely glanced at it. He had, after all, seen it at least three hundred times.

"Welcome!" said a voice which echoed through the lobby.

Alabaster nudged Stanley. "Look, Stanley," he said, "it's your dad!"

Sure enough, there, walking towards the group, was Stanley's father, wearing a smart-looking suit and an obnoxious yellow polka-dot tie.

"Welcome," continued Mr. Brambles, "to the East Stodgerton Museum of Natural History! I'm the curator, Mr. Brambles!"

Stanley braced himself. He hoped his father wouldn't do anything embarrassing.

"Hi, Stanley!" said Mr. Brambles, giving him a little wave. Stanley cringed. Several people giggled.

"I'm Stanley's father," said Mr. Brambles importantly. Stanley ground his teeth. Several more people giggled.

"Hi, Alabaster!" said Mr. Brambles. "Hi, Nancy!" he said to Nell.

"Hi, Mr. Brambles!" said Alabaster brightly.

"Er, hello," said Nell.

"Perhaps you'd like to start the tour," Mrs. Drabdale suggested.

"Eh?" said Mr. Brambles, "The what?"

"The *tour*," said Mrs. Drabdale. "Surely you weren't planning on having us stand here all day?"

"Oh!" said Mr. Brambles. "Ah ... well, I should hope not! The tour, of course! Let's start the tour! On with the tour! This way for the tour, all those on the tour, come this way!"

Stanley wished his father would stop saying 'tour'.

"Our tour begins with our ancient seas exhibit!" said Mr. Brambles, leading the way down a long hall off the left side of the lobby. "Now, 350 million years ago, the world's oceans were very different from the oceans of today!"

"What, didn't they have any water?" someone asked smartly.

"Detention, Miss Schmidt," rasped Mrs. Drabdale.

"Oh, they had water, alright," laughed Mr. Brambles, who hadn't heard Mrs. Drabdale. "But the difference was what was *in* the water!"

He threw open a pair of double doors, and almost everyone gasped as they entered a vast room that had been made to look like the ocean floor. An incredible array of underwater plants and animals was displayed here; it was almost as if a chunk of prehistoric ocean had been frozen in time and sent to the present. For one thing, the lighting was very effective. For another, the models of ancient aquatic plants and animals were hauntingly lifelike, especially the fearsome Dinichthys, which was a focal point of the exhibit. Stanley stared at the huge model fish, remembering his frightening experience with the real thing.

On the way out of the ancient seas exhibit, the group passed by the model of the giant squid. Alabaster nudged Stanley and pointed at it. Stanley nodded; it looked pretty tame compared to the nightmarish kraken they had faced aboard the Ogopogo.

Mr. Brambles led the group down another hall and through another set of doors. "Welcome to the jungle!" he said in a screechy rock star voice. Several people actually laughed.

This next exhibit had been made to look like a prehistoric jungle. The place was overrun with plants, some of which appeared to be real. Sunlight shone down through large skylights in the roof. Mr. Brambles said, "This exhibit represents a forest from the Cretaceous period, which began about 145 million years ago, and ended 65 million years ago, when the dinosaurs became extinct! Now, as we walk along, if you look carefully, you might just see some dinosaurs right here in our re-created jungle!"

"Yeah, but they're just models, right?" someone said.

"Duh, Bradley, of course they're models!" said someone else. "Dinosaurs have been extinct for—"

Suddenly there was a disturbance in the trees behind Mr. Brambles, and a monstrous reptilian head thrust itself out of the foliage.

"*What's that?*" shrieked Bonnie Wart. Stanley rolled his eyes. Obviously it was the head of a Tyrannosaurus, although it must have been a new addition to the exhibit, because he'd never seen it before.

"Eh?" said Mr. Brambles, turning around as people pointed frantically at the Tyrannosaurus head. "Goodness gracious me!" he said, just as the beast's massive jaws opened wide and let out an almost deafening roar.

Hands were clapped over ears, and everyone cowered backwards. The Tyrannosaurus finished roaring and retreated back into the trees. Mr. Brambles turned back to the group, looking a bit dazed.

"Silly me, I'd forgotten all about that," he said smiling nervously. Everyone was staring at him. "It's quite new," he said apologetically. "Er ... *Mike*," he called into the trees, "Why don't you tone down the volume on that roar a smidgeon?"

"You got it, Mr. B," said a voice from out in the jungle.

"Ahem, well," said Mr. Brambles, "Shall we continue with the tour?"

The group stood in shocked silence for a moment, and then several people broke into applause.

"*Awesome!*" they yelled.

"Oh!" said Mr. Brambles, "Well, ah, thank you! This way, please!"

The group continued on through the jungle, but Stanley hung back. Realizing that he wasn't with them, Alabaster and Nell went back to find him.

"Stanley, what are you doing?" said Nell.

Stanley had hunkered down and was peering off into the artificial jungle.

"Stanley?" said Alabaster, "Earth to Stanley! What's up? Is there another dinosaur in there?"

When Stanley still didn't answer, Nell touched him lightly on the shoulder. "Stanley?" she said, "Are you alright?"

Stanley started. "Sorry," he said, glancing up at Alabaster and Nell. "Uh ... I just thought I saw ... something."

"What?" said Alabaster, also hunkering down and peering into the trees.

Stanley looked again, trying to catch another glimpse of what he thought he'd seen. At first he saw nothing but leaves and branches, and was beginning to think he'd imagined it, when suddenly he caught sight of it again, just beyond a particularly dark stretch of underbrush, glinting in a patch of sunlight.

"There!" he said, pointing off into the artificial jungle, "See it?"

"Uh ... nope," said Alabaster.

"I don't see anything," said Nell. "What are we looking for, Stanley? We should get back to the group, come on."

Stanley, though, did not want to get back to the group. He had a feeling that if he left now, he would never be able to find this exact point again. He wanted a closer look at what he'd seen; it was important, he could feel it. "I'll be right back," he said, and with that, he disappeared into the trees.

"Stanley!" said Nell, "Come back!"

Alabaster looked at her. "I'm goin' in," he said dramatically before following hot on Stanley's heels. Nell sighed and muttered something about 'boys' before plunging into the jungle herself.

Stanley could hear Alabaster and Nell following close behind him as he crawled along. He was forced to crawl, because the underbrush had become very thick—so thick, in fact, that it quickly became impossible to stand. The interlacing branches of trees and bushes began to form a kind of roof over the forest floor, blocking out sunlight and creating a surprisingly dark tunnel of leaves and branches.

After at least two full minutes, Stanley became aware that they had been crawling along for quite a ways. How big was this jungle exhibit, anyway? He peered ahead, and was mildly alarmed to discover that he could no longer see the end of the tunnel. Where was the sunlit clearing he'd seen? Had he taken a wrong turn? ... No, that wasn't possible. The tunnel just kept going straight, and there had been no opportunities to leave the path. Also rather alarming was the fact that the tunnel of leaves and branches seemed to be getting darker and darker the further he crawled. What was going on here?

Stanley stopped abruptly, and felt Alabaster crash into him. He said something, but Stanley couldn't hear what it was.

"Okay," Stanley said to himself, "We're lost in the exhibit, or something ... what do we do?"

Going back was out, because there was simply not enough room to turn around, and logically, they must have been getting close to a wall by now. Going by that rationale, Stanley pressed forward. On and on he crawled, with Alabaster and Nell close behind him, while the tunnel grew darker and darker.

Stanley was just starting to feel as if he'd made a very grave mistake, when suddenly he noticed a small point of light not far ahead. Within a minute, it had grown into what he'd been hoping for: the end of the forest tunnel. The three of them emerged from the foliage and found themselves in a large, bright, sunlit clearing. Judging by the sun's position in the sky, it was late afternoon.

"You okay?" Alabaster asked of Nell, who was looking pale and breathing heavily, as if she'd just run a race.

"I'm fine," she said, taking a deep, steadying breath. "It was just a little tight in there, that's all …"

Stanley wasn't paying attention, though, because in the middle of the clearing was the thing he had seen, though how he'd seen it over the distance they'd just covered, was anybody's guess. It was a huge chunk of red crystal, and others like it were strewn about elsewhere around the clearing.

"Wow!" said Alabaster, "Get a load of this! Is that a ruby? We're rich! RICH!" He leaped upon one of the red crystals and clutched it tightly. "This one's mine!"

Unlike Alabaster, Nell had become a bit cross. "That's it?" she said to Stanley, gesturing at the crystal. "You made us crawl all this way just to look at some red rock?"

"They might be rubies, Nell!" said Alabaster. "Prehistoric rubies!"

"Oh, they are not!" said Nell.

Stanley still wasn't paying attention. He was too busy examining one of the crystals. He placed a hand on its smooth surface. It felt pleasantly warm. "It's almost the same," he murmured, "but it's not the right colour."

Nell suddenly grabbed him by the collar, spun him around to face her, and took hold of his shoulders. "*Stanley*, what the *heck* is going on?" she demanded, her bright green eyes boring into his. "What are you talking about?"

Stanley suddenly felt as if he'd just woken up from a long nap. "Uh," he said, trying to get his thoughts in order.

"I want to know what's so important about this red rock," said Nell, still staring intently at him.

"Uh," said Stanley, a bit embarrassed, "I, uh … dreamed about it."

"You *dreamed* about it?" Nell echoed. "You dreamed about a big chunk of red rock in the middle of the Museum of Natural History?"

"Well … no," said Stanley. "In my dream it was blue, and it was … well, rising up out of the jungle, and it was, y'know, *whole*—it wasn't all in pieces." He looked around at the pieces of red crystal. "This one must have been broken …"

"This *what?*" said Nell. "You're dreaming of—of giant, flying jungle jewels? What *are* they? What are they for? Why are they so important?"

Stanley frowned, and thought about it. He really had no idea. "I … dunno," he said at last. "But I've been dreaming of this big, blue crystal in a jungle since the end of June, and there's something really, really important about it … I just don't know what it is yet." It was rather frustrating, trying to explain something that he didn't even understand himself.

Nell sighed. "You're really serious, aren't you?" she said, looking at him searchingly.

Stanley nodded, but didn't meet her gaze. She obviously thought he was being a complete idiot.

"Okay," said Nell, and Stanley looked up at her in surprise.

"What?" he said, "What do you mean, *okay*? Don't you think I'm acting like an idiot?"

"No," said Nell, "But then, I've never really *seen* you act like an idiot, so I wouldn't recognize it if you did, would I? Look, this … *thing* with the crystals is obviously important to you, so let's go back and ask your dad about it."

"My dad?" said Stanley.

"Yeah," said Nell, "If anyone knows something about these crystals of yours, it must be him. It's his museum, after all."

"I wouldn't bet on it," said Stanley, grinning slightly, although it did sound like a fairly good idea.

"Great," said Nell, "Then let's get back. They probably know we're gone, so we're already in trouble, but—Alabaster, *leave it!"*

Alabaster was doing his best to drag a large piece of red crystal across the clearing. "But Nell!" he said, "Don't you think we should bring back a … a *sample?* For, uh … scientific purposes?"

"You're not selling that thing, so just forget it!" said Nell, guessing Alabaster's true intentions.

"Aww, c'mon, Nell," whined Alabaster, "I'll share the profits with you and Stanley!"

"Who do you think is going to want to buy a lump of red rock from a … *weirdo* like you?" she demanded.

"Lots of people!" said Alabaster.

"RRRRGH!" said Nell, "Listen! Even if you could drag that thing all the way back—which you *can't*, because I'm not going to help you, and neither is Stanley—you still wouldn't be allowed to keep it, because it belongs to the museum!"

"How do you know?" said Alabaster. "It's not even *inside* the museum."

"WHAT?" shrieked Nell, "You—you—"

Nell was getting very, very annoyed, but something in Alabaster's voice made Stanley perk up and listen; he didn't seem to be joking.

"Alabaster, what do you mean, *it's not inside the museum*?"

"We're *outside*," said Alabaster, as if it was the most obvious thing imaginable. He pointed upwards. Stanley looked up, and was quite surprised to see not a roof with skylights, but *open sky*. Grim-looking clouds had appeared overhead, obscuring the afternoon sunlight.

"We're outside?" he said half to himself.

"No way," said Nell.

"Yes way," said Alabaster.

"Well then why didn't we notice when we left the building?" said Nell.

"Um," said Alabaster.

"And if we *are* outside," Nell went on, "where are we? I certainly don't remember there being any jungles in East Stodgerton. Of course, I *could* be wrong," she added sarcastically. "After all, I've only lived here six months ..."

Just then, a deafening thunderclap roared down from the sky and smote the clearing with a ground-shaking

BOOM!

With a flurry of wings and feathers, a mass of birds took off in fright from the surrounding trees, just before a torrent of rain came streaming down from the clouds. The three friends were soaked almost instantly.

"Okay," said Nell, her sodden hair hanging into her eyes, "Maybe we *are* outside." She then strode to the edge of the clearing and began poking about in the underbrush.

"Told you," said Alabaster, taking a seat on his chunk of red crystal, apparently unconcerned with his sogginess. "What are you doing, Nell?"

"I'm looking for the stupid tunnel," she said testily, raising her voice to be heard above the cacophonous roar of the falling rain. "I'd like to get in out of this storm."

Stanley went to help her. "I think it was right in here," he said, indicating an area where the branches had created a leafy little overhang.

"Me too," said Nell. "That's odd," she said a moment later, "where did all these vines come from?"

"Dunno," said Stanley, "but let's get rid of them." They both grabbed a handful of foliage and pulled, expecting to find a long, narrow avenue through the trees. What they did not expect to find, however, was a solid rock wall.

"What the—" said Stanley.

"What's *that* doing here?" said Nell.

"The tunnel must be over there," said Stanley, wiping water out of his eyes and pointing several feet to their left. They pulled back another mass of vines, leaves and branches, only to find another section of weather-ravaged stone. They spent almost ten minutes tearing up the edges of the clearing, looking for the way back to the museum. Presently, the rain stopped just as suddenly as it had started, and the blazing afternoon sun shone down on the jungle clearing with an intensity that suggested it was trying to make up for lost time.

Soon, they had torn down a great many branches, enough to see that the rock wall they had discovered did not belong to the East Stodgerton Museum of Natural History; it belonged to some kind of ancient, ruined building. It was nowhere near as large as the museum, but there was no easy way around it, and there were certainly no leafy tunnels leading through it. The three of them stood gaping at the ruin for a time, their wet clothes steaming in the balmy jungle heat.

"Okay," Nell said at last, raising her hands and closing her eyes, "Just what … on earth … is going on here?"

"I dunno," Stanley said, breathing heavily, "but that's where we came through, no doubt about it."

"Well, it can't be!" said Nell. "There's a huge old building in the way!"

"We must have come through it!" said Stanley, his voice rising. Truth be told, he was starting to get scared.

"We didn't!" said Nell, almost shouting, "I'd have remembered burrowing through a ten-million year old piece of rock!"

"*Yeah?*" yelled Stanley, "Well … *so would I!*"

"Hey, hold on a sec," Alabaster said suddenly. Stanley and Nell both looked at him. He was kneeling on the grass in front of the rock wall. Hope flooded through Stanley's chest. Had Alabaster found the way back, after all?

"What is it?" said Nell, pouncing on Alabaster, "*What is it?*"

"Well," said Alabaster, "I'm no rock expert—"

"Geologist," said Nell.

"—but I don't think this ruin is ten million years old. I mean, I don't know what kind of *rock* it is, but it looks like this used to be some kind of Aztec pyramid!"

Nell blinked several times. "Aztec?" she repeated.

"Yeah," said Alabaster. "Well, not exactly, but it sure is close, look at all these symbols. If it's not Aztec, it might be some other Central American—"

"I DON'T CARE IF IT'S THE NOSE OFF THE SPHINX!" shrieked Nell, "I CARE ABOUT FINDING THE PATH BACK TO THE MUSEUM!" She stood up and took a deep breath. "Look," she said, forcing herself to remain calm, "we ... are ... *lost*. I don't know where we are, or how we got here, but I'm soaked, I'm scared, and I WANT OUT OF HERE! HELLO?" she cried, placing her hands on either side of her mouth, "CAN ANYONE HEAR ME? IS ANYONE THERE?"

Stanley decided that Nell had the right idea. "HELLO?" he yelled at the top of his lungs, "HELLLOOOO!"

Presently there came the sound of movement from the bushes at the other side of the clearing.

"Hey!" said Alabaster, "You guys did it! Someone's come to rescue—" He trailed off as a five-and-a-half foot tall lizard stepped out of the foliage. The lizard was built like a human, standing upright on a pair of humanoid legs, with its tail sticking out behind it. Its brownish-red scales were painted here and there with bright red markings, and it was wearing a simple loin cloth with a red-and-white pattern on it. In its hands, it carried a round shield and a short, curving sword.

The lizard glared at the three of them, then made a noise that sounded like a hiss and a cough mixed together. The sound ended with a funny 'pop' from the back of the lizard's throat.

Stanley and Nell stared.

"Uh," said Alabaster, "Hablas Español?"

CHAPTER 5

AN UNEXPECTED REUNION

The lizard cocked its head to one side, clearly not understanding what Alabaster had said. It opened its mouth slightly, and said something else in its strange, lizard-ish language. It made several hissing, coughing and whistling sounds, and finished again with that odd popping noise. It leaned forward slightly, as if listening for an answer.

Nell took a few steps forward. "Uh, hello," she said bravely, "Do you speak English?" She took another step, and the lizard let out a cat-like yowl as it leapt backwards. It raised its sword in a clearly unfriendly way, and bared its sharp, pointed teeth, letting out a long, menacing hiss.

"Get back," said Stanley, pulling Nell backwards by the arm. He glanced sideways at her. Her eyes were wide.

"I think it might attack," she said tensely.

Stanley tried to think of something encouraging to say. "Look," he said as inspiration took hold, "there's three of us and only one of him, and *you* know Karate."

Nell looked at him.

"He's probably just trying to figure us out," Stanley went on. "We just have to show him that we're not a threat—"

Just then, the lizard, who had been eyeing them suspiciously, reared up to its full height, thrust its snout in the air, opened its mouth wide, and let out a series of loud, barking coughs. An instant later, several more lizards came slinking out of the bushes. Like the first one, they all wore red-and-white loincloths, but a few of them had bracelets, or rings, or other pieces of jewelry made from what looked like bronze.

Each lizard was armed with a sword and shield of his own. Some of them had short bows and quivers of arrows slung across their backs.

It was then that Stanley noticed the lizards' feet; each foot had four toes, three of which ended in small, pointed claws. The fourth toe (the 'big' toe), however, was equipped with a large, wicked-looking scythe-like claw. Stanley was instantly reminded of dinosaurs like Deinonychus, Dromaeosaurus, and Velociraptor.

There were now nine armed lizards in the clearing, but once each had taken up a defensive position around the perimeter, a tenth lizard emerged from the trees. This one was obviously the leader. His red body paint was much more elaborate than that of his comrades, and on his head he wore a headdress made of colourful feathers which were still drooping and sodden from the recent rain. He also wore a thick necklace, bracelets, anklets, and a belt, all of which were made of gold. Instead of a loincloth, he wore a skirt made of scaly metal plates. In his hand he held a long spear.

This newcomer exchanged a few quick words with the first lizard. He then looked straight at Nell, pointed with a clawed finger, and made a fluttering hissing sound.

Nell looked at Stanley.

Stanley merely shrugged. He had no idea what to do.

The lead lizard barked loudly, and repeated the fluttering hiss, this time adding a 'click' at the end (but no 'pop').

"We're sorry," said Stanley, not knowing what else to say, "We don't understand you."

The lead lizard made a loud clicking sound, and threw its arms in the air in a very human gesture of disgust and annoyance. It barked something to its warriors, and before Stanley knew what was happening, three of the lizards had each raised a small wooden tube to their reptilian lips. They blew sharply into the tubes, and with a soft *fwoomp*, three tiny darts came flying forth, one of which embedded itself in Stanley's right shoulder.

"Yow!" he exclaimed, yanking the dart free and throwing it away. He looked quickly at his friends. Alabaster was already flat on the ground. Nell had pulled a dart out of her neck, and was staring at it, her mouth open. She looked at Stanley, her eyes wide with surprise and fear.

"Stanley!" she managed to say, before her bright green eyes rolled up into her head and she collapsed beside Alabaster.

"*Nell!*" Stanley cried, "*Alabaster*!" But then he began to feel very dizzy. The jungle swam before his eyes, and everything seemed to melt and turn into great, colourful lumps of green, and blue, and red ...

Stanley was feeling very tired. He stumbled backward and landed on his bottom. He sank back and lay down on the damp grass, unable to keep his eyes open, wanting nothing more than to take a nice, long nap.

Before he fell asleep, though, he heard a series of high-pitched shrieks. The noises cut through his befogged consciousness, and he opened his eyes, forcing them back into focus for just a few more seconds. Fighting to raise his head, he saw that the lizards were running here and there all over the clearing, shrieking loudly and tumbling over one another in a mad rush to escape what looked like a huge, walking lump of fur and leaves, which was chasing them and swinging at them with a large club.

Stanley briefly wondered what in the world was going on, but it was all happening in slow motion, and that seemed very funny to him. He grinned stupidly and tried to laugh, but passed out instead.

The lizards ran off screeching in every direction. A powerful arm lifted the unconscious Stanley off the ground, and bore him off into the jungle.

★ ★ ★

It was dark when Stanley awoke. He tried to move, and found that his arms and legs were quite stiff. He also had a slight headache, so he simply lay there on his back for a time, and tried to figure out where he was. The night air was alive with the sounds of chirping crickets and other insects. Every so often, the piercing cry of some night bird could be heard from somewhere not far off.

Something told Stanley that these sounds were a little too authentic for a museum exhibit.

"I'm still in the jungle, then," he said to himself. "But I still don't know where I am."

He was surprised to find that he was lying on what felt like a soft, furry blanket, with another one draped over him. His clothes weren't damp anymore, but he still felt a bit chilly. He sat up, though the effort made his head throb a bit, and looked around. He appeared to be inside some kind of tent. He could see an oval opening from where he was, and beyond it, he could hear the crackling and popping of a campfire. The fire's warm golden glow stole through the opening, casting a small amount of light around the tent's interior.

It seemed to be of fairly simple make; sheets of something, possibly animal hide, had been sewn together and attached to a framework of long wooden poles. The tent was about fifteen feet across at its base, with a dirt floor. The walls tapered towards the top of the tent, which was more than high enough to allow a tall man to stand up inside. Looking to his left and right, Stanley noticed two more bundles of fur, and was relieved to discover that they contained Alabaster and Nell. They were fast asleep on their backs, lying completely still, except for the slow rise and fall of their chests as they breathed.

Stanley took a closer look at Alabaster, and shook him gently to see if he'd wake up. Alabaster didn't so much as twitch, though, so Stanley left him alone. He leaned over towards Nell, too, and looked down at her sleeping face. A memory of his childhood suddenly floated up from his subconscious, and he was reminded of an occasion on which his mother had read him 'Snow White', back when she still read him bedtime stories. The young Stanley had said that Snow White looked very bootiful, asleep there in the glass case while the seven dwarves stood around it, holding their hats in their hands and looking sad. Mrs. Brambles had thought that this was the cutest thing ever, but even now, years later, Stanley still cringed at the thought of it.

Presently, he realized that he had been staring at Nell for some time. He looked away and coughed embarrassedly, even though there was no one in here besides his sleeping friends. It seemed that someone had heard him cough, though, because just then, there came the sound of approaching footsteps from outside the tent. Stanley immediately lay back down and pretended to be asleep, just before a large, dark shape came climbing in through the oval doorway. Stanley kept his eyes shut tightly, trying to mimic Alabaster's and Nell's breathing.

The dark shape stood there for a second or two, then took a step forward, turned, and knelt down with its back to Stanley. There came the clunky sound of wood being stacked, and then a sharp *'clack' 'clack' 'clack'* as if the person was banging rocks together. Soon, a warm, cozy glow sprang up, accompanied by that familiar crackling and popping. Stanley opened one eye and saw that the stranger had lit a small fire within a ring of stones in the middle of the tent. The smoke from the fire swirled upwards and disappeared through an opening in the conical roof.

The mysterious person poked at the little fire with a stick, then went back outside. Stanley immediately got up and went over to the fire, warming his hands.

"You can come outside if you want," said a voice from outside the tent. It was a low, harsh voice, and Stanley wondered if its owner was entirely friendly. He also wondered how its owner knew he was awake.

"There's a bigger fire out here," the voice went on, "and food, if you want it. You'll probably want to bring one of those furs with you."

Stanley sat there for a moment, and then, deciding that whoever was out there was probably not in league with the nasty lizards who had attacked them, he grabbed his furry blanket and climbed through the oval doorway. Outside, he took a quick glance at his surroundings. He was in a small clearing, in the centre of which was a large fire pit with a roaring blaze crackling merrily in it. Hanging over the fire on a makeshift roasting spit was what looked like a whole pig.

Sitting by the fire was someone covered from head to foot in a mismatch of furs and skins. A pair of furry boots, and clumsily-stitched trousers could be seen beneath the lump of furs, as the someone sat cross-legged by the roasting spit, turning it slowly.

"I didn't expect you to be up so soon," said the someone, not looking up as Stanley approached timidly.

To Stanley, this seemed an odd thing to say. "Uh … why is that?" he asked.

"That dart was coated with the venom of the Crested Viper," said the someone, still not looking at him.

"*Venom?*" said Stanley, as a terrible thought flashed into his mind. "My friends—"

"It's not lethal," said the someone, interrupting him. "It's a powerful sleeping toxin, nothing more. Your friends'll be fine. They won't be feeling too good when they get up, though. Here," he said, holding up what looked like half a coconut filled with some kind of liquid, "drink this."

"Uh," said Stanley, hesitant to accept anything from a strange person living in the jungle.

"Drink it," said the stranger, "It'll help your headache."

"My head's really not that bad," said Stanley truthfully.

"Drink it," the stranger said tersely. "And don't worry," he said, as Stanley took the half coconut, "I'm not going to poison you, or hurt you or anything."

Stanley sniffed the liquid in the coconut. It smelled spicy. He lifted it to his lips and took a sip—a bigger sip than he'd intended, and he coughed and spluttered as an intense burning sensation filled his throat. For a moment he thought he really *had* been poisoned, but the burning quickly passed, and he was left with a pleasantly warm feeling that seemed to spread to his entire body. His headache vanished almost instantly.

"Thanks," he said hoarsely, handing back the coconut.

The stranger nodded slightly.

"Um," said Stanley, not sure how to begin questioning this strange person, "how long was I asleep?'

"A few hours," said the stranger. "The sun only set about half an hour ago. It sets early this time of year."

Stanley looked up at the sky. It wasn't completely dark yet, but the stars were out, and so were the moons.

He gasped. There were three moons in the sky. One was blue, one was green, and the third, barely visible over the treetops, was large and red. "Terra!" Stanley exclaimed, "We're on Terra!"

"Uh, yeah," said the stranger, "I thought that went without saying."

Stanley looked back at him. There was something familiar about this strange person. Something about his voice, the way he talked … Stanley leaned sideways, trying to get a good look at the stranger's face. He couldn't see anything, though, because it was dark, and the stranger's head was almost completely covered by the top half of some big jungle cat's head, which he was wearing like a helmet.

"Who … who are you?" said Stanley.

"What?" said the stranger, turning to look at him. Stanley thought he could see a yellowish gleam in the depths of the cat-head helmet.

"*Who are you?*" Stanley repeated.

The stranger paused, as if trying to decide whether or not Stanley was joking. Then, he reached up and pulled the jungle cat pelt back from his head. Stanley gasped for the second time. Blazing yellow eyes glared at him from out of a black, mostly featureless face, a face that Stanley had thought he would never see again.

"*Grey?*" he said disbelievingly, "Is that … really you?"

It was.

"Yes," Grey said curtly. He glowered at Stanley for a moment. "Is there a problem?"

"What?" said Stanley, "A problem? No, of course not, I just … didn't know it was you, I, er … uh …"

Grey gave the roasting spit a quick quarter turn, then noticed that Stanley was staring at him open-mouthed.

"*What?*" he demanded.

"N-nothing!" said Stanley. "I just … I didn't expect to run into you here—or anywhere!"

"I didn't expect to find *you* here, either," said Grey, as if he were blaming Stanley for something.

Stanley found these words a bit hurtful. It almost sounded like Grey wasn't pleased to see him. Then he reflected that Grey never sounded pleased about anything.

"What's the matter?" snapped Grey, "You keep staring. Are you hungry or something?"

"*What are you doing here?*" said Stanley, jumping to his feet.

Grey looked at him as if he were an idiot. "Cooking dinner," he said, waving at the roasting pig.

"You know that's not what I meant," Stanley countered, taking a step forward.

"Okay," said Grey, "What *do* you mean?"

"*I thought you were dead!*" yelled Stanley, pointing at him accusingly. "You were still on the Titanodon's back when it dove down to the bottom of the ocean!"

"It didn't dive to the bottom of the ocean," said Grey.

"Oh," said Stanley, "Well … I guess that explains—"

"It dove down a little over half a mile, I think," said Grey.

"*Half a mile!*" cried Stanley. Grey just looked at him. "Then what? What did you do? How did you survive?"

Grey scowled. "I swam back to the surface," he said, as if Stanley was being intentionally dense.

"*You swam back to the surface!*" cried Stanley.

"Why do you keep repeating everything I say?" Grey asked savagely.

"Because!" said Stanley, "It's—it's amazing! It's *too* amazing! I almost don't believe it!"

"You think I'm lying?" said Grey, not sounding too concerned.

"No, of course not," said Stanley, "but you have to admit, it's a pretty amazing story! I don't think there are many people who could get dragged half a mile underwater and live to tell about it!"

Grey thought about that for a moment. "No, I suppose not."

"No one else survived, did they?" said Stanley, trying to further prove his point.

"No," said Grey. "There were a lot of bodies floating around down there."

Stanley pictured Grey kicking his way out of the underwater darkness, swimming past hundreds of drowned corpses suspended in the dim, half-lit water. It didn't make for a pleasant image.

"Um … so?" said Stanley, anxious to hear the rest of the tale.

"So what?" said Grey.

"So what happened next?" said Stanley. "This is obviously not interesting to you, but it is to me, so tell me everything!"

"Alright, alright," said Grey. "Once I reached the surface, I grabbed onto some wreckage from the ship—"

"The Maelstrom," Stanley supplied.

"Right," said Grey. "Well, I made a sort of raft, and I paddled till I washed up on shore. That's it."

"Wow!" said Stanley, sitting back down. "That's just … amazing!"

"You said that already," said Grey.

"I know! Because it *is*! I didn't think *anybody* would survive that! And nobody else *did!* … uh …" An unsettling thought suddenly crossed his mind. "Grey?"

"What?"

"You *were* the only survivor, right?"

"As far as I know."

"You didn't see anyone else, uh … swimming back to the surface? Floating on some wreckage?"

"No."

"So … the sorcerer … the masked man you were fighting with—"

"What about him?"

"You don't think he could have survived, do you?" Stanley hadn't thought about the masked man since June, and as pleased as he was to see Grey alive, and to hear his albeit concise tale of survival against all odds, he couldn't help but think that of all the people who had been unfortunate enough to find themselves trapped on the Titanodon's back that fateful day, the ones with the greatest chance of survival were Grey and the masked man. By a longshot.

Grey, however, was shaking his head. "He was dead before he hit the water."

"He was?" said Stanley, feeling morbidly relieved.

"I broke his neck," said Grey darkly. "I felt him go limp and collapse just before we all got sucked down. I think he went further than anyone." He glanced sideways at Stanley. "I wouldn't have done it if it'd been anyone else," he said in a different tone. "It was either him or me … and he almost got *me*." He pulled back his furs and showed Stanley his left shoulder. There was nothing below it.

"Your arm!" said Stanley, horrified. "How did—"

"He cut it off," said Grey. "That's no ordinary sword he had, believe me, I know."

Stanley nodded, his eyes wide. Grey had lost an arm to the masked man. It was a horrid ending to the story. "Wait a minute," said Stanley, another thought springing into his mind, "So that means you swam half a mile, built a raft, paddled all the way back to shore, built a tent, and this campsite, all missing an arm?"

"Yes," said Grey.

Stanley clapped a hand to his forehead. "That's—"

"Amazing, I know," said Grey.

★ ★ ★

"Will Alabaster and Nell be awake soon?" Stanley asked. He and Grey were still seated by the fire, waiting for the meat to finish cooking.

"No," said Grey, "I doubt if they'll be awake before tomorrow afternoon, and even if they are, they won't be in much condition to do anything."

Stanley frowned. "But I'm wide awake," he said, pointing at himself, "and I feel fine."

Grey glared at him. "I was surprised to find you awake after only a few hours. That dart had enough venom on it to knock out a full-grown gorethane."

"A what?" said Stanley.

"Gorethane," said Grey, indicating the pig-like animal roasting over the fire. "Very big, very dangerous. This one's just a baby." He turned the spit twice, then jabbed the glistening carcass with a sharp fork carved from bone.

"A baby?" said Stanley.

Grey looked at him. "They become almost inedible when they get big. The meat gets too tough. For *your* teeth, at least," he added, giving the spit another quarter turn. "That should do it." He took the spit off the fire and thrust it into the ground, then seized one of the gorethane's hind legs and tore it off unceremoniously before handing it to Stanley, who accepted it hesitantly.

"Just say if you want more," said Grey, tearing off a shank for himself. His blank, flat face was suddenly split by a large mouth filled with sharp, pointed teeth. Stanley had never been able to figure out how Grey's mouth worked. One second it was nowhere to be seen, the next, there it was, tearing meat off of a gorethane's leg bone.

"What?" Grey said through a mouthful of meat. "Aren't you hungry?"

"Huh?" said Stanley as Grey chewed loudly, "Oh, uh, sure I am." He took an experimental bite. It tasted pretty good, so he tucked right in; he hadn't realized it, but he was actually *quite* hungry.

Grey cleaned the meat off his bone and licked his lips with his unsettlingly long tongue. Stanley watched as he tore off another shank and bit into it savagely.

"Remember when my Uncle Jack almost *ordered* you to eat breakfast?"

Grey paused in his chewing and glared at him.

"You said you didn't have to eat, and that it was a waste of resources if you did." Stanley couldn't help but grin as he said this.

Grey swallowed his mouthful of meat and belched greasily. "I've gotten used to it," he said, before taking another large bite.

Stanley's haunch of meat proved to be too much for him, so he gave the rest to Grey, who proceeded to finish off the rest of the roasted gorethane, as well. Grey took a long drink from a stout clay jar, then handed it to Stanley. Stanley was almost expecting some other kind of burning, spicy liquid, but it was just water.

After dinner was over, Stanley lay back on the grass with his hands behind his head, and looked up at the stars, while Grey sat and scowled at the fire. The moons were now high in the sky, and the stars were brilliant, as brilliant as they'd been on the high seas.

What am I doing here? Stanley thought to himself as he stared up at the sky. He had thought, of course, that he would never see Terra and its three moons ever again, and now here he was, seemingly by accident. It was almost like a dream.

"Grey?" he said after he'd been gazing at the sky for some time. Grey grunted to show that he was listening. "Do you know where we are?"

Grey's head turned sharply towards him.

"I mean, I know we're here, at your campsite, in the middle of a jungle, but … *where are we?* What part of the world? We're not in Rhedland, are we?"

Grey took a moment to answer. "We're in Verduria. Western continent, southern hemisphere. About five hundred miles from the equator."

For some reason, this didn't surprise Stanley very much. "Hmm," he said. "It sure is chilly for being close to the equator."

"It can get pretty cool at night," said Grey, "but you're still dealing with the after-effects of the viper venom. It'll give you the chills for a couple more days."

"Grey?" said Stanley. He was starting to feel sleepy again.

"Hm?"

"Why didn't the venom work as well on me as it did on Nell and Alabaster?"

"How should I know?" said Grey.

"Well, you've been living in the jungle for a while now, right?" said Stanley. "You seem to know all about it."

"I don't know all about it," said Grey.

"How long have you been out here?" asked Stanley.

"Nine months, maybe less," said Grey.

"Wow," said Stanley. "That's a long time."

"Hm," said Grey.

"Are there any other people around?"

"There's a town north-east of here, on the coast," said Grey. "About thirty miles."

"Why didn't you stay there?" said Stanley.

"Didn't feel like it," said Grey.

"Don't you get lonely?"

"What?"

"Isn't it a bit lonely out here, all by yourself?"

Grey didn't answer. He just sat and stared at the fire for several minutes. Finally, he said,

"I'm going to bed," and he lay down with his back to the fire, and curled up in his furs.

Stanley took the hint that he should go to bed, too. As he started to climb through the opening in the tent, he said,

"You're sleeping out here?"

"I'll be fine," said Grey tersely.

"I thought you didn't have to sleep, either," said Stanley, before he could stop himself.

Grey grunted. "I've gotten used to that, too."

Chapter 6

THE MARUSAI

Stanley woke the next morning to the sound of leaves rustling and birds singing, and of Grey rummaging around inside the tent. He still had his furs on, as well as his hand-stitched boots and trousers. Stanley wondered how in the world Grey had managed to stitch *anything* with only one hand.

Noticing him sitting up, Grey said,

"I'm going to get water, and then I'm going hunting." He slung a short bow and a quiver full of arrows over his shoulder, then picked up the clay water jug. It had straps on it that let him wear it like a backpack. "D'you want to come?"

"Huh?" said Stanley. Had Grey just asked him if he wanted to come hunting with him? "With you?"

Grey scowled.

"Well … yeah!" said Stanley, but then he looked at Alabaster and Nell, both of whom were still fast asleep. "Uh, but do you think it's safe to leave them here?"

"They'll be fine," said Grey. "Nothing will come near the campsite, don't worry."

Stanley got up and followed him out of the tent.

"Here," said Grey, picking up a piece of animal hide which seemed to be covered in leaves. He draped it over Stanley. "Camouflage," he said.

The hide was uncomfortably warm, and smelled musty, but Stanley, not wanting to seem ungrateful, kept it on.

"Take this, too," said Grey, holding up a short, curved metal sword. It looked like the ones the lizards from yesterday had been carrying.

Stanley took the sword wordlessly, hoping very much that he wouldn't have to use it. "Grey," he said, following him across the clearing, "are you *sure* Nell and Alabaster will be okay while we're gone?"

"Yes," said Grey.

"So, no jungle animals will come near them?"

"That's right."

"Um," said Stanley, "yesterday there were these … er … lizards, and they—"

Grey stopped at the entrance to the clearing and pointed at something just ahead.

"Uugh!" said Stanley, when he saw what it was: at the very entrance to the clearing, a severed lizard head had been put on a stick, like some kind of grisly sign post. It was dry and sunken, and had clearly been there a while.

"Did … did you—"

"Yes," said Grey, as he made his way past the head and out of the clearing. "That tells them to stay away from me."

"Who are they?" asked Stanley, trying to change the subject slightly. "They attacked us yesterday, and—"

"I know. I was there," said Grey. "They're Saurians. Lizard people, in case you didn't notice."

"Saurians?" Stanley repeated. Where had he heard that name before?

"Verduria is their home," said Grey. "They live deep in the jungle to the south, but recently some tribes have been moving north. At least, that's what it sounds like. Their language isn't easy to learn."

"You can speak their language?" said Stanley incredulously.

"Sort of," said Grey.

"Well that's pretty good!" said Stanley. "Why don't you talk to them? Maybe you could make friends with them."

"They don't want to be friends," Grey said darkly. "They're not what you'd call *nice*. I don't know about the other tribes, but the ones that live around here—the ones that wear red—well, it's best if you don't run into them."

"The ones yesterday seemed like they were trying to communicate," said Stanley.

"They were," said Grey. "They wanted to know why you were defiling their sacred land."

"Oh," said Stanley. "That's why they shot those darts at us, I guess."

"No," said Grey, "they shot the darts at you because they were planning on taking you back to their camp and sacrificing you to their sun god. Then, they were going to eat you."

Stanley gulped. They walked on in silence for a bit.

"So … why do the Saurians leave *you* alone?" Stanley asked after a few minutes.

"They think I'm some kind of demon," Grey answered, looking sideways at him.

Stanley had the sneaking suspicion that Grey enjoyed that fact.

"Okay," Grey said, as they approached a tall wall of grass, "there's a shallow stream just ahead. Follow me." He crouched low and disappeared into the grass. Stanley followed.

He went on for ten metres or so, crawling through tall grass and bushes, and found himself at the edge of the stream Grey had mentioned. It was wide but shallow, with a rocky bed, and standing in the water maybe thirty yards away, was a herd of strange-looking animals. They looked like a cross between a warthog and a rhinoceros. Their bodies were covered with thick, grey, lumpy-looking skin, and the bigger ones had huge, curving horns above their turned-up snouts, as well as big, wicked-looking tusks sticking out on either side of their mouths.

It was a herd of gorethanes. Stanley could tell what they were, even before seeing the younger ones scampering about in the water, splashing each other while their parents grunted and snorted sociably as they enjoyed a nice, cool drink. Stanley felt a hand grab his shoulder, and let out a small yelp as he was dragged back into the bushes. Immediately, the biggest, toughest, fiercest-looking gorethane looked up and glared at the general area where Stanley had been only seconds before. It grunted loudly, and the whole herd froze.

"Be quiet," said Grey, who had grabbed Stanley's shoulder.

"*Sorry!*" whispered Stanley, "You just surprised me!"

"Shhh," said Grey.

Stanley obeyed.

Several tense moments ticked by, and then the sounds of splashing and grunting could once again be heard from the direction of the herd.

"Okay," said Grey, unslinging his bow and placing it on the ground, "I'm going to shoot one. They're going to scatter, and they probably won't come this way, but they will if they think we're here."

"Uh," said Stanley.

"They probably won't charge," said Grey as he took an arrow out of his quiver and placed it on his bow, "but if they *do*, find a big tree and climb it."

"Uh, okay," said Stanley.

"Make *sure* it's a big one," said Grey.

Stanley nodded, but he wondered whether he might have been better off staying back at the camp. Grey picked his bow up off the ground, opened his mouth, and nocked the arrow with his teeth. He then crept to the edge of the bushes, now using his teeth to draw back the bowstring. Stanley stayed as close as he dared, ready to spring for the nearest tree should anything go wrong.

"Something's wrong," Grey muttered, pulling back and taking the bowstring out of his mouth.

"What?" whispered Stanley.

"I can't see the leader. The head of the herd, the really big one. He should still be there ... we need to leave."

"Why?" said Stanley, but just then, his question was answered as a huge, ugly, piggish head thrust itself out of the bushes right beside them. Small, beady eyes glared fiercely from deep in their cavernous sockets, in a face that looked like something carved from stone.

The gorethane snorted wetly, then raised its head and let fly a thunderous bellow that blew Stanley's hair back and nearly made him fall over. Its breath smelled like a ripe compost heap.

"Run, Stanley," Grey said calmly, as he wound up with his remaining arm and punched the van-sized gorethane square in the snout. Stanley dove from the bushes, listening to the gorethane's surprisingly high-pitched squeal of pain and outrage. He raced back the way they had come, casting about desperately for a tree big enough to scramble up, but none of the big ones had branches that were low enough for him. He could hear the beast stampeding through the underbrush somewhere behind him, but the noise grew fainter and fainter as he ran on. The sounds of heavy feet and splintering wood eventually faded away completely, and Stanley slowed to a brisk trot, just in time to walk right into the severed Saurian head that marked the entrance to Grey's camp.

"*Bleah!*" he exclaimed as he spun away from the head and stumbled into the clearing, throwing off his camouflage and flopping down beside the fire pit. It was then that he realized he was not alone. Standing in front of the tent was a person dressed in a strange suit of armour. The suit covered most of his body, but was not made of great metal plates. Rather, it seemed that small, thin strips of metal had been woven together to form flexible arm guards, shoulder guards, shin guards, leg guards, and a chest piece. The person also wore an odd metal helmet that sloped down at the back. The bottom half of the person's face was covered by a metal mask representing some monster's snarling, fang-filled jaws. Above the mask, sharp, bright eyes regarded Stanley with scrutiny.

"You," said the armoured warrior, pointing sharply at him, "What are you doing here?" He was definitely a man, though he sounded fairly young.

"I could ask you the same thing," said Stanley, trying to catch his breath.

The warrior was undaunted by Stanley's insolence. "How is it that a child like you is to be found this deep in the jungle?" he demanded.

"*Hey!*" said Stanley, "I'm not a child! I'm *thirteen!*"

"There are two others who slumber in yon tent," said the warrior, paying no attention to Stanley's indignation.

"I know," said Stanley, "They're my friends."

The warrior took a step forward. "Your friends have been placed under a sleeping enchantment. You may all three be in very grave danger."

"Danger?" echoed Stanley. "What do you—"

"It is rumoured," the warrior said softly, "that this place is the abode of a *demon!*" He said 'demon' so sharply that Stanley jumped.

"What?" said Stanley.

"A darkness has fallen over the forest in recent months," said the warrior, pacing about the clearing, "A sinister force that frightens animals, and makes them fierce."

"I just got away from some gorethanes," said Stanley. "*They* were pretty fierce."

The warrior stopped and looked at him. "They were not always so."

"They weren't?"

"There is an evil power at work in this jungle," said the warrior, coming towards Stanley, "and I believe that its source is here, in this clearing."

"Here?" said Stanley. What was this guy talking about?

"*Demon!*" the warrior said loudly, raising his head and drawing forth a long, thin, slightly curved sword, "Hear me! After much searching, I have at last found your lair! I have come here today to put an end to your mischief! You will corrupt this jungle no more! If you are not the coward I believe you to be, then show yourself, and face me in battle!"

Stanley stared wide-eyed at the warrior, who had dropped into a defensive stance, holding his sword at the ready.

"*Show yourself, demon!*" the warrior said again. "You will heed me, creature of darkness! In the name of the Marusai, I command you, SHOW YOURSELF!"

Suddenly there came a rustling in the trees and a crackling of snapping branches, and Grey leaped down from above, to land beside Stanley in the middle of the clearing. His furs and trousers were torn here and there, and he looked a tad disheveled, but otherwise, he seemed in good health.

"Grey!" Stanley said, jumping to his feet as relief flooded through him, "You're alright!"

"Stanley," Grey said tonelessly, as usual seemingly unaware that he had just made a spectacular entrance.

"GET BACK, BOY!" shouted the armoured warrior, pointing his sword at Grey. "So, demon, you are not such a coward, after all! So be it. Prepare to die, creature of darkness!"

Grey looked at the warrior with mild surprise in his yellow eyes. He glanced questioningly at Stanley.

"Um—" said Stanley, but before he could get anything else out, the warrior had charged at Grey and thrust at him with his sword.

"*Ha-aaa!*" cried the warrior, as Grey dodged the attack with preternatural speed, "You are fast, demon, but you will taste my steel before long!" He swung his blade in a wide arc, but Grey ducked with plenty of time to spare.

Grey countered with a swift sweep kick, but the warrior sprang nimbly out of the way. He slashed downward and caught Grey in the leg with the edge of his sword. Grey snarled, his sharp teeth coming into view, and rolled away. The warrior took a moment to look at his sword. A few tiny drops of thick, inky-black liquid dripped off the blade and landed on the grass. He had wounded Grey.

"Your hide is thick, indeed, creature," said the warrior, stalking towards Grey, who was back on his feet. "That cut would have severed a normal man's leg!"

"*Stop it!*" yelled Stanley, running forward, but not wanting to get too close to that swinging sword.

"Get back, boy," said the warrior, taking another swing at Grey, "I will have this beast vanquished soon enough." He thrust forward with his sword, and was surprised to have it parried aside by a long, black blade which Grey seemed to have drawn from nowhere.

The warrior backed off and dropped back into his defensive stance. "So, you possess a blade of your own, eh, demon?" he said, breathing heavily. "And you've some skill at wielding it …"

"*He's not a demon!*" Stanley yelled.

"What?" said the warrior, "How can you possibly—"

His question was interrupted as Grey leaped at him and knocked him backwards. The warrior landed on his back with Grey on top of him, holding the point of his black sword inches from his throat.

"Drop your sword," Grey growled.

"Never!" snarled the warrior.

"Do it," said Grey, bringing the point of his sword a tiny bit closer.

The warrior lay there for a moment, breathing heavily.

"Grey," said Stanley. He wasn't sure what Grey was about to do, but he was ready to spring, just in case, even though he could no more stop Grey than he could a stampeding gorethane.

"Drop. Your. Sword," Grey seethed, his yellow eyes blazing.

The warrior grunted as if under a great strain, and then, finally, let his sword fall out of his hand. Stanley kicked it away.

"So be it," said the warrior. "You have defeated me, demon, with the help of your mischievous imp. Finish me!"

Grey glared fiercely down at him, then pulled his sword away from the warrior's throat. "Get up," he said, standing up and putting away his black sword (it seemed to disappear completely).

"Wh-what?" said the warrior, who had closed his eyes.

"I said get up," said Grey, pacing around the clearing and picking up things that had been knocked askew.

"But …" said the warrior.

"GET UP!" roared Grey, and the warrior sprang to his feet.

"What … what trickery is this?" he said. "What manner of demon are you, that spares the lives of mortal men? Do you keep me alive to laugh at my dishonour?"

"*He's not a demon!*" yelled Stanley, making the warrior jump.

"Not a demon?" he said, looking from Stanley to Grey and back to Stanley. "What is he, then?"

"He's … he's … uh …" Stanley paused. What *was* Grey, anyway?

"I am what I am," said Grey simply. "Nothing more, nothing less."

The warrior stood in thought for a time. "Perhaps you are not a demon," he said at last. "I do not feel a sense of menace as I stand in this place … though even here, I can tell that this land is troubled by darkness." He looked back at Grey. "It would appear that I acted with haste and thoughtlessness," he said stiffly. "Such conduct is unbecoming of a Marusai warrior. I have brought dishonour upon myself." He put a fist over his heart, and kneeled on the ground.

Stanley looked at Grey. The warrior was clearly waiting for a word of forgiveness from him.

"Forget it," said Grey.

Stanley wasn't sure if he'd meant, 'forget it, no harm done', or, 'forget it, I'm not going to forgive you'. Whatever his meaning, though, the warrior jumped to his feet and said,

"Thank you, sir, you are most kind."

Stanley would have liked to have had a few words with the warrior regarding his little 'imp' comment, but just then, Nell appeared at the tent's doorway, looking pale and tired.

"Stanley?" she said woozily, "What's going on out here?"

"So," said the warrior, "the sleeping spell is broken?"

"It's not a spell," said Stanley, picking up his sword and handing it to him. "It was the venom of the crested viper."

"Ah," said the warrior, accepting his weapon. "Incidentally," he said once he had sheathed it, "it is considered very rude to handle a Marusai's sword without his permission."

"I was just giving it back to you," said Stanley, slightly taken aback.

Nell climbed out of the tent, but she stumbled, and the warrior caught her before she fell.

"Easy," he said, his proper, chivalric tone softening considerably.

"Where … what …?" said Nell groggily.

"You're alright," said the warrior, as if he himself had rescued her from the Saurians yesterday.

Nell looked up at him, and her green eyes widened. "Who—?" she said feebly.

"Introductions *after*," said Grey, as he handed Nell a half coconut full of the spicy, burning liquid.

* * *

"...And then I ran all the way back here!" said Stanley. The small group was seated around the fire pit: Stanley, Grey, Nell, Alabaster (who had woken up just after Nell) and the mysterious warrior. Stanley had just finished recounting everything that had happened since yesterday, as well as Grey's tale of survival, which Grey had not felt like repeating. Nell and Alabaster didn't know Grey very well (to be fair, though, neither did Stanley), but they seemed pleased enough to see him alive. That is, as pleased as they could be, while fighting off the after-effects of the crested viper venom.

"Well, thank you, Grey," Nell said tiredly, "It sounds like you saved our lives."

"Yeah," said Alabaster, his eyes half open, "we owe you one." He gave Grey a weak but friendly pat on the back. Grey ignored them both.

"How are you feeling?" Stanley asked his friends. Nell and Alabaster were both very pale, with dark circles under their eyes. They were also both wrapped in furs, even though there was a fire burning right in front of them, and the weather that day was balmy, to say the least.

"Pretty lousy," said Alabaster hoarsely, taking another sip of spicy burning-liquid.

"We'll be fine," said Nell, shivering slightly. "*You* sure look good though, Stanley."

"Uh," said Stanley, feeling his ears heating up.

"Oh! Uh, I mean you look like you're feeling good. Feeling *well*," Nell said quickly, a microscopic amount of colour coming back into her cheeks.

"Oh, uh, yeah," said Stanley. "I was only out for a few hours yesterday. I guess the venom didn't affect me as badly as it did you guys."

"Hmm," said Nell, "I wonder why that would be?"

"*Because*," said Alabaster, "Stanley's Wolverine."

"Oh, he is not," said Nell, "And so help me, if you start saying 'bub' again—"

"Of course he's Wolverine, bub," said Alabaster, his sense of humour apparently unaffected by the viper venom, "He's got superhuman healing powers, bub! I thought we'd been over this already, bub!"

"Shut up!" said Nell, massaging her temples. "My head hurts too much to listen to your … *nonsense!*"

"Okay, bub," said Alabaster.

Grey reached out and grabbed Alabaster by the front of his shirt, dragging him forward so that their faces were mere inches apart. "Stop. Saying. Things," he growled.

"My thoughts exactly!" Alabaster said cheerfully. Grey released him. Stanley smirked loudly into his hand.

"Um … Grey?" Nell said a bit timidly, "You don't happen to have anything to eat here, do you?"

"No," said Grey. "I didn't manage to catch anything on our hunting trip today."

"Oh," said Nell.

Grey glowered around the circle. "If everyone's hungry, I'll go catch something right now," he said, getting up and seizing his bow.

"Pardon me," said the warrior, who had been sitting silently across from Grey and looking very mysterious. They all looked at him.

"Forgive me for interrupting," he said politely, "but I have some food with me, if anyone wants it." He opened a small leather bag on the ground beside him, and drew forth something wrapped in a piece of cloth. The something turned out to be a small stack of round, whitish cakes. He passed them around, and Stanley noticed that he gave the first one to Nell.

"Uh … what are they?" said Alabaster, sniffing his cake suspiciously.

"They're called *po-chi*," said the warrior. "They're made from grains and honey. Good for long journeys, they keep well and are nutritious."

Grey scowled at his po-chi, then took a bite. He chewed for a few seconds, then spat it out into the fire pit. He then got up, flung the half-eaten cake on the ground, and left the clearing.

The warrior picked it up and placed it back in his bag. "Po-chi should not be wasted," he said reprovingly. "That fellow … he may not be a demon, but he certainly has the manners for it."

"He's not very sociable," said Stanley, taking a bite of po-chi. It tasted like toast with honey. "He's probably still a bit mad at you for trying to kill him," he added.

"I admitted my mistake," said the warrior. "That should be sufficient."

Stanley shrugged. He still hadn't decided whether or not he liked this mysterious character.

"Are you a Samurai?" Alabaster asked of the warrior.

"A what?"

"A Samurai," said Alabaster, "from feudal Japan? Early twelfth century right up into the eighteen hundreds?"

Nell stared at him incredulously.

"I think," said Alabaster.

The warrior said, "I'm afraid I've never heard of this land you call 'Foodajapan'. My homeland is called Narrone, though I have not been there for some time."

"Who *are* you?" said Nell.

"Oh," said the warrior, as if just remembering something, "Forgive me for not introducing myself earlier." He undid the metal mask covering his face, and took off his helmet.

Stanley was surprised to see that the warrior looked even younger than his voice suggested. In fact, he didn't look much older than him, Alabaster, or Nell. His face was youthful and boyish at first glance, but there was also a certain grimness to it. A thin scar ran diagonally from above his right eyebrow and ended below his left eye. The eyes themselves were bright and sharp, but also hard and cold, as if they had seen a great deal of unpleasantness in their time.

"My name is Mitsuhiro Ryunosuke Akechi," the young warrior said, losing the other three instantly.

"Misty-Roona-Aka-*who?*" said Alabaster, gripping his head in his hands.

The warrior raised an eyebrow. He looked vaguely amused by Alabaster's reaction. "It may be difficult for you to pronounce … you may call me *Ryuno*, for short."

"Ree-oo-no," said Alabaster. "I think I can handle that."

Ryuno smiled. "I am a Marusai warrior," he said. "I have lived by the sword all my life, and fought in many battles."

"You've fought battles?' said Nell. "Like, in wars?"

Ryuno nodded. "The people of my country have been at war for centuries."

"With who?" asked Nell.

"With each other." Ryuno sighed. "The last emperor of Narrone died over seven hundred years ago. He had no children, and left no heir. The clan lords began to squabble and fight amongst themselves, trying to decide who was worthy to be the next emperor. An agreement could not be reached, however, and the larger, more powerful clans soon declared war on each other. Since that time, the scattered clans and families of Narrone have been at war, each trying to wipe the other out, so that in the end, only one clan will remain. And the clan that survives, will rule the land."

"That sounds awful," said Nell.

Ryuno shrugged. "War has been our way of life for almost a thousand years. It's all anyone knows anymore." He looked sharply at Nell. "It is the way of the Marusai."

Nell stared at him, apparently at a loss for words.

Stanley was getting to like Ryuno less and less the more he talked. Sure, it sounded like he'd had a rough life, but he seemed like a bit of an attention hog. Of course, the fact that Nell seemed to be impressed with what Ryuno was saying, might have influenced Stanley's opinion just a tiny bit.

Stanley was trying to think of something to add to the conversation, when, to his delight, Alabaster jumped right in and said,

"You know, Ryuno, I don't mean to be picky, but you're saying it wrong."

Ryuno looked at him. "What am I saying wrong?" he asked.

"Well," said Alabaster, "like I said, I don't mean to be picky, but I *believe* the word is pronounced, '*Samurai*', not '*Marusai*'."

Ryuno stared at him. "Er, I'm afraid you're mistaken," he said, clearly not sure what to make of Alabaster. "'*Marusai*' is the correct pronunciation."

"No no," said Alabaster, "*Sa-moo-rye*."

"Er," said Ryuno.

"Alabaster, *shut up*," snapped Nell, "I'm pretty sure he knows what the right word is."

"Well *I'm* not," said Alabaster. "He keeps saying it wrong!"

"Shut. Up," Nell said dangerously.

"Please, enough of this," said Ryuno. "This is not something over which we should be arguing. You may pronounce the word any way you like. Your name is … Alabaster?"

"Yep," said Alabaster, "That's me, Alabaster Lancaster."

"An interesting name," said Ryuno, shaking Alabaster's hand. "And what is *your* name?" he said, turning to Nell.

"Nell," she said, a bit more pink returning to her cheeks. "It's short for Prunella."

"That's a lovely name," said Ryuno.

"Thank you," said Nell, as her cheeks turned pinker.

"I'm Stanley," said Stanley, butting in and thrusting his hand out at Ryuno.

"Oh," said Ryuno, "I'm pleased to meet you, Stanley."

"How long have you been a Marusai?" Stanley demanded, just as Ryuno started to turn back towards Nell.

"A Marusai begins his training as soon as he is able to wield a sword," said Ryuno, looking back at him.

"How many battles have you been in?" said Stanley.

"Stanley!" said Nell.

"Twenty-three," said Ryuno.

"Twenty-three?" echoed Alabaster.

Ryuno nodded. "It is a small number, compared to those of other Marusai … but then again, I only fought on my own home soil for two years."

"Two years?" said Nell.

Ryuno nodded again. "A Marusai is not expected to fight in earnest until he turns eleven."

"Eleven!" exclaimed Alabaster.

"I fought for two years, and then I was forced to leave when I turned thirteen. I … do not wish to say any more about it."

"You … you've been fighting since you were eleven?" said Nell, placing a hand on Ryuno's arm.

"Yes," said Ryuno. "It is the way of the Marusai."

"How old are you, Ryuno?" asked Alabaster.

"I have been sixteen for a quarter of a year."

Stanley stared at Ryuno. He'd been fighting in wars since he was eleven? Stanley hadn't even been in a fight at school until this year! He'd never been in a war, of course, but he'd learned enough about them to feel a sudden rush of horrified pity for Ryuno, for this warrior who was barely three years older than him.

Mercifully, at that moment, Grey came striding back into the clearing, carrying what looked like a giant, dead chameleon.

"I thought we could use some real food," he said.

* * *

That evening, as they sat around the campfire, Grey suddenly said, "Tomorrow we should leave for Port Verdant."

"We're leaving?" said Nell.

"You can't stay here forever," said Grey.

"Is that the town you told me about?" asked Stanley.

"Mm," said Grey. "It's the biggest town on the continent. Decent enough place, from what I saw of it. You'll be able to get some help there."

"Help with what?" said Nell.

"I don't know, whatever it is that you're doing."

"What exactly *are* we doing?" Alabaster asked of Stanley and Nell.

"I don't know," said Nell. "I thought we might be trying to get home, but we already tried that, didn't we? ... Fine, we'll go to this Port whatever and see if we can figure things out there."

Stanley remained silent. It sounded like Nell was formulating a plan, but he already had a plan of his own. His plan was to look for the towering blue crystal he'd been dreaming about for the past nine months. It was somewhere in this jungle, he just knew it. They'd already found a *red* crystal, although it had been broken. But what *was* the crystal? Where was it, exactly? What was it for? Stanley had a hunch he might find some answers in Port Verdant.

Soon, Grey curled up by the fire and went to sleep. Alabaster said goodnight soon after, and Stanley followed him. The boys laid down on their beds of furs, and Alabaster went right to sleep. Stanley stayed awake, waiting for Nell to come in. After a while, he got up to see what she was doing. He heard voices outside, and saw Nell and Ryuno, sitting side by side with their backs to the tent, immersed in conversation.

Stanley went back to bed and lay there, staring up at the tent's conical ceiling. Nell and Ryuno stayed up talking long into the night. Stanley found it impossible to fall asleep, but not because their talk was loud.

Chapter 7

IT'S A JUNGLE OUT HERE

Stanley woke very early the next morning, because Grey was shaking him rather roughly.

"Get up," Grey said brusquely.

Stanley groaned. He hadn't fallen asleep until very late last night, and his slumber had been interrupted by his usual dreams of blue crystals. "I can't," he murmured, "I'm too tired, just let me sleep …"

"I said get up," said Grey, picking Stanley up by the scruff of the neck and dragging him outside, where he plunked him down by the fire pit.

Everyone else was already up, and in the middle of a breakfast consisting of leftover giant chameleon meat and various jungle fruits.

"Morning, Stanley," Alabaster said cheerfully, as he handed him a funny-looking fruit with brown, leathery skin. Stanley regarded it uncertainly.

"It's really good," Alabaster assured him.

Stanley took a bite, and was surprised to find that the inside was bright blue, and tasted like a blueberry.

"Are you okay, Stanley?" asked Nell. "You look a bit peaked."

Stanley swallowed his mouthful of fruit. "Uh—didn't sleep too well," he said awkwardly.

"More dreams?" said Nell.

"Hm?" said Stanley. "Oh, uh, yeah, actually." Oddly enough, he suddenly found it rather difficult to talk to Nell.

Once they had finished eating, Grey stood up and said,

"If anyone has anything they want to bring, get it now. We're leaving."

"Now?" said Stanley.

"Now," said Grey. He pointed to a pile of bulging leather bags. "Everyone take a water skin. There are streams on the way, but we're probably going to need them, anyway."

"Where are we going again?" said Alabaster, slinging a water skin over his shoulder and stumbling with the weight.

Grey glowered at him. "I'm taking you to Port Verdant. It's north-east of here."

"How far?" said Alabaster.

"A little over thirty miles," said Grey, heading for the entrance to the clearing.

"*Awww*, that sounds far!" whined Alabaster.

"It *is* far," said Nell.

"How long is it gonna take us to get there?" said Alabaster.

Grey let out an aggravated sigh. "I can make it there in less than a day," he said, "but we're going to have to keep a slower pace because of you four. We'll get there by tomorrow afternoon, at the earliest."

"If you are concerned about us slowing you down," said Ryuno, "then go on ahead. I know the way well enough."

Grey scowled darkly at him, but said nothing as he led the way out of the clearing and into the Verdurian jungle.

As they didn't have any heavy luggage to carry, their going was fairly easy. The jungle was dense, but rarely did they have to fight their way through the underbrush; there were paths like the one leading to Grey's camp all over the place, and these they followed for most of the day.

The jungle was a noisy place. By now, Stanley had grown accustomed to the constant cacophony of shrieks and screeches, but every so often a new sound caught his ear, and he simply couldn't ignore it no matter how hard he tried. There was, of course, the usual symphony of bird songs, some of which were very beautiful. At other times, the air was filled with deafening hoots and honks, which Alabaster found very funny.

"*Gloo-gloo to you, too!*" he yelled at an obese toad squatting beside the path and croaking strangely. The toad looked quite offended.

On and on they walked, and it began to get very hot. The overhanging boughs of the trees kept the sun off of the travelers, but it was offensively muggy in the jungle, and they were soon all four of them soaked with sweat (Grey, it seemed, either had a very high heat tolerance, or else he simply didn't have any sweat glands).

Around noon, they came to a stream flowing swiftly and noisily in the same direction as they were walking.

"Water! Water!" croaked Alabaster, flopping down on the ground and crawling towards the stream. He continued to crawl right into the water, and lay there on the shallow, stony stream bed with only his face sticking out. "Aaah," he said, "That's the stuff."

Stanley thought a dip in the stream sounded like a good idea, so he plunged in, as well. The water was wonderfully cold and crisp, and it felt good to be wearing clothes that were soaked with water instead of sweat.

"We'll take a break here," said Grey, clearly realizing that Stanley and Alabaster weren't going anywhere for a while. Nell doused herself in the stream, too, though she had the sense to take off her shoes first.

Soon, the three of them were lying on the rocky banks of the stream, letting the sun dry them off. It was so warm that you could actually see steam rising from their clothes as the water evapourated. Stanley looked around for Grey, and found him sitting under a nearby tree, wearing a pair of sunglasses. Stanley grinned. They were the same ones he'd given Grey during their adventure aboard the Ogopogo. Ryuno, too, was sitting in the shade. He had removed his armour, and was now dressed in a simple shirt (which was stained with sweat around the armpits) and a pair of very baggy pantaloons. He was sitting cross-legged, and looked as if he were asleep.

Stanley glanced over at Nell, who was lying on the rocks beside him. Her hair, being quite a bit longer than his, was still soaking wet, and her bags had been smoothed back from her face. Without even thinking, Stanley said,

"Your hair looks really good like that."

Nell looked at him. "It does?'

"Uh ... yeah," said Stanley, secretly cursing himself for opening his big mouth.

Nell didn't laugh at him, though. She simply smiled and said, "Um ... well, thanks," and went as red as an apple.

Just then, something round and furry came flying out of the trees and landed right on Nell's chest, making her gasp as it hit. She gasped again, as she realized she was looking into the eight shiny black eyes of a huge, bloated brown spider that was almost as big as her head.

Stanley scrambled to his feet and stared at the spider. He'd never seen one so big.

"Eeyugh!" said Nell, her face a mask of disgust as she raised a hand to bat the huge arachnid away. Before she could, though, the spider tensed and hissed frighteningly, before raising its four front legs in an alarmingly threatening stance.

Nell's expression changed from disgust to fear. Her green eyes were wide as she stared at the thick, dark fluid dripping from the spider's fangs.

Alabaster let out a high-pitched shriek, and the spider hissed again. Stanley looked from the spider to Nell. He felt a stabbing rush of furious pain at seeing the frightened look on her face. Without a second thought, he wound up and booted the spider off of her. It was like kicking a furry little soccer ball. The spider went tumbling away and landed on its back, its legs flailing unpleasantly.

Nell leaped to her feet and grabbed Stanley's arm. "That was *so* gross," she said, glaring at the upended arachnid.

Suddenly, with a fat '*plunk*', the spider righted itself. It hissed furiously, legs tensed, and then it leaped straight at Nell.

There was a flash of steel and a sharp '*swish*', and the spider landed at Nell's feet, cut cleanly in two. The legs twitched hideously as the two halves bled nasty green ichor all over the rocks.

Ryuno sheathed his sword. "Are you alright?" he said, placing a hand on Nell's shoulder.

"I'm fine," said Nell, batting him away, "That was just really, really gross. I mean, I'm not afraid of spiders or anything, but that one was just—"

"Really, really big," said Stanley, staring at the cloven arachnid.

"Eeee!" said Alabaster, dancing about and pointing at the corpse.

Grey was suddenly beside them. He knelt down and examined the halves. "Hmmm," he said.

"That is a Verdurian Leaping Tarantula," said Ryuno.

"Gee, do you *think?*" squeaked Alabaster.

"That's its *name*," said Nell.

"Never heard of it," said Grey.

"They are rarely encountered," said Ryuno. "They tend to shy away from larger animals …" He looked grimly at the corpse. "They are not supposed to be this big."

"How big are they *supposed* to be?" asked Nell.

Ryuno held up his right hand. "About this big. No bigger than a man's hand."

"Well look at the size of *this* tubb!" cried Alabaster. "What's the deal?"

"How do you know about this stuff?" Stanley asked Ryuno.

"I read about it," he answered. "A Marusai must train his mind as well as his body."

"Riiight," said Stanley, not wanting to hear another rant about 'the way of the Marusai'. "So why'd this one get so big?"

"And vicious," added Nell. "It wanted to bite me."

"If it had, I suspect you would have died," said Ryuno.

Nell did not look comforted.

"Hey!" said Stanley. "She doesn't need to hear that!"

Ryuno paid no attention to him. "I believe that this creature's size and ferocity are due to the curse that has come upon this jungle."

Grey 'hmphed' loudly.

"This is not mere speculation," Ryuno said, looking sharply at him. "The forest has changed in recent months—this I have already said. The beasts are becoming fierce and dangerous. Insects and spiders grow to unnatural sizes and seek out humans for prey. There is a sinister power at work in this jungle, and while I no longer believe that you, Grey, are the cause, I still feel that it is somewhere nearby … where, though, I cannot say. Would that I could sense the evil, feel it, hear it, and trace it to its source … alas, I can merely observe the effects and hope to find clues to point me in the right direction."

"Are you done?" Grey said brusquely. "We need to get moving again."

* * *

On they pressed through the steamy jungle. The weather only seemed to grow hotter and more oppressively humid as the afternoon wore on.

"Keep drinking water," Grey advised them.

They stayed close to the stream, so there was plenty to drink. At one point, they had to go a little out of their way to avoid a small herd of gorethanes which had laid claim to a section of the stream.

Under slightly different circumstances, Stanley might have found the journey through the jungle interesting and exciting. After all, there was plenty of exotic flora and fauna to see. He loved to explore and discover new things, but fate seemed to be conspiring to make him as miserable as possible. He was quite hot, and his clothes soon became drenched with sweat again. He didn't really have anyone to talk to, either, despite the fact that his two best friends were mere feet away. Alabaster was too busy darting about, poking at things with a stick he'd found. Grey did his best to ignore him, but his exasperation was almost palpable.

Nell wasn't any help, either. All she seemed to want to do was talk to Ryuno.

"I have never heard of this 'Karate'," said Ryuno, after asking Nell if she and her friends practiced any of the 'fighting arts', as he called them. "In my homeland, every child learns an art called *laght-shume*. It is a basic art of self-defense."

Ryuno listened intently as Nell explained Karate to him, and Nell, in turn, was obviously fascinated by Ryuno's explanations of the many Marusai fighting styles.

Stanley, feeling once again that Ryuno seemed like a real show-off, wanted to hear none of it, and stayed at the head of the group with Grey. Grey glanced sideways at him, then at Nell and Ryuno, then back at Stanley. He said nothing, though, and that suited Stanley just fine.

Late that afternoon, after hours of trudging through the hot, steamy jungle, they came to a cliff. The stream went tumbling over the edge in a wide, noisy waterfall.

"There's a way down over here," said Grey, leading the way towards a narrow shelf of rock that sloped steeply down the cliff face. They managed to scramble down without incident, and took a brief rest beneath the transparent curtain of the waterfall.

After they had all caught their breath, Ryuno said,

"If I may make a suggestion ..." All eyes turned towards him. "We have traveled far today," he said. "I do not know how much further we were planning on going, but we are not far from the home of my master. Whether or not you plan to continue on your way, I must stop there and see him. I would like to invite all of you to come with me, and spend the night at his house."

"Sounds good to me," said Alabaster. "I think I'm just about done for today!"

"We should keep moving," Grey said tersely. "We've still got almost two hours of daylight left. I want to put some miles behind us before nightfall."

"Your friends seem quite tired, though," Ryuno said reasonably. "I think they have walked enough for one day."

"They can handle a few more miles," said Grey.

"I think we should stop," said Nell. Grey scowled.

"What do you think, Stanley?" Nell asked.

Stanley scratched his chin. He was certainly tired, and was more than ready to call it a day. On the other hand, if they kept going, they (he) wouldn't have to put up with Ryuno … Of course, continuing now meant that they would have to camp out in the jungle …

He shook his head. He was being a bit ridiculous, wasn't he? Ryuno wasn't a bad guy. He really had no reason to dislike him, did he? And besides, he was offering them a place to stay tonight.

"Hmm … well, why don't we stop for today?" he said, glancing about at his friends. "I'm pretty tired, and … well, it'd be nice to have a roof over our heads tonight."

"Four against one!" Alabaster said, pointing obnoxiously at Grey.

Grey glared ferociously at him. "Fine," he said, "but it'll make our trip tomorrow that much longer."

This didn't seem to concern Ryuno, who simply nodded and said, "My master's house is this way."

* * *

Fifteen minutes later, the small group came to a well-tended footpath which led through a narrow belt of trees. Beyond the trees, a trail of round, flat stones ran across a yard of scruffy green grass, and up to a modest-looking wooden house. It was of fairly simple construction, but the thick wooden beams from which it had been built, appeared to have been sanded and polished, robbing the building of that rustic, 'cabin-in-the-woods' feeling.

"This is the home of my master," said Ryuno, leading the way up the path.

"Pretty swanky," said Alabaster. "Uh, not that *your* place *isn't* swanky," he said glancing sideways at Grey, who simply scowled at him.

"*Master*," Ryuno called, "are you home?"

No answer came from within. "Please wait here," said Ryuno, "I will check and see if he is in."

He mounted the house's front steps, and drew aside a large sliding screen which seemed to serve as a front door. Seconds later, there came a furious shout from inside, followed by several high-pitched shrieks, and the clashing ring of metal striking metal.

"Ryuno!" said Nell, taking a few steps towards the house.

"Wait," Grey ordered, putting his arm out to stop her.

Suddenly, four Saurians came racing out the front door, leaped down the steps, and skidded to a halt in front of Stanley and the others. They were armed with swords and shields, and all four of them had at least one nasty-looking cut somewhere on their hides.

Stanley noticed that the Saurians wore red-and-white loincloths, like the ones from the other day. Their brownish-red scales had also been daubed here and there with red war paint. The lizard-men snarled and raised their weapons, but then they caught sight of Grey, and backed away with much frustrated hissing. Grey sprang at the nearest Saurian and bared his teeth, snarling savagely. The Saurians screeched with alarm, and ran off into the jungle. Ryuno appeared at the front door, sword in hand. Stanley saw that the blade had blood on it.

"Is everyone alright?" Ryuno asked. He looked a bit pale.

"We're fine," said Nell.

"Yeah," said Stanley, "*Grey* got rid of the Saurians. You don't need to worry about them." Nell elbowed him.

Ryuno, who had either not picked up on Stanley's tone, or had chosen to ignore it, simply nodded and said, "Good. Please come inside, I may need assistance."

Stanley and the others followed Ryuno into the house. The interior was sparsely furnished. A low wooden table occupied the centre of the room, and a small stone vase stood in each corner. The floor was made of smooth, polished planks of wood, and the walls looked like they were made of paper sheets attached to a wooden framework. A dead Saurian was lying on the floor by the table in a pool of blood.

"Eeew!" said Alabaster, grabbing onto Nell's arm.

"Knock it off," said Nell, yanking her arm free.

Stanley stared at the lifeless lizard. It was a grim sight. Just then, part of the wall in front of them slid open and Ryuno came into the room, supporting a tiny old man, who was having trouble walking.

"Master," Ryuno said to the old man, "please sit down. Your wound—"

"—Is not nearly as bad as others I have received in my time," the old man interjected. "Fetch me my walking stick, Ryuno, and all will be well."

He had a surprisingly powerful voice for such a feeble-looking old man. Ryuno picked up a short, stout, gnarled stick which had been leaning against the table. The old man took it, and hobbled towards Stanley and the others.

Stanley assumed that the little old man must have been at least seventy, but then he recalled that people from Terra lived longer than those from our world. The man was short, hunched and thin-looking, with a long, white drooping mustache and beard. The top of his head was bald, and what remained of his hair was tied back in a ponytail, like Ryuno's.

"Hum," said the old man, peering at Stanley through thin, slanted eyes which were barely visible beneath his bushy white eyebrows, "So these are the friends you mentioned?"

"Yes," said Ryuno. "This is Nell, Stanley, Alabaster ... and Grey."

The old man peered intently at each of them in turn, gazing into their eyes for what seemed a very long time. "Hum!" he said again, "Hum!" Stanley felt a bit unnerved; the old man had a rather piercing stare.

He stared particularly long at Grey, though not a trace of fear crossed his wrinkled face. Finally, he hobbled back to Ryuno, turned, and bowed gracefully.

"Allow me to introduce myself. My name is Tadakatsu Takeshi Akechi."

He was met with blank stares.

"Again with the impossible names!" said Alabaster.

"*Alabaster!*" cried Stanley and Nell, "*Shut up!*"

But the old man merely chuckled. "Yes, yes, it is rather difficult to pronounce at first. Call me 'Mr. Taki' for short. Everyone else does."

Ryuno *hmphed*. "They should at least address you as Master Takeshi," he said in a low voice. Mr. Taki waved the suggestion aside.

"Nonsense. A man's full name has its place, but imagine the time he would waste, if he used it all the time."

"Well, my name is Alabaster," said Alabaster, stepping forward and grabbing Mr. Taki's hand. Ryuno's eyes widened, as if Alabaster had just picked his nose and wiped it on the old man's robe.

Mr. Taki just smiled, though, and said, "I am glad to meet you, Alabaster." Stanley and Nell gave their names as well, and shook hands with Mr. Taki. The old man then turned to Grey, looking at him expectantly.

Grey simply stood there looking morose, though, and after an uncomfortable silence, Ryuno, sounding annoyed, said,

"My master is waiting for you to introduce yourself."

Grey didn't move.

"In our homeland," said Ryuno, sounding even more annoyed, "to remain silent after someone introduces himself, is considered extremely rude."

Ryuno had obviously not yet learned that *rude* was what Grey was all about.

"What did the Saurians want with you?" Grey demanded.

Ryuno's mouth dropped open, but Mr. Taki merely smiled.

"Ah, so our taciturn friend knows of the lizard men."

Grey scowled.

"They wanted my swords," said the old man, "as well as my blood."

"Your *blood?"* echoed Alabaster.

"Oh yes," said Mr. Taki. "The *Xol'tec* tribe are a murderous, bloody lot. They are identifiable by their red clothing and body paint."

"We, uh, ran into some of them the other day," said Stanley, glancing at the corpse on the floor.

"Indeed?" said Mr. Taki. "That is most unsettling. I must admit, I never expected to see any of the Xol'tecs this far to the north-east." He too looked at the dead Saurian. "Er, perhaps you could remove this deceased warrior, Ryuno?"

Ryuno nodded sharply, then heaved the carcass over his shoulder, and went outside.

"When he returns," said Mr. Taki, "perhaps we can all sit and talk for a bit."

★ ★ ★

Ryuno returned soon after. He wordlessly cleaned up the puddle of congealing blood on the floor, and joined the rest of the group, who were seated at the table.

There were no chairs, but the table was so close to the floor, that there was no real need for them. Stanley and Alabaster sat with their legs sticking out under the table, while Nell and Grey imitated Ryuno and Mr. Taki, who were seated with their legs crossed.

"Now then, Ryuno," said Mr. Taki, "Why don't you tell me about your latest expedition? Were you successful?"

"Not entirely," said Ryuno. "I was unable to determine the source of the forest's … illness." He glanced over at Grey. "I will continue my investigation, though."

Mr. Taki was nodding. "Ah yes … it is an upsetting thing, the corruption of this mighty jungle."

"Excuse me," said Nell, who was sitting beside Ryuno, "but what exactly *is* this 'corruption' you've been talking about? You said earlier that there was some kind of evil power, making the animals vicious—"

"—And the spiders huge," added Alabaster.

Ryuno nodded. "Animals, insects, plants … all are being affected by this strange curse. I have traveled much in the past months, but have been unable to find its source. I'm afraid I know little more than you do, Nell."

Mr. Taki nodded as well. "The jungle has never been a safe place to live, but these days, it is becoming extremely dangerous."

"What about people?" Stanley asked a bit uneasily. "Are … you know, human beings becoming … uh … dangerous?"

"Not from what we have seen," said Ryuno. "The higher species seem unaffected by the curse … for now. Perhaps the effects take longer to manifest themselves in humans." He frowned. "The Saurians, though," he said, scratching his chin, "Perhaps the Xol'tec tribe has fallen under the evil power …"

Mr. Taki was shaking his head. "The Xol'tecs have always been a violent and bloody people, my student. They do not require a curse to act with cruelty and savagery. It is a pity, for the Saurians, as a whole, are just as intelligent as we are."

"But then not *all* the Saurian tribes are evil, are they?" Nell asked.

"Be careful how you use that word, young one," said Mr. Taki, raising an index finger. "The bloody customs of the Xol'tecs may be abhorrent to us, but to them, they are a way of life. They do not think of themselves as evil."

"A Marusai battles not against good, or evil, but against his enemies," Ryuno put in. "It is the *cause* that is important. What seems evil to you, may not be so to someone else." His face became grim. "That does not mean that an enemy should be shown mercy on the grounds that his beliefs are simply different from yours. If it is his way of life that sets him against you, then it is your responsibility to end him, or die by his hand. It is the way of the Marusai."

Stanley rolled his eyes, and was a bit put out to see Nell staring raptly at Ryuno.

"So then, Ryuno," said Mr. Taki, "because who we are determines our view of good and evil, would you say that those things do not truly exist? That there is no universal good, no universal evil?"

Ryuno considered this. "Yes, master, I suppose I would say that."

"What about the corruption of the jungle?" said Mr. Taki shrewdly. "Did you not just say that an evil power is at work?"

"I ... er, yes, I did," said Ryuno.

"Then there is a conflict between your two statements," said Mr. Taki. "You say that there is no such thing as true good or evil, but you also say that the jungle is in the grip of an evil force. The mind of a Marusai must not be conflicted."

Ryuno looked put out, and a bit embarrassed. "But ... but master, surely a power that corrupts in this manner—"

"It is a vile corruption to you and I," said Mr. Taki, "But what of the thing that is causing it? Does it know what it is doing? Is it *trying* to harm the jungle? Do you know its motives, its reasons?"

"No ... no, master, I do not."

"And yet you will not change your view on the matter?"

"That I will not," said Ryuno stoutly. "A Marusai says nothing that is meaningless. He does not go back on his word."

Mr. Taki smiled and nodded. "Then you are still on the right track. Now you must reflect on this, and find the answer that will resolve the conflict, yet still maintain the truth of both your statements."

"I will do this," said Ryuno.

Grey cleared his throat loudly. Everyone looked at him.

"I hate to interrupt," he said, not sounding quite truthful, "but me and these three (he indicated Stanley, Alabaster, and Nell) are on kind of a tight schedule. I want to be out of here as soon as possible, and I want to know if we can expect any more Saurian attacks."

"May I ask where you are headed?" said Mr. Taki.

"Port Verdant," said Grey.

"Hum," said Mr. Taki. "The realm of Men in Verduria. It is also within the realm of the *Oltonac* tribe."

"Great," said Grey, "So we've got two tribes of killer lizards to deal with."

"On the contrary," said Mr. Taki, "The Oltonacs, though a warrior tribe, are much more peaceful than their Xol'tec cousins. They fight only when there is no other option. Many of them even coexist with humans."

"I want to know if we're going to be running into any more Xol'tecs," said Grey. "Anything dangerous."

Mr. Taki and Ryuno exchanged a quick glance.

"I would like to say no," said the old man, "but with the Xol'tecs this far north and east … anything is possible."

Grey scowled.

"But enough of that," said Mr. Taki, "Come, let us have some supper. Then we can all retire for the evening."

⋆ ⋆ ⋆

Dinner consisted of a bland vegetable soup, crunchy cakes similar to Ryuno's po-chi, and meat from another giant chameleon which Grey had caught.

By the time the meal ended, it was very dark outside. Ryuno lit several small oil lamps, and Mr. Taki showed the guests to their rooms. Actually, they weren't rooms, so much as separate screened-off compartments in the room to the right of the dining area. Each compartment had a woven straw pallet, and a cozy wool blanket. The partitions, like the house's front door, could be slid sideways when someone wanted in or out.

Alabaster shuffled into his compartment, and was snoring loudly within minutes. Stanley had planned to go to sleep immediately, as well, but, tired though his body was, his mind was still wide awake.

He couldn't hear any sound coming from Nell's compartment, so she was probably still awake, too. Maybe she'd like to get up and chat for a while, or go out and look at the stars.

"Nell?" he said quietly to the darkness, "are you awake?"

No answer.

"Nell?" Stanley said again.

Still not a sound.

Stanley got up and pulled back a section of the partition. Nell was not in her compartment. Where was she? Stanley threw off his blanket, got up and tiptoed back into the main room. A single candle burned on the table, but no one was there. Outside, the crickets were chirping loudly, but there was another sound, too—the sound of voices.

Curious, Stanley pulled open the sliding screen at the back of the dining room, and found himself in another large, open room, with a thick blue mat on the floor. A sliding screen at the back of this room had been left open, and the voices were coming from outside. Stanley crept out quietly onto a wide porch. A pair of fat paper lanterns hung from the roof, illuminating a short flight of wooden steps leading down. These he descended, and found that he had entered a kind of garden. A narrow stone path meandered off among blocks of well-tended vegetation. The moons were shining brightly in the sky, and their light reflected off the surface of a wide, tranquil pond ringed with stones.

On the other side of the water was an open space surrounded by trees, in front of a high wooden wall. Two people were there, the owners of the voices Stanley had heard. Still curious, he made his way quietly around the pond and hid himself in a bush with large, drooping leaves. He was close enough now to see that the two figures were Ryuno and Nell.

Stanley felt an odd pang shoot through his stomach. What was she doing out here with him?

It looked like they were talking. Stanley felt his face getting hot. It wasn't nice to be spying on them like this. He was just deciding that he should sneak back, when Ryuno finished whatever he'd been saying, then turned and walked away. Nell nodded, and did the same thing, only she began to walk straight towards Stanley's hiding place. This was certainly odd behaviour. Had they just had an argument? Was Nell mad at Ryuno? A sudden warm ray of hope lit up in Stanley's chest, nullifying the unpleasant pain in his stomach.

But what was happening now? Nell was only a few feet away from him, and she was looking off into the distance as if daydreaming. Ryuno, however, had stopped at the garden wall, and turned back to face her. There was something in his hand.

A sword!

Stanley's eyes widened. What was going on here? Ryuno suddenly raised his weapon, then dropped into a menacing-looking stance. Was he going to attack Nell? He was! Stanley now felt a cold, bitter fire spring to life inside him. He had to save Nell! But what could he do? He was unarmed, and would be going up against a guy who was three years older than him, and had been a sword expert since he was eleven.

But he had to do something. He crouched down, shoulders hunched up, ready to spring. His heart was pounding in his chest. He began to feel a bit lightheaded. The moonlight seemed to fade from the garden. His vision was becoming cloudy, but he could still see Ryuno and Nell clearly. Suddenly, Ryuno charged at Nell. He was attacking her when her back was turned! He moved with unearthly speed, and with a noiselessness that seemed impossible. Within the space of a heartbeat, Ryuno had closed the distance between himself and Nell, raised his sword, and swung it at her unprotected back.

The blow did not connect, however, for at the very last second, Nell spun round with a speed to rival Ryuno's, and parried his weapon aside with a sword of her own.

Clunk! went the swords as they connected.

Clunk? What kind of sword goes clunk? The answer was simple: wooden ones.

Stanley stared for a moment, then let out a huge sigh of relief. Of course the swords were made of wood. There had been no flash of steel in the moonlight. Ryuno was obviously showing Nell some sword techniques, not attacking her.

"*Idiot!*" Stanley said under his breath, hitting himself on the forehead with his palm. It had certainly been a close call. He'd come very close to leaping out of the bushes and sinking his claws into Ryuno.

Claws? He blinked and shook his head. *Claws?* Where did that come from? He had come very close to leaping out of the bushes and tackling Ryuno, *that* was what he'd been thinking. He hit himself on the forehead again, then sat quietly and listened. Now that Nell and Ryuno were closer to his hiding spot, Stanley could hear what they were saying. He still felt bad about spying, but if he moved or tried to leave, they would see him, or at least hear him.

"That was very impressive," Ryuno was saying, sounding almost awed.

"Oh," said Nell, sounding quite flattered, "Er, thank you."

"And you say you've never used a sword before?"

"No. I mean, yes … I mean, no, I haven't. I've used a bo-staff, and kamas, though …"

"I have never heard of these weapons, though I know what a staff is. These kamas—they are not swords?"

"Um, no, they're … well, they're kind of like little sickles, almost …"

"Well, regardless," said Ryuno, "you have just demonstrated a command over the sword that I have never seen in a beginner. It would take most people at least a year to be able to handle a sword half as well as you can."

Nell said nothing. Stanley assumed that she was blushing furiously. The idea did not make him feel better.

"What is more," Ryuno went on, "you seem to possess many of the senses and abilities prized by all Marusai warriors. You are very fast on your feet. Your movements are graceful and beautiful, but precise. You attack without projecting, without showing your opponent what you are about to do. You seem able to think ahead, and guess what your opponent's next move will be. And most impressive of all, you parried my last attack. Do you know what that attack is called? It is called the *Shyin-Venn*, the *Silent Shadow*. The one who uses this move must have complete control over himself, and have knowledge of his surroundings. To perform this attack correctly, the Marusai must move quickly and silently. If it is done perfectly, then the victim hears nothing, not even the sound of steel cleaving air."

"I didn't hear anything," Nell said quietly.

"That is because I did it correctly," said Ryuno. "I have practiced the Shyin-Venn for countless hours in this garden, and only here can I execute it flawlessly. And yet still, you blocked me."

"What does that mean?" Nell asked.

"It means you would make a fine Marusai," said Ryuno.

Stanley ground his teeth.

"Me?" said Nell.

"You could not have heard my approach," said Ryuno. "Either you felt a change in the movement of the air, or felt my footfalls …

or perhaps you merely sensed what was happening. However you did it, you did it. While there are few Marusai who could ever hope to master the Shyin-Venn, fewer still are those who can counter it."

There was a brief pause.

"Ryuno," said Nell, her voice very quiet.

"Yes?" said Ryuno.

"...Did you say that my movements were ... graceful and ... beautiful?"

"Yes, I did."

"...No one's ever called me beautiful before." She took a step towards Ryuno.

And Stanley turned away. He had to get out of there, it didn't matter if they saw him. He just had to get away. He crept out of the bushes, biting down on his tongue. He could feel a roar of fury trying to fight its way up from the depths of his burning chest. He slunk back around the pond and ran back up the path and into the house. He yanked open his compartment screen and dove onto his straw pallet, burying his face in the woolen blanket. The roar of fury finally burst forth, but the blanket did a nice job of muffling it.

Stanley rolled over and lay there panting, staring wide-eyed at the ceiling. What had just happened? Why was his heart racing? Why did it feel as if fire and ice were waging war inside him? Why did he feel a seething and inexplicable hatred for Ryuno?

Somebody's jealous! sang a nasty little voice inside his head.

"I am not jealous," he muttered to himself. "Nell's my friend. I was worried about her. It was a surprise, that's all. She's just my friend."

But when his friend came in some time later to go to bed in the compartment next to his, he didn't speak to her. He just lay there, pretending to be asleep.

"Stanley?" Nell's voice came wafting through the partition. "Are you awake?"

Every fibre of Stanley's being screamed at him. *Say something! Talk to her! Say* anything!

But he didn't. He just lay there, until finally, Nell went to sleep, and the sound of her deep, rhythmic breathing mingled with that of Alabaster's, and with the other night sounds of the jungle.

It was a long time before Stanley fell asleep.

Chapter 8

THE GATES OF PORT VERDANT

Stanley dozed fitfully through the night. He kept waking up and wondering where he was, then falling back to sleep for a while, until finally, at about 5:30, he woke with a start and wondered why he felt so miserable. Then he recalled last night's events, and the war between fire and ice in his stomach began anew.

"Like I'm gonna be able to get back to sleep now," he muttered.

"Another armour fish!" Alabaster murmured from the next compartment.

Stanley decided to get up and maybe take a quiet, early-morning walk in Mr. Taki's garden. The thought of splashing cold water on his face seemed like a good idea. Tiptoeing out from his sleeping compartment, he made his way towards the sliding door, but in the dim early morning light, he didn't see the huddled lump lying in the middle of the floor. With a loud exclamation, he tripped over the lump and landed hard on the wood floor.

"Wha's gon'on?" said a sleepy voice.

"Nell?" said Stanley, picking himself up off the floor. He was surprised to discover that the lump he'd tripped over had in fact been *her*, wrapped up in her blanket.

"Stanley?" Nell said, her speech slurred with sleep, "Whasmatter?"

"Er, nothing," said Stanley, as Nell sat up and stared at him with half-lidded eyes. "Why are you out here?"

Nell looked around groggily. "It was a bit too tight in there," she murmured, gesturing feebly at her compartment.

"Oh, right," said Stanley, understanding instantly. Nell was claustrophobic.

"Weaftagetup?" said Nell.

"Huh?" said Stanley, "Oh, no, no, we don't have to get up yet. Go back to sleep."

"Okay," Nell said pleasantly, before flopping back onto her pillow.

Stanley gazed at her sleeping face for a moment. Her hair was quite messy, and she had some grime on her right cheek. She looked very peaceful, and very pretty. Stanley remembered what she'd said to Ryuno last night:

No one's every called me beautiful before.

Stanley made a noise of disgust and left the room. Out in the main room, he was heading for the rear sliding screen, when he heard Mr. Taki's voice from the other side.

"Have you given thought to yesterday's question?" he asked.

It was Ryuno's voice that answered. "I have, master, but I do not have an answer. I wanted to speak to you about something else."

"Oh?" said Mr. Taki's voice.

"It's about … the girl, Nell."

Fire and ice clashed together again in Stanley's stomach.

"Indeed?" said Mr. Taki. "What about her?"

"Master, she … ah, that is, she … er—"

"Choose your words and speak them," said Mr. Taki calmly.

"Yes, master. Right. She … I think she could be a Marusai."

Stanley took a sharp breath. Was he hearing correctly?

"Really?" said Mr. Taki. "That is a bold claim to make of one who has never held a sword."

"But she *has*," said Ryuno, sounding excited.

"She has?" said Mr. Taki.

"Last night," said Ryuno. "I gave her a practice sword, just to see how she carried herself with it. She practices a fighting art, you see, something called *Karate*, I believe."

"Hum. And?"

"And I … I was amazed, master! It was as if she had already had years of training with a blade."

"And you think this is a result of her training in … er …"

"Karate. Yes, but only partially. The art of Karate does not involve sword combat. But she handled the practice sword like … like … well, not like a master, but—"

"Like an apprentice?" Mr. Taki offered.

"Like an apprentice who has long been ready for her final test," said Ryuno.

"There are many who have a natural inclination for the blade," said Mr. Taki.

"Master," Ryuno said solemnly, "she blocked the Shyin-Venn."

There was a pause. "You used the Shyin-Venn on a person who has never fought before?"

"They were only practice swords, master—"

"I do not care! The Shyin-Venn is not to be used in such a manner! That you would use it on … on one who is not even a novice!"

"I would not have done it if I had not been completely sure."

"You were *not* completely sure! Be mindful of your words, student!"

A pause.

"Forgive me, master … you're right, I was not completely sure."

"You go back on your words, young one. That is not the way of the Marusai."

"But it *is* the way of the Marusai, to recognize talent, and draw it out by any means necessary."

Mr. Taki sighed. "And you recognized this talent?"

"Yes, master."

"…She blocked your Shyin-Venn?'

"She did."

"…You performed it correctly?"

"Of course, master. Only in the garden—"

"—Can you do it perfectly, I know. Hum …"

"Master?"

"If what you have told me is true … then perhaps she is worthy to become a Marusai."

Ryuno sounded extremely happy. "We could start training her today! She can stay here, and train, benefiting from your wisdom and experience!"

"Ryuno … I already have an apprentice."

"But—"

Stanley had heard enough. He yanked the sliding screen open and marched into the back room. Mr. Taki and Ryuno looked at him with surprise.

"I'm sorry, I couldn't help overhearing," said Stanley, crossing the room and stopping in front of the other two.

"Stanley," said Ryuno, "what are you doing up?"

"I couldn't get back to sleep," said Stanley, "I had a lot on my mind."

"Well would you mind leaving for a moment? You're interrupting—"

"Good!" said Stanley, cutting him off.

"Excuse me?" said Ryuno, clearly taken aback.

"Good," Stanley repeated. "I'm glad I'm interrupting you! Look, I'm sorry for listening in on your conversation, but there's no way Nell is staying here."

Ryuno frowned. The scar across his face made him look quite fierce. "This conversation was not for you to hear."

"It wasn't for Nell to hear, either, I guess, eh?" Stanley fired back. "You were just going to make a bunch of decisions for her on your own? Without even asking her?"

"Of course I was going to ask her," said Ryuno. "I just—"

"Wanted to run it by your master to see if it was alright?" Stanley supplied. Mr. Taki glanced meaningfully at Ryuno.

"Well … yes," said Ryuno.

"Yeah?" said Stanley, "Well what about running it by her friends? What about running it by *her?"*

"I always consult my master," said Ryuno defensively.

"Oh yeah?" said Stanley, "And if he said it was okay, what then? You'd tell Nell that she *has* to become a Marusai? That's it's her destiny? That it's the *Way of the Marusai?"*

Ryuno looked very put out. Stanley's legs began to shake. Adrenaline was pumping through his system. It was rather thrilling to be standing here, telling Ryuno off. There was something he wanted to say, but he knew he shouldn't. The more he tried to stop himself, though, the more it bubbled and seethed, until finally he erupted like an insolent little volcano:

"Or do you just want her to stay so you can make out with her again?"

Ryuno's eyes went wide. He didn't know exactly what the expression meant, but he guessed enough from Stanley's tone, to become really angry. "How dare you!" he said indignantly, taking a threatening step forward.

"Enough!" said Mr. Taki, stepping between the two boys. "This discussion is over for now. Stanley, I apologize for not including you and your friends in our conversation. It would seem that even old men sometimes forget their manners. As for *you*, student," he said, turning to Ryuno, "I would suggest that you be more mindful of yourself, your feelings, and your actions."

"I will, master," Ryuno said humbly.

"I also hope," continued Mr. Taki, "that your reasons for wishing to train this girl, are the right ones."

"Yes, master," said Ryuno, not quite giving a straight answer.

★ ★ ★

Stanley spent the next hour in the garden, sitting by the pond, watching the sun rise. Mr. Taki had brought him a few crispy honey cakes, but he only nibbled at one of them. His mind was preoccupied with thoughts of Nell. He tried to wrap his mind around these horrible jealous feelings he was having. His thoughts seemed to be having a heated shouting match inside his head.

You like Nell! You like her! Face the facts!
But she's your friend! How can you like your friend?
Doesn't matter how! You do! Who better to like than your friend?
But you hang out with her! She's just a friend!
But if she's your friend, that proves you already like her!

Stanley clutched his head in his hands. In addition to his conflicting thoughts, there was also the battle raging in his stomach, between fire and ice. What was he supposed to do, walk up to Nell and confess his feelings? He had seen and confronted some pretty scary things on his adventures, but he doubted he could ever muster the courage to do *that*.

He shook his head. It was all way too much to deal with, especially after four hours' sleep and no breakfast. He picked up a honey cake and took a bite.

* * *

It wasn't long before everyone was up and eating breakfast at the table in the dining room. Stanley couldn't help but think murderous thoughts every time he saw Ryuno say something to Nell.

"You okay, Stanley?" said Alabaster, noting the look on Stanley's face.

"Hm?" said Stanley, "Oh, yeah, I guess … just … tired."

Alabaster. Here was the one person in whom he'd always been able to confide. He could tell Alabaster everything, all his thoughts and feelings concerning this crazy business with Nell.

Just not right now, though.

Grey sat there morosely, after devouring six honey cakes in one gigantic bite. Alabaster had applauded at this, making Stanley and Nell laugh. Ryuno looked vaguely repulsed; Mr. Taki ignored it completely.

"We should leave within the next half hour," Grey said shortly, getting up from the table. "If there's anything you need to bring, get it now. I'm going to fill the water skins."

"Why does he keep calling them *skins?*" said Alabaster.

Nell looked at him. "Because that's what they are?"

"*What?*" said Alabaster, "Those things are actually made of *skin? For real?*"

"What did you think they were?" said Nell.

"I … I dunno!" said Alabaster.

"Er, before we leave the table," said Ryuno, standing up himself, "I would like to … ah … propose something to you all." He waited for Grey to sit back down before continuing. "Actually, this is directed mainly at … er, Nell, although I'm sure you will all no doubt want to hear it."

Stanley ground his teeth.

"Nell," said Ryuno, "I will be blunt. I told you last night that you possess certain qualities … you have the makings of a Marusai warrior."

Nell had gone bright red, and was looking uncomfortable.

"That said," Ryuno continued, "I would like to offer you the chance to train in the ways of the Marusai—to one day become a great and noble Marusai warrior in your own right."

Nell stared at him. "Excuse me?"

"I want to see you trained in the ways of the Marusai," said Ryuno, leaning towards her and smiling. "Your abilities already rival those of many full-fledged Marusai warriors. Properly trained, you could become one of the greatest Marusai *ever*."

"*Whoa!*" said Alabaster, gawking at Nell. "That'd be *awesome!*"

Awesome was not the word Stanley would have chosen. "How long does it take?" he asked loudly. He couldn't believe Ryuno was doing this.

"Pardon?" said Ryuno.

"How long does it take?" Stanley repeated. "How long does it take to become a Marusai?"

"It is different for everyone," said Ryuno. "Though I have no doubt that Nell could complete her training in as little as three years."

"Three years?" said Stanley, "She'd have to stay here for three years? You can't ask her to do that!"

"I don't have to ask," said Ryuno. "For a Marusai, such commitment is expected."

"Well, sorry, but she's not a Marusai, so—"

"*Stanley*," Nell said sharply, "I can speak for myself."

"But—"

Nell glared at him, then turned back to Ryuno. "It's nice of you to offer, Ryuno," she said slowly, "but I could never stay here for three years. I have a home, and a family … they're far away, but I can't just leave them."

"We will send a letter to them," said Ryuno, starting to sound a bit desperate. "You can visit them sometimes, you need not leave them forever—"

"It's not that simple," said Nell, glancing at Stanley and Alabaster. "We … come from very far away. We're lost, and we don't know how to get home. That's why we're going to Port Verdant, to find some help. Stanley knows someone who might be able to take us home …

"Besides," she said, looking again at Stanley and Alabaster, "I could never leave my best friends." She looked up at Ryuno. "I'm sorry," she said. "Maybe someday I could do it … but not now."

Stanley felt the fire in his stomach deal a crushing blow to the ice. Ryuno looked very disappointed.

"I … understand," he said, nodding slowly. "I just thought—"

"It's okay," said Nell, patting his hand.

"If we're just about done here," said Grey, "I'd like to get a move on." He headed for the back door. "I'll be out front in a few minutes," he said to Stanley, Alabaster, and Nell. "Wait for me there."

"Well, it would seem that this is where we part," said Mr. Taki. "It has been a pleasure to have you as guests in my home."

"Thanks!" said Alabaster, leaping up and wringing the old man's hand. "Thanks, Ryuno," he said, shaking hands with him as well. "Maybe we'll see you 'round."

Nell thanked Mr. Taki, and while Stanley was shaking hands with the old man, he saw her hug Ryuno and kiss him on the cheek. The ice in Stanley's stomach rose up powerfully, and he glared at Ryuno, before leaving the room without another word. Alabaster followed him, and Nell came out just behind him.

"Why didn't you say goodbye to Ryuno?" she asked Stanley.

"He looked a bit busy," Stanley said coolly, not meeting her gaze.

"What's *that* supposed to mean?" said Nell, putting her hands on her hips.

"Nothing," Stanley muttered, staring at his shoes. He felt like a bit of a jerk, talking to Nell like this, but he really just wanted to be away from here … away from Ryuno.

"Okay, fine," said Nell. "Alabaster how are you?"

"Not great," Alabaster confessed. "I think that soup last night disagreed with me!"

Back inside the house, Ryuno watched the three of them sitting on the front steps. His master joined him.

"Have you given any more thought to my question?" the old man asked.

Ryuno nodded. "Yes, master. And I finally have an answer."

"I would hear it."

"Good and evil do not exist on the battlefield," said Ryuno. "That is why it is said that the Marusai do not fight for or against either of them."

"Hum," said Mr. Taki.

"Good and evil, however, do exist elsewhere," said Ryuno.

"Really?" said Mr. Taki. "Absolute good and absolute evil? Where do they exist?"

Ryuno pointed at the three friends. "*There* is absolute good, master. Loving friendship."

"Hum," said Mr. Taki. "But what if someone says that your definition is incorrect? There are those who would seek to destroy that loving friendship. What of them, what of their thoughts and beliefs?"

Ryuno looked squarely at his master. "That," he said quietly, "would be absolute evil."

Mr. Taki smiled. "You have done well in resolving this issue," he said after a moment. "Yes ... the student must one day stop learning from the master ... but the master must never stop learning from the student."

"These three," said Ryuno, nodding at Stanley, Alabaster, and Nell, "there is something about them ..."

"Ah, so you have noticed it, too," said Mr. Taki.

"It is difficult to explain," said Ryuno. "They are young—"

"As are you."

"—And yet, they seem ... older. Especially the girl—especially Nell."

"You can see it in their eyes," said Mr. Taki. "Their eyes have seen much. Their souls have endured things that ordinary folk their age would never have had to endure. They are already old beyond their years, that much is plain ... becoming adults before their time. I am surprised and pleased that you were able to see it."

"Old beyond their years," Ryuno mused.

Mr. Taki sighed. "Yes. It is a tragic thing."

"But master, to be old beyond one's years—to be older in mind than in body ... is that not the way of the Marusai?"

"It is," said Mr. Taki. "And that has always saddened me."

* * *

"What's taking so *long?*" groaned Alabaster.

"Next time, help," said Grey, coming around from behind the house carrying four bulging water skins. "It'll make the wait shorter."

"It was just a simple question," Alabaster muttered as he slung a skin over his shoulder.

Just as they were all about to strike off into the jungle again, Ryuno appeared at the front door of the house.

"Wait!" he cried, catching up to the group.

"What did we forget?" Grey demanded.

"Nothing," said Ryuno. "I am coming with you."

"*What?*" said Stanley and Nell together (although their tones of voice were quite different).

"I am coming with you," Ryuno repeated. "My master says that my apprenticeship is complete. I am now a true Marusai, and so am free to do as I please and go where I wish."

"If we decide to let you tag along," said Grey.

Ryuno frowned. "I assure you, Mr. Grey, I will pull my own weight, and then some. A Marusai is never a burden, and most people would be grateful to have one traveling with them."

Stanley *hmphed*. He could think of a few ways in which a Marusai could be a burden. One of those ways was illustrated right then and there, as Ryuno turned to Nell and said,

"And, if I accompany you, I can train you in the ways of the Marusai as we travel."

"Oh," said Nell, a bit surprised by this, "Well, uh … okay, that sounds … nice."

Stanley bit down on his tongue.

"Excellent," Ryuno said happily. "I will teach you everything I know."

"Do not overstep yourself, young one," came Mr. Taki's voice from behind them. The little old man came hobbling down the front steps to join them on the path. "You may teach others what you know, Ryuno," he said, approaching the group, "but be mindful of your place. Although you are a full-fledged Marusai now, you still have much to learn. Just because an old man cannot teach his student anything more, does not mean that the student stops learning. Now, it is up to you to travel and learn on your own. Life is your master now, Ryuno. Do not forget that."

"I will be ever mindful of this," said Ryuno, bowing humbly.

"Excellent," said Mr. Taki. "And remember, anyone who wishes to learn the way of the Marusai from you, may do so—but you are no Marusai master, Ryuno, and no one can become a Marusai until they are trained by a master."

"Yes, mas—yes sir," said Ryuno.

Mr. Taki smiled. "Well then, that is all I wanted to tell you. Off you go then … and do come back and visit once in a while."

"I will," said Ryuno, bowing again. Mr. Taki bowed as well, then turned and went back into the house.

"Is he going to be okay?" Nell asked, as they continued along the stone path, towards the belt of trees.

"He'll be fine," said Ryuno. "My master—er, my *former* master, has dwelt in places far more dangerous than this. He was a great warrior in his time."

"The operative word being *was*," said Alabaster.

Ryuno looked askance at him. "He may appear frail, but he can still fight. He is more than a match for any Marusai master."

* * *

Soon, Mr. Taki's house was far behind them. The group pressed on through the jungle while the sun rose slowly into the sky, bringing the temperature up with it. It was another hot, steamy, sticky day in the Verdurian jungle, and everyone was soon sweating profusely (except for Grey, of course). Stanley wasn't bothered nearly as much by the heat, as he was by Ryuno, who spent the entire journey gabbing to Nell about how great it was to be a Marusai, and what it means to be a Marusai, and all the things a Marusai could learn. By noon, he was so sick of hearing about the way of the Marusai, that he joined Grey again at the head of the procession. He didn't feel like talking to anyone, and Grey was the perfect company if you wanted to be completely ignored.

"Something's bothering you," said Grey. So much for being ignored.

"It's nothing," said Stanley, glaring ahead at the endless procession of trunks and boughs. Grey didn't press the issue.

Twice they stopped to rest, and both times, Stanley was forced to sit at a distance from the others, lest he overhear Ryuno's complete re-telling of the entire history of the Marusai.

"If I hear the word 'Marusai' one more time, I'm gonna puke," he muttered to a small red lizard. The lizard stuck its tongue out at him and scurried off into the bushes.

"Whatcha doing, Stanley?" said Alabaster, flopping down beside him.

"Oh, nothing much," Stanley answered listlessly, "Just thinking."

"Sounds strenuous!" said Alabaster.

Despite his bad mood, Stanley couldn't help but chuckle. "It *is*, actually. You should try it sometime!"

Alabaster laughed. It was a very genuine, care-free sound. It made Stanley smile.

"Is something bugging you?" Alabaster asked after a moment.

Stanley sighed. "Nah, it's nothing."

"You *sure*?" said Alabaster. He glanced meaningfully back to where Nell and Ryuno were sitting.

"Yeah, I'm sure," said Stanley, slightly alarmed by Alabaster's shrewdness.

"Well, okay, if you're sure," said Alabaster, getting up. He disappeared into the bushes, and a few seconds later, leaped out beside Ryuno and Nell, roaring at the top of his lungs. Nell shrieked, and Ryuno tried to jump to his feet, but fell over in the process.

Stanley laughed. Good old Alabaster, always trying to lighten the mood. Nell was laughing as Ryuno picked himself up. He looked a bit embarrassed, and proceeded to inform Alabaster about how dangerous it was to sneak up on a Marusai like that. Alabaster then began to joke with Nell. Ryuno looked annoyed by this.

"Serves you right, Mr. hot-shot," Stanley muttered.

★ ★ ★

It was late afternoon when, after pushing through a dense thicket, they found themselves at the edge of a vast, open field bordered on the right by a massively-wide river emptying into the sea from the south. The jungle had come to an abrupt end, and not far ahead, beyond the field and at the bottom of a gentle slope, there stood a town.

Stanley was instantly reminded of Port Silverburg and Ethelia. This was obviously a Rheddish city, one of the many colonies that Uncle Jack had told him about.

"That's Port Verdant," said Grey, pointing ahead with his remaining hand.

"And *that* is the Armadon River," said Ryuno, mostly to Nell. "Said to be the longest river in the world."

"Finally," said Alabaster, "I thought we were *never* gonna make it!"

As its name would suggest, Port Verdant was built right on the seashore, its Eastern edge hugging the banks of the Armadon. It was larger than Port Silverburg by a fair margin, though it did not extend very far inland. Its harbour occupied almost all of the town's coastline, but there weren't many ships moored at the moment.

The buildings, most of which were built from white or sandy-coloured stone, were placed fairly close together; the streets all looked quite narrow.

"Let's go," said Grey, leading the way down the sloping green field towards the town. As they approached the town gates, they found themselves on what looked like the remains of an old stone road. The road was in a state of advanced disrepair; many of its interlocking stones were missing, and scruffy-looking weeds had sprung up between the ones that were left, which were old, weathered, and cracked. The road's condition improved slightly as they drew closer to the town, but not by much.

Within about ten minutes, they were standing in front of the town wall. The wall's white stone was almost completely obscured by a vast growth of vegetation, probably some kind of tropical creeping vine. It looked rather fetching.

The gate itself seemed to be the one place where the vine did not hold dominion over the wall. A pair of huge metal doors stood open, revealing a stout wooden portcullis, which currently closed off the entryway. Beyond, Stanley could see, through the gaps in the portcullis, a bustling street filled with people.

Just outside the gate, an old man with a long grey beard was seated on a wooden stool, his chin on his chest, snoring loudly. He wore a tarnished metal helmet, a shirt of chainmail, and a pair of battered, dented greaves over his trousers. A long pole with a flag on it was propped against the stone wall, and an old, blunt-looking sword was grasped half-heartedly in the old man's gauntlet-clad hand.

"Guess he's a guard," said Alabaster, peering intently at the old man.

"Guard, indeed," said Ryuno disdainfully, "asleep at his post—I've never seen anything like it. No Marusai would ever let something like this happen."

"He's just an old man," said Nell, "give him a break."

"Yeah," said Stanley, anxious to join Nell in berating Ryuno. "They probably just have him here because he doesn't have to do much. It doesn't look like too many people come through here."

Ryuno frowned, and muttered something about the way of the Marusai.

Grey took a step towards the old man and cleared his throat loudly. The old man just went on sleeping, a silly smile on his wrinkled face. Grey took another step forward, reached out, and rapped hard with his knuckles on the man's helmet.

TONK, TONK, TONK

The old man's head bobbed comically with each hit, but he still refused to wake up. Grey glanced back at the rest of the group, then turned back to the sleeping man. He leaned forward so that their faces were almost touching, then opened his mouth with its sharp, gleaming white teeth.

"WAKE UP!" he roared.

The old man grunted and slowly opened an eye. "Eh?" he said sleepily, "What's all this—" He caught sight of Grey's ferocious visage directly in front of him, and his eyes opened wide with alarm. "*Great Scott!*" he exclaimed, springing to his feet and raising his sword shakily. Grey lazily batted the weapon out of his hand and seized him by the front of his mail shirt.

"Grey!" shouted Stanley, racing forward, "Stop! Take it easy!"

Grey glared at him, then at the old man, whose eyes were wide as saucers, then back at Stanley. "I was just about to explain to this kindly old gentleman, that we're not here to look for trouble," he said.

"Oh, well why didn't you say so?" said the old man, struggling feebly. Grey released him, and he dropped to the ground and landed on his backside.

"Sorry about that," said Stanley, helping him to his feet.

"Quite alright, er, no harm done," said the old man, dusting himself off and glancing apprehensively at Grey. He went to retrieve his sword, whose blade had sunk several inches into the ground. "Urrf!" he grunted, trying to pull the sword free, "Ummmf! My, but it's stuck!"

Grey took a step towards the old man, who let out a frightened squeak and sprang out of the way. Grey grasped the sword's hilt and drew it effortlessly out of the ground. He returned it to the old man, who said an embarrassed 'thank you'.

He turned around and spent a solid minute wrestling his sword back into its sheath. Finally, he turned back to face the group, straightening his helmet and smiling pleasantly.

"Uh … so, can we go in?" said Stanley.

"In? Ah! Yes, yes, of course!" said the guard. Stanley and Grey moved forward, but the old man stopped them.

"But first," he said, raising his right hand, "I'm going to have to see some identification."

"What?" said Grey.

"Identification?" said Stanley.

"Fraid so. We can't let just anybody into the city, now can we? Gotta make sure you're on the level! Identification, please!"

Alabaster marched up to the old man. "You don't need to see our identification," he said, passing a hand in front of his face.

"What?" said the guard, "I don't?"

"Oh for pity's sake, jus' let 'em in, Frank," came a voice from atop the wall. "They're the on'y ones've come by since that explorer fellow, an' they hardly look dangerous! If they make any trouble, we'll jus' toss 'em out again, simple as anythin'."

The man atop the wall clearly hadn't gotten a good look at Grey or Ryuno, which was probably just as well, because the next instant, old Frank said,

"Alright then," and yelled, "RAAAAAIIISE THE GATE!"

With a groan of protesting metal and wood, the portcullis slowly lifted up. Frank sprang aside, grabbed the flag pole, stood at attention, and recited,

"Welcome to Port Verdant, principal Rheddish Colony of Verduria, and gateway to the continent! Please enjoy your—eh?" He blinked at Stanley and the others as they passed, then stared after them, his mouth hanging open. "Here now!" he called after them, "Did you lot just come from the jungle?"

"You better believe it!" Alabaster called back.

"Well my word!" Frank exclaimed, before sitting back down on his stool and falling asleep.

Chapter 9

A RELATIVE MEETING

They were now walking through what looked like a market area. Stalls and shops and kiosks were squashed as close together as possible on either side of a wide thoroughfare, and people were milling about, buying fruit from one stand, beads from another, and haggling over the price of meat. Stanley overheard part of a conversation between two middle-aged women:

"Have you heard about the famous explorer who's staying in town?" the first woman was asking.

"Heard about him?" said the second, "I've *seen* him!"

"You *have?"*

"Yes! He's staying at the Imperial Garden Hotel, just up the street!"

"Really?"

"He's been there for the past few nights, telling stories about his adventures! He's been out in the jungle for weeks!"

"The jungle? My word! How did he ever survive?"

"Oh, he must be one of these survival experts. I'm sure he knows *everything* there is to know about the jungle!"

The two women continued to talk, but by now the group had moved on, and Stanley could no longer hear what they were saying.

"So," said Ryuno, causing the others to stop, "what do we do now?"

"We should find a place to stay for the night," said Grey, looking up at the sky.

The sun was sinking low on the horizon. Soon it would vanish behind the vast jungle to the west.

Stanley peered down the street, and caught sight of a large, elegant-looking sign. Painted on it in stylish, loopy letters were the words *Imperial Garden Hotel.* "How 'bout there?" he said, pointing at the sign.

Grey scowled at it, then at the dignified-looking building to which it was attached. "Too expensive," he said shortly.

They passed by the hotel on their way up the street. The doors were wide open, and Stanley could see a crowd of people inside. Suddenly, a loud voice from within exclaimed,

"Jackson Lee? I know a Jackson Lee! He's a relative of mine—my uncle, in fact!"

Stanley froze. The rest of the group was already a good ways down the street before they noticed he wasn't with them.

"Stanley," Nell called, "what are you doing?"

"Come here!" he said, waving her towards him.

He peered through the doorway, into a large, open room. It seemed to be a restaurant, or a pub; there were scores of people crammed into every available space, huddled around tables or standing shoulder to shoulder along the walls. At the far end of the room, leaning against the bar and holding a half-empty pint glass in his hand, was a young, bespectacled man who looked as if he could have been Stanley's older brother.

He was tall, lanky, and had a long, thin face. He looked like some kind of explorer, clad in a khaki shirt and pants, with a battered-looking pith helmet perched on his head. Stanley noted that (unlike some people he knew) this man at least had the sense to wear sturdy-looking boots on his feet, instead of sandals with navy blue socks pulled up to his knees.

"A pirate?" said the man, in response to one of the other patrons' questions, "Good lord, Uncle Jack, a pirate? Well, I don't know … if he is, he's never mentioned it. But then, I haven't seen the dear old fellow for quite some time! I suppose anything is possible."

"What's going on?" said Nell. She and Alabaster had just appeared at Stanley's shoulder.

"That guy's talking about Uncle Jack," said Stanley, pointing at the man in the pith helmet.

"He is?" said Alabaster. "Really?"

"Well, I must say," the man said loudly, "I've never heard of Uncle Jack doing any of *that!* You must be talking about another Jackson Warrington Lee."

A disappointed murmur ran through the crowd.

"Er, ah," said the young man, looking around, "But then again, maybe you *aren't!* Maybe we're talking about the exact *same* Jackson Warrington Lee!"

Another murmur ran through the crowd, this one full of excitement and interest.

"How 'bout that?" said Alabaster, "It sounds like that guy knows Uncle Jack, Stanley!"

"We should talk to him," said Nell. "Maybe he can help us get in touch with your uncle."

This sounded like a good idea to Stanley. He plunged into the crowd, Alabaster and Nell close behind him, and after many an 'excuse me' and several 'sorries', found himself right up at the front. Nell gave him a small shove, and he stumbled out of the crowd.

"Hello there," said the young man with the pith helmet, "little young to be in the pub, aren't you?" Several people laughed.

Stanley was surprised to suddenly notice what looked like a gorilla standing beside the young man. The gorilla was dressed in much the same way as the man, minus the pith helmet. He stood there silently in a very un-gorilla like fashion, his back straight, his hands clasped behind him. He looked bored and a little embarrassed.

"Ahh, no need to be alarmed, my young friend!" said the man, noticing Stanley staring at the gorilla. "*This* is my faithful companion, Koko!"

Koko rolled his eyes and sighed.

"He saved my life out there in the jungle," the young man went on, "So I made him my number one expedition partner! But enough about all that. What can I do for you, me buck?"

"Uh," said Stanley, tearing his eyes away from Koko, "I … was just wondering …" He glanced over at Nell and Alabaster. Nell was twirling her hands as if to say *'out with it!'* Alabaster was giving him a 'thumbs up'.

"Uh," Stanley said again, feeling rather warm in the face, "I … did you say you knew a Jackson Warrington Lee?"

"That I did," the young man said heartily. "Why? Do you know him too?"

Stanley cleared his throat. "Well ..." he glanced again at Alabaster and Nell. Nell was nodding, and Alabaster was trying to be funny by doing the opposite.

"Yes," said Stanley. "He's ... uh, my great uncle."

There was a general intake of breath throughout the room. The young man set his glass down and peered intently at Stanley.

"Your great uncle?" he said.

Stanley nodded.

"Does he live in a town called Westport?" the young man asked.

"Yes!" said Stanley. "Well, usually—"

"Well then you must know Rose and Robert!" said the young man excitedly, "Rose and Robert Brambles?"

"Yes!" said Stanley, "They're my mom and dad!"

"Eureka!" cried the young man, "Then you're Stanley!"

"Yeah!" said Stanley.

The young man thrust out his right hand. "And *I* am Algernon Petrie, adventurer and explorer extraordinaire! But please, call me Algie! I'm your mom's cousin! So I guess that makes me your ... what, second cousin? Incredible!" He shook Stanley's hand vigorously, then said, at the top of his voice, "I'd like to take this opportunity to introduce one of my esteemed relatives, whom I've just met face to face for the first time! Everyone, meet Stanley Brambles!"

The room broke into thunderous applause, and Stanley was trying to figure out what he'd done to merit it, when something caught his eye. In a dark corner of the room, he'd seen something ... something white ... what was it? He was starting to think he'd imagined it, when ...

There it was again. The room seemed to darken, and the sounds of Algernon talking and people laughing seemed to grow faint. Stanley could see it clearly now. It was a face, a face as ghostly white as freshly fallen snow. He stared at the face, and saw that it belonged to a woman. She looked quite young, maybe a few years older than Ryuno, and she was extremely pretty, in an unsettling kind of way. She was dressed all in black, and was almost completely hidden in the shadowy corner. Long, straight curtains of raven-black hair hung down on either side of her face. She wore what looked like black lipstick, and far too much black eye makeup. She stared directly at Stanley, her eyes cold and dark. It felt as if an icy claw were clutching at his chest. He looked away for an instant, and when he looked back, the woman had gone. Had he really seen her? And if so, who was she? Probably just someone who lived around here. Maybe she was an actress, or a street performer. But how had she disappeared so suddenly … and why did he feel so cold when he looked into her eyes? His thoughts were interrupted as Algernon draped a long, spindly arm around his shoulders and started to tell the crowd what a genius his father was.

"You should see this museum!" he said enthusiastically. "Rose's husband, Bob (we're great friends) plans all the exhibits himself! He's a genius, a certifiable genius!"

Just then, there was a slight disturbance in the pub. The crowd parted as a group of grim-faced soldiers came striding into the room. They were all dressed like old Frank at the gate, but they didn't look very friendly.

"Mr. Petrie?" said the one in the lead. She looked fairly young—probably in her mid-twenties. Her blonde hair was pulled back in a short ponytail, and a deep, vivid horizontal scar ran across her face just beneath her eyes, making her look extremely fierce.

"That's me," said Algernon, "but please, call me Algie!"

"Mr. Petrie, if you would be so good as to come with me," said the soldier.

"I don't see why not," said Algernon good-naturedly. Koko, however, stepped forward and grasped him gently by the shoulder.

"Algernon, maybe you should find out where they're going," he said in a deep, even voice.

"Good thinking, Koko," said Algernon. "See here, my dear!" he said to the soldier, "I *demand* to know where you're taking me!"

"To the home of the governor," said the soldier, her eyes narrowing. "He'd like a word with you."

"The governor?" said Algernon, "Sounds great! Lead on, MacDuff!"

"Algernon," said Koko, "Perhaps you should find out exactly *what* the governor wants with you."

"You can tell your pet there to relax," one of the other soldiers said truculently. "The governor just wants to talk to you. We're not dealing with a criminal offense here."

Koko sighed and rolled his eyes again. He looked offended.

"Now wait just a minute!" said Algernon, "Koko is no pet! He's my number one—"

"Save it," said the lead soldier. "The governor is waiting."

"Wait!" said Algernon, looking at Stanley, "I insist that my cousin, Stanley, come along, too."

"*And my friends, Alabaster and Nell,*" Stanley whispered.

"And my friends, Alabaster and Nell!" said Algernon.

"Fine," said the soldier, signaling to her men and leading the way towards the door. Stanley motioned for Nell and Alabaster to follow him, and fell into line behind Koko.

Outside, the lead soldier stopped short in front of Grey, who was at least a head taller than she was, and still dressed in his furs and hand-stitched trousers.

"You got a problem, nature-boy?" she asked.

Ryuno stepped out of the shadows, ready to draw his sword. "*You* will be the one with the problem, if you do not release our friends," he said, glaring fiercely at the soldiers.

"Wait!" said Stanley, "It's okay, they aren't going to hurt us. Right?"

"R-r-right," said the lead soldier, at whom Grey had just bared his teeth. "Er … are these two friends of yours, Petrie?"

"Hm? I don't … er … ah, *yes!*" said Algernon, as Stanley nodded furiously at him.

"O-okay," said the soldier, "The, uh … the governor's house is this way …"

⋆ ⋆ ⋆

It was rather a long walk to the governor's house. As night fell over Port Verdant, the streets emptied quickly. All over town, doors were slamming shut and locking, and groups of soldiers appeared on almost every street corner, weapons drawn.

It was a much less cheerful place than Port Silverburg or Ethelia, and Stanley found the difference unsettling.

"Is the Rhedland Freedom Festival over?" he piped up. One of the soldiers glanced back at him.

"We can't afford to bother with that sort of thing," the man said grimly. "Back in Rhedland, they can make merry all they want, but this is Verduria. We've got too many problems to waste time with *festivals.*"

"That's enough, Hawkins," said the lead soldier. "No need to worry these people with Verduria's troubles. They'll learn all about them soon enough, I'm sure."

"No time for festivals and parties?" said Algernon, "What a shame! Why is Port Verdant so devoid of cheer?"

"You've been in the jungle for six weeks and you can't figure it out?" said Hawkins.

"You can ask the governor," said the lead soldier. "He can no doubt explain it better than we can."

"Ah yes, the governor!" Algernon said genially, "When do we get to meet the old chap?"

"We've got a ways to go yet," said the soldier, "And I wouldn't call him an 'old chap' to his face if you know what's good for you. The governor isn't one to suffer nonsense."

"Oh pish-tosh," said Algernon, "anyone governing a tropical paradise like *this* must be a decent enough fellow—you probably just have to get to know him a bit!"

The soldiers scoffed and shook their heads.

"Hey, not bad, eh?" said Alabaster, nudging Stanley. "The governor! We seem to meet all the important people, wherever we go!"

"We weren't actually invited," Nell told him quietly. "I don't know how happy he's going to be when he sees that Algernon's brought a whole group of people along."

"Well, if he's anything like Mr. Crane, I think we'll be fine," Alabaster said knowingly.

"It doesn't *sound* like he is," said Nell, glancing at the soldiers.

"Maybe he's a friend of Uncle Jack's," said Stanley, feeling suddenly hopeful.

"And maybe he's not!" said Nell, looking rather alarmed. "For goodness' sake, don't mention your uncle! This governor might have been an enemy of his!"

Stanley gulped. He hadn't thought of that. Now that he considered it, he could see that throwing Uncle Jack's name around was really not a wise idea. After all, he'd once been the most feared pirate in the world … what if the governor had been working for the old emperor, or for Chamberlain? Stanley suddenly felt a bit foolish.

A little over half an hour later, the small procession arrived at a large wrought-iron gate in a high stone wall. Part of the metal in the middle of the gate had been worked into the shape of a capital letter 'C'. Beyond the gate, a smoothly-paved driveway ran across a sweeping lawn dotted with neatly-trimmed shrubs, to a great marble fountain. Beyond the fountain, a flight of wide steps ran up to the front door of a colossal white house. Stanley was reminded of Uncle Jack's mansion back in Westport. Huge pillars supported the front porch, and the building's wings, which extended a good distance to the left and right, both had three floors, and at least thirty windows each on this side.

The lead soldier pressed a button which was fixed to a metal plate set into the stone wall. Seconds later, another soldier came marching out of a small hut just inside the gates.

"Evenin', Lieutenant Breaker," he said through the iron bars. "What business brings you to the governor's residence?"

"I'm escorting a guest of His Lordship's," said the lieutenant.

"A whole *party*, looks like," said the man inside the gate.

The lieutenant sighed and glanced at the group behind her. "They insisted on coming along."

"Well, if the governor doesn't want 'em, we can get rid of 'em easy enough," said the gate guard. "Gw'on through."

The gate swung open, and the soldiers led the way up the drive, around the fountain, and up to the mansion's big wooden front doors. Lieutenant Breaker grasped a metal knocker shaped like the head of a wild boar (or perhaps a gorethane), and gave three smart taps.

The doors were opened seconds later by a gaunt, elderly man in an impeccable black suit. He peered haughtily out at the group on the doorstep.

"Mr. Petrie and his—er—party," said the lieutenant.

"Very good," said the man in the suit, opening the doors wider and stepping back.

"Right," said the lieutenant, "in you go." And with that, she and her men turned and descended the front steps and made their way back towards the gate. Stanley and the others stepped uncertainly over the threshold and into a vast, cylindrical entrance hall with a marble floor, white walls, and a spiral staircase leading to the upper floors.

"This way, please," the man in the suit said pompously, leading the way across the hall to another pair of doors to the left of the staircase, which he opened, waving the group down a long hallway whose walls and floors gleamed in the light of at least a dozen hanging lanterns spaced a regular intervals. Stanley noted that these lights seemed to be electric, as their glow was clearly not being supplied by flame.

Presently, the man in the suit stopped in front of yet another door, and knocked softly on the spotlessly-white wooden surface.

"Come," said a deep, commanding voice from the other side.

The man opened the door and went in. Algernon followed on his heels, puffing out his chest and swinging his arms with exaggerated enthusiasm. He seemed to be enjoying himself. Koko followed, looking very embarrassed. The rest of the group went in, with Grey bringing up the rear.

Stanley looked around. They were now standing in a large, round room. The walls were adorned with paintings, some of which looked extremely old. An unlit chandelier hung down from the high ceiling. Beneath it, a small collection of high-backed chairs was placed in a loose semi-circle around an enormous fireplace. In front of the fireplace, in whose grate a huge fire was crackling wildly, a man was standing with his back to the group, his hands clasped behind him. He was dressed in a long, blue coat, with white pantaloons and great black boots. His head was covered with a very long and curly wig which reached down to the middle of his back. He did not turn around as the group entered the room, but stayed where he was, apparently staring at the flames leaping before him.

The man in the suit cleared his throat. "Ahem! Presenting Mr. Algernon Petrie and his party."

The man in front of the fire remained motionless for a time, then slowly turned to face the group. The guards who had brought them here had been a grim-faced lot, but this man made them seem like a fun-loving bunch by comparison. The room's dim lighting threw the man's face into relief; it seemed to consist entirely of harsh lines and ridges. Clearly, this was a man accustomed to frowning.

Stanley was forcibly reminded of Ezekiel Chamberlain, former regent of the Rheddish Empire. The man standing before him also bore no trace of warmth or laughter in his cold, grey eyes. Stanley hoped, for all their sakes, that that was where the similarities ended.

"So," said the man, "I send my soldiers out for one person, and they bring me seven." He frowned darkly. "Which one of you is Petrie?"

"That would be me," said Algernon pleasantly, raising his hand. He advanced on the grim-faced man and thrust out his hand with a very unnecessary flourish. "Algernon Petrie at your service," he said, grinning broadly. "But please, call me Algie!"

The look on the man's face suggested that he would fling himself into the fireplace before he ever called Algernon 'Algie'.

"I am Charles Cromwell," he said, ignoring Algernon's hand, which was still waiting expectantly to be shook, "Governor of the Verdurian Colonies. Perhaps you could take a moment to explain to me who these … *people* are," (he motioned towards the rest of the group) "and why they are here, when I called for you, and only you, Mr. Petrie."

"Oh!" said Algernon. "Well! … Er, yes, as to that—er—*ah*!" He threw an arm around Koko's massive shoulders. "For starters, *this* is my faithful sidekick, Koko!" he grinned broadly and jostled Koko chummily. Koko sighed, and bowed low to Cromwell.

"Governor," he said shortly.

Cromwell nodded. "And?" he said, after a brief pause.

"And," said Algernon, glancing awkwardly at the rest of the group, none of whom he had met before today, "Er—ah … oh, well, *this*," he said, grabbing Stanley by the arm and dragging him forward, "is my cousin, Stanley! And—and—er, *these* are his friends!" He made a sweeping gesture which encompassed the rest of the party.

"And do they have names?" said Cromwell coolly, glancing disinterestedly at them.

"Er," said Algernon. He glanced sideways at Stanley, a definite hint of desperation in his eyes. It was clear that he needed a bit of help.

Putting on his very bravest and most businesslike manner, Stanley piped up, "These are my friends, Alabaster and Nell."

Nell stepped forward and dropped into a flawless curtsey, even though she was wearing jeans, and Alabaster made a ridiculous bow, sticking his right foot out and twirling his hands as he said, "Enchanté."

Nell sprang out of her curtsey and elbowed him roughly in the stomach. Stanley, flushing furiously, jumped in front of them both and glanced embarrassedly up at Cromwell.

"Charmed, I'm sure," said the governor, not sounding particularly amused. "And what about you?" he said to Ryuno, who was standing proud and tall behind Nell and Alabaster.

"I am Mitsuhiro Ryunosuke Akechi," said Ryuno, bowing low.

"A Marusai," Cromwell said with minimal interest. "I wouldn't have expected to find one of your kind roaming my city. Not that I'm complaining, of course—we can always use another sword. Oh, and forgive me if I refuse to waste time trying to commit your name to memory."

Ryuno looked a bit taken aback by this. It looked like he was about to say something else, but Cromwell was apparently done with him for now. His cold, hard eyes came to rest on Grey, who was standing silently at the rear of the group, still decked out in his furs and hand-stitched clothes.

"And you, sir," said Cromwell, gesturing in Grey's direction, "may I have your name?"

Grey was silent for a moment before answering. "Grey," he said flatly.

"Hmm," said Cromwell glancing around at his 'guests', "well, Petrie, I'm sure you have a good reason for bringing this lot along ... let's get to business, shall we?"

"Er—yes, let's," said Algernon.

"Wilfred," said Cromwell to his butler, "Please send in the others, will you?"

"Very good, sir," said Wilfred, bowing his way out of the room.

"Please sit, Mr. Petrie," said Cromwell, gesturing towards one of the high-backed armchairs.

"Oh, thank you," said Algernon, taking the seat offered to him.

"I'm afraid the rest of your party will have to stand, or sit themselves on the floor," said Cromwell, not sounding too concerned. "As you can see, seating is limited."

Ryuno made a small noise of annoyance. He clearly did not approve of the governor's manners.

Stanley was just wondering who Cromwell had meant when he'd said *the others*, when the door opened, and with a *click clack* of claws on marble, in slouched a muscular, humanoid lizard. It was a Saurian warrior.

Alabaster shrieked loudly and leaped into Nell's arms. She dropped him immediately, and grabbed hold of Stanley's arm. Stanley didn't look at her, but his heart had suddenly begun to hammer in his chest and he felt suddenly brave—brave enough to take on a Saurian, maybe.

But he didn't get the chance, fortunately. With a metallic swish and a flash of polished steel, Ryuno's sword was out of its sheath and pointing squarely at the lizard, who had stopped short with a surprised look on its face. It then bared its teeth and snarled, then glanced uncertainly at Grey, who had just done the exact same thing.

"STOP!" roared Cromwell, stalking forward, "Lower your weapons, you fools!"

"What is the meaning of this, Cromwell?" said the Saurian in perfect English. Its voice had a certain hissing quality to it.

Cromwell shoved Grey and Ryuno aside. "I must apologize for my other … guests," he said to the Saurian. "Clearly they have never met any of your kind before."

"*I* have," Grey said darkly, glaring ferociously at the lizard.

"Wait!" said Ryuno sharply, "This Saurian is not of the Xol'tec tribe!"

"I sincerely hope not," hissed the Saurian, and Stanley could see that this was true. This Saurian, whose scales were vibrantly blue instead of rust-coloured, was wearing a loincloth with a green pattern on it, instead of a red one.

Ryuno sheathed his sword and kneeled before the Saurian. "Please forgive me," he said humbly. "I acted in haste, and without thought."

The Saurian waved a clawed hand. "A common mistake among humans," he said, "Although among my people, it is an insult punishable by death."

Ryuno got to his feet, his expression neutral.

"*What* is going on in here?" Another man had come into the room while Ryuno and Grey were squaring off against the Saurian. He was tall and thin and looked to be in his late thirties. He had shoulder-length hair, which was black, and made his somewhat pale skin look even paler.

"A slight misunderstanding, Father," said Cromwell.

"Father?" said Alabaster, "*That* guy's your *father?*"

The black-haired man laughed; it lightened the mood wonderfully. "No, lad, not that kind of father. I'm a clergyman—a chaplain, actually."

"He's a priest," Nell muttered, noting Alabaster's blank look.

"Nigel Blake, at your service," said the priest with a little bow. "Just call me Blake, though, everyone else does. Two first names, right?"

He smiled, then looked around at the group gathered before him, his expression changing to one of polite puzzlement.

"Unexpected guests, Father," said Cromwell, before Blake could ask who they all were.

"Ah," said the priest. He scanned the group again, and his gaze fell on Stanley. His eyes suddenly widened, and a look of something like disbelief crossed his face. Stanley stared back, slightly puzzled by the odd reaction. No one else seemed to think anything of it, and Father Blake quickly looked away.

"Temoc," he said, noticing the Saurian, "It's good to see you again."

The Saurian, whose name appeared to be Temoc (the priest had pronounced it *Tay-muk*), nodded shortly and said, "Likewise, hass Blake."

Stanley wondered briefly what *hass* meant, but then Father Blake was saying,

"Please, who are the rest of these good people? I think some introductions are in order."

"Later," Cromwell said sharply. "Dinner will be served soon, but right now I'd like to get down to business. Please, everyone, come in and sit down."

Stanley, Alabaster, Nell, Ryuno, and Koko took seats on the floor, while Algernon, Temoc, and Father Blake each took a chair. Grey remained standing.

"No doubt you're wondering why I've called you here this evening," said Cromwell, pacing back and forth in front of the fireplace. "Let me begin by giving you some … unsettling news." He cleared his throat. "Ezekiel Chamberlain, Regent Lord of the Rheddish Empire, has fallen."

Clearly, Cromwell expected everyone to gasp with surprise at this 'unsettling' news, but not one of them so much as flinched. After all, four of them had been there to witness Chamberlain's downfall, and Algernon wasn't even from Terra. The others probably weren't too concerned with Imperial affairs, with the possible exception of Father Blake, who said,

"Chamberlain … so he's … dead? What on earth happened?"

"No one knows," said Cromwell, "but his ship, the Maelstrom set sail from Ethelia nine months ago, and hasn't been seen since."

"That's 'cause it was *destroyed!"* Alabaster said dramatically. All eyes turned to him.

"How could you possibly know that, *boy?"* said Cromwell, eyeing Alabaster suspiciously.

"Because I was—*oof!"* Stanley and Nell had just elbowed Alabaster simultaneously.

It was no doubt very important that Cromwell did not find out that they'd witnessed the destruction of the Maelstrom and her crew firsthand.

"Well?" said Cromwell, glaring at Alabaster, "Speak up!"

"He's just joking," said Nell, clamping a hand over a protesting Alabaster's mouth. "He just does it for attention. Of course he wasn't. Really. There."

She said these last three words while staring fiercely into Alabaster's eyes. Alabaster finally seemed to get the picture.

Cromwell made a noise of annoyance. "Of course, I should have known. That's why *I* never include *children* in this sort of thing. I'm sure you have your reasons for having them in your party, Petrie, but I don't know what they might be."

"Er," said Algernon.

"We're technically teens," said Alabaster.

"Back to the business at hand," said Cromwell, taking no notice. "Chamberlain has been declared dead, killed in the line of duty. The wreckage of a ship, confirmed to be the Maelstrom, washed up on our shores some time ago." He glanced meaningfully at the group. "The capital is in an uproar, of course, but recently, a new regent has taken control of the throne."

Stanley's insides squirmed. A new regent? Would it just be another Chamberlain?

"Currently, I am not at liberty to divulge the identity of the new regent," said Cromwell, "but I can tell you that he was not appointed—he seized the Capital, and has declared martial law until he can get things under control."

"This doesn't sound good," said Father Blake.

Cromwell held up a hand. "Don't worry too much about it. The new regent is a decent enough man, and will do all he can to restore order to Rhedland."

"I would like to know what this has to do with us," said Temoc, sounding a tad impatient.

"I'm getting to that," said Cromwell. "With Rhedland in its current state, all resources are being used to re-stabilize the country. Because of this, the colonies have had to fend for themselves for the past while. Rhedland has been unable to spare any soldiers or supplies, so we have had to become completely self-sufficient.

"Now, as a colony, we've already *been* fairly self-sufficient for a good number of years, but there's a problem. In recent months, Verduria, the continent, has become increasingly hostile. Something has happened, something that seems to be affecting the jungle and its creatures. Plants and animals that were once harmless and docile have become fierce and dangerous, and those creatures that were dangerous to begin with, have grown more dangerous still."

Cromwell's expression had become very grave. "We are now fighting a losing battle against the jungle itself. My city has already suffered attacks by marauding beasts from the forest, not to mention the red Saurians. Many Rheddish citizens have died, and people are fleeing the other colonial cities for the safety of Port Verdant, the largest and best-defended settlement on the continent." He took a deep breath. "It is getting to the point where I have begun to seriously consider evacuating the colony. If things get much worse, that's exactly what's going to have to happen."

"To flee would indeed be wise," said Temoc. "Humans are ill-suited to life in the jungle. Even my people, who have dwelt in these lands for millennia, are having problems dealing with this new threat."

"If it comes to it, we will flee, yes," said Cromwell, "But I'm not ready to give up just yet. I want to find the source of this … corruption, and put an end to it, if possible."

Stanley glanced at Ryuno, who was nodding enthusiastically.

"I have been trying to do just that," the Marusai said importantly.

"That's good to hear," said Cromwell. "Because I think I know exactly where the source *is*."

Everyone was listening intently.

"I've heard tell of a place deep in the jungle," said Cromwell, "Far to the south of here, in the very heart of the continent. No human has ever set foot there, and as far as I know, no Saurian, either."

Temoc raised his snout. "You are speaking of *Quetzal-Khan*," he said slowly. "The Lost City …"

"Precisely," said Cromwell.

"A lost city?" said Algernon excitedly, "Fantastic! I *love* lost cities! The mystery, the intrigue! The *danger!*"

Stanley heard Koko sigh heavily at this.

"That's good to hear, Mr. Petrie," said Cromwell, looking down his nose at Algernon, "Because if there's one thing I can guarantee, it's danger."

"What exactly are you proposing, Governor?" said Father Blake.

"I am proposing an expedition," said Cromwell, "to find the Lost City of Quetzal-Khan."

Temoc hissed derisively. "Quetzal-Khan is a myth. Even my people know that."

"Do they now?" said Cromwell. "I suppose, then, that your people have explored the continent in its entirety? Hmm?"

Temoc shifted in his seat. "No, we have not … we are not explorers—"

"Of course not," said Cromwell. "Your people have been too busy slaughtering each other over the past five thousand years to spend any time on something as *trivial* as exploration."

"We are warriors!" growled Temoc, clutching the arms of his chair with his clawed fingers.

"Of that, I am *constantly* aware," said Cromwell, waving the Saurian's words aside.

"Governor," said Father Blake, "I'm still not clear on the purpose of such an expedition—"

"The purpose will be threefold," said Cromwell. "First, to find the source of the taint that affects this land."

"And you believe it to be in this Lost City, of all places?" said Blake.

"Second," said Cromwell, ignoring him, "to recover the treasure of the Lost City—"

"Treasure?" said Algernon. Stanley's ears perked up, too. He looked at Cromwell, suspicion growing in his mind. Was this going to be just another treasure hunt? The search for Uncle Jack's treasure had been an incredible experience, and after all, they had been trying to *protect* the treasure, not steal it. What were Cromwell's motives, he wondered?

"Oh yes," said Cromwell, noticing the look of acute interest on Algernon's face, "you will be well paid for your efforts, you can be sure of that. Assuming you survive, of course."

"And what is the third purpose of this proposed quest?" Temoc enquired, sounding as if the whole idea was nonsense.

"Ah," said Cromwell, rubbing his chin, "The third purpose, yes …" he went over to a picture of an old castle hanging on the wall, and moved it aside. Behind the picture was a recess in the wall, in which sat a small iron safe. Cromwell fiddled with the combination and opened the safe, drawing forth an ancient-looking scroll.

He unrolled the scroll carefully, and held it up for all to see. It was covered with symbols—some kind of ancient language, perhaps—but in the middle was a simple drawing—a faded charcoal sketch, which made Stanley sit up and gasp. The drawing looked like this:

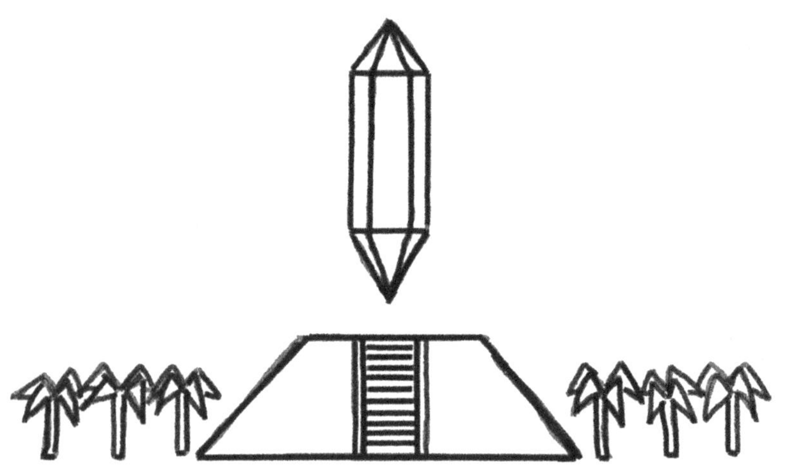

It was as if someone had drawn a picture of his recurring dream: a huge crystal, rising out of the jungle—of course it was rising, because it was floating—floating above some kind of building, a pyramid …

"What—what is that?" he asked breathlessly, pointing at the drawing with a slightly-trembling hand.

Cromwell glanced haughtily at him. "This is …" his eyes flitted over to Temoc, who was also staring raptly at the scroll. "Temoc, would you care to do the honours?"

The Saurian got to his feet and approached Cromwell, reaching out slowly for the scroll. He took it in his clawed hands and gazed reverently at it for a moment.

"This," he said softly, "is a precious relic …"

"A treasure of your people?" Cromwell offered.

"Not of *my* people," said Temoc, still staring at the scroll, "This is a record left behind by the Teo-Huan—the Ancient Ones."

"Ancestors of yours?"

"No," said Temoc, "The Teo-Huan were not Saurians … they are those who were here even before my people. They are the ones who built the first cities." He looked up from the scroll, his eyes bright. "My people warred with them for a thousand years … this was long ago. The Teo-Huan are little more than a myth, these days."

"And they are the ones who made this scroll?" said Cromwell.

Temoc nodded. "If this is genuine—and I believe it is—then this scroll … came out of Quetzal-Khan."

"That much, at least, I was able to figure out myself," said Cromwell, a note of impatience in his voice.

"So—it really exists," Temoc muttered, gazing again at the scroll with wide eyes.

"But what's the *picture* of?" said Stanley, rather more loudly than he'd intended.

Temoc looked at him. "The picture represents—forgive me, this dialect is very old and difficult to translate. These characters seem to represent … Sky … Jewel … Weapon."

"Ooh!" said Alabaster, "Sounds sinister!"

"Sinister or not," said Cromwell, "I want it found."

"A weapon …" mused Father Blake.

"Something on your mind, Father?" said Cromwell.

"I'm merely wondering why you would seek such an artifact."

"For now, my reasons will remain my own," said Cromwell.

"But why tell *us* about it?" said Blake.

"Because," said Cromwell, "I feel that you are the individuals best suited to such a quest. Temoc knows the jungle, and will serve as a guide. Petrie is, from what I've heard, an expert on ancient civilizations, and has been living out in the jungle for some time."

Algernon cleared his throat self-consciously.

"That is," Cromwell went on, "up until the point where his—er—assistant brought him into town unconscious and half dead."

"Er, well," said Algernon, tugging at his shirt collar, "I wouldn't go so far as to say I was *half* dead—I was just a bit tired, you see, and—"

"You, Father Blake," said Cromwell, cutting Algernon off, "Are also something of an historian, are you not? That's what I surmised from your personal records, of course."

"Ah," said Blake, "Well, yes, I suppose I do possess a good deal of knowledge concerning our world's past."

"If you prefer," said Cromwell, "you need not go any further than Daruna Abbey. I would ask, though, that you make the abbey's library available for the rest of the party."

"Of course," said Blake. "The library holds a wealth of old histories and documents. I'd be more than happy to do some research on my return."

"Splendid," said Cromwell. "In that case, I think our meeting is over. Preparations have already been made for your departure."

"Departure?" said Algernon. "What departure?"

Cromwell looked at him as if he had just asked what two plus two was. "Your departure for your journey," he said shortly. "You'll be leaving tomorrow morning."

"Tomorrow!" exclaimed Algernon.

"Uh, excuse me," said Nell, suddenly raising her hand. Everyone turned to look at her.

"Er," she said, her cheeks turning pink, "I think there's been a mistake."

"What sort of mistake?" said Cromwell, frowning at her.

"Well, the thing is—we, the three of us," she said, indicating Stanley and Alabaster, "aren't really supposed to be here—"

"Wait!" said Stanley, "Nell—"

"We're not part of this expedition," she said, pressing on but looking sideways at Stanley. Her expression demanded to know why he was trying to interrupt her.

"*What?*" said Cromwell, "Not part of—*Petrie, is this true?*"

Algernon jumped as if he'd just been stung. "Huh?"

Cromwell wiped his face with his palm. "Is what this girl says true? Are they not really part of your team? *Do you even know who they are?*"

"Yes!" said Algernon. "I mean—well, technically no, I suppose, but they could be! Wait—what I mean to say is, I didn't before today, but I do now, and Stanley's my cousin, so there you are, and, well, they may not be part of my team *officially,* but they can come along, too, eh?"

Cromwell stared. "THAT'S NOT YOUR DECISION TO MAKE, PETRIE!" He finally roared.

"Oh!" said Algernon, cowering back in his chair. "It's not? S-sorry about that—"

"This was a top-secret meeting!" said Cromwell. "I can't have every bloody street urchin in town being briefed on matters of colonial security! Good god, man, what's wrong with you?"

"We're sorry," said Nell, coming to Algernon's defense (he looked like he was about to cry). "We didn't know how important this was. We—"

"*But* we do now," said Stanley, "So—you can count us in."

"*What?"* said Nell.

"Count you in?" said Cromwell. "I'm surrounded by lunatics! The three of you have no training, no experience, and as it turns out, no *business* being here! Is anyone else here *not* part of Petrie's team?"

Grey and Ryuno raised their hands.

Cromwell collapsed into the nearest chair, pinching the bridge of his nose. After a brief silence, Blake asked,

"What happens now?"

Cromwell sighed heavily. "*Now* you will all enjoy a lovely dinner while I sit here and try to figure out how to salvage this situation. My first instinct is to throw this lot in jail to keep them from blabbing the contents of this meeting over half the empire—"

"We won't say anything," said Nell, sounding worried. "We promise!"

"We'll see," said Cromwell. "Until further notice, you are, it seems, my guests. Just don't leave this house—or I *will* have you thrown in jail."

★ ★ ★

Dinner that evening was a tense affair, at least for Stanley and Nell. They spent the entire time trying to keep themselves from yelling at each other as they shoveled their food home, each pointedly avoiding the other's gaze.

After the meal, Wilfred the butler showed them all to their rooms. Alabaster bade his friends a hasty goodnight, leaving Stanley and Nell alone in the hall.

.Nell stood there expectantly, arms folded in front of her. "So are you going to tell me what that was all about?" she said after a moment of awkward silence.

"What *what* was all about?" said Stanley.

"Don't play dumb with me!" said Nell. "You know what I'm talking about—why are you so desperate to go on this stupid trip they're planning?"

"Why are you so desperate to *not* go?" Stanley returned.

Nell's expression changed to one of disbelief. "Are you serious? Are you honestly asking why I don't think we should go *back into the jungle?"*

"I don't—"

"Giant spiders," said Nell, cutting off whatever Stanley was going to say and starting to number off points on her fingers. "Killer lizard-men. Angry rhino-boars. And those are just the things *we've* seen! What about this *dark power* everyone's talking about? You think they were kidding when they said how dangerous the jungle is? Cromwell's even talking about evacuating the entire colony! And you want to *stay?* To go back into that death trap?"

Stanley had to admit that Nell was making some good points.

"We're here by *accident*," she went on. "We need to focus on getting home—can't you see that? This place is dangerous, and we're lucky to be alive! Doesn't that bother you at all?"

"Sure, but we've been through worse," said Stanley, thinking back to their adventure on board the Ogopogo.

Nell stared at him. "That's *not* the takeaway!" she said in exasperation, "If the only lesson you learned from that—*trip*—was that *we've been through worse*, then you—you—*rrrgh!"*

"That's not all I learned," Stanley said defensively. "But I know that danger is part of going on an adventure—but—well, you go anyway, 'cause what's at the end is worth the risk."

Nell raised an eyebrow. "So the ends justify the means? What if people get hurt? What if they die? What if *we* die? Would it still be worth it?"

"Er—"

"What do you *want* out of this anyway? You still haven't told me why you're so desperate to do this."

The short answer was the crystal. Deep down, almost on some kind of subconscious, primal level, Stanley knew that he had to find it, had to see it for himself. If not, he'd never stop dreaming about it. And he had the disturbing feeling that if he didn't, he would eventually go insane.

This was the answer he gave Nell, but there was another answer, one that he might not even have been able to put into words just then. It was more of a feeling, a feeling that *this* was where he belonged—Terra. Over the past while, he'd had the faintest inkling that his mundane life back on Earth was *wrong* somehow, like an ill-fitting pair of shoes. He felt lost, in a way, adrift and without purpose (hardly an original thought for a teenage boy, perhaps), but since he'd come back to Terra, he'd once more felt the thrill of adventure, the call of this mysterious, savage planet that was similar, yet so different from his own. He needed to be here, needed to embark on another adventure, to face the terrors of the jungle. But he could never say as much to Nell.

"Not your dreams again," she said, running a hand through her hair.

"I know it sounds crazy—" Stanley began.

"Yeah, kinda," said Nell, "But I certainly believe you're having them—even that they might be important, especially based on that scroll—but it's still not worth risking our lives for."

Stanley sighed. Maybe Nell was right. The more he tried to think of it from a logical perspective, the more he found himself agreeing with her. Not that that made his need for answers any less acute.

"Wait for them to come back," she said reasonably. "We're stuck here for now, anyway—assuming we don't get put in jail—so why don't we just work out a plan to get home, and maybe they'll be back from their super-dangerous trip before too long, and they can tell you all about the crystal."

Stanley nodded. The question of their participation in the expedition had already been answered, after all.

"Okay," said Nell, smiling a little. "Well … I'm glad we worked that out."

"Me too," said Stanley.

"Alright, well … um … see you tomorrow?"

"Yeah—yeah, for sure."

"Okay. Well—'night!"

"G'night," said Stanley, as Nell turned and zipped into her room. He sighed heavily and opened the door to his own room, stepping through into the blueish evening gloom, glancing around at the shapes of a massive four-poster bed, a comfy-looking easy chair, and a large antique wardrobe. He flicked on the light and saw that a pair of blue and white striped pajamas were folded on the bed, beside a pair of clean jeans and a t-shirt, and, most importantly, fresh socks and underwear. Attached to them was a note which read, *for your personal use.*

Grateful at not having to sleep in his clothes again, Stanley disrobed and went into the adjoining bathroom to clean himself up and brush his teeth. He'd never thought a shower could feel so good, and as he climbed into bed and lay down in cozy comfort for the first time in what felt like forever, his thoughts began to wander.

Why was he here? Had he been brought back to Terra for a reason, or was it all just a coincidence? Somehow he doubted it—to arrive here, in Verduria, so close to the crystal from his dreams, just as an expedition to find it was getting under way …

He sighed and closed his eyes, feeling a rush of disappointment at not being included in the adventure, despite Nell's very sensible and convincing arguments. One way or another, he had to learn more about this crystal, this 'Sky Jewel Weapon'. What was it? What did its name even *mean?* And why was it so important to him? He simply did not know. For now, he would just have to live with that, as well as with the feeling that his one purpose in Verduria was to find this mysterious Weapon.

Chapter 10

FAREWELL TO THEE, PORT VERDANT

The air was thick with the sound of chirping insects and singing birds. The sun was high in the sky, and a bright flash of light caught Stanley's eye. He looked up, and saw, not far off, a massive, floating blue crystal. *The* crystal! The sunlight was glinting off its multi-faceted surface. He could see now that the crystal was hovering above a colossal building—a pyramid with a flat top like the one he'd seen in the drawing on the scroll.

With a feeling of elation, he set off towards the pyramid at a run. At last, at long last, he was going to unravel the mystery of the crystal …

But then suddenly the sun went out. It didn't set; it simply vanished, as if someone had just flicked a giant celestial light switch. A hideous, evil laughter rang through the sudden darkness, and the blue crystal began to glow ominously. An instant later, a brilliant blue-white light flared from the crystal, blinding Stanley with its glare. There was a sound like a thousand windows being smashed, and then …

A tinkling explosion of breaking glass snapped Stanley out of a sound sleep. He sat up in bed and looked around at his darkened room.

Something was wrong.

From outside he could hear shouts and screams—cries of alarm. A reddish-orange glow was filtering through the curtained windows, giving him a very bad feeling. A series of *pop-pop-pops* rang out from somewhere not far off, and a loud, clanging bell began to toll. Human shouts and cries were answered with bestial roars and shrieks. Stanley got reluctantly out of bed and crossed the room. With a bit of trepidation, he pulled open the curtains of the middle window and peeked out into the night.

Across from the mansion's huge front yard, the dark shapes of Port Verdant's buildings meandered lazily down towards the town harbor, beyond which the deep blue expanse of the southern ocean stretched out to the horizon, lit by the three moons of Terra. Here and there, fires had sprung up in town, forming a rough line of burning buildings that led east, towards the city's main gate. Movement from close by grabbed Stanley's attention. A group of figures was milling about in the street outside the mansion's front gate, but it was difficult to make out who they were.

There came several more *pops*, and then a great, united roar of what sounded like triumph. The great iron gate was smashed open, and at least a dozen torch-wielding Saurians came charging towards the mansion, their hoots, shrieks, and roars easily audible over the relentless *clang-clang-clang* of the town alarm bells.

Stanley sprang away from the window as the lizard-men approached. Had they followed him and his friends all this way? Thinking quickly, he grabbed the fresh clothes that had been laid out for him, and was just pulling on his shirt when the middle window exploded inward, showering the floor with broken glass. The rock that had been used to break the window was followed promptly by a small flaming sphere about the size of a tennis ball.

The fireball exploded as it hit the floor, coating the far end of the room in burning liquid. Stanley scrambled for the door as the flames began to lick their way across the floor, and was just about to grab the door handle when Alabaster burst through.

"Stanley!" he yelled, "Wake up! We're under attack! The house is on fire!" He looked around at the steadily-growing blaze and said, "Oh."

"Come on!" said Nell from behind him, grabbing Alabaster by the shoulders and hauling him backwards out of the burning room. Stanley rushed out after them, and Nell took a moment to close the door behind him.

"Keep it from spreading," she muttered.

"Stanley!" Alabaster gasped, "I never would've thought: *You*—an *arsonist!*"

"Oh shut up," said Nell, "this is definitely *not* the time, Alabaster. We need to—"

"*There you are!*"

The three of them looked up to see Father Blake standing near the top of the stairs. "Come on!" he said, waving them towards him.

A door suddenly burst open nearby, and Grey sprang through, followed by an alarming gust of flame that came belching out into the hall.

"Building's on fire," he said tonelessly as he walked past them towards the stairs, his clothes singed and smoking.

"*Move!*" yelled Blake, prompting Stanley, Alabaster, and Nell to jump to their feet and follow him down the steps as fast as they could.

Blake led the way down into the main hall, where Governor Cromwell and several soldiers of the town guard were crouched behind an improvised barricade of overturned furniture. Each soldier had a long rifle trained on the front doors, which were starting to buckle as something outside pounded on them with a merciless, relentless *BOOM! BOOM! BOOM!*

Lieutenant Breaker was crouched beside Cromwell, hefting a small, sleek submachine gun—a much more modern-looking weapon than those of her companions.

"What the *hell* are *you* still doing here?" snarled the governor, his long wig sitting slightly askew on his head.

"I had to make sure everyone got out," said Blake.

"What's happening?" Nell said loudly, "What is this?"

"Saurian raiding party," said Cromwell, as Blake did his best to usher his charges towards a door at the rear of the room. "Never seen one so brazen, but I'm being told that *some* damn fool left the east gate open, so we can hardly blame the lizards for trying. No offense, Temoc."

"None taken," said the blue-skinned Saurian, who was standing behind a nearby pillar, a short, curved glassy-looking black sword clutched in his hand.

Another *BOOM* shook the hall, and the doors began to crack and splinter, clinging desperately to their failing hinges.

"OUT!" barked Cromwell, and Blake all but shoved Stanley and the others through the back door.

The priest closed the door behind him, and led the small party through the mansion's cavernous kitchen. "Service entrance," he said, stopping by a nondescript door in the far corner, "Let's go."

Just before the door closed behind him, Stanley heard Cromwell roar,

"*Here they come! Give 'em hell, boys n' girls!*"

And then the service door swung shut, muffling the sounds of breaking wood, gunfire, and reptilian war cries.

★ ★ ★

Father Blake led them through the winding streets of Port Verdant as the fires burned and the alarm bells rang. At first, the situation seemed extremely grim, but the further they went from the governor's mansion, the calmer things became. Before long, they had made it to the docks. The sky was filled with smoke lit by the glow of the fires still burning here and there throughout the city.

Blake began to pace back and forth, looking up at the ships moored in front of him. He seemed to be searching for one in particular.

"Hooo," said Alabaster, taking a seat on a nearby wooden crate, "Must … take … rest."

"No time for that now," said Blake. "We need to find you a place to hide. Somewhere fireproof, ideally. Here!"

He was pointing at a good sized metal steamship with a great water wheel affixed to its stern. The vessel looked sturdy, but had clearly seen better days.

"You want us to hide out on a boat?" Nell said doubtfully.

"For now, yes," said Blake. "You'll be safe from the fires, and in my experience, Saurians aren't interested in shipping."

"But what if it sets sail while we're hiding?" said Alabaster. "The high-seas hijinx might be hilarious and heartwarming!"

Blake stared at him.

"But you know what?" Alabaster went on, "I bet we'd all learn some valuable lessons in the end."

"Is he alright?" Blake asked, cocking a thumb at Alabaster.

"That's a very good question," said Nell.

"I'm not hiding on some tub while the Saurians are messing up the place," Grey growled. "I should've stayed back there and helped them fight—"

"Well I, for one, am glad you didn't," said a strange voice.

They all looked up to see a young woman step out of the shadows of a nearby warehouse. Her long, straight black hair framed a hauntingly-beautiful face that was as white as a sheet of paper, save for her shiny black lips and excess of dark makeup around her eyes. She was dressed like some sort of soldier—her feet were shod with big black combat boots, into which were tucked the cuffs of her baggy cargo pants. She wore black, fingerless leather gloves and a simple black t-shirt with no sleeves.

It was the woman Stanley had seen at the Imperial Garden Hotel. He stared at her, eyes wide, and was about to ask who she was, but Grey beat him to it.

"Who the hell are you?" he asked disinterestedly. The woman smiled mirthlessly.

"Don't see how that matters," she said, her voice smooth and even. "What *does* matter, is that I'm here to bring you back."

Grey *hmphd*. "Back where?"

"Nine months ago you escaped from the dungeons of the Imperial Palace," said the woman. "Cell nine-two-three. Prisoner two-four-six-oh-one. *Grey*."

Grey's eyes narrowed. "Bounty hunter," he muttered darkly.

"Bounty hunter?" echoed Alabaster. "*Sweet!*"

"Looks like you have me at a disadvantage," said Grey.

"Yes, I do," said the woman, just before she leapt at him, drawing two curved black knives seemingly from nowhere. The weapons whistled through the air as she took a great double-handed swing, missing Grey's face by millimetres as he lurched backwards, dropping into a quick on-the-spot turn. His own mysterious black sword was out in an instant, and he finished his spin by deflecting his attacker's next dagger-swing, countering with a savage upward thrust that she dodged easily.

"Not bad," said the woman, executing an impressive backflip and landing in a menacing crouch. "I'd heard how dangerous you are, and you don't disappoint—even after being *disarmed*." She nodded at his missing appendage.

"You're funny. I like you," said Grey, clearly not meaning a word of it.

The woman grinned and sprang at him again, and Grey backed away, defending himself as she rained blow after blow upon him.

"Mr. Grey!" said Blake, "Do you need help?"

"*Get out of here!*" Grey roared. "It's me she wants, just go!"

"He's right," said the woman.

"Come on," said Blake, "do as he says."

"NO!" Stanley yelled. "Not this time." He wasn't going to leave Grey again—not like this. This time he'd help him. Somehow.

Grey half-turned, probably to tell Stanley to stop being an idiot and *run*, but the woman took immediate advantage of the distraction by kicking him hard in the jaw, snapping his head back and dropping him to the ground with a heavy *thud*. She was on him in an instant, straddling his torso, her left knee pinning his right arm. She placed one of her daggers against his throat and leaned in close, looking into his yellow eyes.

"I'd *prefer* to bring you back alive," she said tauntingly, "but I don't *have* to."

Grey's face was the picture of bestial fury—his sharp teeth were out, and his eyes were blazing like two extremely small and angry suns.

All at once, though, the anger vanished from his face, and his eyes went wide. "*Lucrecia?*" he said, his tone miles softer than any Stanley had ever heard him use.

The woman froze. She stared down at Grey for several long moments.

"How do you know that name?" she said through gritted teeth.

Grey shifted beneath hear, and she leapt off of him, landing well out of reach.

"*Answer me!*" she yelled, brandishing a knife at him as he picked himself up off the ground.

"I don't know," said Grey, "It just—popped into my head."

The woman pursed her lips and scowled darkly at him for a few seconds, then turned and ran off down the docks, vanishing into the darkness.

Grey immediately dashed after her, his footfalls fading quickly as he, too, ran off into the night.

"Wait! Grey!" said Stanley, perhaps thinking of following after him.

"Not you, too," said Blake, his hand falling on Stanley's shoulder.

"I gotta go find him!" said Stanley, shrugging him off.

"He can handle himself," said Blake. "You, on the other hand—"

He trailed off as the sounds of Saurian shrieks and roars came echoing down the street, accompanied by the distinct *clack-clack-clack* of claws on stone.

"Lovely," said Blake. "They probably heard all that carrying-on, and now—come on, up the gangplank. Get down to the hold and stay hidden." He waved Stanley, Alabaster, and Nell ahead of him, and indicated a stout metal door towards the rear of the ship's cabin, which he pulled open for them.

The sounds of approaching Saurians were getting louder, so Nell and Alabaster reluctantly started down the stairs to the hold. As he followed his friends, Stanley turned back to Blake. "What about you?"

Blake sighed. "I'm going to see if I can find your friend."

And with that, the door swung shut.

It was dark in the hold of this ship, but a series of long, thin rectangular windows just below the ceiling let in a sparse amount of light, at least enough for them to see that they were in a large room packed with wooden crates and boxes.

The three friends found a decently-sized hiding place in a sort of box-canyon formed by three piles of crates, and sat down, huddled in the darkness.

"Man, what a night," said Alabaster. "The intrepid trio makes yet another daring escape, eh?"

"Yeah," said Stanley, "I sure hope everyone got out of there."

Alabaster *hmmd*. "Well, Cromwell seemed to think we were the last ones in the house, so …"

Stanley nodded.

"What I want to know is what that *fight* was about!" said Alabaster. "Sheesh! Who *was* that bleached babe? Some kind of … death mime?"

"I dunno, but I saw her back at the hotel when we met Algernon. She must have been following us."

Alabaster sighed happily. "Super-tough and intimidating bounty hunters! Every time I think this adventure might be lacking that little something, *pow!* Special delivery: awesomeness."

Stanley smiled in spite of himself.

"Not to mention, it adds another strong female character to the mix," said Alabaster. "There hasn't been many of those in this story of ours."

"What?" said Stanley.

Alabaster shrugged. "You have to admit, our epic adventures have been a bit of a boys' club. You, me, Uncle Jack, Benjamin, Pericles—and Grey—and now we've got Algernon, Koko, Ryuno, Temoc, that Blake guy, Grey again—Nell's like the only girl! It must be a bit tough on her, not having another female around. Hey Nell? What'ya think?"

Stanley turned to his left and saw that Nell, who had been sitting quietly while he and Alabaster chatted, was now sound asleep.

"Ohh," said Alabaster. "Oh well, no need to wake her up."

"You know what though?" said Stanley, "You should ask her about that when she wakes up. I bet she'd appreciate it."

"Huh. Okay," said Alabaster, "I will. So. What now? How do we know when it's safe to come out?"

"I guess we just wait for Blake to come back," said Stanley. "Or Grey ..."

"Cool," said Alabaster, yawning hugely. "In that case, I'm gonna catch a few more zees. You okay to keep watch?"

"Me? Er—yeah, sure," said Stanley. He felt he was too worked up and worried about the fates of Grey and the others to sleep, but his eyelids soon began to droop, then fell closed, and within five minutes he was snoring and dreaming of the great glowing blue crystal floating above the jungle, blissfully ignorant of the fact that in a few short hours, he would be much closer to it.

Chapter 11

ROLLIN' ON THE RIVER

"Ah-HA! Stowaways!" said a voice.

"Uh?" said Stanley, blearily opening an eye. Before he could fully come to his senses, a large pair of hands grabbed him by the front of his shirt and dragged him roughly to his feet, where he found himself face-to-face with an angry-looking riverboat crewman.

"So! Three of you, enh?" said the man, glancing at Nell and Alabaster as they jumped to their feet. Stanley struggled, but couldn't free himself.

"Unhand him, you fiend!" cried Alabaster, latching onto the man's forearm, which was about as thick as Alabaster's waist.

"Get off, ya grubby urchin!" snarled the crewman as he tried to break Alabaster's grip.

"Stop it!" said Nell, "Wait, let us explain!"

"There'll be time enough for explainin' when I take you three to see the captain!" said the crewman. "And I'll tell ya this much—he's even less fond of stowaways than *I* am! I wouldn't be surprised if he has you thrown overboard. Now let's—"

Suddenly there was a brief flash of metal, and before the crewman knew what was happening, a long, thin blade swept out of the darkness behind him, and came to rest against his throat.

"Awk!" said the crewman.

"Not another sound," said a soft, calm voice from behind the crewman, who promptly shut his mouth.

"Let the boy go," ordered the voice.

The crewman's hands sprang open, releasing Stanley, who stumbled backwards to be caught by Nell and Alabaster.

"Now," said the voice, "I am going to put my sword away. If you try to run or call for help, it will be the last thing you ever do. Do you understand?"

"Y-y-*yes!"* stammered the crewman, his eyes popping. The polished blade disappeared. The owner of the voice stepped out from behind the crewman, and into the lamplight.

"Ryuno!" cried Nell, springing forward and throwing her arms around him. Alabaster coughed conspicuously, and Nell quickly broke the embrace.

"What!" said the crewman. "You're just some punk kid! You got some nerve, threatenin' me with a knife!"

"Sword," said Ryuno. "And *you* have some nerve, *sir,* threatening to throw my *friends overboard*."

"I—I—aw, come on, I wasn't actually—I was just tryin' to scare 'em, that's all. Put the fear o' god in 'em, y'know?

"Good," said Ryuno.

"What are you doing here?" Nell asked.

"And where *is* here?" added Alabaster. "I mean, I know we're on a boat—but are we moving?"

Stanley had just noticed that the air was filled with a faint but angry-sounding mechanical growl which suggested that the ship was indeed on the move. His eyes widened as the implications of their situation hit him.

"Yeah, o' course we're moving," said the crewman. "We're on the Armadon, at least six hours south o' Port Verdant."

"What!" Stanley and Nell said in unison.

"How long did we sleep?" said Alabaster, sounding impressed.

"No!" said Nell, "This is a mistake! We're not supposed to be here!"

"I *know!"* said the crewman.

Nell looked helplessly at Stanley. "This is—ugh, of all the—we need to get off! We need to get back to Port Verdant!"

"Whoa whoa," said the crewman, raising his hands, "that's a decision for the captain."

"Can we talk to him?" said Stanley.

"I've been tryin' to get you to talk to 'im for the past five minutes!" spluttered the crewman. "But okay, okay, c'mon, follow me."

The crewman led the way up the stairs from the hold and out the door. Stanley and the others stepped out onto the main deck, blinking and squinting in the bright late-morning sunshine. The 200-foot steamship was indeed on the move, ploughing through the dark, greenish waters of the Armadon River at a brisk pace. At her stern, a huge, tired-looking water wheel turned with dogged consistency, churning the river water into a roiling foam while further forward, a pair of rusty old smoke stacks belched greasy black smoke into the air high above.

"That engine sounds awful," Nell remarked, looking up at the smoke.

Of all the places Stanley had expected to find himself today, the middle of the Armadon River had not been high on his list. He gazed out over the water at the wildly overgrown river bank a hundred yards away.

"C'mon," said the crewman, "let's get this over with. Plenty o' time for sight-seein' later." He led them towards the bow, to a door marked

-BRIDGE-

and knocked smartly on the solid metal.

"Yep," said a voice from inside.

The crewman opened the door and slouched through, followed by Stanley and the others.

The room beyond was filled with dated-looking machinery (although it was some of the most advanced technology Stanley had seen on Terra): dials, gauges, and levers were placed seemingly at random all over the walls. At the front of the room, before a huge window, a young man sat at a console covered with buttons and blinking lights. Behind him, manning the ship's steering wheel, was a squat, barrel-chested old fellow with a bushy grey beard, clad in a once-smart-looking blue naval uniform.

"Bah!" said the bearded man, "I'm gettin' good an' sick o' this. We're crawlin', here! Who's in engineering today?"

"Bradford, cap'n," said another man in the far corner, staring intently at a row of what looked like pressure gauges.

"Get 'im on the horn and ask 'im why I hired 'im!" Barked the captain. "Chief engineer an' he can't get this old girl above twenty? Shameful!"

"Right, sir" said the man in front of the window, picking up an old-fashioned telephone receiver from the console in front of him.

"Well?" said the captain, looking over his shoulder at the new arrivals to his bridge, "What is it, Mr. Grant?"

The crewman who had found Stanley, Alabaster, and Nell saluted sloppily and said,

"Located some stowaways, sir. Down in the hold."

The captain sighed. "Wonderful. Gibbons, take the helm."

The man in the back corner rushed over to grab the wheel, while the captain sauntered over to scrutinize his new passengers.

"Hmph!" he said, frowning down at them, "Ya picked the wrong boat, I'm afraid, lads and lassie. We're not goin' anywhere fun today. Where're you tryin' to get to? Ethelia? Port Silverburg? This here's a *river* boat. Not bound for the open sea."

"We know," said Nell, "And we're sorry—we didn't mean to—uh—stow away. We just hid here during the Saurian attack and—er—fell asleep."

The captain chewed his tongue for a bit, then shrugged. "Makes sense, I s'pose. No one in their right mind'd want to hop a ship headin' for the heart o' the jungle."

Stanley breathed a sigh of relief. It was starting to look like they weren't in trouble, after all.

"I'm so glad you understand," said Nell. "We don't want to bother you—you could just drop us off—"

"Drop you off?" said the captain. "Uh-uh. That I *can't* do. We're almost a hundred miles out of Port Verdant! If I let you off around here you'd be some critter's lunch in about ten seconds flat!"

"A hundred miles!" said Alabaster.

"I know—embarrassing, isn't it?" said the captain. "*Should* be 150, but we're havin' engine trouble. Or *engineer* trouble, maybe."

"But—wait," said Nell, "This is all a mistake! We're not supposed to be here! We need to go back to Port Verdant!"

"Not gonna happen," said the captain, shaking his head. "We're behind schedule as it is, so I'm afraid you're stuck with us. Or *we're* stuck with *you,* more like."

Nell looked completely stunned. "This can't be happening," she muttered.

"We'll let you off when we dock at Daruna Abbey," said the captain. "They might be able to help you there."

Stanley's ears perked up at the mention of the abbey. Hadn't Cromwell said something about it last night?

"Until then," the captain was saying, "you lot're gonna be workin' for your keep."

"*What?*" said Alabaster.

"Hah!" laughed the captain. "Thought you'd sneak aboard my ship an' get a nice little pleasure cruise out of the bargain? Dream on!"

"But we didn't mean to!" said Alabaster.

"That's not my problem," said the captain. "My problem is that four street urchins decided to become *sea* urchins, and now we got four more mouths to feed! So you're gonna pay your way by helpin' me fix this old girl up. Speakin' of which, welcome aboard the *Empress Hildegarde,* the fastest, sturdiest riverboat in the Empire! ... Well, it *would* be the fastest if I had a half way decent engineer—"

Just then, a filthy, sweaty man in soot-blackened coveralls appeared in the doorway. "You wanted to see me, cap'n?" he said breathlessly.

"Not really," said the captain, "but seems like it's the only way to get you to do your job! You're fired, *Chief Engineer Bradford,* if you can't get this tub up to speed!"

"S'not my fault, cap'n!" cried Bradford. "That hunk o' junk engine's fallin' apart! I don't have enough men down there to fix everythin'!"

"If I wanted excuses I'd've—er—gotten an ... *excuse machine!"* spluttered the captain.

"*Weeeak,*" said Alabaster.

"We just plain don't have the know-how to fix 'er, sir," said Bradford. "She could conk out at any minute! We need a ... a mechanical *genius* to get 'er up to scratch."

"Nell's a mechanical genius," Stanley blurted. All eyes turned towards him. "Uh—"

"Who?" said Bradford.

"Uh—sorry," said Stanley, glancing awkwardly at Nell, whose cheeks were turning red. "I didn't—"

"Hey, yeah!" said Alabaster, "Right here—Nell, mechanic extraordinaire! *She* knows engines!"

Bradford blinked. "She does? *Her?"*

"I—well, ah—*yes!"* said Nell, after receiving a sharp nudge from Alabaster. "Yes I *do* know engines. Is there a *problem* with that?"

"Well, you're a—I mean, I've never seen—"

"A female mechanic? *Tuh!"* said Nell, folding her arms.

"Sure, sure," said Bradford, "but you're, what, ten years old?"

"Thirteen!" said Nell.

"Oh," said Bradford.

"I want to see this engine," said Nell, shoving her way through the group and out the door. "I've been listening to it for the past ten minutes and it sounds like you're about to blow a piston. When was the last time anyone oiled it? Have you checked the gears? Are any of them stripped? I bet they're stripped. You'd better have some replacements—"

She set off towards the engine room, Bradford trailing behind, trying to answer her questions. Ryuno darted out of the room and followed after them.

"Huh," said the captain, looking dazed. "O-kay … I guess she's on engine duty. Now as for you two …"

⋆ ⋆ ⋆

Stanley and Alabaster were put to work swabbing the decks, a chore that was much more arduous aboard a 200-foot steamship with two levels than it was on a tiny single-mast vessel like the Ogopogo. Crewman Grant supervised their work, and managed to make the situation even more boring by regaling them with tales of the Empress Hildegarde's phenomenally unremarkable history on the Armadon.

After about an hour of swabbing in the hot sun, Stanley heard someone call his name, and was surprised to see Algernon waving enthusiastically at him from the other end of the deck.

"Stanley! Cousin!" Algernon came running towards him, slipped on the wet deck, and went skidding into the cabin wall, knocking over Alabaster's mop bucket and drenching himself in soapy water.

"Algernon!" said Stanley, as Koko swooped in out of nowhere and helped Algernon to his feet, "This is *your* ship?"

Algernon shook his head. "No, no, not at all (thank you, Koko). *But* our friend, Governor Cromwell commissioned her for the journey to the Lost City!"

"Here!" said Crewman Grant, "That's privileged information, that is. You're not s'posed to just throw that around!"

"Everyone on board has been briefed," said Koko.

"Not them," said Grant, pointing at Stanley and Alabaster.

"Actually, we technically have," said Stanley.

"Oh," said Grant. "Well … okay."

"So did everyone survive?" Alabaster asked brightly.

"Survive what?" said Algernon. "Oh, right, the attack. Yes, yes, no worries there. All hands accounted for, and all that. Blake and Temoc are around here somewhere."

"What about Grey?" Stanley asked hopefully.

"Oh—right—tall, dusky fellow? I thought he was with *you*."

Stanley's face fell. Grey, it seemed, would not be coming with them.

"Cheer up, noble cousin," said Algernon. "I'm sure we haven't seen the last of him. Come on, we're just off to get some lunch. Join us!"

Stanley glanced at Crewman Grant, who sighed and nodded.

"Excellent!" said Algernon. "To the mess hall! Follow me!"

The mess hall was a wide room packed with sailors crowded around several rough plank tables. Algernon led the way to a smaller, round table off to one side, at which were seated Temoc and Father Blake. Blake smiled and raised a hand, while Temoc gave an almost imperceptible nod.

"There you are," said Blake as Stanley and the others sat down. "Er," he said, noting Stanley's expression, "Is everything alright?"

"I—uh—I don't know, exactly," said Stanley. He felt relieved to see some familiar faces (even if he'd only met their owners yesterday), but he wanted to know how they'd come to be in this situation.

"What happened to you?" he asked Blake as he sat down. "You said you'd come back to get us ..."

"I did," said Blake, "but you were already asleep. I'm afraid I couldn't find Mr. Grey."

"But we were supposed to stay back in Port Verdant," said Stanley.

Blake raised his eyebrows. "But—wait—I thought you wanted to join the expedition."

Stanley paused.

"At least, that's the impression I got at the meeting," said Blake, looking doubtful.

"Well—yeah, I did, but we—er—decided after that it—uh—might be best if we stayed behind ..."

Even as he said these words, Stanley knew they weren't really true. Not for him, at least. Nell had convinced him that a journey into the jungle was a bad idea, and he'd agreed with her at the time, but now, here, aboard this steamship as it chugged southward surrounded on all sides by savage jungle, he felt that he *did* want to join the expedition after all, and though he didn't really have the slightest idea of what to expect, he felt fortunate to have been given a second chance.

"Blast it," said Blake, looking mortified. "I'm sorry, Stanley, I completely misunderstood. I thought your plan was to come with us—especially after the governor threatened you with *prison*."

"He was serious?" said Alabaster.

"Cromwell is a hard man," said Blake. "I've only known him a few months, but he has no compunction about—er—*removing* people who *inconvenience* him.

"Oh my!" said Algernon.

Stanley took a moment to think that one over. This information, at least, would probably make it a bit easier to explain things to Nell the next time he saw her.

"Again, I really am sorry," said Blake. "I'll do whatever I can to help you get home—we'll look into some options when we get to the abbey."

"Yeah, okay," said Stanley, although he was starting to think that since they were already here, maybe it would be best to stay on board and see the expedition through. After all, the trip was going well so far, and they had already gone a hundred miles, much further south than Stanley, Alabaster, and Nell had been when they'd first arrived on Terra. If things stayed as calm and quiet as they were now, he and the rest of the party were in for a relatively easy journey.

Being an experienced adventurer, Stanley should have known that in the wilds of Terra, things never stay calm or quiet for long.

Chapter 12

ATTACK ON THE EMPRESS HILDEGARDE

Nell was a bit upset about Blake's mistake, but she wasn't surprised that she, Stanley, and Alabaster were now bound for the lost city of Quetzal-Khan.

"Well I certainly didn't think we were on some holiday cruise," she said testily when Stanley broke the news to her after lunch.

She and Ryuno returned to the engine room soon after, leaving Stanley and Alabaster to their own work. They had finished with their swabbing, and were now charged with touching up the Empress Hildegarde's once-white coat of paint.

"Just do the parts that need it," said Grant, dropping off the last of twenty paint cans for the two unhappy boys. Stanley made a face. There wasn't a single square inch of ancient paint on this level that wasn't peeling, dirty or rust-stained.

"Boy, painting this boat sure is *fun,*" said Alabaster loudly as a group of sailors walked by. "I feel sorry for all these poor guys who don't get to do any painting at all. It's sad—they could be having the time of their lives—just like me!"

"I think most o' the lads've read that one," said Grant, laughing.

"When the heck was Mark Twain ever on Terra?" Alabaster muttered as he dipped his brush.

The Empress Hildegarde continued on its way up the Armadon River. It was largely thanks to Nell's work in the engine room that the decrepit old steam ship was going anywhere at all. Nell, in fact, seemed to have been made an honourary member of the crew, which was not particularly surprising, considering that her knowledge of machinery vastly outstripped that of the ship's head engineer.

Stanley and Alabaster, meanwhile, painted and painted and painted as the long, hot hours dragged by. It was so unbelievably humid that Stanley started to doubt whether the paint would ever actually dry, and annoying bugs kept landing on the walls and getting stuck, messing up the finish.

"Ah—don't worry about that," said Grant, when he noticed Stanley re-painting a section for the third time. "This ain't the Grecarian Wall you're paintin'!"

At length, the sun began to sink towards the western horizon. Evening came on quickly in the Verdurian jungle, and it wasn't long before even the wide Armadon River was cloaked in twilight. Stanley and Alabaster were nowhere near finished painting the cabin walls, but it would soon be too dark to see what they were doing.

The door to the bridge burst open, and the captain waddled out onto the deck, producing a small metal whistle from his pocket. Stanley and Alabaster covered their ears as the captain blew the whistle, which was far louder than its size would suggest.

"Right-o, everyone," he yelled. "That's it for today! Let's find a good spot to stop for the night. Night Watch, you're on duty in half an hour!" He turned to Stanley and Alabaster. "Well!" he said, folding his arms, "You lads look like something the cat dragged in!"

He was right. The boys were dirty, sweaty, disheveled, and covered with paint. Stanley was in no mood for playful jibes, and Alabaster was so tired that he simply tossed his paint brush in the can and curled up on the deck with his eyes closed.

The captain found this most amusing. "Ha ha ha haaah!" he laughed, "Not used to working all the live-long day, eh? Well I'd *get* used to it if I were you! And besides, you know what they say: an honest day's work never hurt anyone!"

"I'm gonna need more paint," Stanley muttered darkly.

"Ha ha haaah!" the captain laughed again. "I think not, lad. You've done enough for one day, both of you. Go get cleaned up, then you can head down to the mess hall and get something to eat." He turned and bellowed at a passing crewman, "*Go tell Engineer Bradford to cut the engines! It's past 7:30!*"

"Aye cap'n," said the crewman, saluting as he hurried off towards the engine room.

Stanley stood up and stretched. He felt surprisingly alert and energized, unlike Alabaster, who seemed to actually be asleep. "C'mon, Alabaster, get up," said Stanley, gently shaking his friend.

Alabaster opened his eyes and yawned. "That captain's a merciless slave driver!" he said, his speech slurred with fatigue.

"Ah, he's not so bad," said Stanley.

Alabaster *hmphed*, then yawned again.

Presently, the rumbling and chug-chug-chugging of the engine died down, and the great waterwheel slowed and stopped, leaving the Empress Hildegarde to drift along serenely, before the river's current stopped its momentum.

The door leading to engineering opened, and Nell appeared on deck, looking tired and grimy, but thoroughly pleased with herself.

"What a great day!" she said, when she saw Stanley and Alabaster. "I've never worked with an engine like that, ever! I mean, it's old and rusty and it's a piece of junk, but it's—I mean, it's a steam engine, technically, but it's way smaller than you'd think—it's more like an I.C., but it still has a boiler, even though—"

"Steampunk. Nice," said Alabaster.

"Er—that's great Nell," said Stanley, who was glad she was happy, but simply couldn't get excited about engines.

"One of the pistons was totally worn out," Nell went on. "The thing could have blown at any moment! The whole engine had to be shut down so we could remove it. It was totally corroded! No one could remember the last time they even oiled the thing. Luckily they had another one handy."

She paused to take a breath, and Alabaster immediately leapt into the breach, saying,

"Boy, Nell, after all that mechanical mumbo-jumbo, you must be starving! … hint hint."

Nell missed the point completely. "Are you kidding? Who could possibly think of food after working with the most amazing engine I've ever—"

"Me too!" interrupted Alabaster, as he started to nudge her towards the mess hall. "Absolutely famished!"

"You can tell us more about the engine while we eat," said Stanley, helping to usher her along. "I want to hear more about the … um …"

"Pistons!" Alabaster supplied, opening the door and almost shoving Nell through. "Fascinating things, those pistons."

"Oh all right," said Nell rolling her eyes, "I guess I could eat *something*."

"That's the spirit!" said Alabaster, stepping back and making a ludicrous bow. "Right this way, mademoiselle."

Minutes later, they were seated at one of the dingy wooden tables, about to tuck into three steaming plates of

"Beany weenies?" said Alabaster disappointedly.

The cook, a big, beefy bald man with an eye patch and tattoos all over his arms, squinted fiercely at him. "And what's wrong with good old fashioned weenies and beans, eh?" he said, clearly daring Alabaster to make some crack about the food.

"Nothing!" Stanley said quickly. "Beanies and weens are great. *I mean—*"

"You don't have any sea scorpion, do you?" said Alabaster.

Nell's mouth fell open.

"Sea scorpion?" said the cook. "*Sea scorpion?*"

"We're sorry," Nell said hastily, "he doesn't mean anything by it—he just doesn't know when to keep his mouth shut. He—"

She was interrupted as the cook leaned his head back and let out a great booming laugh.

"HAW!" he said, his face now drawn up in a big grin, "HAW HAW HAW! Sea scorpion! Of course, lad, I've got a whole crate of them in the galley! HAW HAW HAW! I'll get out my gold stock pot and boil one up right away!"

And with that, he shuffled off to the galley, chortling merrily to himself. Nell glared at Alabaster.

"You have absolutely no tact, you know that?"

"What do you mean?" said Alabaster, "I have *lots* of tact! Look, now I'm going to be getting a sea scorpion, instead of beany weenies! You can't wrangle a deal like *that* without a bit of tact … What's tact?"

Nell looked at Stanley for help, but frowned darkly as she saw that he was trying hard not to laugh out loud.

"You two are totally hopeless," she muttered, scooping up a spoonful of wieners and beans, while Stanley snorted with suppressed laughter.

Just then, someone called Stanley's name from across the room. He looked up to see Algernon coming towards him, followed closely by Koko.

"Hello you three," he said, straightening his glasses and beaming at them. "Mind if we join you?"

"Oh, uh, no, of course not," said Stanley, shifting over on the bench.

"Thank you!" said Algernon, as he and Koko sat down beside him. "We've just been dining with the captain, Father Blake, and that lizard fellow, Tectonic," he said, his voice full of excitement. "We've been planning our route!"

"Route?" said Stanley, as Nell and Alabaster glanced at each other. "What route?"

"Our route to adventure and glory!" said Algernon, "Our route to fame and fortune! Our route to the Lost City of Quetzal-Khan!" With a flourish, he pulled a piece of paper out of his pocket and spread it on the table, while Koko sighed heavily. The paper was a map of Verduria. Algernon pointed to a long, crooked blue line which seemed to cut the entire continent in half.

"This is the Armadon River," he said, "and we are currently right—about—*here*." His finger was resting on a point about a half inch from the dot labeled *Port Verdant*. "And in another day or so, we should be *here.*" His finger traced the river for about another half inch, and stopped by a smaller dot, labeled *Daruna Abbey*.

"And where's the Lost City?" asked Stanley, looking closely at the map while Nell took her turn to sigh heavily.

"Ah," said Algernon, "Well—the thing is, you see—"

"We don't know," said Koko, in his deep, even voice. "You'll notice that most of the map is covered with these green lines."

Sure enough, almost the entire section of the map south of Daruna Abbey was blank, save for dozens of diagonal green lines.

"Verduria is a largely unexplored continent," Koko went on. "Very few expeditions to the interior have ever returned, and those that did, didn't manage to bring back much in the way of useful information."

"So you're saying we really don't have any idea where we're going?" said Alabaster.

"Temoc knows more than most," said Koko, "But to be honest, it's mostly lore and hearsay. When we stop at Daruna Abbey, Algernon is planning on spending some time in the library. It's possible that they have some better maps and information there."

"Quite right, Koko," said Algernon, nodding vehemently. "Couldn't have said it better myself. If anyplace has got a more complete map of Verduria, it'll be the Abbey."

Stanley nodded too, more to himself than to Algernon. Spending some time in this library sounded like a good idea—although he would be making use of it for slightly different reasons.

He wanted information on the Lost City itself—or, more accurately, on its connection with the giant flying blue crystal.

They finished their simple supper, and made their way back out to the main deck.

"Oh yes, I've been to Costa Rica several times," Algernon was saying to Alabaster. "Been all over Central America, in fact. The Aztecs and Mayans are a specialty of mine."

"How did you get *here*, though?" asked Stanley.

"Now that is a good question," said Algernon with a short laugh. "It was the darnedest thing. I was on my way up the Yucatan Peninsula with my expedition party, when it happened—"

"You got suddenly transported to this world through some as-yet unknown means?" said Alabaster.

"No," said Algernon, "I had to go to the bathroom. We parked the truck, and I charged into the bushes. I'd eaten a three-bean burrito for lunch, you see, and—" he paused meaningfully. "Well, it was a desperate situation, to say the least. So there I was, a man on a mission, trying to get a little privacy, when suddenly, there it was!"

"A mysterious portal through time and space?" said Alabaster.

"No, an outhouse," said Algernon.

Stanley blinked. "An *outhouse?"*

"Yes!" said Algernon. "It was a godsend. And the odd thing was, it was made of stone!"

"Please tell us you're joking," said Nell.

"I know what you're thinking," Algernon said quickly, "and no, I did *not* do a number two in an ancient Mayan ruin. It really *was* an outhouse—the strangest one I've ever been in, but … well—"

Stanley and Alabaster were looking doubtful. Nell was shaking her head.

"No, really!" cried Algernon, "It wasn't some old ruin! It couldn't have been more than a few years old! It even had running water! … though I'm a monkey's uncle if I have the slightest idea how it worked … Oops! Sorry, Koko, no offense!"

"None taken," murmured Koko.

Algernon cleared his throat. "Anyway, when I came out, I'd completely lost my bearings. I went back towards the road, only to find that there was no longer a road, at all! Everything looked different. I wandered for hours, trying to find my party, and it started to get dark. I was flat out terrified for a while there, and I think I panicked, because … ah …"

He paused and cleared his throat once more.

"That is to say, I was afraid that my friends would get worried without me, so I raced around trying to find them, and I, er, must've taken a bad step, because the next thing I knew, it was morning, and Koko here was lugging me through the jungle on his shoulders."

He clapped Koko on the back. "And we've been inseparable ever since, right partner?"

"Hm," said Koko.

"And now, here we are, ready to plunge into the heart of a continent no one's ever heard of! Who *knows* what amazing discoveries await us?"

TOOO-WHEEEEEE!

Stanley and the others jumped as a loud whistle blast assaulted their eardrums.

"Eight o'clock, lads!" yelled the captain, putting his whistle away. He caught sight of Stanley and Alabaster, and laughed. "Har har har! You two sprats oughta think about turnin' in pretty soon—you've got another big day ahead o' you tomorrow!"

Stanley made a face. He was not looking forward to another day of menial labour.

The captain laughed again, then turned to Algernon. "So, Mr. Petrie, how're you enjoying the journey so far?"

"Oh, I'm having a wonderful time, just wonderful! But I must say, I am anxious to strike off into the jungle."

"The jungle?" said the captain, "Hah! Give me the river any day. Ah, but to each his own, I s'pose. Speaking of the jungle, though, where's the rest o' your group? That Saurian fellah, an' Blake, an' that young lad with the funny name?"

Algernon started to say *I don't know*, but his words were drowned out by a strange sound from out in the jungle. Everyone immediately fell silent and listened. It sounded like an insect's song, similar to the long, constant trill of a cicada. Unlike a cicada's song, however, this sound was almost painfully loud, and sounded like nails on a chalkboard—a horrid, almost metallic grating shriek that seemed to gouge its way into their brains.

The sound seemed to be coming from close by, on the river's western bank.

"What in heaven's name is that hideous noise?" said Algernon, holding his hands over his ears.

"Got me," said the captain. "I've never heard anything like it."

Stanley screwed up his face against the noise and put his fingers in his ears. The chirping of crickets and the whine of cicadas were the sounds of pleasant summer nights, but this sound ...

This sound spoke of madness and terror. It felt to Stanley as if there were jagged shards of glass spinning through his brain, and no matter how hard he tried, he couldn't block it out.

BOOM!

A nearby explosion made Stanley open his eyes. The nightmarish chirping had stopped abruptly, and the captain was now holding a long rifle in his hands. The barrel was still smoking.

"That shut 'em up," the captain said grimly.

Indeed, the jungle had gone silent.

"Boy, what the heck was that?" said Alabaster.

"Whatever it was, I guess it's gone now," said Nell.

But Stanley wasn't so sure. He continued to stare at the western bank, and it felt as if something was staring back at him. Suddenly, two points of pale greenish light appeared among the dark jungle foliage.

Two more points of light appeared beside these, and it wasn't difficult to tell what they were.

They were eyes.

"Did someone fire a gun?"

Father Blake had just appeared on deck, accompanied by Temoc and Ryuno.

"Nothin' to worry about," said the captain, "Just scarin' off some jungle pests."

"It is unwise to make such a loud and sudden noise, even this close to the coast," said Temoc.

While they were speaking, at least thirty more pairs of luminous green eyes had appeared in the trees by the river's edge. Stanley was feeling very uneasy. As if conjured by his feelings of trepidation, thunder began to roll ominously overhead.

"There's something in the trees over there," he piped up. Everyone looked, and several gasps were heard.

"Just some jungle critters," said the captain. "Trust me, it's nothin' to worry about."

By now there were at least sixty pairs of eyes gleaming out of the darkness of the jungle.

"Just checkin' us out, that's all," said the captain, sounding less and less sure of himself.

"Temoc, what are they?" said Father Blake.

The Saurian shook his head. "I do not know—I have never seen eyes like those. They do not give me a good feeling."

"Nor me," said Ryuno. "It might be best to leave this area."

"What, and go blunderin' up the river in the dark?" said the captain. "Hit a herd o' gorethanes? We'd run aground before we went a hundred yards.

For once, Stanley found himself agreeing with Ryuno. "I think we should keep going," he said, turning to the captain, who looked back at him with mock surprise and said,

"Oh really? Well seein' as how *I'm* the captain o' this bleedin' vessel, you'll have to forgive me if I decide not to act on the advice of a grubby wee wharf rat like *you!"*

"Hey!" said Alabaster and Nell in unison.

"Now just a moment, captain," said Algernon, "Stanley here is my cousin, and I—"

He was interrupted by another peal of thunder, accompanied by a loud splash and a shout from one of the crewmen.

"*Captain!*" yelled the man, "Something's in the water, sir! Starboard side!"

Stanley's gaze snapped instantly to the river bank. Something had indeed dropped into the water and was swimming towards the Empress Hildegarde. He could see the surface ripple, as well as the distorted glow of the thing's pale green eyes.

"*Steady on, lads,*" yelled the captain, rifle at the ready.

There was a brief pause as the swimmer reached the side of the ship, and then the thing broke the surface, erupting from the water and latching on to the hull.

Stanley and the others backed away towards the cabin wall as the thing began to climb with a click-click-click of claws on metal. Seconds later a long, spindly, multi-jointed leg appeared from over the railing, followed by a pair of luminous eyes. In one quick move, the creature heaved itself up onto the railing and perched there like a gargoyle.

Stanley's first impression was of a giant earwig. It was an insect, that much was plain enough; its six legs clutched the railing rightly, its short wings folded tightly against its thorax. Its glowing green eyes took up most of the space on its diamond-shaped head, beneath which a pair of large and savage-looking mandibles opened and closed at regular intervals. The creature's most unusual feature was its long, flat, segmented tail, which ended in a pair of massive pincers.

The huge insect sat there on the railing, staring at nothing in particular, while its antennae waved and twitched in the night air. Thunder rolled again, and one of the crewmen said,

"What the hell is it, captain?"

As soon as the man spoke, the insect's eyes locked onto him, and it made a low, menacing clicking sound with its mandibles.

"Oy!" exclaimed the man, alarmed at the creature's reaction, "What're you looking at, ya ugly beast!"

The insect made a louder clicking sound and pointed its antennae at him. Slowly, it started to creep down off of the railing.

"Don't move!" shouted the captain, springing forward and pointing his rifle at the giant earwig. The creature went rigid, locked eyes on him, and raised its clawed tail over its head like a scorpion. A split second later, it sprang at the captain, letting out a grating shriek as it did.

Stanley, Alabaster, and Nell jumped out of the way as the insect leapt, but the captain caught it in the thorax with a blast from his rifle. The giant earwig was blown backwards, where it landed in a crumpled heap at the edge of the deck.

No sooner had the corpse hit the deck, when there came a nasty sizzling sound. To everyone's astonishment, the greenish ichor which seemed to serve as the creature's blood began to bubble and steam, and in less than ten seconds, had eaten its way through the deck, leaving a ragged, smoking hole.

"What in the hellfire," muttered the captain.

"That thing's got acid for blood!" cried the crewman.

Just then, there arose from the jungle the same grating cicada song they'd heard earlier. Stanley rushed over to the railing, Alabaster and Nell close behind him.

"Look!" said Nell, pointing towards the river bank, but she needn't have bothered. Even in the dim evening light, they could see that something was out there. The entire jungle seemed alive with writhing shapes and luminous green eyes. Dozens of dark forms were emerging from the trees, dropping into the water and thrashing about, making the river froth and boil.

"*They're coming towards the ship!*" yelled Stanley.

"*Battle stations!*" Roared the captain. "Engine crew! Get this old girl moving! On the double!"

Temoc, Blake and Ryuno excused themselves as the crew sprang into action, but before they could all arm themselves or get the engine going, the swarm of giant earwigs reached the ship. At first, it sounded like rain falling on metal, but not a drop fell from the dark roiling clouds above.

It was the sound of scores of clawed feet digging into the hull of the Empress Hildegarde, as their nightmarish owners scaled the side of the ship.

With an ear-piercing scream, the first giant earwig leaped onto the main deck railing and sprang at the captain, who leveled his rifle and fired. The creature's head disintegrated in a spray of green ichor as it was blown right out of the air and into the water. Several gobs of the stuff landed on the deck, burning holes in the solid metal.

At least ten more giant earwigs gained the railing, most of which were blown away by the other crewmen, who had managed to locate firearms of their own. The Hildegarde's engine lurched to life, and the great paddle wheel began to slowly turn as the scene descended into a riot of explosions, muzzle flashes, and screams, both human and insect.

One of the crewmen was set upon by a pair of the monsters. He hit one with a blast from his shotgun, but the other dodged swiftly out of the way, and managed to grab him with its massive tail-claw. The last anyone saw of him was the look of shock and horror on his face as he was dragged over the railing and into the river.

"PETRIE!" roared the captain, taking out two more earwigs with a single rifle blast, "WHAT TH'HELL ARE YOU DOING? GET YOUR PEOPLE OUT OF HERE!"

"Eh?" said Algernon, looking extremely pale.

"TO THE BRIDGE WITH YOU! ALL OF YOU!" yelled the captain, pointing to the nearby door.

Just then, Ryuno reappeared from below decks, followed closely by Temoc and Father Blake. Ryuno was clad in his full battle armour, and Temoc was brandishing a short curved sword and round shield. Even Blake was armed: he was holding a long, black sword which looked a bit odd when coupled with his simple traveling clothes. Before anyone could say anything, Ryuno darted forward, and in one blindingly fast movement, drew his sword from its sheath in a wide arc, cutting a giant earwig in two as it leapt through the air.

"NO!" bellowed the captain, "LOOK OUT! DON'T TOUCH THE BLOOD!"

The insect's ichor gushed forth from its cloven halves, drenching the deck. Miraculously, no one was hit, but it burned straight through to the hold in a matter of seconds, leaving a small chasm that would have to be jumped across.

"*My ship!*" cried the captain, "Look what you're doing to my ship, you sword-swingin' bastard!"

"The condition of your ship is secondary to our survival!" said Ryuno, decapitating another giant earwig.

"*Would you prefer we left them alive?*" roared Temoc, stabbing a third before it could drag another man to his doom.

The Saurian pulled out his sword, then hissed loudly as the acid ate away at the blade. He cursed, and threw away the now-useless weapon. As if sensing his lack of weaponry, one of the earwigs came at him, screaming hideously and snapping its tail claw. Without hesitation, Temoc swung his shield at the insect, smashing it into the cabin wall, pinning it. Removing his arm from the shield strap, the Saurian stepped back and delivered a savage kick to the inside of the shield, crushing the giant earwig against the wall.

Father Blake impaled another of monstrous insects on his black sword. The thing shrieked and struggled, but Blake calmly braced a foot against its shiny exoskeleton, and pulled the blade free, booting the creature overboard in the process.

Blake turned around, and his eyes widened as he caught sight of Stanley, Alabaster, Nell, and Algernon cowering against the cabin wall.

"What on earth are you doing out here?" he demanded.

Ryuno was suddenly beside them as well. "You! All of you! Get out of sight! Now! This is a time for warriors!" He and Blake quickly led them to the bridge. He shoved Stanley through, followed by Alabaster and Algernon.

"Hey!" said Stanley, indignant at this kind of treatment, even during a giant earwig attack.

"Koko!" cried Algernon, "Where's Koko? Don't tell me those *things* got him!" he was close to hysterics.

As if on cue, Koko jumped down from the cabin roof. He was breathing heavily, and had a nasty-looking cut on his cheek. The knuckles of his right hand were smoking slightly. "I'm here, Algernon," he said breathlessly. "Sorry for the delay. He followed Algernon onto the bridge, and Nell was about to go through the doorway, as well, when Ryuno reached out and grasped her shoulder.

"Wait," he said.

Nell looked back at him with surprise. Wordlessly, Ryuno reached behind him and drew a second sword from a sheath strapped to his back. It looked like his other blade, except that it was notably shorter.

"Nell—I want you to have this. I was going to wait for a better time, but … please, take it." He held the sword out to her, head bowed.

Nell's mouth had fallen open. "Ryuno, I can't—"

"Take it!" said Ryuno vociferously, raising his head and looking at her. "Take it and fight with me!"

Nell continued to stare, and Temoc roared, "*Take it or leave it, Marusai, we have no time!*" before leaping on a giant earwig and wrestling it to the ground.

"WHAT THE *HELL* ARE YOU LOT DOING?" bellowed the captain. He was looking at the small group huddled by the door to the bridge, and so didn't notice the giant earwig creeping up behind him. Nell's eyes widened as she saw the creature raise its tail, claws wide, aiming right at the captain's neck.

Stanley barely even saw what happened next. One second, the shortsword was resting on Ryuno's palms. The next, it was whistling through the air, and when it stopped, it didn't drop to the ground, because Nell was holding it. The scene seemed to freeze for a moment:

The captain, staring horror-struck at the claws that were inches from his throat, the giant earwig, a look of insectoid surprise in its glowing eyes, and Nell, who was now beside the monstrous bug, holding the shortsword straight out beside her.

Then the giant earwig collapsed, cut cleanly in two. The captain swore loudly and his legs gave way. He gaped at the dead insect as its spilled blood burned yet another hole in the deck.

Finally, Nell lowered her sword and turned around. Stanley stared at her; he had never seen her look like this before: her face wore a look of deep concentration, but her eyes blazed with a cold fury. She looked completely serene, unmindful of the battle raging around her.

Suddenly another earwig skittered down from the roof and hissed loudly at Nell. She calmly raised her sword and dropped into a stance almost like the one Ryuno used.

But the captain, who had become a bit unhinged by his near-death experience, panicked. He raised his rifle and fired, just as Ryuno yelled

"NO!"

The insect shrieked as its exoskeleton shattered, and its green ichor sprayed out in a wide, sizzling burst, painting the cabin wall. Ryuno made a horrified noise.

Nell had been standing close to the giant earwig.

Very close.

Stanley's fingers clamped down on the doorframe. He couldn't see Nell. It took a moment for the implications of what had just happened to sink in. He stared. His face went white.

And then something inside him exploded.

"*NOOOOO!*" he roared, and it did not sound like his voice. His fingers clamped down even harder on the doorframe, and there was a squeal of protesting metal. He sprang forward, knocking Ryuno out of the way.

"Stanley!" cried Alabaster, rushing to the door. He stopped short as he noticed the deep score marks in the doorframe.

Stanley was nearly blind with rage. He raced around the deck looking for Nell, but couldn't find her. She was gone! The acid must have gotten her. He would kill the one responsible! But the giant bug was already dead, its blood eating its way through the ship, because the captain had shot it.

The captain.

Stanley rounded on the captain, and began stalking towards him. Idiot. He was responsible. He shot the giant earwig while Nell was standing right behind it.

The captain recoiled as Stanley approached, his eyes wide with fear and confusion. Stanley reached for him. He would make the captain pay for what happened to Nell. He would do it with his bare hands …

Only they weren't his hands. They were claws. Great black talons, long and sharp. The claws of a wild beast. Why did he have them? Where were *his* hands?

Never mind, said a voice. Just use them.

"Lord o' mercy, *help me!*" cried the captain.

Do it, said the voice. Destroy him. Make him pay.

But suddenly a strange feeling came over him.

"What … what am I doing?" said Stanley.

Thunder boomed again, louder than ever, and the first drops of rain began to fall.

A pair of hands grabbed Stanley by the shoulders. He looked up and saw Father Blake staring at him intently.

"*Fight it!*" yelled Blake.

"Wh-what?" said Stanley.

"Fight it!" Blake repeated. "Don't give in!"

"Give in to what?" said Stanley, "What are you talking about?" He suddenly felt very lightheaded. Lighting flashed as Blake released him and he fell down onto the deck. A searing pain suddenly shot through his skull, and he groaned, clasping his head with his hands.

His claws.

He blacked out then, and the next thing he knew, he was in the river. He coughed and spluttered, swallowing a lot of water, which made him cough more. It was difficult to stay afloat. Thunder roared overhead, and the sound of the rain was almost excruciatingly loud. He struggled feebly, but just couldn't muster the strength to swim. He tried to call for help, but he could barely make any noise. No one would have heard him over the din of the storm, anyway. Finally, his arms and legs gave out, and he sank beneath the surface.

But then he was moving again! He could feel the water rushing by him. He felt his back hit the bottom, and almost reflexively he spun around and dug his fingers into the rocky riverbed. He felt himself being pulled backwards, then upwards, and moments later he was out of the water, and on the grassy river bank, coughing and vomiting as his body forced the water out of his lungs. He collapsed then, and lay very still, barely even breathing, as the rain pelted him and the storm raged overhead. He did not dream.

Chapter 13

PRISONERS

Stanley awoke in a cold, dark somewhere. His head was pounding and he groaned with pain. A faint, golden light was shining on his face, and he shut his eyes against it. He lay still for a time, waiting for his headache to pass.

Presently, he felt well enough to open his eyes and look around. He was lying on the damp stone floor of a tiny room. It was perhaps eight feet long and five wide, and devoid of any kind of furnishings. He sat up and shivered. No wonder he was so cold—his clothes were soaking wet. He looked around at the damp stone walls, then at the room's only door. It was closed tightly, but a small barred window three quarters of the way up allowed a bit of light to shine through. Torchlight, Stanley guessed, by its flickering quality.

"This is a prison cell," he muttered to himself, and for one wild moment he thought he was back in Ethelia, back in the dungeons of the Imperial Palace. But no, this was definitely a different dungeon.

"Why do I always end up in jail?" he said to no one in particular. He tried to remember how he came to be in this situation. He recalled the attack on the Empress Hildegarde, but after that, he had only brief flashes and images.

He remembered being confined to the bridge … he remembered getting very angry … and then being under water … and then being here. He'd obviously had another blackout. But why had he been angry?

Suddenly he remembered. Something had happened to Nell. Ryuno had given her a sword, and she'd gone to fight the giant earwigs. The image of the captain shooting one of the monsters flashed into his mind. Nell had been standing behind it, and the thing's acid blood had sprayed out …

"No!" Stanley growled, gritting his teeth and forcing the image from his thoughts. "Think of something else. She's alright. She's alright. She's probably with the others."

The others … where *were* the others? Had they managed to fight off the giant earwigs?

A sudden noise from outside the cell made Stanley sit up and listen. All other thoughts were pushed from his mind as someone outside said something in a strange language. It sounded like an animal's growls and hisses. There came a sharp metallic *click* followed by the sound of a door swinging open on squeaky hinges. It sounded like it was the door right next to Stanley's cell.

The strange hissing voice spoke again. Stanley was sure he'd heard this kind of speech before. Another voice answered, also in a growling hiss. There was a loud *whack!* followed by the sounds of a scuffle, and then the first voice spoke again.

Stanley was breathing hard, listening intently. It sounded like someone had just been beaten up. There came a low grunt from next door, and then an odd slithering sound. A figure passed by Stanley's cell. He couldn't get a good look at it, but he could tell that it was dragging something behind it. The figure's clacking footsteps faded away.

Stanley shivered. Who had just been taken away, and to what end? Why was he, Stanley, in here in the first place? Who were his captors? Several tense minutes passed, in which Stanley stood stock still, listening for any sound, anything that could tell him where he was.

Then he heard footsteps approaching. The *clack-clack-clacking* echoed dismally off the stone walls; it sounded as if two or three pairs of clawed feet were coming closer and closer. The footsteps stopped, and with a thrill of horror, Stanley realized that the owners of the feet were right outside his cell. He stumbled back from the door just as someone stepped in front of the window, blocking out the torchlight. There was a guttural hiss as someone outside fumbled with a key ring and started to unlock the door.

Stanley huddled in a corner of the cell, frightened of what was going to happen to him when his captors dragged him away. He closed his eyes and hid his face in the crook of his elbow. He wished there was somewhere to hide. He wished he could just turn invisible and sneak out of this terrible place.

The door creaked open. Torchlight flooded into the cell. Stanley stayed very still. He pushed himself as hard as he could into the wall, wishing with all his might that he could be hidden.

Someone stepped into the room. Stanley could hear them breathing. Maybe if they thought he was asleep, they'd leave him alone. The someone let out a loud exclamation, like a surprised bark, prompting the two other figures out in the hall to poke their heads into the cell. They said something in their strange language, and the first figure turned around, answering in a clearly frustrated tone.

Stanley risked a peek at the situation. The first figure barked at one of its companions and pointed at the torch on the wall outside. One of the others took the torch out of its bracket and brought it into the cell. The torch was very bright to Stanley after so long in the dark, and he squinted in its flickering light, but was now able to see his captors clearly.

They were Saurians. Their reptilian faces were obvious, as were their clawed feet, each with a large sickle-shaped talon on the big toe. These Saurians were dressed differently from the ones Stanley had seen before: they wore long, black robes, and their skin appeared to have been painted black, as well—the blackness was smudgy and uneven, and lighter patches could be seen around their eyes and nostrils. Had Stanley not been so terrified, he might have wondered what tribe these strange creatures belonged to.

The first cloaked Saurian wore a gold circlet on his head, with a single white feather sticking up from it. He was clearly in charge here, and showed it by snatching the torch from his underling. He held the torch high, his eyes roving back and forth, scrutinizing every inch of the chamber. Several times he looked into Stanley's corner, gazing right into his eyes, but didn't react to him at all.

The feathered Saurian lowered the torch, leaned his head back, and sniffed the air. His snout swung back and forth, then stopped. He turned to his underlings, and thrust the torch back into the hands of the one closest to him. He then threw his clawed hands in the air and proceeded to shriek and roar, while the other two croaked apologetically.

Stanley watched all of this with uncomprehending fascination, and before he knew it, the three Saurians were out of the cell, their footsteps clacking away into the distance.

He hardly dared move. What did it mean? He'd been right there in plain view, huddled up in a ball, yes, but certainly not hidden. The one with the feather had even sniffed around for him! How could they possibly have missed him? Perhaps they had been looking for someone else, but if that were true, why had they not even registered his presence? And why had they left the door open?

THE DOOR!

Stanley had to make a conscious effort to keep from crying out with surprise and relief. The Saurians had left the cell door wide open, which meant that they clearly thought the room was empty. But why would they think that? There was no way they could have missed him. Something must have happened. He'd been sitting there, wishing he could hide, wishing he could become invisible. Was that it? Had he somehow turned invisible? The idea was pretty far-fetched, and even if he *had* turned invisible, the Saurians would surely have smelled him.

The sound of more clawed footsteps out in the hall reminded Stanley that he didn't really have time to be sitting here thinking. The footsteps came closer and closer, and another cloaked Saurian passed by his cell. He waited for the footsteps to fade away, then carefully poked his head out the door. To his left, a long stone hallway extended into the distance. Many more wooden doors could be seen, most of which were also open. To his right, there was about thirty more feet of hallway, and then an arch, through which he could see stone steps leading up. Just before the archway, the hall made a sharp left turn, but Stanley was only interested in the stairs.

His pulse pounding in his ears, he crept along as silently as he could, listening hard for the sound of claws on stone. He reached the point where the hall turned, and peeped around the corner. Another torch-lit hallway extended into darkness. It, too was empty. Stanley relaxed a bit and headed for the stairs. He slunk stealthily from step to step, his wet shoes making small squishing noises that sounded annoyingly loud to his own ears. At the top of the stairs was a landing, and another flight leading up. The walls were covered with strange carvings and symbols, but Stanley paid them no mind; any minute now, more Saurians could come clack-clack-clacking down the stairs, and he didn't want to be here when that happened. He started up the second flight of stairs, his arms and legs shaking as adrenaline raced through his bloodstream.

He was almost at the top of the second flight when a horrible thought entered his mind. What had happened to the others? Where were Alabaster and Nell, and Algernon, Temoc, Blake, Koko, Ryuno, and the Hildegarde's crew? What if he, Stanley, wasn't the only one in here? What if his friends were all down there, huddled in tiny cells, with no hope of escape?

Stanley nearly moaned out loud at the thought. He was close to freedom, so close to escaping … but maybe he *was* the only one down here. Maybe everyone else had escaped, or not been captured at all. There had been enough open doors down there to corroborate that theory …

Maybe they were all dead.

"No," Stanley whispered. "Not that. No way."

Maybe his friends were down there and maybe they weren't, but there was no way he was going to take the chance. He had to be sure. He had to go back down.

He was far from pleased at the prospect of returning to the strange Saurian dungeon, but he squared his shoulders, took a deep breath, and let out a surprised "*Whoa!*" as the ground beneath him gave a mighty lurch, knocking him off his feet and down the staircase. He landed at the bottom of the steps with a great *thump* and a short groan, as the ground continued to shake. He was in considerable pain, having rolled his ankle and landed badly on a few of the stone steps, but his greatest concern right now was that his fall had seemed horrendously loud, and at any moment, a dozen Saurians were sure to come charging down the steps to see what all the noise was about.

About a minute passed as Stanley lay there gasping and listening for the approach of his doom, but as the brief earthquake faded away, it soon became apparent that no one had heard his unfortunate and ill-timed spill. With a bit of effort, he sat up and checked himself for injuries. He'd landed hard on his right side, and it hurt to breathe too deeply. His right arm was also aching, and it felt as if his knees and shins had been skinned pretty badly. He gingerly pulled up the legs of his jeans, which were now torn here and there, and saw that he had only a few small nicks and cuts. There was some blood, and it seemed to be a bit more than one would usually find issuing from such small, shallow wounds, but Stanley really didn't know much about that sort of thing.

Presently, he started to feel a bit better; it didn't hurt to breathe anymore, and when he tried to stand, he found that he could do it with very little trouble at all. He experimentally put his full weight on his right ankle, and there was no pain—just a slight stiffness.

Reflecting that maybe his luck hadn't completely run out after all, Stanley started down the next staircase. His side was still twinging slightly, and he clutched it absently with his left hand, but he was much more concerned about the possibility of running into a pack of bloodthirsty Saurians. At the bottom of the stairs, he paused, his heart pounding. He strained his ears for anything, even the slightest sound that would betray the presence of an enemy, but all was quiet down here in the dungeon, save for the low, calm crackling of the torches on the walls.

Stanley peeked around the corner. Nothing down the hallway to his right, nothing straight ahead. So far so good. It was time to begin his search. But *where* to begin? He supposed he'd have to go around checking every single cell with a closed door ... but how long might *that* take? He had no idea how big this place was; maybe there were two floors. Maybe there were *three* floors—five, *ten!* He shook his head and pushed these thoughts from his mind. There was no point in panicking, and no matter the size of the dungeon, he had to start somewhere. He set off down the hallway in front of him, and almost had a heart attack when he heard a noise. It was faint, but there was no mistaking it: someone had just let out a low groan.

Stanley froze, listening hard. The sound had definitely come from somewhere behind him, but there were no footsteps to accompany it, so whoever had made the noise was probably not moving around.

A prisoner! Stanley's heart leapt. He wondered who it was. One of his friends, perhaps? He hoped so, but either way, he was off to a good start. He crept quietly back towards the staircase, checked that the hallway to the left was still empty, and turned the corner. He went along slowly, checking every door he came to, listening for any unusual sound. Most of the doors down this hall had been left open, too, and the ones that were closed didn't seem to have anyone in them.

Suddenly he heard it again: a low, painful groan, but it was much closer this time, maybe two or three doors down. Something dropped onto his head, and he started with surprise.

"Guh!" he exclaimed, quickly brushing whatever it was off of him. With a quiet *plop*, a big orange and black tarantula landed on the stone floor. This one seemed to be of normal size, for once, and Stanley let out a sigh of relief as it scuttled away.

"Who's there?" said a voice from close by. Stanley froze. Someone had heard his grunt of surprise, but they were speaking English, with suggested that they might be friendly; one of his captors would surely have hissed something at him.

All the same, Stanley decided to play it safe until he knew what he was dealing with. He waited a few moments, then silently approached the room from whence the voice had come. Peeking around the doorframe, he was surprised and dismayed to find himself in the doorway of what looked like a medieval torture chamber.

Most of the space in the room was occupied by six rectangular stone tables, each of which had a horrible dark stain on its surface. The walls were covered with strange and frightening carvings; most of them seemed to depict Saurians doing nasty and painful things to one another. Stanley's blood ran cold as he examined a carving that clearly showed a group of robed Saurians cutting off a prisoner's arms and legs and throwing them onto a nearby pile of severed limbs. It was like looking at a grisly stone comic book.

The wall to Stanley's left was adorned with a wide assortment of mounted weapons, from small, sharp knives to huge double-handed swords, all displayed as if they were part of a museum exhibit. His gaze came to rest on a pair of swords, still in their scabbards, that looked suspiciously like Ryuno's. He glanced again at the tables, and was surprised to notice that one of them was occupied.

Lying on the flat stone surface, his wrists and ankles bound with ropes that seemed to come up through slots in the table, was a Saurian warrior. He was a sorry sight: he'd been badly beaten, and was still bleeding from multiple wounds in his blue, scaly hide. Stanley cautiously crept over to him. It had obviously been he who had spoken a few minutes ago, but he hardly seemed to be breathing. Was he even still alive?

Stanley's jaw dropped when he realized that he knew this Saurian.

"Temoc!" he exclaimed, before he could stop himself. Temoc blearily opened a swollen, purple eye and looked at him.

"You," he said weakly. He turned his head, grunting with the effort. "What in the name of Sotzol are *you* doing here?"

At first, Stanley thought Temoc was angry at him, but the Saurian smiled and gave a short, harsh laugh. "If I worshiped any gods, I would say they work in strange ways," he said, trying unsuccessfully to sit up. "I had given up on any hope of rescue. It is good to see that you are still alive, Stanley—and not just because you have the ability to release me." He strained emphatically against his bonds.

"Oh, uh, right," said Stanley, feeling like a bit of an idiot for just standing there while poor Temoc was tied to that awful table. He cast around for something with which to cut the ropes binding the Saurian's wrists and ankles.

"That one will do," said Temoc, nodding towards a short knife with an odd rectangular blade on a nearby table. Stanley went to pick it up, but recoiled when he saw that the blade was covered in blood.

"What is wrong?" said Temoc, the tiniest hint of urgency in his voice.

Stanley gulped. "There's blood on it—"

Temoc stared at him. "This concerns you?"

"Well—yeah, kind of," said Stanley.

"Blood or no blood, I need you to cut me free," said Temoc. "Will you help me?"

Stanley, realizing that now was not the time to be grossed out to the point of inaction, took a deep breath, gingerly picked up the knife, and brought it over to Temoc.

"Be quick," hissed the Saurian, "our time is short. They will be back soon. Do not worry about wounding me—if you do, it will bother me but little compared to what I have already endured."

Stanley supposed that this was probably true. Temoc's body had been scored with dozens of deep cuts—it looked like whoever had made them had tried to carve all kinds of strange, curling lines and symbols into his skin. He pressed the blade into the rope around Temoc's left wrist, and sawed back and forth a few times. The rope sprang apart, and Temoc grabbed the knife from Stanley, and in three swift movements, severed the ropes binding his other limbs. He climbed off the table and dropped to his knees in front of Stanley, touching his snout to the ground.

"I thank you most deeply," he growled.

Stanley stood there for a moment, not quite sure how to respond, when there came the sound of approaching footsteps from out in the hall. Temoc jumped to his feet and let out a low hiss.

"They return," he muttered, as the clacking footsteps drew nearer. His reptilian brow furrowed, and he said, "You will hide. I will lay here and feign incapacity." He climbed back on to the table and laid down. "When they are all in the room, complacent in their surety of victory, *then* we will *strike*." He laid his head back, closed his eyes, and let his jaw go slack. Stanley cast around wildly for a hiding place, and dove behind the table furthest from the door. He was just starting to wonder if he'd heard Temoc correctly (had he said *we* will strike?), when three cloaked Saurians came slouching into the room.

Stanley peaked around the corner of the table, and recognized the Saurian with the white feather and gold circlet. He and his subordinates were carrying an array of strange instruments, all of which seemed to be geared towards inflicting intense pain. The third Saurian was also carrying a stout vase with an evil, snarling face carved into it.

The cloaked Saurians gathered around Temoc, who was doing a commendable job at pretending to be comatose. The feathered one growled something to his comrades, both of whom answered with a sharp clicking sound. He then positioned himself at the foot of the table, in front of Temoc's feet, and produced what looked like a large pair of pliers.

He began to recite something, possibly some kind of Saurian scripture, but he didn't get far, for, as he leaned in to close the pliers around Temoc's left big toe, Temoc sprang into action. He made a swift sweeping kick with his left foot, catching the feathered Saurian in the wrist with his five-inch toe claw. The claw slashed open the black-painted hide; the feathered Saurian's shriek of surprise and pain was cut off abruptly, as Temoc raised his right foot and dealt him a savage heel-kick to the jaw.

The other two cloaked Saurians roared loudly and sprang backwards as Temoc leapt up off the table, the small rectangular knife clasped in his right hand. The cloaked ones had each drawn weapons of their own: short, curved swords of shiny black stone. They snarled savagely, baring their sharp, pointed teeth. Temoc snarled back, but his knife seemed a tad pathetic compared to the two swords being brandished at him. This did not phase Temoc, though. He hurled the knife at the Saurian on his left, and leapt at the one on his right, raising his arm and bringing his elbow crashing down on the crown of his foe's head.

The remaining cloaked Saurian stared, jaws agape, as his companion crumpled to the floor, then turned and tried to flee, but got tangled up in his own robes, before Temoc grabbed him and hit him in the jaw with a powerful elbow-strike. The cloaked Saurian reeled drunkenly for a moment, a ridiculously vacant look in his eyes, and then collapsed alongside his fallen companions.

Temoc propped himself up against one of the stone tables to catch his breath. Stanley came out from his hiding place.

"Uh—are you okay, Temoc?"

Temoc looked up at him, breathing heavily. His face was a mosaic of cuts and bruises, his left eye now swollen completely shut. He was still bleeding from the myriad open gashes all over his body.

"I've never felt so *alive*," he said, grinning savagely.

"*What in the name of—*"

They both looked up sharply. There in the doorway stood Father Blake. He looked a tad disheveled, but otherwise seemed to be in good health.

"Temoc!" said Blake, "And Stanley? What in the *world* are you doing here?"

"Get in!" snarled Temoc, stalking towards Blake and grabbing him by the front of his coat, before propelling him unceremoniously into the room. The Saurian took a quick look out into the hall, then came back in and pulled the door closed.

Blake was staring wide-eyed at them both, particularly at Temoc, as if he half suspected that the wounded Saurian was really some foul zombie, freshly risen from the grave.

He definitely looked it.

"We were captured by the Xol'tecs, obviously," said Temoc, coming back over to join the other two. "I'd thought the same of you, but clearly you managed to avoid them."

"Yes," said Blake. "But I was able to track them. I'm sorry it took me so long to get here."

Stanley, who was starting to feel as if this were all some kind of bizarre dream, suddenly shouted, "*What's going on here?"*

Blake and Temoc stared at him.

Frustrated by the blank looks on their faces, he continued, "What *is* this? Where are we? What happened? What are we *doing* here?"

Blake and Temoc glanced at each other.

"What's the last thing you remember?" said Blake calmly.

Stanley frowned. "What's that got to do with—"

"Just tell us," said Blake.

Stanley thought for a moment. "The boat—the Empress Hildegarde. We were attacked by giant bugs. That's the last thing I remember. Oh, and falling in the water, I think …"

"That's all?"

"Yeah—well, and waking up here."

Blake and Temoc exchanged another glance.

"We lost track of you after the sinking of the Hildegarde—"

Stanley's jaw dropped. "It *sank?"*

Blake nodded solemnly. "The—*blood* of the giant insects was … highly acidic. Too much of it was spilled, and it ate right through the bottom of the hull."

"By the end, they were throwing themselves into the water wheel," added Temoc. "Sacrificing themselves to destroy us."

Stanley racked his brain, trying to remember the events being described to him.

"The Hildegarde started to sink, and the captain ordered us all to abandon ship," said Blake. "We all swam for shore, but … many didn't even make it off the boat. I think the storm scared the creatures off, which is probably the only reason any of us are still alive." He sighed heavily.

Stanley had to steady himself against the table to keep from falling over. Their entire expedition—crippled, obliterated, just like that. And he'd *wanted* to come along. How could he have been so stupid?

"Are they … are they all—"

Temoc interrupted him. "There were some survivors," he said gravely. "I think, at least, that none of our travelling companions are dead."

Stanley felt his stomach unclench a bit.

"That's right," said Blake. "I'm sure we all made it to shore … many of the Hildegarde's crew weren't so lucky."

They were silent for a time, and then Temoc said,

"Now is not the time for talk. We should be escaping from this place, with the rest of our party intact. If possible." He took a few steps towards the door, and stumbled. Blake caught him.

"We're not going anywhere with you looking like this," he said.

"I am fine," said Temoc.

"You're *not* fine," replied Blake. "Look at yourself—you're a wreck."

"I can still fight," Temoc snarled, shrugging him off. "I felled these three *ruchas*, did I not?" He indicated the unconscious cloaked Saurians on the floor.

"And now you can barely walk," said Blake.

Stanley agreed that Temoc hardly seemed in any condition to go elbowing his way out of a prison, but he was deeply troubled about the fate of the others. He wanted to rescue them as soon as possible, although with Temoc in his weakened state, their chances seemed much slimmer. Struck by sudden inspiration, he looked squarely at the Saurian and said, in his toughest, coolest voice (which was still pretty high-pitched),

"You're no good to us dead."

Blake suppressed a smile, but Temoc looked sharply at him, then slowly nodded his head.

"Let's see to those wounds," said Blake. "You're going to need real medical attention, but we can at least try to keep you from getting any worse." He reached into his coat and drew forth a small leather bag. From this he took a bottle and what looked like a roll of cloth. "Now this may sting a bit," he said as he unscrewed the cap.

Temoc snatched the bottle. "I think I can handle it," he growled.

⋆ ⋆ ⋆

"Ssss!" Temoc hissed through gritted teeth, as he used a cloth to dab at the deep cuts covering his body.

"I told you it would sting," said Blake. "It's rubbing alcohol."

"I'm not complaining," snarled Temoc. "It's a better pain than the wounds themselves."

Another earthquake briefly gripped the dungeon, causing the ground to vibrate beneath them. Small bits of dust and rock came cascading down from the ceiling, loosened by the tectonic movement.

"Might be a good idea to get outside," Blake muttered.

Stanley agreed—he was feeling more and more anxious the longer they stayed in this horrible room. "Shouldn't we hurry?" he said. It wasn't that he felt no concern for Temoc, but terrible thoughts were floating around in his mind every time he thought about Alabaster, Nell, and the others.

"Yes," said Temoc, setting the bottle down and reaching for the roll of bandages. "The sooner we get out of this place, the better."

Blake produced a small pocket watch and glanced at its face. "3:30," he said. "We've got some time left."

Stanley was confused by this, but Temoc, who had begun to dress his own wounds, paused and looked quizzically at Blake.

"I didn't know you were so familiar with Xol'tec customs," he said, sounding impressed.

"Not all of them," said Blake with a shrug, "but I did notice that the red moon is full tonight."

Temoc nodded, then turned to Stanley. "The red moon is an important part of Xol'tec culture," he explained, as he resumed his bandaging. "They revere it just as much as they do the sun—perhaps even more so, for they *fear* it. Once a month, when the red moon is full, a ceremony is held—the *T'Lopan Xoln.* The Feast of the Blood Goddess."

Stanley gulped. He already didn't like the sound of this ceremony.

Temoc continued, "The Xol'tecs believe that the red moon is the eye of the Blood Goddess, *Chimé Xoln'ec.* They believe that when the moon is full, the goddess is angry and hungry, and if she does not receive a sacrifice before the night is over, she will strike the sun from the sky. There is no doubt in my mind that our companions are to be this month's sacrifice to Chimé Xoln'ec.

"Then we have to save them!" Stanley burst out.

"We will," said Blake calmly, "but first we need a plan. It's 3:30 now, and sunrise won't be for another two hours at the earliest. Our only chance is stealth. We need to find a way to get out of here without alerting the entire city."

"*City?*" Stanley echoed.

"We are in *Teno-Xol-Zan*," said Temoc. "The Xol'tec capital city. The City of Blood."

Stanley felt a cold surge in his chest, and he shivered. The Xol'tec capital city. How were they ever going to get out of this?

"It is not as bad as it sounds," said Temoc, as he finished bandaging himself up. He now looked like some kind of bloody Saurian mummy. Stanley was reminded of how Grey had looked when he'd first met him. He wondered where he was right now, and what he was doing. He'd almost half expected him to come bursting into this dungeon to save them all, but it was looking less and less likely that that was going to happen. He sighed heavily.

Temoc was still speaking. "The Xol'tecs, as a people, have been slowly dying out for centuries. Their population has dwindled, and still they refuse to abandon their barbaric and bloody practices. This, their capital, was once the mightiest bastion in all Verduria, but now it is a crumbling, ruined shadow of its former self. It is an aged warrior waiting for death."

"The Xol'tecs that remain are still extremely dangerous, though," said Blake. "We've had more than enough proof of that. It'd be very bad to underestimate them."

"You are correct, *hass* Blake," said Temoc, bowing his snout briefly. "But I think that is enough history for the time being. Now is the time for *action.*"

"First we need to *think*," said Blake. "We can't go up there, swords swinging, and expect to get away."

They spent a few moments in thought. Every second felt like a hideous waste of time to Stanley, but Blake was right. What could they do against a city full of Saurians? He glanced down at one of Temoc's unconscious torturers.

"Why are these guys in black?" he asked suddenly. "I thought Xol'tecs wore red."

Temoc looked up. "They are *priests*," he said disdainfully. "They paint their bodies black, and wear black robes and cloaks to mark their station." He wrinkled his nose. "They also never bathe."

This gave Stanley an idea.

"We'll wear the cloaks!" he cried, jumping up and spreading his arms in a *Ta-daa!* gesture.

Temoc stared blankly at him, but Blake's eyes lit up.

"Of course! Why didn't I think of that? Excellent idea, Stanley!"

"It does not sound excellent to me," said Temoc. "To don the foul robes of a priest … it is … it is to invite the most horrible curses."

Blake looked squarely at him. "I thought the Oltonnacs abolished the priesthood," he said, as he knelt down and began pulling off one of the priests' robes.

"We did," said Temoc.

"Which means you no longer follow the ancient religion of the Saurian people."

"We do not."

"Then surely you don't believe in some superstitious nonsense about these robes being *cursed*."

Temoc paused for a moment, then laughed out loud. "Well said, *hass* Blake, well said." And with that, he knelt down and yanked the robes off the priest with the feathered circlet.

Soon, the three unconscious priests were wearing considerably less, and Stanley, Temoc, and Blake had been reduced to three walking heaps of mouldy, stinking, filthy fabric.

"It's no wonder that curse rumour got started," came Blake's muffled voice. "I'd believe *anything* was cursed if it smelled this bad."

"Just try to keep from thinking about what is *causing* the smell," said Temoc.

Stanley thought about it, and immediately wished he hadn't. The robes smelled like the inside of a gym bag full of used bandaids.

Temoc and Blake spent a few moments tying up the priests. "Better not to have them roaming free," muttered Temoc, before kicking the one with the feather in the face. "*That* one was about to remove my great claws," he said, as if it were the ultimate insult, which, Stanley supposed, it probably was.

"Come on," said Blake, leading the way towards the door. "We still have some time before sunrise, but we've got a lot of work to do." Temoc and Stanley followed after him. On his way out the door, Stanley suddenly remembered something. He raced back to the wall covered with weapons (or rather, he *stumbled* back; his robes were miles too big for him), and looked closely at two of the swords—the ones he'd noticed earlier. Close to, he was almost a hundred percent sure that they were Ryuno's. Of course, one had been given to *Nell*, but …

A faint heat crept through his stomach, and he seized the swords, one in each hand, and headed for the door.

"We have to take these," he said to Blake and Temoc.

"Too cumbersome," said Temoc. "Try this one." He held out one of the curved black swords used by the Xol'tec priests.

"No," said Stanley, "I'm not going to use them—we just need to bring them with us."

Temoc shook his head.

"It's important," said Stanley.

Temoc frowned at him from under his hood, then glanced at Blake.

"We'll take them," said Blake. "Here, I'll carry the longer one, Stanley."

Temoc shrugged.

"Thanks," said Stanley, hiding the shorter sword in the folds of his robe. Blake smiled and gave him a quick nod.

"Are we prepared?" said Temoc.

Stanley and Blake nodded gravely.

"Very well," said Temoc. "Then let us move."

⋆ ⋆ ⋆

"Hold here for a moment," said Temoc. Stanley and Blake obeyed.

They had reached the top of the second staircase, and were now in a small room with a single doorway leading outside. Cool, fragrant night air was wafting through the opening, along with the unmistakable sound of chirping insects. The fresh air felt wonderful to Stanley after breathing the stale air of the dungeon for so long, and it was especially good compared to the foul mustiness of the Xol'tec robes. Stanley pulled his hood back and marveled at how much people took fresh air for granted.

"Wait here," said Temoc quietly. "I am going outside to get a brief glimpse of our surroundings. I will be back soon." He slipped quietly out of the room, and his footsteps faded away almost instantly.

Stanley and Blake stood there for an awkward moment.

"Er—good to be out of there," said Blake.

"Oh, uh, yeah—it is," said Stanley.

There was a brief silence, and then Blake said,

"How did you escape, if you don't mind my asking?"

"Huh?" said Stanley.

"From your cell, I mean," said Blake. "They did put you in a cell, didn't they?"

"Oh, right," said Stanley. "I guess they did."

"You *guess* they did?"

"Er—yeah—sorry, yes, they did put me in a cell."

"So how did you get out?"

"Um," said Stanley. He was feeling a bit uncomfortable. If he told Blake what had happened, Blake would surely think he was crazy, or at least lying.

"I'm not accusing you of anything," said Blake. "I'm just trying to figure something out."

Stanley looked up at him, and thought for a moment. What *had* happened, anyway? "Well," he began slowly, "When the Saurians came to get me, I just … I dunno, I just sort of curled up and tried to hide, and …"

"And?" said Blake.

Stanley paused, trying to find the right words. "It was like they couldn't see me," he finally managed. "They looked right at me, but then they just left, and they didn't close the door. That's how I got out."

Blake looked pensive, and started to scratch his chin. "Hmm," he said.

Stanley frowned. His story didn't seem to have surprised Blake very much.

Just then, a noise from outside made them jump.

"Can we talk more about this later?" said Blake, as he and Stanley retreated towards the staircase, lest something unfriendly come barreling into the room.

"Er—yeah, sure," said Stanley.

An instant later, Temoc returned. He was slightly out of breath, and it took him a moment to explain what was going on.

"We must do something now," he said in response to Blake's questions. "Something is amiss—the ceremony is already starting."

"*What?*" said Blake.

Stanley felt his stomach drop. If the ceremony had already started … "What does that mean?" he asked a bit frantically, although he had a pretty good idea.

"It means our friends are in a lot more trouble than we thought," said Blake.

"Follow me," said Temoc, heading for the door. "We must go swiftly. Keep your faces hidden, and if we meet anyone, stay calm and do not say anything. It is fortunate that we are dressed like this—no one will dare to challenge us, and very few would be brave enough to start a conversation with a priest. Come." He went out the door, followed closely by Blake.

Stanley took a deep breath, pulled his hood back over his head and followed them out into the night.

They were now walking down a narrow street of rough cobbled stones, with buildings looming in closely on either side. Some of them were two or three stories high, and Stanley marveled at how difficult it must have been to hoist the huge stone blocks used to build them.

This street appeared to be part of a residential area; the box-like, flat-roofed buildings all had the look of houses or apartments, but not one of them seemed to be occupied; the windows were all dark, and no sounds of life came from within.

There was something sinister about the silent emptiness of this block; Stanley had a distinct sensation of being watched, but by who or what, he could not tell. Maybe it was just the way the dark windows seemed to stare at him, like the vacant eye sockets in a massive row of giant skulls.

Like back in Port Verdant, the buildings here were covered with plant life. Vines and creepers were everywhere, hanging from roofs and climbing walls; but somehow, the foliage didn't seem at all unwelcome. It seemed that, instead of trying to take over, the jungle had reached a compromise with the architecture, so that one was now an integral part of the other.

It was all very strange to Stanley, but his thoughts were interrupted as the night breeze carried a new sound to his ears. It sounded like music—a high, mournful piping accompanied by a steady drum beat. Along with the music, there arose on the night air a weird sort of screeching howl that could only be a vast number of voices raised in song—although this was clearly a song that no human vocal chords had ever supplied.

"We must be getting close," Blake said in an undertone.

"Very," said Temoc. "They have begun the Song of Blood. This is not good." He and Blake began to jog, and it was all Stanley could do to keep up with them. He fumbled absentmindedly with his cloak, trying to keep it from tripping him up, while the words *Song of Blood* rang repeatedly through his thoughts.

The music and singing grew louder and louder, and Temoc suddenly stopped, holding up a clawed hand and diving into the shadows of a nearby doorway. Blake and Stanley huddled in next to him, Stanley making every effort not to breathe too heavily.

"We are at the edge of the city square," Temoc said quietly. "I would not be surprised if every Xol'tec in Teno-Xol-Zan is there."

"What's our next move?" asked Blake.

"Our friends are no doubt the intended sacrifices. They will be at the top of the Great Pyramid in the centre of the square, along with the Xol'tec high officials."

Stanley listened intently, his heart hammering in his chest.

"We are fortunate to have approached the square from the south-west," said Temoc. "There will be far fewer revelers between us and the pyramid, and, hopefully, no soldiers."

Stanley felt his stomach clench. They had to go to the pyramid. Of *course* they had to go to the pyramid.

"Wh-what happens when we get to the pyramid?" he asked, nervously.

"We will ascend the steps, and rescue our friends," said Temoc. "Our disguises will enable us to get very close without arousing any suspicion." He reached over and clapped Stanley on the shoulder. "You were very clever in coming up with the idea to wear these robes. You have performed admirably thus far—with courage and intelligence."

Stanley felt his face turn red.

"I will not force you to come with me, *hass* Stanley," Temoc went on. "You may hide here, if you prefer. Your honour will not be sullied."

"No, I want to come, too," said Stanley. Somehow, hiding here, alone, was even more unappealing than charging into a massive crowd of dangerous lizard-people.

Temoc smiled from under his hood. "It is good to hear you speak these words," he said. "Your skills may well prove helpful to us."

"Skills?" Said Stanley, but before he could ask what Temoc was talking about, Blake hunkered down in front of him and gripped his shoulder.

"I need you to listen carefully," he said, looking Stanley square in the eye. He took a deep breath and paused, as if he wasn't sure what to say next. "I want you to stay close to me, and if it happens again, try to force it into your hands."

Stanley stared. "Wh-what?" he stammered, "What are you—"

"I think you know," said Blake, as he let go of Stanley's shoulder and held up his right hand. For a moment, Stanley simply stared incredulously, mildly worried that Blake had gone out of his mind. But then, with a soft, bony creaking sound, the hand went black and changed into a large, bestial paw with long, clawed fingers.

Stanley gasped. Blake flexed his monstrous fingers, and solemnly regarded the hand.

"You've seen this kind of thing before, I think," he said gravely.

Stanley nodded slowly, his eyes wide.

"I saw your hands turn into the exact same thing on board the Empress Hildegarde," said Blake. "It's happened before, hasn't it?"

"Uh—I don't know," said Stanley. "I think it did, but I didn't know for sure—" Temoc interrupted him. "We are out of time," he said distractedly. He had been peering around the corner of the building, and not really paying attention to the exchange between Blake and Stanley.

"Alright," said Blake, nodding at Temoc, but he turned back to Stanley. "Just remember," he said deliberately, "Focus it into your hands. Keep it away from here." He tapped his forehead with a clawed finger, and then his hand changed back to normal.

"Okay," said Stanley, still not quite sure what Blake meant. His mind was now spinning with all sorts of questions, but he was clearly going to have to wait for the answers.

"With me," hissed Temoc, and the three of them rounded the corner, and entered the city square.

CHAPTER 14

ESCAPE FROM THE CITY OF BLOOD

The vast city square was a riot of colour, sound, and movement. Huge torches on tall wooden poles cast their flickering light over the great open expanse, illuminating the forms of thousands, perhaps tens of thousands of Saurian revelers. It seemed as if the entire city was gathered here; Xol'tecs of every age were standing shoulder to shoulder, jostling one another excitedly, or dancing in time with the high-pitched whistle of some strange wind instrument. Ancient, wrinkled old Saurians leaned on gnarled walking sticks, while females clutched tiny babies closely. Here and there, slightly older Xol'tec children raced around their parents' legs, hitting each other with sticks and chirping happily.

In the centre of the square was a colossal structure, a massive monolithic ziggurat, hundreds of feet across at its base. Stanley was briefly reminded of the pyramids of Egypt, but had he known more about such things (or had Alabaster been with him), he would have realized that the structure very closely resembled an Aztec or Mayan step-pyramid from Central America.

The Saurian pyramid consisted of four terraces, each one smaller than the one below it. The pyramid rose to a point at least one hundred feet above the square, where it was topped by a small building, probably a temple of some sort. Each terrace was lit by a massive torch at each of its corners, and the hunched, hooded forms of black-robed priests could be seen slowly ascending an extremely steep flight of stone steps on the east side of the structure. A small group of figures was gathered before the temple at the top of the pyramid, but Stanley could not make out who or what they were.

He was sure, though, from what Temoc had said, that at least some of them were his friends. He felt the weight of the short sword hidden beneath his robes. He was not comforted.

Temoc shouldered his way into the crowd, Blake and Stanley following him in a line. He didn't have to shoulder far, though. As soon as the nearby Saurians saw that three priests were coming towards them, they did all they could do to get out of the way, bowing and hissing submissively as the three went by. Stanley found the procession through the square to be a bit surreal. These were the same people who were about to sacrifice his friends, and who had tried to kill him not so long ago. He made sure that his face was well concealed; he could only imagine what would happen if any of the Xol'tec citizens saw a human face peeking out from the folds of a priest's robe.

It took them several minutes to make their way through the crowd to the base of the pyramid. Between the crowd and the building, an open space had been cleared, in which huge, towering bonfires burned at regular intervals. Around each fire danced a group of costumed Saurians dressed in brightly coloured robes with elaborate head dresses and masks covering their faces. Disquietingly, some of the costumes seemed to include actual bones—a particularly energetic dancer sported what looked like part of a ribcage covering his chest, while another wore shoulder-coverings made of reptilian skulls.

Stanley gulped and tried to focus on the various musicians. There were groups of them here and there, huddled at a safe distance from the dancers. Some were playing simple drums, thumping out a steady, unrelenting beat. Others plucked on odd-looking curved stringed instruments with long slits carved up their sides. The most common instrument appeared to be a wooden two-pronged flute with holes drilled along its length. These supplied the fast, high-pitched tune that soared out over the square and into the night as the players' clawed fingers danced from hole to hole, almost too quickly for the eye to follow.

The music was beautiful in a haunting way, but it failed to distract Stanley from the grim business at hand, especially when he saw the heads.

As he, Blake, and Temoc reached the base of the pyramid, where two priests were standing with crossed arms and sullen looks on their black-painted faces, he glanced to his left and saw a hideous sight.

It was a severed head, mounted atop a wooden pike, like a grisly totem. The head was dry and sunken, not much more than a skull, but it was definitely human. The mouth hung open with a lazy, tired tilt of the jaw, and the eyes were dark, sightless caverns. Not far away, several more almost-mummified heads were displayed similarly.

Stanley instantly felt his insides clench and churn, and he fought to keep the contents of his stomach from heaving themselves upward. Breathing heavily, he shut his eyes and stumbled sideways, dropping to his hands and knees. Blake and Temoc stopped short and turned sharply to look at him. Blake was instantly at his side, helping him to stand up, making sure his hands and face were still covered by his robes.

"Are you alright?" said Blake in a barely audible whisper.

"Yeah," gasped Stanley, struggling to his feet. He didn't think he'd be throwing up any time soon, but his legs felt shaky, and his torso seemed to have heated up about twenty degrees; his armpits were sweaty, and his heart was pounding uncomfortably in his chest.

A low murmur rose up from the surrounding Saurians, and a nearby musician, a drummer, chuckled quietly. Not quietly enough, however, for Temoc immediately straightened up and stalked towards him. The drummer's eyes went wide, and he started to get up, but Temoc was already upon him. He dealt the drummer a swift backhanded blow to the snout that sent him sprawling to the ground. Temoc then stomped on the drum, breaking it with a loud *crunch*. He turned and came back towards Stanley and Blake, ignoring the drummer's apologetic grunting and hissing as he cradled the remains of his instrument.

Stanley was at first shocked and confused by this display, and had come very close to yelling *Wait! Stop!* But Blake put a hand on his shoulder and said, again in a very low whisper,

"Don't say anything—he has to punish him—otherwise it would look very suspicious, and we'd probably be found out in about five seconds."

Stanley looked at him, then at one of the real priests at the foot of the steps, who nodded approvingly at Temoc.

Stanley understood: you do *not* make fun of a priest.

Blake helped him along, and at the base of the pyramid, the priest who had nodded at Temoc handed Stanley a short stick, and said a few words to him. Nonplussed, Stanley accepted the stick hesitantly. What was he supposed to do with it? Hit the drummer who had laughed at him? He felt panic start to form in his stomach, but then Blake whispered,

"*Walking stick,*"

and Stanley understood. He clutched the stick in his right hand, keeping his skin covered by his voluminous sleeve, and leaned on it with overexaggerated feebleness. He nodded briefly at the priest, who returned the nod and went back to staring ahead at the crowd. Blake patted Stanley on the back, and they started up the great stone steps, following Temoc closely.

It took them a few minutes to climb the steep steps to the top terrace of the pyramid. Up close, the temple at the pyramid's top seemed much bigger than it had from down in the square. Stanley looked back the way they'd come, and saw the thousands of Saurians of Teno-Xol-Zan reduced to tiny, colourful toy versions of themselves. The music from down below floated up and mixed strangely with the low, cool whistle of the night wind. In the sky above, the clouds had cleared, at least for now, letting the moons and countless stars shine down on the scene of revelry and veiled horror below. The great red moon, in particular, seemed to be taking a special interest in the proceedings; it was huge and full, looking not so different from a gigantic red goddess's eye …

Blake tapped him on the shoulder and they both shuffled across the terrace towards the temple building which crouched there like a squat, square gargoyle.

By now at least three dozen cloaked priests had gathered about the front of the temple, surrounding a low stone table near the top of the staircase. Stanley stood between Blake and Temoc, muscles tensed. Now that he was here, at the top of the pyramid, surrounded by an entire city of Saurians, it began to dawn on him that he really had no idea what they were going to do, or how they were going to get out of this. Temoc and Blake seemed to know what they were doing, but, capable though may have been, Stanley once again felt blind panic stirring inside him.

As if sensing his unease, Blake put a reassuring hand on his shoulder.

Just then, a great metallic crash, like the sound of a colossal gong rang through the night. Down below in the city square, the music and dancing halted instantly. Hundreds upon hundreds of reptilian faces looked up at the pyramid, their collective gaze fixed on the top terrace where the priests were gathered.

The sudden silence was strange, and hung over the scene like an invisible, sound-proof blanket. Even the night animals of the jungle had gone quiet, probably having been driven away temporarily by the sounds of music and celebration.

Far away, Stanley could hear the sound of chirping insects start up again. The wind whined over the top terrace of the pyramid, making odd *whoo*-ing noises in his ears.

There was a soft rustling as the priests turned as one towards the temple building behind them. A figure emerged from the dark doorway, and the priests began to back away as it came towards them.

The newcomer was another priest—that much was made clear by his black-painted skin and his robes, but this was obviously a priest of some importance. He carried a long staff of dark wood with a large and ornate headpiece—a disc made of gold covered in strange symbols. At its centre was set a huge red gem worked into the shape of an oval. It looked like a staring red eye.

Also unlike his fellows, this priest did not wear a hood. Instead, he wore a crown-like headdress topped with white feathers. It didn't take Stanley long to realize that the 'crown' was actually a jawbone, with sharp, pointed teeth, grinning hideously from atop the priest's head.

This character was the Xol'tec high priest, and though he was an imposing sight, his presence did not affect Stanley or Blake the way it did Temoc.

Temoc felt fear and anger rise up inside him. When he was a child, he and his people, the Oltonnacs, had lived under the bloody rule of the priesthood. They, too, had once worshiped the Blood Goddess, Chimé Xoln'ec, as well as the rest of the Saurian pantheon, and he had seen many of his family and friends sacrificed to the bloodthirsty gods of Verduria.

There had once been a high priest like this one in Temoc's hometown; a dark and wicked creature who delighted in the pain and death of others. Even the emperor clove to the will of the priesthood, whose black, bloody grip closed tighter and tighter until the common people, pushed to the brink by fear and poverty, rose up and wiped out every last one of them.

It was brought to light that the priesthood had been hugely corrupt, hoarding the wealth of the Oltonnac nation for themselves, while cultivating a religion of torture and murder. The abolition of the priesthood had been the first step on the road to a better life for the Oltonnacs, who were now a reasonably wealthy warrior tribe, and the largest in Verduria, next to the Xol'tecs.

Now, standing here in the midst of this Xol'tec festival, all the terrible memories of dark and bloody years past came flooding back to Temoc, and he trembled with rage and horror. Every fibre of his being roared at him to spring forward and end the high priest's foul existence, but he mastered himself, and kept silent. The abolition of *this* priesthood would have to wait for another day.

The high priest raised his arms, holding his staff high. He spoke, then, and though it sounded like a series of frightening dinosaur sounds to Stanley, Temoc understood every word.

"*The Blood Moon has waxed full!*" cried the high priest, his snout raised to the heavens. Down below, in the city square, the crowd murmured,

"*The Goddess! Praise the Blood Goddess!*"

"*The Blood Goddess demands sacrifice!*" yelled the high priest. "*She shakes the earth in Her anger!* Who *has angered the Goddess?*"

"*We*," answered the crowd, "*we have angered her.*"

"*You!*" roared the high priest, pointing accusingly down at the multitude below him. "*You have indeed angered Her! She should rip open the ground and strike the sun from the sky! But She will not do this, for we, the Faithful, have been granted the divine knowledge: the knowledge of* appeasement!"

"*Appease the Goddess, lest She strike the sun from the sky*," the crowd almost sang.

"How *do we appease the Goddess?*" demanded the high priest.

The response was a single word: "*Blood.*"

"BLOOD!" screamed the high priest. "*The blood of those who have angered Her!* You," he made a sweeping gesture with his free hand, and the entire crowd seemed to cringe. "*You should* all *be made sacrifice for angering the Goddess! But …*"

He paused for effect.

"*She is merciful. She demands only a* small *sacrifice—a paltry few, so that all the rest may live.*"

"*Merciful … She is Merciful.*"

"*But marvel* further *at Her grace and mercy,*" the high priest roared, "*For* She Herself *has provided the sacrifices! Bring forth the prisoners!*"

At this there was a general intake of breath, followed by a tense silence. Temoc had been fiercely grinding his teeth while the high priest harangued the crowd below, but Stanley, who had no idea what was going on, looked around in surprise as, with a flourish, the high priest pointed to the temple.

Out of the building came a short, grim procession: a line of between ten and fifteen people was being led across the terrace by a pair of priests with white-feathered gold circlets on their heads. Stanley couldn't see who the others were, for they were draped in long, white hooded robes. They were obviously prisoners, though, for they were all bound together by a length of rope tied about their necks. The prisoners were brought to the left side of the flat stone table. One of them stumbled, and a priest cuffed him sharply, forcing a muffled cry from underneath the hood.

Stanley stiffened. The cry had come from Alabaster, there was no doubt in his mind. His heart, already beating quickly, began to race, and presently the scene seemed to darken. He felt a furious need to save his friends, but also a helpless hopelessness; what could he do against a horde of bloodthirsty Saurians?

Why can't you do something? He demanded of himself. *Why are you always the one to stand there and watch while other people to everything? Why do you have to be so useless?*

He clenched his teeth, and felt every muscle in his body tense. A powerful, burning anger was building behind his eyes. But it didn't exactly feel like anger anymore, not quite. It felt like something else …

"*Bow before your holy emperor!*" roared the high priest, as Temoc watched the prisoners line up beside the stone altar. He briefly considered that it was strange the way such a nondescript piece of rock could evoke in him such a feeling of horror and revulsion, and then the Xol'tec emperor emerged from the temple. He was dressed magnificently in robes of red and green and yellow and blue. His arms and hands were covered in gold bracelets, bangles and rings, and a forest of gold chains and jeweled pendants hung about his neck and chest. His head was topped with a headdress of vibrantly colourful feathers, with a red jewel set in the middle above his forehead. It was much smaller than the one on the high priest's staff.

Temoc made a sour face as the emperor approached the altar and raised his arms in a gesture similar to the one the high priest had made earlier. Unlike the high priest, this 'emperor' evoked in Temoc only feelings of pitying disgust. This Saurian represented the pitiful, stunted remnant of a once-mighty and honourable people. Probably not even a direct member of the royal family, he would have been chosen by the high priest for his slow wit, his lack of imagination and ambition, and for his malleability. This so-called 'emperor' was nothing more than a puppet, and Temoc knew it; he had seen almost the exact same thing years earlier.

"*Beloved ones*," said the emperor in a simpering drawl, "*join me, join together, as we make peace with the great and merciful Blood Goddess!*"

A cheer rose up from the crowd, and the high priest struck the stone floor with the butt of his staff.

"*Let the blood of the female be spilt first!*" he growled, "*For it will be the sweetest!*"

"*Even if it* is *from a stinking ape*," said one of the other priests in an undertone, and several others laughed nastily.

Temoc and Blake tensed as one of the hooded, white-robed figures was untied and pulled out of the line. One of the other prisoners cried out, and Stanley's stomach dropped as he recognized Ryuno's voice.

"NO!" yelled the Marusai, "Take me! Take—"

CRACK

One of the feathered priests punched hard into the folds of the hood, and Ryuno's cries were abruptly silenced.

The other feathered priest brought the first prisoner up to the altar. Stanley's pulse pounded in his ears. He knew who this hooded person must be, but did not want to believe it.

The priest pulled back the hood. The light from the moons and the torches fell on a pale face topped with a dark mat of chestnut hair.

It was Nell.

Stanley caught the briefest glance of her face before the priest shoved her onto the altar. He'd almost cried out upon seeing her, having been unsure of her fate ever since the attack on the Empress Hildegarde. He had, in truth, feared that she was dead, but hadn't allowed himself to entertain the possibility. His relief at seeing her alive was short-lived, though.

A whole rainbow of emotions blazed through his heart all at once: he felt shock, surprise, elation, relief, happiness, and an odd burning in his chest that he couldn't quite identify … but these were followed by feelings of betrayal, injustice, and helplessness. Was he to learn that Nell was still alive, only to have to watch her die mere minutes later? And what of his other friends? Was the same true of them?

"It's not fair," he said to himself, although it sounded like a different voice.

His vision started to go cloudy, the whole scene growing darker and darker before his eyes. He felt as if he was going to pass out.

And then he remembered what Blake had told him:

If it happens again, focus it into your hands.

A light went on in Stanley's head. He understood, or at least thought he did.

Don't pass out, he told himself, shaking his head to try and clear it. *Focus it into your hands*, he recited in his head. *Into your hands …*

He held his hands up before his eyes. His vision had gone very dark and blurry.

Into your hands …

He felt the muscles in his hands clench almost painfully, and he screwed up his face in an expression of intense concentration. *Into your hands*, he kept saying to himself. All the anger and negativity he was feeling … he would put it in his hands, get it away from his mind, just like Blake had told him. He gritted his teeth and his hands began to shake.

"Into your hands," he almost growled, and his vision suddenly begin to clear. He could hear a strange rushing sound in his ears, as if a river were raging somewhere not far off. The scene grew brighter and brighter, clearer and clearer, but his hands seemed to be growing darker and darker and darker.

All at once, the rushing sound stopped, and he could see and hear everything clearly. He no longer felt like passing out, and his angry and negative feelings were all but gone, reduced to a vague heat in the back of his head. He looked at his hands again, and his eyes went wide.

There, in place of his own hands, seen clearly now for the first (but not last) time, was a pair of large, taloned paws, each as black as coal. He stared and stared at these monstrous appendages, half refusing to believe what his eyes were shouting at him as truth.

He flexed his fingers, and the black clawed fingers with their big bony knuckles flexed as well. He made a fist, and the black hand did the same.

"I did it," he said, rubbing the paws together and poking himself to test the sharpness of the claws. "I focused it into my hands ..."

All this happened quite quickly, but when Stanley turned to look for Blake, he was surprised to see that the priest and Temoc were no longer beside him. A tiny burst of panic lit up inside him, but he rationalized that they couldn't have gone far. It wasn't easy to locate his friends in the sea of black cloaks and hoods, but his gaze soon fell on two completely-covered priests standing just behind the Xol'tec emperor. They hadn't been there a moment ago, so they had to be Blake and Temoc. Picking up his walking stick in one clawed hand, Stanley slowly shuffled over to join them, his heart thundering in his chest.

Temoc had begun to slowly inch his way closer and closer to the high priest, with Blake close behind him. He thought it best if Stanley stayed put for now; the boy was brave and clever, but hardly a warrior in his own right. If things went badly, he, at least, might have a chance at escape.

Temoc's plan was to wait until the last possible second, and then take the high priest hostage. He wished he could have shared this plan with the others, but he'd only just thought of it, and to speak now in a foreign tongue, even in a whisper, was too risky. He hoped that Blake at least was ready for what was coming. The human priest was quick and wise, and most importantly, good in a fight—this Temoc had seen firsthand.

He glanced to his right and saw that Stanley had joined them. So be it. He slowly drew forth the curved sword concealed in his robes, and nodded briefly to Blake. It was almost time to strike.

The high priest had begun to speak again, hissing and spitting and growling at no one in particular. Stanley was breathing heavily; his mind was clear, but he still had no idea what they were going to do. Nell was lying face down on the altar while the high priest screeched out some Saurian diatribe. He needed to do something.

He looked down at his hands, and nodded to himself, his jaw set. He would probably have to use them as weapons.

The high priest finished speaking, and the entire city square went quiet. A faint, steady drum beat started up, and he drew forth a short, wicked-looking knife. The blade was curved like a sickle, and Stanley realized that it was made from a Saurian's big-toe-claw. It didn't take much imagination to guess what that knife was for.

Temoc recognized the sacrificial dagger before it was even fully free of the high priest's robes. The priest grabbed the girl by the hair and hauled her upwards. There were tears streaming down her cheeks, but her face was set, a mask of defiance, even in the face of death.

Temoc drew his sword and made a move. The high priest was oblivious to this, and opened his mouth to say something, perhaps a final, idiotic religious recitation, when a great shrieking cry split the silence from somewhere close by.

For an instant, Temoc, Blake, and Stanley thought they'd been found out, that all was up, and they were as good as dead.

Temoc wheeled around, ready for a savage, if brief fight to the death, but the one who had cried out, another priest, was not looking at him.

He was looking at Nell, staring wide-eyed and pointing with a shaking hand.

"*Look!*" shrieked the priest, though all Stanley heard was "*YEET!*"

"*Look! The sacrifice—she bears a* mark!"

A general murmur rose up among the priests. There were a few shouts of "*Mark? What mark?*"

The high priest dropped his knife, let go of Nell, and turned to face the others. His face was frozen with reptilian shock and surprise. He stood there for a moment, eyes wide and haunted, and said, in an almost dreamlike voice,

"*The mark … the red moon … the mark of the Blood Goddess!*"

All eyes locked on Nell, who looked about with wide eyes. There was a collective intake of breath, from Stanley, too, for he could see what had caused the priests' strange reaction.

Nell had an angry-looking wound on her face. It looked like a ragged cut or a bad burn, and, uncannily, it formed the shape of a crescent starting above her left eyebrow, curving towards her ear and ending below the eye. Being relatively close, Stanley could see that the crescent shape was actually made up of a series of smaller wounds, but it didn't take a very great stretch of the imagination to tell what it looked like.

"*The moon! The mark of the Blood Goddess!*" wailed one of the priests. "*We are damned! We cannot sacrifice one who is marked by the Goddess!*"

"*But she is one of the apes!*" said another.

"*It matters not,*" a third said grimly. "*A mark of the gods is a mark of the gods.*"

"*But there must be a sacrifice!*"

Down below, the citizens of Teno-Xol-Zan were sensing the confusion, and began to shift and mutter uneasily.

Blake and Stanley were poised, ready to spring into action, but Temoc stepped forward.

"*The ceremony must stop!*" he said in the Saurian language. "*The mark is a sign of our folly. There must be no sacrifice this night!*"

This was a huge gamble, but it could mean that they could get out of this without a fight.

"*What madness is this?*" yelled one of the priests.

"*We must stop the ceremony!*" cried another. "*Who knows what the Goddess will do if we harm those She has marked?*"

"*It is only the female who is marked,*" shouted the high priest. "*The rest must be sacrificed! The Goddess demands blood!*"

There was much nervous murmuring at this, and a few more cries to stop the ceremony. Seeing the dissent among the ranks of the priests, Temoc pressed his advantage.

"*The high priest is a fool and a fraud!*" he roared.

The high priest's eyes went wide, and he stared at Temoc as if he'd just slapped him.

"*He cannot hear the words of the Goddess,*" Temoc continued, "*He cannot even interpret so blatant a sign as the mark on this girl's face! He is a madman who knows nothing of the gods—he seeks only to further his own misguided plans!*"

"*You DARE—*" growled the high priest, but he was interrupted as several other priests cried out,

"*He disobeys the Goddess!*"

"*Depose him!*"

"*Kill him!*"

The emperor, looking worried and afraid, raised his arms and tried to call for quiet, but his reedy, whining voice was drowned out as the Xol'tec priesthood polarized into two squabbling factions: one supporting the high priest, and the other clamouring for his dismissal (at the very least).

It was bedlam atop the great pyramid, and the arguing priests began to fight with one another. Within the space of a minute, the top terrace was transformed into a miniature battlefield as the situation escalated into an all-out brawl. Priests were punching, scratching, and kicking each other, making liberal use of their wickedly-sharp toe-claws.

Temoc turned to Stanley and Blake. "This is our chance," he said loudly over the din of the fight raging around them. "Help me lead the rest of our companions out of here, and for the sun's sake, don't get in anyone's way."

Blake swiftly crossed the terrace and took hold of the rope connecting the line of prisoners, then tugged on it sharply, leading them towards the stairs.

Stanley helped Nell down off the altar, and, suddenly inspired, cut the ropes binding her wrists with the claw of his right index finger.

She rubbed her wrists briefly, staring at him with mild apprehension. He lifted his hood for a second so she could see his face. She looked immediately relieved, but still a bit nervous.

"Your hands," she whispered.

"I'll explain later," said Stanley, "we're getting out of here."

She took hold of his hand when he offered it, hesitating for only a moment before allowing him to lead her towards the stairs, as well.

"*Wait!*" roared Temoc. "This way! There is another stairway on the other side of the pyramid! Follow me!"

Stanley, Nell, and Blake followed, with their friends in tow. None of the battling priests paid them any heed as they skirted the edge of the terrace, and a few tense moments later, they found themselves at the rear of the temple building.

Temoc used his sword to cut everyone free. Slowly, they all drew back their hoods and stood there staring uncertainly at the three black-cloaked figures before them.

Stanley was sure he'd never felt more relieved. There was Alabaster, looking very confused and a bit frightened. Behind him stood Ryuno, looking grim and fierce, blood still flowing slowly from his nose where the priest had punched him. Algernon and Koko were here, as well, along with several members of the Empress Hildegarde's crew, including Mr. Grant.

"What is the beadig of this?" Ryuno said thickly.

"It's okay," said Stanley, pulling back his own hood, "It's us!"

Alabaster's face lit up. "Stanley!" he cried, and rushed towards his friend. He raised his hand for a high five, but stopped short as he caught sight of Stanley's monstrous black claws.

Alabaster gaped at them for a few seconds, then looked up and said, "Sweet claws. You okay?"

"Yeah," said Stanley, letting his hands drop to his sides. "You?"

Alabaster nodded. "Pretty good, I think," he said, smiling uncertainly. "You really stink," he added after a moment. Stanley grinned at him.

Meanwhile, Blake and Temoc had shed their own cloaks, and the crewmen from the Empress Hildegarde came forward to shake hands with both of them. They ignored Stanley, but he didn't really care. Algernon came over, apparently at a loss for words, and wrung Stanley's hand for a good thirty seconds before Koko gently placed a hand on his shoulder.

"R-R-really good to s-see you," Algernon managed. He turned away to talk to Koko, and Stanley, looking around for Nell, saw that Ryuno had already found his way over to her. He thought briefly that this should annoy him, but at this moment, he was so glad to see his friends again that nothing could ruin his good mood. Except, perhaps, for the next thing that Temoc said.

"We are not out of this yet," the Saurian said bluntly, and everyone turned to look at him, expressions of elation and relief vanishing from their faces.

"We have already lingered here too long. We still have to get off this pyramid, cross the square, and escape the city. If we move now, we may have a chance."

"But—" Ryuno began, but Temoc interrupted him.

"If you wish to live, then follow me, and say no more."

And with that, he threw his fetid cloak to the ground and started down the stairs. Stanley and Blake did the same, and the rest of the group followed silently.

There was no one waiting for them when they finally reached the base of the pyramid. The brawl on the top terrace had presumably ended; there were no more sounds from above, but even if there had been, they would have been drowned out by the clamour of the crowd on the other side of the city square.

This side, however, seemed to be empty. A wide, open section of cobbled stones spread out before them. Beyond this, a line of buildings rose up like a sudden miniature mountain range. The shadowy alleys between them spoke of safety and escape. If they could just get to that first line of buildings …

There was no one around. Now was as good a time as any. Temoc waved them all after him, and they started out across the square. The distance between the pyramid and the line of buildings seemed nightmarishly long.

They were more than half way across the square when a loud, screeching cry split the night from somewhere behind them. Stanley looked back and saw, high on the top terrace of the pyramid, the shape of the Xol'tec high priest, silhouetted against the red moon. The priest cried out again and raised his staff high over his head. Stanley had no idea what the high priest was saying, of course, but he could tell that the Saurian ruler was not pleased at seeing his prisoners fleeing across the square.

The high priest let out a series of barking coughs, and within seconds, a squad of Xol'tec warriors, fully armed and armoured, came racing around the southern side of the pyramid. Upon seeing Stanley and the others, they roared savagely and charged.

"MOVE!" Temoc yelled, "Don't stop! What are you doing? MOVE, I SAID!"

They all sprinted as fast as they could; they were a mere thirty yards from the edge of the square, but the Xol'tec warriors were very quick on their feet. Algernon stumbled, and Koko immediately grabbed him around the waist and hauled him onto his shoulder.

Stanley and Alabaster were decent runners, but were no match for a race of creatures whose ancestors had been the reptilian equivalent of cheetahs. Nell lagged behind slightly; she seemed to be having trouble running, but Ryuno had caught hold of her elbow, and was helping her along.

They reached the cover of the buildings with the Xol'tec warriors a mere twenty yards behind them. Stanley hung back as Blake and Temoc caught up with the rest of the group.

"FLEE!" roared Temoc, as he turned round and prepared to face the Xol'tecs singlehanded.

"No!" said Blake, "*You* run! You're no match for all of them, especially with your wounds! I'll handle them. GO!"

Temoc started to argue, but their time had run out. The Xol'tec warriors were mere paces away.

Blake turned to face them and swiftly raised his arms above his head. The Xol'tecs belted out a savage war cry and leapt at him, weapons held high for the killing blow.

But not a single sword or spear point touched him; an instant later, three of the Saurians were lying dazed on the ground, having crashed headlong into a wall of darkness that, until a few seconds ago, had not been there.

Stanley's jaw dropped. He had seen something like this before. Blake stood there, arms now at his sides, before the tall, translucent wall. It seemed to be made out of undulating black mist, but was as solid as stone; four more Xol'tecs bounced off it as they tried to charge through, and the rest were pounding futilely on it with their fists and the butts of their weapons. Arrows flew from Saurian bows, only to splinter harmlessly off the mysterious wall of darkness.

Stanley and Temoc gaped at Blake.

"What magic is this?" said Temoc sounding awed and maybe a little afraid.

"How did you do that?" Stanley demanded, stepping forward and pointing accusingly at Blake with a clawed finger.

Blake turned to face him, ignoring the Xol'tecs as they continued to attack the wall. "This is *not* a good time for questions," he said sharply. "I'll tell you whatever you want to hear once we're safely out of this city. I thought you two would be wise enough to appreciate the pointlessness of discussion at a time like this." He brushed past them, and added over his shoulder, "Come on. Our friends are waiting for us."

Stanley and Temoc glanced at each other, both feeling the slight sting of Blake's words, then silently followed him into the dark alley.

The wall of darkness dissolved twenty minutes later.

CHAPTER 15

WE'RE NOT OUT OF THE WOODS YET

They fled down the muddy, uneven path, splashing through puddles and stumbling over roots until they were all soaked, filthy, and sore. It was dark under the trees, and Stanley was only partially aware of the shadowy boughs as he jogged along behind Father Blake.

The jungle was alive with the shrieks and shouts of the Xol'tec Saurians; they were in the woods now, searching for their captives, and it was truly a terrifying thing to hear their harsh reptilian voices echoing among the trees. At times, their barks and roars sounded horribly close, as if an entire war party was mere paces behind; gradually, though, the voices faded into the distance.

The group had been jogging for quite some time, and they soon began to slow with fatigue. Up ahead, there was a loud *splash* and a groan from Alabaster. Stanley and Blake caught up with him a few seconds later, and found him crawling forward through the mud.

"Must—escape—lizards!" he gasped, dragging himself along the sodden path.

"Great scott, he's delirious," said Blake.

"No, he's just joking," said Stanley, as he leaned down to help his friend. "You okay, Alabaster?"

"Yeah ... little bit ... tired," puffed Alabaster as Stanley helped him to his feet.

Up ahead, the rest of the party had stopped and was meandering back up the path to see what was happening. Temoc came splashing up from somewhere behind them. He hardly seemed winded at all.

"Why have we stopped?" he demanded.

"We need to take a break," said Blake.

Temoc shook his head. "We are still too close to the city. We need to put some distance between ourselves and Teno-Xol-Zan. Their search parties will easily be able to reach this far in their sweeps."

"These people are tired," said Blake. "We can't just keep running, especially not while it's this dark. Best thing to do, I think, would be to find someplace close by to hide, at least until sunrise. I'm sure the Xol'tecs will be surprised and confused when the sun comes up despite the wrath of their *unappeased* goddess."

Temoc looked slightly stunned for a moment, and then his face lit up with an almost frightening grin. "Hss hss hss," he hissed, in what appeared to be the Saurian equivalent of laughter, "Of course! You are wise, indeed, *hass* Blake. They will get quite a shock when they see that the sun rises with or without their mad rituals." He composed himself instantly. "We are still not out of danger yet, though. Everyone, we must get off the path and find a sheltered place to hide. Follow me."

He waved them all after him, and disappeared into the bushes.

Soon after, Temoc called a halt. They had arrived at what seemed to be the base of a rocky hill.

"Pity that there is no cave here," muttered the Saurian.

There was, however, a huge overhanging stone that jutted out from the hill, which at least provided a dry spot upon which to sit.

Soon they were all huddled together under the overhang.

"M-my word it's ch-ch-chilly out here at night," Algernon managed through his chattering teeth.

"Can't we light a fire?" asked one of the riverboat crewmen.

"That would be very unwise," said Temoc. "Even if we did have dry kindling, the Xol'tec search parties would be upon us in an instant."

"Oh, er, right," said the crewman.

"Way to use the ol' noodle there, Donnie," said one of his mates.

"Brrr," said Algernon. He was shivering badly. Koko looked askance at him, then put a big hairy arm around him and clasped him firmly.

"Ack!" said Algernon. "Ahem! Th-thank you, Koko, that's better already."

"Don't mention it," muttered Koko.

Stanley grinned at the comic image, despite their situation. He was cold and his clothes were damp, but he was glad to be huddled in with his best friends on either side of him. He was acutely aware of Nell's arm pressed up against his. He glanced at her briefly and winced. Even in the pre-dawn gloom, the wound on her face was plain to see. She seemed to be sleeping, but then her eyes opened, and she met Stanley's gaze. She gave him a small smile, then said "Ow," and brought a hand up to her face.

"Are you okay?" Stanley asked lamely.

"Yeah," Nell said, a bit weakly.

"Does it hurt much?"

"M-hm." She closed her eyes again.

Stanley felt his face heating up. "Uh—sorry for the stupid questions!" He planned to shut his fool mouth then and there, but then Nell smiled and said,

"It's okay, they're not stupid." There was a pause, and Stanley nearly jumped up and cracked his head on the rock when Nell took hold of his hand.

"Your hands are back to normal," she said quietly, and they were. Not a trace of the big black talons remained.

"Huh," said Stanley.

Nell looked at him. "Can I put my head on your shoulder?"

Stanley's eyes widened. *Keep cool,* he told himself.

"Uh, y-yeah, go ahead," he said, and then cursed himself for making an unintentional joke.

Nell said nothing else, though, and soon she was sleeping peacefully again, her head resting on his shoulder. Stanley felt like a superhero. Or at least, an extraordinarily tired superhero.

"I must go and search the area," said Temoc to the group at large. "You," he said, pointing at Ryuno, "Will you accompany me?"

Ryuno looked up from where he was sitting. He had two black eyes and his nose was swollen and crusted with dried blood. "Pardon be?"

"You are a warrior, and familiar with life in the jungle, yes?" said Temoc.

"I ab Barusai," said Ryuno, sitting up straight and trying to look regal. His nose sounded completely stuffed, though, and ruined the effect. "I will accobady you." He got up, glanced back briefly at Nell, and graced Stanley with a fierce scowl before following Temoc out into the jungle while the Saurian began to explain Xol'tec tracking techniques.

"Hey, look," Alabaster said suddenly, "It's getting brighter! The sun's coming up!"

Sure enough, what little they could see of the sky was now a lighter shade of blue, with a faint purplish glow off to the east. The night was almost over.

Soon after, when the first hint of orange appeared in the eastern sky, a great cry went up from somewhere a long way off.

"Sounds like the Xol'tecs are having an interesting morning," said Blake. He glanced around at the others. Everyone else was sound asleep. He went over to Stanley and regarded him thoughtfully for a time. "It's always tiring at first," he murmured to himself. He frowned, then shook his head, and left the shelter of the overhang to wait for Temoc and Ryuno.

⋆ ⋆ ⋆

Stanley groaned and blearily opened his eyes. His whole body felt terribly stiff, and it took a few moments before his limbs would move properly. Nell was still fast asleep beside him, her head still resting on his shoulder. It seemed she hadn't moved at all during the night.

He and Nell were the only ones left under the rocky outcropping; everyone else was out in the clearing, which was now filled with sunlight. It looked to be late morning.

Temoc ducked his head under the overhang. He looked tired, but calm. "Good—you are awake," he said. "I was just coming to rouse you. We are moving out soon—wake your female."

"Okay," said Stanley, before realizing what Temoc had said. "What! Wait, I—I mean, she's—Uh," but Temoc was already gone.

Awake for barely three minutes and already feeling embarrassed, Stanley gently shook Nell's shoulder.

"Nell? Time to get up."

"Mnh?" Nell slowly raised her head and looked around sleepily. "What time is it?" she murmured.

"Dunno," said Stanley. "Still morning, I think."

"Hm," said Nell, rubbing her eyes. In daylight, the wound on her face looked much worse. The previously thin crescent was now very red and swollen, and the redness seemed to be spreading. She definitely looked the worse for their harrowing experience in the Xol'tec city; she hardly seemed able to stay awake, and her skin was pale and clammy, making the painful red of her wound even more vivid.

"Are you okay?" said Stanley.

Nell smiled weakly. "Yeah, I'm okay." Her voice was sounding more strained every time she spoke. "I think I'm just coming down with a cold. No big surprise after last night, huh?"

"Stanley!"

Stanley looked up and saw Blake waving at him. He wanted to stay and make sure Nell was alright, but when he turned back to her, she said,

"Go ahead, I'll be out in a minute."

Stanley nodded, then got up and went over the where Blake was standing.

"I hope I wasn't interrupting anything," he said as Stanley walked up.

"Huh? Oh, uh—nope," said Stanley.

"Well," said Blake, "Temoc says we've got to get moving soon, so I thought you might want to return these to their owner." He held out the two swords that Stanley had taken from the Xol'tec torture room.

Stanley looked at the swords, then over at Ryuno, who was seated apart from the rest of the group, looking morose.

"I think he'd be pleased to see them again," said Blake.

"Oh … yeah," said Stanley, remembering the way Ryuno had looked at him last night, "Um … maybe *you* should give them to him. I mean, you carried them all this way, and—"

Blake interrupted him. "But it was your idea, and you're the one who found them. Go on, give them, to him. I think you're the best person to do it."

Stanley hesitated. He half expected Ryuno to yell at him for one reason or another, but in this situation, he thought the young Marusai would forgive him for handling his swords. Besides, the whole reason he'd taken them in the first place, is that he thought Ryuno would be sad to lose them.

Finally he nodded, took the weapons from Blake, and set off across the clearing.

"Uh, Ryuno?" he said.

Ryuno looked up and Stanley gave a small start. The Marusai's face was practically one big bruise. Both his eyes were blackened, and his nose had become a swollen purple lump. It was clearly broken.

"Oh—Stadley," Ryuno said thickly, "whad is id? Dode led by abbearance alarb you—I look worse thad I feel."

"R-right," said Stanley. "Um, well, listen, back in the city there, I—"

Ryuno suddenly jumped to his feet. "Dell!" he exclaimed, and sprang forward, almost bowling Stanley over in the process.

Stanley whirled around and saw Nell lying on her back several feet away. Ryuno was already kneeling beside her, and Stanley felt a great chill pass through him.

"Omigosh! What happened?" he said as he ran over.

"She's faided," said Ryuno. He touched the side of her face, then quickly withdrew his hand. "She's withfever!" he exclaimed. "This girl is very sick! Sub-wud helb be here!"

His eyes locked on Stanley, and he scowled darkly. "Did you dot realize thad she had a fever?" he seethed.

Stanley had not expected this line of questioning, and was taken aback by Ryuno's sudden change in demeanor. Was he really angry?

"Um," said Stanley, "Well—"

"You were sittig by her the entire dight!" Ryuno said, his voice rising. "Could you dot feel the heat cobing off her? Could you dot tell she was *ill?"*

Stanley was at a loss. Nell had seemed a bit under the weather last night and this morning, but not sick to the point of passing out.

"She said she was okay—" he began.

"IDIOT!" roared Ryuno, cutting him off.

Stanley felt his whole body seize up; he couldn't think of a single thing to say.

"What's going on here?" said Blake, "Who's calling for help?"

Ryuno was frantic. "Dell has faided, and is ruddig a very high fever! We bust do subthig!"

Blake knelt down beside Nell and put a hand on her forehead. "Good lord, she's burning up."

"I didn't know!" said Stanley, "She seemed okay until she fainted!"

"It's okay, no one's blaming you," said Blake.

Stanley glanced at Ryuno and received a fierce frown for his trouble.

Nell stirred and her eyes fluttered open. She gave a small groan and squinted in the sunlight. "Wh-what?" she managed.

"Shh," said Ryuno. "Try dot to talk."

"That wound is looking pretty bad," said Blake. "It's probably infected—that would account for the fever. I think she's going to need medical attention."

"We are days away frub eddy settlebets!" said Ryuno. "We deed to do subthing *dow!*"

"As you *just said*, we're far from any settlements," Blake replied sharply, "And I can assure you that losing our heads and shrieking at each other will *not* help her."

Ryuno gaped at Blake as if he'd just struck him, then promptly shut his mouth.

"I'll talk to Temoc about finding some herbs that might help, but other than that, our goal should be to reach Daruna Abbey as soon as possible."

"Daruda Abbey?" echoed Ryuno, "How do we ged there frub here?"

"The first step will be getting back to the river. If we move out now, we should be able to get there before nightfall." Blake stood up and addressed the group at large. "Listen, everyone, we've got to get moving. Once we get to the river, we'll be able to—"

"The river?" interrupted crewman Grant of the Empress Hildegarde, "As in, the place where we got attacked by giant killer bugs?"

"The abbey is on the eastern side," said Blake. "Once we cross, it shouldn't take more than a full day's walk to get there."

"It'll be *zero* days walk for us if we get eaten by bugs," said Grant, the other crewmen chiming in to support him with a few *hear hears*. "You lot can do wat'cha like, but we're heading back to the port, right lads?"

"You will not make it," said Temoc. "It is at least a three day walk, and more than half that time, you would be going through Xol'tec territory."

"Yeah?" said Grant, "Well, I'd rather take my chances with the lizards than get eaten alive by a mess o' giant earwigs. For all we know, you could be a spy, and them Zotecs, or whatever you call 'em are your mates, waitin' to ambush us soon as we get back to the Armadon!"

Temoc let out a savage growl and sprang towards crewman Grant, who cried "Oy!" before falling on his backside. The Saurian dragged the man to his feet and snarled,

"If you were not as *ignorant* as I know you to be, I would *kill* you where you stand. If you do not wish to accompany us, then *go*. Confirm my suspicions that that you are a pack of fools, and go die in the jungle. You will not last a day, I promise you." He released Grant and went off to brood by a nearby tree.

Crewman Grant, visibly shaken but trying valiantly to hide it, said "I don't need this. C'mon lads, we make for Port Verdant. Leave this sorry lot to the bugs."

With that, the last members of the Empress Hildegarde's crew disappeared into the jungle. Their journey north would be far from pleasant.

* * *

Soon after, the remnants of the crippled expedition were moving along a narrow, overgrown path, heading southeast through the Verdurian jungle. Nell was in no condition to walk, so Temoc spent some time fashioning a crude travois out of sticks and vines. He pulled her along for a good while, until he collapsed on the path and could not get up again without help. The Saurian was exhausted, and his condition was aggravated by his hastily-bandaged wounds.

Temoc was soon able to walk again, but Blake refused to let him pull the travois.

Nell at first protested the idea of being pulled along like someone's luggage, but Blake gently assured her that she needed to rest as much as possible, and that the uneven ground of the jungle path was no place for someone with a high fever.

Temoc also assured her that in her weakened state, she was a much more attractive target for predators.

"Not quite sure where Temoc was going with that," said Alabaster as he and Stanley took their turn to pull the travois.

"Yeah," said Stanley distractedly. He was now more worried than ever about Nell's safety, and had come to terms with the fact that he would surely have to fling himself into the jaws of some giant jungle carnivore to protect her.

"Don't worry," said Blake, who was walking along a short distance behind them. "We're keeping an eye out."

Eventually, Ryuno wrested control of the travois from Stanley and Alabaster, claiming that they were being too rough with it. He pulled the device for the rest of the journey, but Stanley made sure to stay close the entire time.

Finally, as the afternoon sun began to sink low towards the western horizon, the beleaguered expedition reached the banks of the mighty Armadon River.

"Finally," said Blake as they all sat down to rest.

Ryuno laid down the travois and went to sit in the shade. Stanley sat down beside Nell, but was so tired he could barely sit up. Alabaster flopped down beside him.

"Ooh, my achin' feet," he groaned as he peeled off his shoes and socks. "Ugh. Blisters."

Alabaster's bare feet were covered in painful-looking blisters, some of which had burst, and begun to bleed.

Temoc came over to look at Alabaster's feet. "Your foot-pads seem inadequate for long journeys. Hold here for a moment." He got up and began to root around in the bushes beside the path.

"I probably couldn't get up if I wanted to," said Alabaster, "but it was nice of him to give me the illusion of choice!"

Stanley smiled at Alabaster's ability to remain affable even in the face of sore feet. "Want me to help you over to the water so you can soak your feet?"

"That would be ill-advised," said Temoc, hunkering down beside Alabaster. "It would be better not to tempt the river beasts with the scent of blood."

Stanley's and Alabaster's eyes widened.

"River beasts?" said Alabaster.

"What kind of river beasts?" asked Stanley.

"Various fish, reptiles, and parasites," said Temoc. "Let me see your feet." He took hold of Alabaster's right foot, and nodded. "Hold still."

The Saurian stuffed a handful of leafy green plants into his mouth, chewed briefly, then spat the masticated pulp all over Alabaster's foot.

"Gah!" cried Alabaster, reflexively yanking his foot away. Temoc instantly seized his ankle and began to rub the chewed plant matter into Alabaster's blisters.

"This is totally revolting!" said Alabaster, staring transfixed as Temoc worked. "I—I love it!"

"Hold still," growled the Saurian, now taking hold of Alabaster's left foot.

As a rule, Stanley wasn't easily grossed out, but it did sort of look like Temoc was throwing up on Alabaster's feet.

"Let that sit for a time," said Temoc. "Your feet will feel better soon. Just make sure not to wash them for at least five hours."

"Five hours!" echoed Alabaster. "You mean I have to put my shoes back on with my feet like *this?"*

"Obviously," said Temoc. "Now you," he said, turning to Stanley.

"Huh? Me?" said Stanley.

"Yes. Remove your footpads."

"Um, okay." Stanley took off his shoes and socks. Aside from being dirty and smelly, his feet were fine.

"Hm," said Temoc. "Good, yours are undamaged." He then moved on to Nell, who was resting peacefully on the travois nearby. Stanley turned to watch as Temoc begin to chew another handful of the green plant. The Saurian spat a bit of the pulp into his hand, and began to work it into the wound on Nell's face.

"What is that stuff?" asked Stanley.

"This plant is called *ko-toll*," said Temoc, spreading the green goo carefully over the fiery red wound. "It is used to make a strong healing salve. I would have preferred to apply it earlier, but it only grows close to water."

"Oh," said Stanley, feeling relieved. "So will that stuff—you know, cure her?"

"No," said Temoc. "It should slow the poison, but it will not be enough to purge it, especially after it has been left so long."

Stanley's relief evaporated instantly. All Temoc had done was delay the inevitable. He looked down at Nell's pale face. Her eyes had dark circles under them, and her lips were almost grey. He wished he could do something.

"Her survival now depends on speed," said Temoc. He clapped Stanley on the shoulder with a clawed hand. "Do not be discouraged, *hass* Stanley. My people are *built* for speed."

He got up and went over to speak to Blake, leaving Stanley to ponder his words.

Chapter 16

THE RIVER GOD

"Attention everyone," said Blake.

About a half hour had passed since they'd stopped to rest, and for most of that time, Blake and Temoc had been engaged in intense discussion, while Algernon hovered close by, trying to get his two cents in.

"Yes, ah, listen up everyone," Algernon said unnecessarily. Blake gave him a look.

"Right," said Blake. "We've decided that we need to keep moving."

"Staying the course," said Algernon.

"Er," said Blake, "Yes, we're continuing on in hopes of reaching Daruna Abbey tonight."

"As soon as possible," said Algernon.

"I just want everyone to know that we realize that night travel is not usually advisable in the jungle, but we have people who need medical attention, and another night out here followed by even more walking would be disastrous."

"Not a good idea," said Algernon.

"Rather than ford the river and walk the rest of the way, Temoc has opted to construct a raft which we will sail upriver to the abbey. They have a secure harbor, and this way, we won't get lost."

"It's a better option all around," said Algernon.

"Do not for an *instant* think that this will be an easy journey," said Temoc.

"Temoc," said Blake, "I don't think you need to—"

Temoc ignored him. "Travel in the jungle at night is a dangerous game. Many more predators are active at night, and the further south we go, the greater the danger will be."

"Temoc—"

"Rafting the river is completely different from riding in a great metal tub. Our chances of survival are low. In the likely event that we should fall beneath some beast's claws and fangs, I would strongly advise you all to die bravely, and with honour."

There was a brief silence as everyone stared wide-eyed at Temoc, and then Blake said,

"Thank you, Temoc, for your encouraging words."

The sarcasm was lost on the Saurian who said, "You are of course most welcome, all of you. Now, I need everyone of able body and sound mind to help construct our raft. Speak to me and I will assign you a task. Let us begin now!"

⋆ ⋆ ⋆

Temoc quickly explained his raft plan: A network of boughs would be lashed together with vines, and placed on top of a collection of floating deadwood. The whole thing sounded more than a bit ramshackle to Stanley, but then, he hadn't spent his life eking out an existence in a savagely dangerous jungle.

Stanley was assigned to accompany Temoc in finding dead logs. Algernon, too, had been given this task, and contributed by supplying an armload of twigs, which Temoc unceremoniously slapped out of his hands without a word.

Fortunately, Temoc knew exactly what they were looking for, and within three quarters of an hour they had dragged a fine collection of cork-like logs down to the water.

"I really do wish I could be of assistance" Alabaster drawled as Stanley hauled a cork-log almost as tall as he was out of the bushes.

"Th-thanks," grunted Stanley, "You're the greatest!"

Soon, all the vines, boughs, and logs were gathered on the river bank, and Temoc set about putting it all together. The bamboo-like green boughs were tied together with strong leathery vines. Stanley quickly became familiar with the figure-eight knot Temoc showed him, and finally, just as the sun disappeared behind the western treetops, the raft was set afloat on the mighty Armadon River.

Nell was carefully laid in the middle on her travois, and everyone else piled on, soaking their shoes and pant legs in the process.

"So much for not getting my feet wet," said Alabaster.

"Do not expect to stay dry on this journey," said Temoc, pushing off from the river bank with a long wooden stick.

"We'll cross the river and stay close to the eastern bank," said Blake, taking up a pole of his own. "The water is pretty deep around here, so we'll do our best to travel in the shallows whenever possible. Let's stay as quiet as possible, and be on the lookout."

"For what?" asked Stanley.

"Anything," said Temoc.

* * *

They crossed the river in less than half an hour, and began paddling southward when they were beneath the overhanging boughs of the eastern bank.

The raft, such as it was, had not been designed with comfort in mind, and its passengers were soon wet and miserable as it bobbed haphazardly in the current. The spot where Stanley was sitting kept dipping below the waterline, so he was thoroughly soaked from the waist down. He tried not to focus on his discomfort, and looked up at the darkening sky as a distraction.

The stars were coming out, and the reddish-purple glow of the setting sun was almost gone. The moons of Terra had begun to rise; the small blue moon had already cleared the treetops, and its green sister wasn't far behind. The large red moon wasn't yet visible, but thinking about it brought Stanley's mind back to Nell, and he tore his gaze away from the brilliant sky to look down at her sleeping face.

She'd been asleep most of the day, and the longer she slept, the more worried Stanley became. What if she never woke up again?

Alabaster interrupted his thoughts by saying

"Boy, do I ever have to go to the bathroom."

"How bad?" asked Stanley.

"Pretty bad," said Alabaster. "All this water isn't helping, either."

"It'd probably be best if you could hold it for a bit," said Blake.

"I don't think I can," said Alabaster. "Can't we pull over? I'll just go in the bushes."

Stanley peered into the dense, dark foliage of the nearby river bank. It didn't look like an easy place to stop the raft, let alone a safe one. Not far off, something roared savagely.

"Or maybe I'll try holding it," said Alabaster, as they all stared wide-eyed at the dark bank.

"For now, at least," said Blake. "Till we've put a bit of distance between us and whatever *that* was."

⋆ ⋆ ⋆

Almost an hour later, Blake piped up,

"Ah, look, there's a little beach—why don't we stop there so Alabaster can—er, do his business?"

"We are making excellent time," said Temoc. "I would prefer not to stop."

"Don't worry about me," said Alabaster. "I already went."

"*What?*" said Stanley, Blake, and Temoc in unison.

"I already went," repeated Alabaster. "When you gotta go, you gotta go."

"Er … oh," said Blake.

"Eew!" said Stanley, "I thought I *imagined* the water getting warmer!"

"What are you talking about?" said Temoc, turning around. "He went nowhere. He has been here the entire time."

"Er," said Blake, "*To go* is a euphemism for urination, Temoc."

Temoc's eyes widened and he rounded on Alabaster. "You made *tipli* here? Right in the river?"

"Nope," said Alabaster, "I made *pee.*"

"*Haaacch!*" snarled Temoc. "*Why would you mark territory out here? Who knows what it will attract?*"

"Attract?" said Stanley.

"Some creatures are attracted to the scent of tipli in the water," Temoc said in an exasperated tone.

"Well if I'd known *that* I wouldn't have gone," said Alabaster.

Stanley gave him a look.

"Okay okay, so maybe I would've," said Alabaster. "I'm sorry, I couldn't hold it anymore!"

"Well, nothing seems to have noticed us yet," said Blake.

Just as he spoke, there came a loud, gurgling groan from somewhere off to their right. Everyone froze.

"Wh-what was that?" whispered Algernon.

When no one answered, he repeated, "*What was that?*" a bit louder, and the groan sounded again.

"*Shud ub, for the sake of the gods,*" Ryuno whispered loudly.

Stanley's breath caught in his throat. The groaning sound had come from somewhere close by, probably from the river itself. It bore a disturbing similarity to the sounds made by the armour fish that had attacked Uncle Jack's ship last summer. If this thing wasn't an armour fish, it was probably just as big.

The groan came again, this time much closer, and was accompanied by the low splashing sound of something dipping stealthily beneath the water's surface. Stanley could have sworn he'd seen a flicker of movement less than ten yards away.

"Temoc," Blake said quietly, "There's something here …"

Temoc had been silent since the first groan, and seemed to have been frozen in place.

Something big brushed the raft, causing it to lurch ever so slightly. The thing, whatever it was, remained submerged, except for the tip of its tail, which broke the surface, showing a line of five wicked-looking spikes, each almost as long as Stanley's arm.

Temoc saw the spikes, too, and drew a sharp breath through his teeth.

"What is it?" Blake asked in an undertone.

"It is a *Shio-Khan,*" Temoc breathed. "A river-god."

"A god?" squeaked Algernon. "An actual *god?*"

"It might as well be," said Temoc, his voice shaking slightly. He drew a steadying breath. "A Shio-Khan is perhaps the largest, most dangerous creature in all of Verduria."

"Oh great," said Alabaster.

"It is a primordial thing," continued Temoc. "An unstoppable force of nature, like the storm and the tide. It is of the Earth itself; it is the will of the jungle made manifest."

"Temoc," said Blake, "I need to you tell us something that can *help* us."

"Forgive me," said the Saurian, "but there are no documented cases of anyone surviving a Shio-Khan attack."

The water off the raft's starboard side began to ripple ominously.

"We need to get to shore *now,*" said Blake, jabbing his wooden pole into the water and starting to paddle.

The pole was suddenly wrenched from his hands and pulled into the dark depths of the Armadon. Blake almost lost his balance and fell in, but Stanley grabbed hold of his coat tails, saving him from the titanic jaws that erupted from the water an instant later.

A cavernous, tooth-filled maw surged forward out of the churning river, unleashing a deafening roar accompanied by a horrendously-foul plume of fishy reek. Dark river water cascaded off of a reptilian head more than eight feet long and covered in bony, glistening scales.

Being an aficionado of all things prehistoric, Stanley was instantly reminded of Deinosuchus, a gigantic Cretaceous crocodile large enough to eat a Tyrannosaurus. This thing, this 'river-god', was much larger even than Earth's nightmarish 'Terrible Crocodile', and could have easily made a light snack of the eight puny morsels who had wandered into its territory, but just before the beast could clamp its jaws shut on the rickety little raft, Temoc drew a long knife from his belt and, bellowing a Saurian war cry, sprang forward, right into the titanic crocodile's gaping maw, plunging the knife into the beast's hard palate.

The behemoth stopped abruptly, mere inches from the raft, then reared up out of the water, letting out a long and terrible bellow of surprise and pain. It thrashed its head from side to side, trying mightily to dislodge Temoc from its jaws.

"Get to shore, all of you!" Blake ordered, as he drew his long black sword from inside his coat. Algernon obeyed instantly, flopping unceremoniously into the water and promptly sinking.

While Koko dove in to save Algernon, Ryuno hoisted Nell onto his shoulder and grabbed a nearby hanging vine, swinging deftly to shore.

"What about you?" cried Stanley, as Blake braced himself at the edge of the raft.

"I've got to help Temoc."

Just as Blake readied himself for a heroic leap into the fray, the river-god rolled on its side and lashed out with its long, spiked tail. Blake ducked as the tail swept the raft with a dire *whoosh*, but Stanley wasn't nearly as fast.

The tail struck him on the side of the head with enough force to lift him off his feet; he flew limply through the air and hit the water with a sharp *splash*, sinking almost immediately out of sight.

Crouching on the edge of the raft, Alabaster stared transfixed at the spot where Stanley had been only seconds before. He couldn't move. What had happened? Where was his friend? He felt something wet on his face, and when he reached up to touch it, his hand came away smeared with blood. The image of the tail hitting Stanley flashed through his mind.

"Come on," growled Blake, grabbing Alabaster by the back of his shirt and leaping from the raft, a split second before the river-god's tail came crashing down, obliterating the ramshackle little vessel.

They reached the river bank, and Blake hauled Alabaster out of the water.

Alabaster knew they were all in danger, but all he could seem to do was sit there and stare. There were things going on around him, but he couldn't focus on anything. He knew he should be feeling something, anything, but he seemed to have gone numb. The only thing he could see clearly was the image of Stanley's

(lifeless)

body falling into the river.

Stanley …

"STANLEY!" Alabaster suddenly cried, leaping to his feet. He tried to say more, but was instantly ill on the river bank. Blake put a hand on his shoulder.

The priest looked up as the river-god let out another earth-shaking roar. Temoc had escaped its jaws and was now swimming madly towards the shore. The beast was close behind him, and gaining fast. He wasn't going to make it.

"I'll be right back," Blake said to Alabaster, standing up and preparing to jump back into the river.

The monstrous crocodile was right behind Temoc now, its jaws gaping, ready to come crashing down on its prey.

Suddenly the river exploded as something came surging up from the murky depths. The something blasted out of the water in a herculean leap that carried it twenty feet through the air, to land on the river-god's fearsome head.

The thing was difficult to make out, since it was completely black, but its humanoid shape was revealed against the rising blue moon as it leapt through the air.

Temoc gained the bank and dragged himself out of the water gasping for breath, his bandages, now filthy and sodden, hanging off of him like clumps of grey seaweed. Mere metres away, the giant crocodile and the strange black thing from the river depths had become locked in a savage battle.

The black creature was raining blows on the river-god's scaly head, and tearing at its thick hide with knife-like claws. It also seemed to be trying to wrap long strands of itself around the giant crocodile, almost like a spider's web.

The river-god, meanwhile, was trying futilely to turn its head and bite the strange creature, thrashing madly in the dark water in an attempt to dislodge its attacker. The beast's spiked tail whipped through the air, but the black thing dodged the killer blows with preternatural agility.

The river-god's struggles grew feebler as the battle wore on, and it exercised its final advantage by diving beneath the surface.

The water churned and boiled as the two combatants continued their battle underwater, but abruptly, the disruption stopped.

Moments later, the still form of the colossal crocodile floated to the surface. The beast was dead.

Alabaster, Blake, and the others stared in stunned silence as the massive corpse was picked up by the current and carried slowly out of sight.

"Wh-what on earth *was* that?" Algernon whispered.

There was a sudden disturbance in the water near the bank, and the slayer of the river-god slowly clambered out onto the shore. The thing crawled forward a short distance, then collapsed.

They all stared down at the creature's prone form.

"Whad is id?" said Ryuno wonderingly. "Could id be … a debud?"

"I don't think it's a demon," said Blake. "Let's have a look here—"

"Take care," said Temoc, inching forward and sniffing tentatively at the creature. "You saw what it did to the Shio-khan."

"Yes, I did, thank you," Blake replied drily.

"Is it dead?" squeaked Algernon.

"No," said Blake, placing a hand on the thing's neck. "It's breathing, and I can feel a strong pulse here."

Alabaster shuffled over to get a better look.

The creature was jet-black all over, and its head and back seemed to be covered with sleek overlapping armour plates. It was lean but muscular, with large claws on its hands and feet. Alabaster stared long at the hands, then at the thing's face, which was mostly blank, lacking a visible nose or mouth. Blake carefully lifted one of the creature's eyelids, revealing a faintly-glowing, solid purple eye.

The thing was surprisingly reminiscent of Grey, if smaller and more bestial.

They all jumped back as it suddenly gave a violent twitch, and then, with a soft, and slightly wet bony creaking sound, seemed to shrink and dissolve. Pale, smooth skin began to show through the thick, leathery black hide. In a matter of seconds, the claws, armour plates, and corded muscle were gone, replaced by the form of a brown-haired, slightly skinny teenage boy.

It was Stanley.

Abyss

Stanley looked around and found himself surrounded by darkness.

Where am I? He wondered. *How did I get here?*

He thought for one panicked moment that he might be under water, but that couldn't be, since he was dry and able to breathe.

It was very dark here, wherever here was, but there seemed to be a faint blue light coming from somewhere. He listened for any sound that could give him a clue as to where he was, and thought he could hear muffled noises from far off, but they were soon gone, if they had ever been there at all.

Suddenly, Stanley felt very afraid. He sensed movement close by, and felt something drop into his pocket; it felt like a big marble. Pulling the object out, he was temporarily blinded by a bright golden light.

The light didn't penetrate very far into the surrounding blackness, but it lit the area enough for him to see the horror on the ground a few feet away.

Stanley screamed as he caught sight of the horror, and thought that he would surely go blind after seeing this awful, flailing, thrashing, twitching monstrosity.

It was huge, black and shapeless, seeming round and spherical one moment, then long and trunk-like the next. It would flatten out like a pool of tar, and then seem to burst into a million writhing maggots, only to reform a second later.

The thing's form and shape cannot be described, but there were legs, definitely, many legs and arms, clawed and multi-jointed, and tentacles, as well. In fact, it seemed as if the thing was trying to decide what sort of limbs it should have.

What frightened Stanley most about this apparition, were the eyes.

At first, the thing was covered with horrid, bulging, juicy glowing eyes, some red, some bright electric blue, some a vivid black-light purple. These eyes would disappear and reappear, staring at Stanley with indecipherable intent.

As he watched, the horrific thing seemed to grow smaller, and as it did, his fear seemed to diminish as well, until he was filled more with a vaguely repulsed curiosity than with outright terror. He was now looking at this creature the way he might look at a big weird bug. It had shrunk to the size of a large dog, and its twitching and flailing were growing feebler and feebler.

The thing seemed to have decided on purple as its eye colour, perhaps as a compromise between red and blue. It peered at him out of two baleful purple eyes, and reached out with a tentacle that turned into an arm.

Frankly, the thing looked tired.

"Er … what are you?" Stanley asked tentatively.

"Er … what are you?" the thing gasped back at him.

Stanley's eyes widened. "Hey! You're—have I seen you before?"

"Hey! You're—have I seen you before?" the thing repeated.

Stanley scratched his head. He'd definitely dreamed this before, hadn't he?

Experimentally, he said,

"Leave me alone."

"Alone," said the thing, now looking intently at him. "Not … alone."

"Not alone?" said Stanley, "What do you—"

"Stanley? Stanley, are you okay?"

It was Alabaster's voice. Stanley felt relief flood through him.

"Alabaster!" he cried, "Alabaster! I'm here! Can you see me?"

"Stanley!" said Alabaster's voice, "Wake up, you're having a nightmare."

"I am?" said Stanley, "but I'm not even asleep … am I?"

"Stanley," said the thing, "Wake up, you're having a nightmare."

"Maybe I *am* asleep," Stanley said aloud. "But if I am, how do I wake up?"

"Sta … nley," gasped the thing. "Night … mare …"

Suddenly a blinding white light shone down from above, and the next thing Stanley knew …

Chapter 17

DARUNA ABBEY

The light began to fade, and a large, blurry dark shape appeared. Stanley blinked a few times, and the shape came into focus.

It was a face.

It was Alabaster's face.

"Hey Stanley!" Alabaster said brightly as Stanley blinked dazedly.

It was a great relief to see his friend, but where was he?

"Hey Alabaster," Stanley managed. His entire body ached, and trying to sit up brought on such an intense wave of dizziness that he had to lie back down.

"Oof!" he said, flopping back onto his pillow. "I feel …"

"Awful? Horrible? Terrible?" said Alabaster.

"Yeah," said Stanley, smiling in spite of his condition. He looked down at the clean white linen of his bed, then at the small beeping box on the table beside him. "Is this a hospital?"

"Yes," said a voice that was not Alabaster's.

A pretty young woman in a long white robe and a hat that looked like a big folded napkin had entered the room. She walked up to Stanley's bed and said,

"How are you feeling this morning?"

"Uh," said Stanley, apparently at a loss for words as the woman gave him a dazzling smile.

"He's feeling pretty rough," said Alabaster, patting Stanley bracingly on the shoulder.

"Oh, that's too bad," said the woman. "Can I get you anything?"

Stanley was still trying to figure out just what he was doing here, and where *here* was, for that matter. "Sorry, but … er … where am I? What am I doing here? How did I get here?'

"Oh!" said the woman, "I'm sorry, I didn't realize—is this the first time you've been up?"

"Yeah!" said Alabaster. "He was asleep all yesterday. Boy, if I had a dollar for every time Stanley's fallen unconscious and woken up somewhere else …"

"Huh!" said the woman, "Nobody tells me anything around here. I'm sorry, Stanley, you must have a hundred questions. You're in the hospital wing of Daruna Abbey—I'm sure you've heard of the abbey if you've spent any time in Verduria. I'm Sister Marie, the head nurse. Well, I'm the *only* nurse, but … well, I also have a degree in history, but the nursing field just *called* to me, so I went back to school and …" She paused and cleared her throat. "And I'm rambling. Sorry. Stanley, you've been asleep since Monday night, when brothers Richard and Leon brought you and your friends to the abbey."

At the mention of *friends*, Stanley sat straight up.

"Are they okay? Are they here?" he asked, before falling back onto his pillow.

"Easy, try to stay calm," said Marie soothingly. "They're fine."

Stanley breathed a sigh of relief. Everyone was fine. He still had no idea what had occurred between Monday night and today, but at least his friends were safe.

"I have to go, but I'll be back in a little while," said Marie. "Try to get some rest, okay?"

"Okay," said Stanley, with a small nod.

"Can I stay?" asked Alabaster.

"I think we should leave him alone for a while," said Marie.

"Aww!" said Alabaster.

"I need to go down to the dispensary. Would you like to come with me? You could join me for lunch after."

"I'd love to!" exclaimed Alabaster, practically leaping up out of his chair.

Stanley looked on in amazement as Alabaster followed Marie towards the door, then turned around and mouthed the word *Hot* while fanning himself with his hand.

Just then, the door opened and Blake entered.

"Oh!" said Marie. "Father Blake! Hi! … I mean, *hello*, it's good to see you. Er, thank you for visiting the infirmary."

Blake smiled slightly and said, "Good to see you too, Marie. And please, call me Nigel."

"Oh, right, of course," said Marie, clearly flustered. "Sorry."

"Nothing to be sorry about," Blake said warmly.

Marie cleared her throat self-consciously. "Ahem! Er, well, I'm going down to get some lunch in a little bit, er, if you wanted to, ah—"

"We both are!" said Alabaster, leaning in and lightly tapping Blake with his elbow.

"Actually, I was hoping to have a word with Stanley, if that's alright," said Blake, raising an eyebrow at Alabaster. "Is he awake?"

"Oh, why, yes, he is," said Marie. "Ah …"

"I won't be too long," said Blake. "Hopefully I'll have time to come meet you downstairs after."

"Really? Well—Yes! Yes, that sounds great," said Marie. "Er, see you later, then!"

And with that she swept out of the room with Alabaster close behind her.

Blake approached Stanley's bedside and sat down in the chair vacated by Alabaster. "Glad to see you're finally awake," he said. "How are you feeling?"

"Tired," said Stanley. "Sore, stiff, headachy—"

"I won't keep you long," said Blake. "I just wanted to talk to you about what happened on the river."

"The river?" said Stanley.

"Yes," said Blake. "Do you remember any of it?"

"Um … I remember the raft … and the crocodile—"

"After that."

Stanley shook his head.

Blake sighed. "I'd better bring you up to speed."

He proceeded to relate the events and aftermath of the river-god's attack. Stanley's eyes grew wider and wider as Blake went on. It wasn't possible, was it? A savage blow to the head, a bizarre creature leaping from the river depths to attack the massive reptile …

A bizarre creature that was apparently *him*.

Blake was looking at him intently, his chin resting on his palm. "By all rights you should be dead," he said flatly. "I'm glad you're not, of course, but I need to know the reason."

Stanley was at a loss. "What *happened* to me?"

"I'm not entirely sure," said Blake, "but I have the beginnings of a theory. I've seen this sort of thing before."

"You have?" said Stanley. "When?"

Blake help up his hands, and an instant later they were replaced by a pair of now almost familiar black claws.

"Every time I look in the mirror. My office is on the fifth floor. Come see me when you're feeling better, will you?"

Stanley nodded.

"Good. Thank you. Sorry, this is just—well, this, ah, situation hits a bit close to home, if you catch my meaning. Get some rest. I'll see you later."

Blake got up and headed for the door. He paused and turned back to Stanley. "I'd appreciate it if this could remain between us for now," he said. "I mean, the others saw what happened, but they don't know the full extent of it. I'm not even sure *I* do."

Stanley nodded again. Apparently satisfied, Blake returned the nod and left the room.

"That was interesting," said a voice, making Stanley jump with surprise. He'd thought he was alone in here; Blake had obviously thought so, too.

This voice, though, was not at all unwelcome.

"Nell?" said Stanley, "Is that you? Are you alright?" His confusion and apprehension evapourated almost instantly, giving way to elated relief at knowing that she as finally safe. The curtains to Stanley's right parted, and there was Nell, propped up in the bed next to his. Stanley's mouth dropped open at the sight of her. She still looked pale and sickly, with a dark patch under her right eye. Her left eye was covered by a large square padded bandage held on by strips of surgical tape.

Stanley could barely speak. "Your eye—"

Nell gave him a small, tired smile. "Don't worry, it's still there. The doctors just bandaged me up after they cleaned out that acid burn on my face."

"Acid?" said Stanley, horrified at the prospect but relieved that nothing terrible had befallen her eye.

"They had another word for it," said Nell, settling back onto her pillow. "*Caustic bio-toxin*, or something. They said they'd never seen anything like it. It gave me a pretty bad infection, too. They've got me on all kinds of antibiotics … you know, you can push that little button on the side of your bed to prop it up."

"Huh?" said Stanley, still stuck on *caustic bio-toxin*.

"Like this," said Nell, smiling a bit more easily now as she demonstrated the wonders of the adjustable hospital bed.

"Oh!" said Stanley, finding the control button on his own bed. "Neat!"

Nell sat back and watched him fiddle with the control for a moment, then said,

"So it happened again, huh?"

"What?" said Stanley, finally easing himself up into a sitting position.

Nell was looking at him intently. Her smile had faded. "You lost control again. Of … whatever it is. Your *power*."

Power.

Stanley looked down at his hands as the word resounded in his mind. Up until now, he hadn't thought about it that way, had, in fact, been for the most part in denial about the possibility of anything being at all amiss.

But no, there was obviously something to all of this. He'd seen the claws enough times, and for an extended period not so long ago.

He looked up to see Nell watching him.

"Alabaster told me what happened," she said quietly. "It shook him up pretty badly."

Stanley was silent for a moment. Anything that could shake Alabaster must have been horrific, indeed.

"You really don't remember anything?"

"No," said Stanley. "It's like I wasn't even there."

Nell nodded and looked away. "I'm sorry, I'm not trying to pester you or anything. It's just so hard to believe … I wasn't *all there*, either." She looked back at him and smiled. "I'm just glad you're okay."

"Zguh!" said Stanley. "Uh, me too. I mean, I'm glad *you're* okay, too. Really glad." His face suddenly felt like it was on fire.

Nell's smile widened. "I'm still pretty tired," she said. "I'm gonna go back to sleep. Feel better!"

"You too," Stanley managed, as Nell closed the curtain. She settled back into her bed while Stanley silently cursed himself for being a tongue-tied babbling idiot.

Nell fell asleep almost immediately, but Stanley spent a good half hour frantically wondering how much of an idiot he'd just made of himself, and whether or not Nell had gone back to sleep because she was unbearably annoyed by his lack of verbal tact.

Finally, he managed to convince himself, with ninety percent surety, that she had indeed just been tired, and did not think that he was a complete buffoon.

With that settled, Stanley was free to ruminate on the implications of the past few days' events. His mind began to spin with questions. Did he really have some kind of superhuman power? Did such a thing even exist? Could he really be sure of what did and did not exist anymore?

And where on earth could such powers come from? He was an ordinary kid from East Stodgerton, for goodness' sake.

Or was he?

Loud though the clamouring thoughts in his head were, Stanley soon fell asleep himself.

His questions, for the moment, would have to remain unanswered.

* * *

Stanley woke later that evening from his first untroubled sleep in a long while. He stretched, sat up without difficulty, and looked up at the clock on the wall. It was a quarter past seven. The deep orange rays of the setting sun were floating tiredly in through the tall windows in the western wall, and Stanley, not feeling the least bit tired, threw off his covers and jumped out of bed.

His bare feet hit the cold stone floor, and he realized that he had no clothes aside from the pajamas he was wearing. He did a quick search of his surroundings, but his clothes were nowhere to be found.

He had just sat down to think about where they might be, when the door swung open and in came Sister Marie, holding a big tray with two covered plates on it.

"Oh, hello," she said pleasantly. "I didn't know if you'd be awake yet. Good timing, though—care for some dinner?"

"Dinner?" echoed Stanley. The word sounded almost alien to him; it seemed like ages since he'd had anything even closely resembling *dinner*. "Uh, yes, please! Thank you!"

Marie set one of the plates down on Stanley's bedside table and went to check on Nell.

Stanley lifted the cover and was almost overwhelmed by the delicious smells that wafted out.

Dinner consisted of a pile of flat, leafy vegetables which took up half the plate, a warm buttered bun, and a big slice of ham-like meat. The meat was a bit tough (it was Gorethane, as it turned out), but Stanley didn't even notice, and wolfed the whole thing down in three bites. He wasn't sure if he'd ever been hungrier, and had polished off the entire plate by the time Sister Marie came back from checking on Nell.

"Someone was hungry," she said with a small giggle.

Stanley cleared his throat self-consciously.

"Nell's still asleep, so I just left her food for when she wakes up," said Marie as she gathered up Stanley's cutlery. "Poor thing. She'll need a lot of rest for the next little while."

"How is she?" Stanley asked quickly. "I mean, I talked to her a bit earlier, but—"

Marie smiled. "She'll be fine. Her fever's gone, so right now she just needs to sleep." She reached down and picked up a small pile of clothes from the foot of Stanley's bed. "You, on the other hand, look ready to be released. These are for you."

She placed the clothes at Stanley's feet and started towards the door. "You're welcome to take a look around the abbey, if you like—not much goes on around here at night though. A few areas are off limits to visitors, but they're locked anyway. I think you're staying in one of the guest rooms on the fifth floor. Oh, and Ni—ah, Father Blake wanted you to come see him as soon as you were up. I'll take you up there once you're dressed."

"Oh, yeah—okay, thanks," said Stanley.

Sister Marie waited outside while Stanley got out of his pajamas and into the jeans, plaid button-up, and hiking boots that she'd brought him. For borrowed clothes, they fit surprisingly well.

Out in the hall, Stanley said,

"Er, Sister Marie—"

"Just Marie is fine," she said with a smile.

"Oh, uh, okay," said Stanley. "I just had a question."

"Ask me anything," said Marie.

"Well, this might sound weird, but—do you know how I got here? I mean, I don't think I was awake when we all arrived, so …"

"That's true," said Marie. "You and Nell were both unconscious. We were all really worried. It was lucky Brother Richard found you. He was out on patrol in the Monitor, and picked you and your friends up. Kind of miraculous when you think about it."

"What's the Monitor?" asked Stanley.

Marie cleared her throat. "It's an armoured battleship from—er, Azuria, and we're not … exactly supposed to *have* it, but the way things are in the jungle these days, it's the only way to get around. Brother Richard converted it into more of a science vessel, which makes me feel a bit better about having it around." Marie paused and laughed nervously. "Goodness, I talk *way* too much. The abbot wouldn't be too pleased if he knew I was blabbing about the Monitor to visitors!"

"I won't tell anyone," Stanley assured her.

"It's not a big deal," said Marie. "After all, you were all on board for a good hour or so."

As they walked, Marie told Stanley a bit about the history of Daruna Abbey. Apparently it hadn't always been a monastery; the abbey itself used to be a fortress, and though it was a very old building in its own right, it had been built on top of the remains of an even older structure.

"There's a huge underground complex beneath us," said Marie. "No one ever goes down there, though. I think it was mostly filled in when the abbey was built."

"Didn't anyone want to explore it?" asked Stanly, thinking of how Alabaster's parents would have felt at the discovery of some ancient ruin, especially one on another world.

"Oh, sure. And they did," said Marie. "At least, as much as they could. As far as I know, most of the artifacts found down there were sent back to Azuria. That's where the original survey team was from."

"What *is* Azuria?" Stanley asked.

"You've never heard of it?" said Marie.

"Er, no," said Stanley.

Marie *hmmd*. "Well, I guess that's not too surprising. Azuria isn't really a place you can easily visit."

"It's a country?"

"Yes … but it's also a city. And a continent. They call it the 'continent that never sleeps'. They've got the most advanced technology in the world, but they're very isolationist. It's almost impossible to get in or out, and they don't accept many visitors."

Stanley pondered Marie's words. Not even Uncle Jack had ever said anything about Azuria, and he'd been all over the world.

"They've got all sorts of things in place to keep outsiders out," Marie went on. "Many of us here are *from* there, in fact. That's why we have so much advanced medical equipment. Er—don't go spreading *that* around, either. Ah, here we are!"

By now they had reached a door at the end of a mostly-empty hallway. Marie took a deep breath. "I'll just knock and see if he's in." She cleared her throat self-consciously.

"Sure," said Stanley, not quite sure why she was telling him this.

She paused for a moment, then knocked smartly on the wooden door.

"Yes, come in," came Blake's voice from the room beyond.

Marie grinned at Staley, then opened the door and led the way in.

The room beyond was more like a library or a museum than an office. Bookshelves lined the walls, and much of the floor space was occupied by stacks of books, piles of papers and boxes, and heaps upon heaps of what could only be classified as *junk*.

Amidst the junk, though, were many interesting artifacts; Stanley marveled at a massive antique globe similar to the one at Uncle Jack's house; this one, however, obviously depicted Terra, as it included models of the three moons, which were slowly orbiting the miniature planet. Amazingly, the moons did not appear to be attached to the globe.

Towards the back, near the room's only window, was a colossal wooden desk heaped high with books and papers. Seated behind the desk with three ancient-looking volumes open before him, was Blake.

"Good evening, Father Blake," said Marie, sounding a tad breathless as she entered the room.

"Hello Marie," said Blake, setting his pen down and looking up from his work. "How are you?"

"Oh, fine, thank you," said Marie.

Blake smiled uncertainly at her. "Er, what can I do for you?"

"Hm?" said Marie, sounding a bit dazed. "Oh! Ah, no, I just, er, brought Stanley up to see you—"

Stanley, who had been hovering uncertainly in the doorway, took a few steps into the room.

"Stanley!" said Blake, his face brightening, "Excellent, glad to see you up and about. Come in, come in and have a seat." He waved Stanley towards a stout wooden chair in front of the desk. Stanley came forward and sat down while Blake spent another minute or so writing furiously on a sheet of paper.

"There," he said with finality, setting down his pen and shifting a pile of books so he could talk to Stanley. "Now—er—" he paused, and Stanley realized that Marie was still standing behind him.

"I'm sorry Marie, was there anything else you needed?" Blake asked her.

"Hm?" said Marie, sounding again like she was being roused from a deep daydream. "Uh! No, sorry, I just—um—nothing! No problem, I'll just, ah, head back down to the infirmary."

"Er, alright," said Blake. "Would you mind closing the door on your way out?"

Marie straightened her back and cleared her throat. When she spoke again, her tone was much more formal. "Certainly. Good evening, Father Blake."

"Nigel," said Blake, as she turned to leave.

"Pardon?" said Marie, looking back at him questioningly.

"Nigel is fine," said Blake. "You can call me Nigel. Remember?"

Marie smiled uncertainly, then hurried out of the room, forgetting to shut the door behind her.

It was Blake's turn to look a bit dazed. "So," he said after she'd left, "how are you?"

"Fine," said Stanley with a shrug.

"Well, that's good news, at least," said Blake, "even if it *is* only half-true."

"Huh?" said Stanley.

Blake smiled. "What I mean is, you're obviously feeling better, but I can tell that the events of the past week or so have weighed heavily on you. At the very least, you must have a lot of questions."

He got up from his desk and picked up one of the ancient-looking books he'd been reading. "I've been doing a lot of research while you were in the infirmary," he went on, pacing back and forth as he flipped through the stiff parchment pages.

"Based on what I already know, I'd say, right off the bat, that you, Stanley, possess the power to manipulate shadows and darkness—in short, the powers of a Shadow Lord."

Stanley stared. Whatever he might have expected Blake to say next, this wasn't it.

"The Shadow Lords," Blake went on, "were the masters of the Shadow *Legion,* a race of creatures said to have existed eons ago, before the sun came into being."

He held the book out for Stanley to see. The pages were obviously very old, and seemed to have been written by hand. The text was some sort of spidery runic language that Stanley couldn't identify if his life depended on it, but there were also drawings interspersed with the text.

These seemed to depict an array of strange creatures, all coloured completely black. Much of the alien menagerie resembled terrestrial animals, but some, including what appeared to be a blob covered with eyes, were bizarre in shape, and bordering on grotesque. Turning the pages, Stanley was confronted with a familiar image.

"Grey," he murmured.

"Hm," said Blake, "There were—according to legend, of course—a great many humanoid members of the Shadow Legion. Some were apparently human at one time … men and women who gave themselves over to darkness."

The archaic sketch depicted a tall, black, hairless humanoid form with no visible nose, mouth, or ears. It appeared to be clad in a suit of plate armour.

"There *is* a striking resemblance," said Blake. "Although if your friend were a real shadow legionnaire, I doubt if he'd be able to survive in sunlight. I would've liked to have had a chat with him. Did he ever tell you anything about himself?"

"Not really, no," said Stanley. "He doesn't really like to talk about himself. Or *anything*, actually."

"Well, that's fine," said Blake. "His story can wait for another day."

Stanley continued to flip through the ancient book.

"It's said the Shadow Legion was the world's first race," said Blake, consulting his notes. "They were rulers of the planet—their empire spanned the globe for … well, a mind-bogglingly long time."

Stanley was only half listening, so enthralled was he by the astonishing array of creatures that appeared before him with every turn of the page. Was Grey a member of this ancient race?

"We can leave the history of the Shadow Legion for another time," said Blake, taking back the book. "It's all myth and legend, anyway—you won't find too many people these days who know about it. I'm actually almost done working on a Rheddish translation of it, if you'd like to have a look. It's a fascinating read."

"Oh, uh, sure, thanks," said Stanley.

"Now," said Blake, "What I'm most concerned with at the moment, is *you*." He sat back down at his desk and put his hands together, thoughtfully regarding Stanley over his steepled fingers. "To put things simply, you have extraordinary powers. I've seen them manifest themselves enough times to know what they are, and, as you now know, I've had enough experience of my own to recognize them in others.

"Essentially," Blake went on, "I have two goals. First, I want to train you in the use and control of your abilities."

"Train me?" Stanley echoed.

"Yes," said Blake. "I've seen your shadow powers in use three times, the third being some sort of full-form corporeal manifestation … but a manifestation of what, I'm not sure … which brings me to my second goal, which, I think, would benefit both of us. I want to understand your powers, Stanley, and by doing so … hopefully understand my own."

Stanley could still scarcely believe that any of this could be real. Blake had to be mistaken. How could Stanley Brambles, an ordinary kid from East Stodgerton, have the powers Blake was talking about? Where would he have gotten them in the first place?

"But," said Stanley, "I don't—I mean, why—"

"Breathe," said Blake.

Stanley took a breath. "I can't really have these—magic powers. I'm just a regular, ordinary person, I—"

"Firstly, they aren't magic," said Blake, cutting him off. "Far from it. And secondly, you're *not* ordinary. Why do you say that? Because someone *said* you were? Because events in your life have led you to believe that you're unimportant and easily overlooked?"

Stanley said nothing.

"Trust me," said Blake, "you are an extraordinary individual. As are all people in their own way. Now, bearing that in mind, watch this."

Blake suddenly leapt up from his desk and thrust his right hand towards the ceiling. A split-second later, the hand was clasping the hilt of a long black sword that hadn't been there a moment ago. He swung the sword deftly from side to side, parrying the attacks of an imaginary foe, then finished with a strong upward swing.

"Shadow sword," said Blake. "Sword of Darkness, Umbral Blade—there are lots of names for it." He presented the sword for Stanley to examine.

Stanley had seen Blake use this sword a number of times. The jet-black blade was completely matte. It was cool to the touch, but felt more like stone than metal.

"What's it made of?"

"Shadowmass," said Blake as Stanley ran his fingers along the blade. "*Dark Matter* is the more modern word for it, I think. Pure darkness—careful, it's exceedingly sharp."

Just as Blake finished speaking, Stanley caught the side of his thumb on the blade's edge.

"Ow!" he exclaimed, yanking his hand away and cradling the wounded digit. A thin stream of blood issued from the cut.

"Not to worry," said Blake. "Keep an eye on that cut."

Stanley looked closely at his thumb, and his jaw dropped open in amazement as the wound promptly stopped bleeding and proceeded to close itself. In a matter of seconds, all that was left was a barely-noticeable line of new, pink skin.

For several long moments, all he could do was stare at the place where the wound had been. He looked up at Blake, who nodded shortly and said,

"Greatly-accelerated tissue regeneration. I'm sure you already suspected as much."

Stanley couldn't decide which was more incredible—the super-fast healing or the ridiculously-sharp sword that had appeared from nowhere.

"Pure darkness—*true* darkness isn't just an absence of light," said Blake, turning the sword slowly in his hand. "It's a real, tangible material. Just about anything that has *mass* also has shadowmass. It's usually not visible to humans, since our vision is based on light. One aspect of your power, like mine, is the ability to concentrate and project this mass into physical form. For example, I've seen you project your shadowmass into claws a couple of times."

Stanley nodded.

"Claws are a very basic and primal weapon," said Blake, casually changing his hand into a black, taloned paw. "I'm not surprised that it was your first successful projection."

Stanley looked down at his own hands, half expecting them to suddenly change shape. "Can you do it whenever you want?" he asked.

"Generally, yes," said Blake, as his claw dissolved back into a normal hand. "You'll be able to do it, too, with practice."

"It only seems to happen when I don't want it to," said Stanley.

"I think your abilities are triggered by emotion," said Blake. "Most likely strong negative ones—anger, fear, anxiety … you were clearly afraid during the attack on the riverboat—and you went into a bit of a rage when the captain accidentally injured your friend."

Stanley remembered the attack, but the events afterward were still blurry and half-formed in his mind. "I can't remember what happened," he said. He found the lapses in memory more worrisome than the fact that he had the ability to spawn savage, rending claws out of thin air.

"I know," said Blake. "I've been thinking about that, and I have a theory. I suspect that for some reason, your powers are much more 'active' than any case I've seen before."

Stanley briefly wondered exactly *how many* cases Blake had seen.

"Judging from the incident on the river with the Shio-Kahn, I'd almost go so far as to suggest that your shadowmass has a mind of its own. Very peculiar."

This didn't sound like good news to Stanley.

"While I doubt your powers can be called a secondary entity, I *do* think they may be incredibly strong—so strong that when they activate fully, you lose consciousness, and your base emotions take over. This would mean that if you get angry, you might lose control and become very violent."

"No!" said Stanley. "That's—I don't want that, *at all*. I already hurt someone that way. It was a bully at school, and, I mean, I don't like him, but I can't go around clawing people—"

Blake raised an eyebrow. "So this goes back further than I thought. I didn't realize this had happened before I met you."

"It was probably a couple weeks ago," said Stanley. "Till now I thought I must've imagined it, but—now I know is was … me."

The notion that he, Stanley, was truly responsible for Danny Briggs' injury was very unsettling. It gave him a horrible feeling in the pit of his stomach.

"I—I don't want it," said Stanley, his voice rising. "There's got to be a way to get rid of it—I can't keep it, I can't—"

Blake reached out and gripped his shoulder firmly. "There's no getting rid of it, Stanley. I'm afraid this is just something you're going to have to learn to live with. I can help with that."

"NO!" Stanley suddenly yelled, wrenching his shoulder free, "I don't want to hurt anyone! I don't *want* swords and claws! GET IT OUT OF ME!"

Stanley's voice had almost turned into a snarl as he raged at Blake. Vaguely, he was aware that his outburst seemed mostly unwarranted, but it was getting harder and harder to think clearly. It felt as if a fire was starting inside him, threatening to explode out of him at any moment. He doubled over in sudden agony, sure that his chest was about to split in two.

Blake's voice suddenly cut through his thoughts.

"Remember what I told you," he said sternly. "Focus it into your hands—get it away from your mind. Just like last time."

"*Rrrrg,*" said Stanley. He remembered Blake giving him this advice back in the Saurian city, and tried desperately to repeat the process. As before, he held his hands up in front of his face, his entire body shaking with undue wrath, and willed all his anger to flow into his clenched fists.

It happened much more quickly this time; the boiling, burning feeling in his chest and skull just seemed to melt away, running down through his body and along his arms. Seconds later, his mind was clear, and his hands were claws.

"Well done," said Blake, as Stanley slowly straightened up, breathing heavily.

"S-sorry," Stanley gasped, "For … yelling like that."

"Don't worry about it," said Blake with a smile. "It was an emotional trigger—not your fault. I think the unusual nature of your powers makes you much more susceptible to bouts of anger. Your powers want to come out and do their job—they want to work, and if they're activated by your anger, then *part* of the job is to make you as angry as possible."

The situation was still sounding less than ideal to Stanley.

"I don't want to get angry like that," he said, experimentally flexing his talons.

"No, of course not," said Blake. "And that's why you'll learn to control yourself. Eventually you won't even have to struggle like this—you'll be able to internalize the whole thing, deal with it by reflex. Then, you'll just get angry the way you usually do—no more losing your head. And you'll be manifesting claws and swords on your terms. Speaking of which, let's turn those claws into something else, shall we?"

"Er—how?" said Stanley.

"Think of the shadowmass as clay," said Blake. "You just need to concentrate, visualize the form you want it to take. You can shape it any way you want."

Stanley stared at his claws. He tried to concentrate on a sword, like Blake's.

Nothing happened.

"I just … think of something?"

"Yes," said Blake, "but it's also an act of will. You can think about making a fist, but nothing will happen if you don't actually *do* it."

Stanley tried to concentrate harder, willing the blackness to change, but his claws didn't so much as twitch.

"You need to accept that the shadowmass is an extension of your body," said Blake, starting to pace back and forth. "Try something a bit simpler: make the claws longer."

"Longer?" Stanley repeated.

"Yes, just grow them," said Blake.

Almost instantly, the already impressive claws grew at least three inches.

"Whoa!" said Stanley. It was a strange sensation, as if his fingers were being sucked into a vacuum cleaner.

"There you go!" said Blake, beaming. "You did it."

Stanley gaped at his claws in amazement. "I—just thought about it—it's like the picture in my mind was happening."

"That's pretty much it," said Blake. "It's as simple as willing it to happen. Once you're used to it, you'll wonder how you ever had trouble with it. It's like learning to whistle."

Stanley clenched and unclenched his fingers, wondering just how long his claws could grow. He focused his thoughts, and was delighted to see the claws grow another few inches. The longer they grew, though, the more difficult it became.

"Don't strain yourself," said Blake. "Shadow powers have limits, just like anything else."

Stanley relaxed, and the claws dissolved almost instantly.

"Oops!" he said, looking at his hands in surprise.

"Not to worry," said Blake. "This is a good point to stop, anyway."

Stanley suddenly felt lightheaded, and stumbled backward, nearly falling flat on his back.

"Careful," said Blake, darting forward and grabbing hold of Stanley's arm to steady him. "Are you alright?"

"Yeah," said Stanley a bit listlessly, "I just suddenly felt … really tired."

"Take a seat," said Blake, guiding him back to the chair in front of his desk. "You're just not used to controlling your powers. You'll develop your endurance as you go. This is just a muscle you're not used to using."

Stanley leaned back in his chair and closed his eyes. He had a headache, and it felt as if the room was spinning around him.

"I'd like you to be in complete control of your powers as soon as possible," said Blake. "My plan is for training sessions every day, for at least an hour, probably more."

"Every day?" said Stanley.

"It's important," said Blake. "The last thing you want is another episode like the Shio-Kahn."

Or Danny Briggs, Stanley thought to himself.

"Tomorrow we'll work on manifesting your power at will—you need to be able to do it without the emotional trigger, and once you're able to do *that,* you can start practising."

Stanley took a deep breath. This sounded like a lot of work.

"Now, *before* tomorrow evening, I'd like you to do some heavy thinking," said Blake. "Think about how long you've had these powers, and any incidents over that period when they may have activated. Have you had them all your life, or are they a more recent development? We'll talk about it tomorrow. How do you feel?"

"Tired ... but better," said Stanley.

"Good," said Blake. "In that case you're dismissed. I'll see you back here tomorrow evening at, say, seven o'clock?"

"Sure," said Stanley, getting up from his chair.

"Alright. See you then." Blake picked up his pen and returned to his research. Stanley, feeling a tad awkward at this abrupt dismissal, paused on his way out the door.

"Er—Father Blake—" he said, turning back towards the huge desk.

"Just Blake is fine," said Blake, looking up from his books. "D'you have a question?"

"Yeah," said Stanley. "I was just wondering—where did you get *your* powers?"

Blake was silent for several moments. "I was born with them," he said simply.

"Did—I mean, how old were you when—"

"I could use them from birth," said Blake.

"Oh," said Stanley. "Okay. Well—goodnight."

"Goodnight," said Blake.

Stanley let himself out into the hall and closed the door behind him. It was surprisingly dark out here—it seemed odd that the hallway lights would be turned off, as it wasn't even nine o'clock yet.

The huge windows let in enough moonlight from outside to see, but the effect of the ghostly blue outdoors glow on the old gothic architecture was a bit unsettling. Stanley walked over to one of the windows and peered outside.

The window looked eastward down over the abbey's grounds. Stanley could see a wide, open courtyard which ran from the main building to a tall stone wall that encircled the property. Beyond the wall loomed the jungle, a shapeless, leafy mass of shadow. Near the horizon, the blue moon, full and bright, cast its glow over the treetops and bathed the courtyard in a cool light.

Something down in the courtyard caught his eye. Had something moved down there? Maybe someone was out for a night walk. Stanley was just about to turn away from the window when he saw it again. He watched as a pale figure stepped out from the shadows near the outer wall. It looked like a person, but it was impossible to tell who it could be. Whoever it was seemed to be dressed in some kind of tattered robe that blew raggedly in the night wind.

There was something strange about this figure, but Stanley's attention was suddenly captured by the sound of movement behind him. He whirled around, heart racing, and scanned the shadowy hallway.

"Hello?" he said, not sounding particularly brave. He was aware of an odd sensation throughout his body, as if an undulating force was radiating out from his head and chest, and flowing out through his limbs. His lightheadedness returned, and he realized what was happening.

"Into your hands," he muttered to himself. "Focus it into your—"

Just then, a ghostly white face and hands emerged from the darkness.

"Stanley, I'm really sorry, I—"

"AAAARGH!" Stanley cried out and leapt way from the apparition, arms raised defensively, his breath coming in short, seething gasps.

Then he noticed that this 'ghost' had arms, legs, and running shoes.

"Alabaster?" said Stanley, as his friend stepped uncertainly into the moonlight. "Wow! You scared me! I—"

Alabaster was staring at him, a shocked look on his face. It was then that Stanley noticed that he once again had big black claws in place of hands. Even though he'd just been looking at them for the past hour, their sudden appearance was a surprise.

"Whoa!" he exclaimed. "I'm really sorry, Alabaster, I didn't mean for them to come out—it was, uh, an *emotional trigger*—"

Alabaster laughed nervously. "Heh! That's okay, no harm done. At least you didn't claw me!"

Stanley stared at him, and then suddenly burst out laughing. Alabaster started laughing too, and soon both of them were howling with mirth, barely able to stay standing.

Finally they managed to calm down.

"Phew!" said Stanley, trying to catch his breath, "That … that was really not funny … at all."

"Hah!" said Alabaster. "I know! But sometimes … all you can do is laugh. Hooo!"

Eventually, the two boys composed themselves.

"As I was trying to say," said Alabaster, "sorry for sneaking up on you—I didn't mean to scare you."

"That's okay," said Stanley. "It's not really your fault. This place is pretty creepy with the lights off."

"I *know,*" said Alabaster vehemently. "Sweet claws, by the way."

"Oh, right," said Stanley, looking down at his monstrous hands. He concentrated on banishing the big black paws, and was very pleased when they melted away a moment later. He almost fainted, then, and had to sit down for a spell before he could walk again.

"You okay?" said Alabaster.

"Y-yeah," gasped Stanley. "Just … tires me out."

It took some time before Stanley could get up, but soon he and Alabaster were walking easily down the moonlit hallway, although Stanley wanted nothing more than to just lie down and sleep right then and there.

"So what were you doing lurking in the shadows like that?" asked Stanley.

"Um," said Alabaster, "I was originally planning to, y'know, do some exploring, but, surprisingly, it's not quite as much fun by yourself—not here, anyway. I mean, it seems like at night, someone flips a big switch and all the lights turn off, and the spookiness turns *on!* Anyway,

Nell's still down in the hospital wing—or infirmary, or whatever—so I thought I'd come find you and see how long you were going to be. I figured I'd just wait outside 'till you were done—I think I nodded off for a while there when you were trying to lengthen your claws."

"What!" said Stanley, "You were outside the entire time? Listening in?"

"I guess so," said Alabaster, scratching his head. "Hmm. Sorry 'bout that—I wasn't really thinking."

"Well ... I guess it's okay," said Stanley. "I was just going to tell you everything tomorrow, anyway."

"That's the spirit!" said Alabaster, nudging Stanley chummily. "So: claws, check. Greatly accelerated healing factor: check."

"Huh?" said Stanley.

"Just going over my mental list," said Alabaster. "A few more steps and you'll pretty much be Wolverine! For real!"

Stanley laughed, but the humour of Alabaster's 'list' was dampened by the notion that this was real life, not some comic book.

"Ah, home at last," aid Alabaster, stopping in front of the door to their shared room. He opened the door and the light from Alabaster's bedside lamp spilled out into the hall. It was a welcome change from the spooky gloom of the hallway, and it felt good to close the door against the endless night outside.

Alabaster went into the bathroom to brush his teeth, but Stanley was so tired that he just flopped down on his bed and closed his eyes.

It had been a trying day: he now knew beyond a doubt that his powers were real. That much, he thought he could accept, but the main question bouncing endlessly through his thoughts was *where*. Where had he gotten these strange 'shadow powers'? And *how,* for that matter. Had he been born with them, like Blake? Somehow he didn't think so, but the more he through about it, the more tired he became.

When Alabaster came out of the bathroom, Stanley was fast asleep.

CHAPTER 18

TRAINING DAY(S)

"So what's the plan for today?" asked Alabaster, his mouth full of scrambled eggs. He and Stanley were finishing their breakfasts in Daruna Abbey's dining hall. The room was very long and barely wide enough to accommodate a huge rectangular table that took up most of the floor space.

"Hmm, I dunno," said Stanley, setting down his orange juice. "I'm supposed to go back and see Blake later on, but nothing before that."

"Sweet," said Alabaster."That means we should be able to get some serious exploration done. Think this place has any secret passages? Hey—we should go see if Nell can come, too."

Stanley's stomach clenched slightly at the mention of Nell's name.

"Or not?" said Alabaster, trying to decipher Stanley's expression.

"No no, we should totally go see her," Stanley said quickly.

"Cool," said Alabaster. "You just looked sort of ill for a split-second there, I thought maybe—"

"Stanley! Cousin! There you are!"

Stanley and Alabaster looked up to see a beaming Algernon coming towards them, followed closely by Koko.

"Er, hi Algernon, hi Koko," said Stanley, as Algernon plunked himself down on the other side of the table.

"I can't tell you how glad I am to see you up and about," Algernon said enthusiastically. "I was literally worried sick. Literally!"

"Oh," said Stanley, "Well—it's great to see you, too, Algernon, I'm sorry you weren't feeling—"

"Bedridden!" Algernon said dramatically. "Just an absolute wreck, wasn't I, Koko?"

"Yes, that's ... an accurate way of putting it," said Koko.

"Scootch over a smidgeon, would you old chap?" Algernon said pleasantly, nudging Alabaster out of the way.

Koko sighed heavily. "Algernon, he was seated there before you—"

"Pish-tosh, Koko," said Algernon, obnoxiously waving his words aside. "I've got important things to discuss with Stanley. You don't mind, do you, Albert?"

"Uh, I guess not, if it's important—"

"There you go," said Algernon. "Good man. Now. Stanley," he said, leaning forward conspiratorially, "I've been up in the library these past couple days—doing research, and all that."

Koko cleared his throat.

"Oh, yes, Koko's been helping, too, and we've found more than a few *very* interesting books."

"Er ... that's great," said Stanley.

"It is!" said Algernon. "We've found some great leads to this lost city of Shakka-Kahn—"

"Quetzal-Khan," said Koko.

"Precisely," said Algernon. "Now, more than ever, I'm sure that the Lost City really exists! Look, it's all right here in this book." He produced a large, leather-bound volume from his bag and started flipping through it.

"The librarian said that book was not to leave the library," said Koko.

"What kind of library doesn't let you take out books?" Algernon returned. "I'm not keeping it, anyway—I'll bring it back."

"I think the restriction was based on the book's age, value, and rarity," began Koko, but Algernon interrupted him.

"Here we go! Apparently this account was written down by a monk hundreds of years ago. It seems he met someone from the Lost City itself. *Quetzal-Khan, the City of the Gods, is a realm of wonder,* according to this monk. *An ancient people live there, wise and powerful, and wealthy beyond imagining!* There's talk of buildings made of solid gold, and reservoirs filled with jewels! Nice enough to look at, I'm sure, although if these fantastic treasures are real, they *should* be in a museum. Ah! Now here's the really interesting bit. Remember that scroll Governor Cromwell showed us back in Port Verdant?"

Algernon turned the book around so Stanley could see.

Stanley's jaw dropped. Most of the page was taken up by a painting so vivid and life-like that it could have been taken right from his dreams:

A great stone building, a pyramid very similar to the one in Teno-Xol-Zan. Above the pyramid, suspended in the air, was a colossal blue crystal. It was as if Stanley's dreams had been committed to paper.

"That's it!" he exclaimed, gripping the book tightly. He began to read the archaic text below the painting:

Today, my new friend told me more of his homeland. When asked, he seemed unfamiliar with the concept of wars and armies, though he confirmed that his people were proficient in the use of many different weapons. Most astonishing was his description of a device supposedly 'created by the gods themselves'. He explained, in detail, the use of this incredible, if improbable machine.

Called the 'Klaxl Lakt' by his people, the device's name translates roughly to 'Moon-Killer'. Why anyone would want to kill a moon is beyond me, but apparently the machine was created eons ago, in preparation for some great event. I asked my friend why someone would deem it necessary to destroy our moons, but he did not know. He told me that at the fated hour, the 'chosen one' would activate the machine, and unleash the power of the gods.

Stanley set the book down on the table. This was it. This was what he'd been dreaming about: this 'Moon Killer'. The Sky Jewel Weapon.

But *why?* He'd obviously never seen it, never even imagined that such a thing existed. Frankly, it sounded rather sinister. Why destroy a moon?

"I need to go the library," he said, before getting up from the table, the massive book tucked under one arm.

* * *

The library was a vast two-story room packed with towering bookshelves. Extremely tall sliding ladders allowed access to the highest shelves, and Alabaster, spying one close by, immediately sprang aboard and managed to travel a good fifty feet before the librarian, a thin, bony woman in a black dress with a frilly white collar and cuffs, noticed what was going on.

"*Young man, get down from there this instant!*" she shrieked.

Stanley had to fight to keep a straight face as Alabaster hopped down off the ladder and jogged back to join him by the door.

"Sorry about that," said Alabaster, bowing slightly to the librarian. "There's just some things that you *gotta* do."

"Bravo!" said Algernon, applauding Alabaster's hijinx while Koko shook his head minutely.

"Gentlemen!" cawed the librarian, "This is a *library*—a place of study and *quiet* contemplation. If you can't behave like civilized people, you *will* be asked to *leave*."

"We'll be good," Stanley said quickly, elbowing Alabaster. "*Right?*"

"Ow!" said Alabaster. "I mean, *right*, yes of course, we'll be good. Very good. And civilized. Civil, too, of course."

"Not to worry, Sister Bernadette," said Algernon, "they're under *my* supervision."

"Well that makes me feel *so* much better," said the librarian. "I take it you've come to return that book?"

"Eh?" said Algernon.

"*The Chronicles of Frederick Whipple,* first abbot of Daruna Abbey? The very old, very valuable book that is not to leave this library, but is for some reason tucked under this young man's arm?"

"Ah," said Algernon, taking the book back from Stanley and peering at the embossed title as if he didn't know what it was. "About that—"

"I'll return it to its case," said the librarian, snatching the book from Algernon.

"Wait!" said Stanley. The librarian fixed him with her beady gaze. "Er, sorry, but do you think I could look at that for a bit, please?"

The librarian *hmphed*. "Well, since you seem to be the most *civilized* young man in this group, I suppose so. But under *two* conditions. One: Bring it right back to me when you're done. This book does *not* leave the library again, alright?"

"Alright," said Stanley.

"And *two,"* said the librarian, "Keep *him* away from it, for heaven's sake." She nodded at Algernon, who cleared his throat self-consciously. "He almost spilled a cup of coffee on it yesterday."

"A minor accident!" said Algernon. "And after all, Koko's wonderfully absorbent fur ensured that disaster was averted!"

Koko sighed.

"I'll take good care of it," said Stanley.

"Good," said the librarian, handing him the book. "Off you go then, find yourself a table."

"I'm gonna go sit by the window," Stanley said to Alabaster.

"Okay. I'll meet you over there."

Clutching the large and heavy volume, Stanley found a table by the library's large, circular window, and sat down to read. He found the spot that Algernon had shown him, and continued from where he'd left off.

Dishearteningly, there wasn't much else about this 'Moon Killer' device, and after skimming page after page for any further mention of it, he decided to look elsewhere. He was just about to close the book when suddenly one of the pages came loose. For a moment, Stanley thought that he'd damaged the book, and that he was effectively doomed. Feeling his face heat up and his pulse quicken, he looked around to make sure that the librarian wasn't bearing down on him with mayhem in her eyes, then picked up the fallen page to assess the damage.

Upon touching the paper, though, Stanley realized that it wasn't actually a page from the book; pages 532 and 533 were right there, side by side. In fact, the page in Stanley's hand didn't even seem to be actual paper. It was more rigid, and had a slight sheen to it. It was almost as if it had been laminated, but it didn't feel like plastic. The side Stanley was looking at was blank, but on the reverse was some kind of map. It was a large land mass surrounded by water. It seemed to depict the continent of Verduria, although it was much more detailed than any map he'd yet seen of the 'green continent'. Amazingly, this map seemed to be animated. In the far south of the continent, a blue dot was slowly blinking. Stanley had to close his eyes and look again to make sure he was seeing properly, but there it was, a blinking blue dot on what seemed to be a laminated piece of paper.

He touched the dot with his index finger, and his mouth fell open as a bright yellow line quickly traced its squiggling way to the blue dot from a point farther north on the map. At the point where the yellow line began, there was now a tiny yellow arrow, pointing east. Stanley stared thoughtfully at it for a moment, then looked out the window at the morning sun as it climbed towards its zenith.

Experimentally, he held the map out in front of him and turned to his right. As he did so, the tiny arrow turned, too, so that it was now pointing south.

"Wow," said Stanley, "It's like a GPS." As far as he knew, though, GPSs couldn't tell you which way you were facing, and were certainly not made of laminated paper. He whipped the page back and forth and watched the arrow spin wildly in place. He made a mental note to show this strange map to Blake the next time he saw him.

THUD!

"GAAH!" Stanley cried, jumping up from his seat and banging his knees on the underside of the table in the process.

"Oops, sorry!" said Alabaster, who had supplied the noise by dropping a stack of books on the table.

"SHHH!" hissed the librarian from somewhere out among the shelves.

"I've been researching the local fauna," Alabaster said proudly, taking a seat while Stanley caught his breath. "Check it out—*armour fish!*"

He showed Stanley a page of a modern-looking book entitled, *Monsters of the Deep*. The photo of the armour fish was impressive, but Stanley wanted to show Alabaster the map.

"Look at this!" He handed the map to Alabaster, who looked at it and nodded.

"Okay—a map of Verduria. Very nice."

"No, it's more than that," said Stanley. "Look—that blue dot there? It blinks!"

"Okay, that *is* pretty cool," said Alabaster.

"I think that's where the Lost City is," Stanley said excitedly. "And this yellow line is the route! It's almost like Uncle Jack's Memory Mirror."

"Hmm," said Alabaster, thoughtfully scratching his chin. "Neat." He looked at the map for a time, then set it down and picked up *Monsters of the Deep.* "*Now,* are you ready for *this?*"

Stanley was about to voice his frustration over Alabaster's lack of interest in his map, when Alabaster turned to the page labeled

KRAKEN

His blood ran cold as images of the attack aboard Uncle Jack's ship flashed through his mind: the horrible, oily black tentacles twisting and flailing in the fog, the baleful yellow eyes, the gnashing teeth, and the terrible, cavernous mouth …

Stanley was also forcibly reminded of the spike that the creature had fired into his shoulder in its death throes. The spike that had made his whole body feel like ice, and that had put him to sleep for four days …

"Not quite as scary as the one we saw, eh?" said Alabaster. "No weird tentacle-eyes, no scary tentacle-teeth … red skin, white shell—and apparently they have *beaks!*"

Stanley stared open-mouthed at the page without seeing it. Why hadn't he thought of it before? Truth be told, the kraken attack had been the most frightening experience of his adventure, if not his entire life. Maybe his mind had blocked out the details to save him from having to remember.

He'd had a cut on his hand before the kraken attack, hadn't he?

And afterwards, when he woke up, the cut was gone, wasn't it?

Alabaster was watching him uncertainly. "Uh, Stanley? You okay?"

"Do you think I got my powers from the kraken?" Stanley blurted. Alabaster blinked, clearly not expecting this line of questioning.

"Er—"

Stanley sprang up from the table and made a beeline for the library doors.

"Stanley, wait!" Alabaster called after him.

"SHHH!" said the librarian.

* * *

Stanley reached the abbey's main staircase almost at a run, and leapt up the steps two at a time. He was only half-aware of Alabaster loping along gamely a few paces behind. Gaining the top of the grand staircase, he set off down the east fifth-floor hallway at a brisk pace.

"Stanley, come on, wait up," gasped Alabaster. "Where are we going?"

"I need to find Blake," said Stanley, refusing to slow down.

They reached his office, but the door was closed and locked; no one seemed to be inside.

"*Darn it!*" growled Stanley, pounding unnecessarily hard on the door.

One of the monks poked his head out from a nearby room to see what all the noise was about. "Father Blake is out for the day," he said flatly. "What's that in your hand, boy?"

He was looking at the strange map Stanley had found.

"Uh, just a note for Blake," said Stanley, deftly sliding it under Blake's office door, just in case the monk decided to take it away from him.

The monk shook his head and slammed his door, muttering about vows of silence.

"Where could he have gone?" said Stanley, as he and Alabaster made their way back to their shared room.

"Stanley, talk to me!" said Alabaster. "What did you mean about the kraken giving you powers?"

Stanley stopped and looked at him. "Remember when it shot that—*spike* at me?"

"Yeah," said Alabaster, "Yeah, I do … so, you think it might have somehow transferred its … weird *essence* into you?"

"I dunno," said Stanley, "but I'm pretty sure that's the point where my cuts started healing super fast."

Alabaster's eyes lit up. "Yeah! That's when you became Wolverine! Wow! This is awesome. Not only do you have super powers, but now we can trace your origin story. Can I play myself in the movie? *Stanley Brambles: Origins!*"

Stanley laughed in spite of himself.

"Okay," said Alabaster as they reached the door to their room, "let's think back. After the kraken staked you, you got accelerated regeneration. What happened after that?"

Stanley thought for a moment. "Well let's see … we went to Ethelia … met that weird guy in the mask—"

"Brrr," said Alabaster. "What a creep *he* was."

"And Ethelia is where I met Grey," said Stanley.

Alabaster *hmmd*. "They seemed to have strangely similar powers. D'you think there's a connection?"

"I don't know," said Stanley, thinking back to what Blake had told him about the mythical Shadow Legion. "I really think Blake knows something, though. That's why I need to talk to him."

"Well, in the meantime, you know who *I* think we should talk to?"

"No, who?"

"*Whom*."

"What?"

"Nell."

"Nell?"

"Yeah—I think we should see what *she* thinks about all this. We were going to see her earlier, anyway, right?"

"Oh yeah," said Stanley, feeling a bit bad about having forgotten all about visiting Nell. "Okay, let's go."

★ ★ ★

Soon after, they arrived at the door to the infirmary.

"Oh, hello," said Sister Marie, who answered the door in response to Alabaster's knocking.

"Uh, hi," said Alabaster dazedly.

"Er, we were wondering if Nell was awake yet," said Stanley, glancing sideways at Alabaster.

"Nell?" said Marie, raising her eyebrows. "Oh—she was discharged earlier this morning, actually."

"Really?" said Stanley. "Okay—uh, thanks."

★ ★ ★

"I wonder where she went," said Alabaster, as he and Stanley made their way up into the main hall. "So—what now? Back to the library?"

Stanley glanced out a nearby window and noticed a small gathering of people over by one of the gardens.

"Looks like something's going on out there," he said, half to himself.

"Let's go see!" said Alabaster.

They made their way out through the abbey's huge front doors and crossed the courtyard to where the group of priests and nuns had gathered.

"Quite the display," Stanley heard one of the priests say.

"Yes," said another, "they're very skillful."

Stanley and Alabaster edged their way around the crowd to see what had captured their attention. About ten yards away, two people were going through a series of slow sword movements. One was Ryuno, and the other was

"Nell!" Stanley exclaimed, quite a bit louder than he'd intended.

Nell looked around at the sound of her name. Her left eye was still heavily bandaged, but she seemed much livelier than she did yesterday. She paused in her swordplay and smiled when she caught sight of Stanley.

"Stay focused," said Ryuno, who was standing beside her. His nose was bandaged up, with a strip of metal running up the bridge and held in place with surgical tape.

Nell gave Stanley a little wave, then returned her attention to her swordplay.

Stanley couldn't help but stare; Nell was very good. She was mimicking Ryuno's actions exactly, going through each flowing movement as though she'd done it a million times before. Now and then Ryuno would pause to correct her.

Nell's movements became a little less confident, and Ryuno frowned at Stanley after having to correct her for the fifth time.

"You *must* stay focused," Ryuno told her. "Block out all distractions and annoyances."

"I know," said Nell, "I'm trying."

"Annoyances?" said Alabaster, "I think he's talking about *us!*"

"Yeah," said Stanley, weighing the pros and cons of jabbing Ryuno with a clawed finger.

"*Trying* implies the acceptance of *failure,*" snapped Ryuno. "A Marusai must *do,* not *try.*"

"Don't screw up, Nell!" called Alabaster, at which point she promptly dropped her sword.

"If you don't mind," Ryuno said loudly, "this is an important training session. Please leave so that this student can learn."

"Boys, leave them be," said one of the nuns.

"If you're looking for something to do, I can put you to work cleaning the stables," said a priest.

"Uh—" said Stanley.

"*Thank you*, but we really *must* be going," said Alabaster, grabbing hold of Stanley's arm and backing away towards the abbey.

"I'll meet you at lunch," Nell called after them.

Stanley fumed for the rest of the morning. Ryuno certainly had some nerve, telling him and Alabaster to leave, and calling them 'annoyances'. That nun and priest were no better, either. Who did they think they were? Nell was Stanley's friend, and Alabaster's, not theirs!

At lunch, the boys were half way through their smoked meat sandwiches when Nell came in, sweaty and out of breath.

"*Whew,*" she said, plunking herself down at the table and draining half a pitcher of water in one go, "It's *hot* out there today."

"Finally, you're free!" said Alabaster. "Free from the clutches of that—that *madman!*"

"Ryuno is *not* a madman," said Nell. "He's just very serious about the way he trains people."

"So he's actually training you?" said Stanley, "Like, to be a Marusai like him?"

"Kind of. I guess," said Nell shortly. "Why, is there some problem with that?"

"No," Stanley said quickly. "I just—I dunno, I didn't think you wanted to, that's all."

"Well," said Nell, "I find it fascinating and fun, and I really like learning to swordfight, *okay?*"

"Okay, fine!" said Stanley. "Why are you getting all mad about it?"

"I'm not," Nell shot back. "You're the one who's sitting here deriding me for no good reason. You interrupt me, distract me, and make me look like an *idiot* in front of—in front of all those people, and now you're talking like me training to be a Marusai is some big stupid idea!"

"I never said that!" said Stanley.

"It was your tone of voice," Nell returned.

"Guys, guys," said Alabaster, "There's no need to fight over this. You two have some real common ground here."

They both stared at him.

"We aren't fighting," said Nell.

"Yes you are—over nothing," said Alabaster. "Especially since Stanley totally understands where you're coming from."

"I do?" said Stanley, "I mean—I *do!* Because, you see, I … uh …"

"He's doing some training of his *own,"* Alabaster supplied.

"What?" said Nell.

"Yeah," said Alabaster. "Since Stanley's super powers are the real deal, Blake is teaching him how to control them. It's very comic-book-esque."

"You've got to be kidding," said Nell.

"No, it's *true,"* said Stanley defensively. "And I don't see why you get to derive *my* training right after giving me a hard time about *yours."*

"*Deride,"* said Nell. "And this is completely different. I can't believe he's encouraging you! You can't seriously think it's a good idea to try and … *develop* something you have no control of. What's Father Blake thinking, anyway?"

"I *can* control it," said Stanley, "and that's *exactly* what Blake is teaching me to do."

Nell was silent for a moment. "It just makes me worried," she said in a softer tone. "There's something about this … *power* of yours that I don't like. It seems unnatural. I mean, where does a person get the ability to—I dunno, spawn claws? Turn into a monster? It's more like a curse, if you ask me."

"We think it was the kraken," said Alabaster. "Sticks him with a projectile, and then *BAM!* Super powers."

Nell looked ready to roll her eyes at Alabaster's theory, but then her brow furrowed as she thought it over. "What if it's a disease?" she said suddenly. "What if it *kills* you? You should be in a hospital, Stanley, not *practising* with it!"

"The last thing he needs is a hospital," laughed Alabaster. "He's got super-accelerated healing, remember? Just like Wolver—"

"*Will you shut up and let* him *speak?"* Nell snapped. Alabaster shut his mouth and flinched as if she'd hit him. He looked a bit hurt.

Stanley's limbs were tensing, and he felt a familiar heat in his chest.

"You don't have to yell," he said, his own voice rising, "and if you really want to know what I think, I agree with Alabaster—once I've trained enough, I'll be able to completely control it, *and* it protects me from getting hurt. I'd be dead now if it wasn't for this power, did you know that? Dead! That crocodile would've cracked my head wide open! You still think it's a bad thing?"

The heat in his chest was trying to rise up to his head, but with barely a thought, it swiftly drained away, and his hands transformed.

Nell stared at the claws, her jaw clenched.

"Are you going to attack *me* now?" she asked quietly.

"What?" said Stanley. "No! I just—"

"So much for being able to control it," said Nell in a disgusted tone as she got up roughly from the table. "Looks like you still have a lot to learn."

"This *is* how you control it!" Stanley said as she turned and marched away towards the entrance hall. "Nell? Wait, come back! *Nell!"*

She ignored him completely and left the room without a backward glance. Stanley sat there for a moment, completely flabbergasted. Why in the world was Nell so mad?

"I wonder if Ryuno was giving her grief for messing up her training," said Alabaster. "Maybe I shouldn't have yelled *don't screw up* at her."

"Yeah, maybe," said Stanley, allowing himself a new possible reason to dislike Ryuno. He looked down at his claws. "I'm sure *these* didn't help, though," he said, willing them to evaporate. The claws disappeared with their now-familiar bony creaking sound. "I think I should ask Blake how to keep them from appearing altogether."

⋆ ⋆ ⋆

"Well," said Blake when Stanley asked him later that evening. "You can either learn to master your emotions, or cause your shadowmass to appear in a different form or place. Now, control of your emotions is, at this stage, easier said than done, since you're now much more susceptible to them than you used to be. Choosing an alternative form for the shadowmass is probably your best bet for now, although it'll take practice."

"How do I do it?" Stanley asked.

"Exactly the same way you make the claws," said Blake. "Claws, sword, axe, whatever form it takes, it's all done the same way. Now, if concealment is what you want, you could always just form it into a shell, or an extra layer of skin—anything that'll fit under your clothes, really. You could even turn it into a t-shirt, if you wanted."

"That sounds good," said Stanley.

"We'll get started on that right away," said Blake. "There is another option, though, if you're interested. It's pretty advanced stuff, but I suspect you might be able to handle it."

"What is it?" said Stanley.

"Direct shadow manipulation," said Blake. "You add shadowmass to your own shadow, and that opens up a whole new category of abilities. If you've got the skill for it, you can change your shadow into something completely new, or even turn invisible."

"Alright! That sounds great."

"Remember, it's extremely advanced shadowcraft," said Blake. "Don't feel bad if you can't master it—although, again, I think you'll find you have a knack for it."

Blake looked thoughtful for a moment, then said, "Before we get started, Stanley, I'd like to discuss your powers. Have you given any thought to what we talked about yesterday?"

Stanley took a deep breath. "Yeah … er—I think I might have an idea where I got my power, but … it might sound kind of weird."

"I expect it'll sound *very* weird," said Blake, "But weirdness and I are well-acquainted. Let's hear it."

Stanley nodded and took a deep breath. "This past summer, back in June, I went on a trip with my great uncle Jack. On the way to Ethelia, we ran into this fog …"

He proceeded to relate every detail of the kraken attack. As he spoke, Blake sat very still, his face expressionless.

"...And when I woke up, it was four days later. And I was totally healed, too."

Blake was silent for a long while, his brow furrowed, his right hand clenched and resting against his chin. Finally, when the silence was getting uncomfortable, he looked sideways at Stanley and said,

"I think you may have encountered one of the most powerful shadow creatures that ever lived." He got up and began flipping through one of the many books on his desk. "No legend tells of a shadowform like the one you've described ... by no means am I the foremost authority on this sort of thing, but ... I think you're extremely fortunate to be sitting here today."

Stanley couldn't help but agree.

"I've just never heard of *anything* like this," Blake went on. "What on earth *was* this thing? ... I guess we'll never know."

He almost sounded disappointed. "Well, just one more thing to add to my list of research, I suppose." He snapped the book shut. "Alright. We're behind schedule. Come on, on your feet, Stanley. We've got work to do."

The rest of the evening was spent trying to get Stanley to create a shadow sword. Claws were all well and good, but they were really a sign that more work needed to be done.

Stanley felt a notable sting when Blake told him this, essentially repeating what Nell had said earlier.

After an hour and a half, Stanley was still unable to manifest a sword.

"*Come on,* Stanley," said Blake, pacing back and forth, "with your potential you should be able to spawn a shadow sword without even thinking! You need to focus."

"I'm trying," said Stanley, visualizing a sword with all his might. But it was no good; the best he could do was a spiky protrusion jutting out of his thumb.

To make matters worse, every time he used his power, he felt as if he'd just run a race.

"Your power does seem to be more reactive than anything else," said Blake. "It's important that we correct that."

Without warning, he suddenly sprang forward and brought his sword swooshing down in a sweeping overhead arc. Stanley didn't even have time to wonder what madness had possessed Blake before the midnight blade was mere inches from his forehead.

Not knowing why or how, he took a half step backwards and, quick as a flash, brought his left arm up in a defensive posture that Nell had shown him.

There was a loud *clang!* as the sword made contact, and the next moment, Blake was flat on his back on the floor.

"Wha!" exclaimed Stanley, nearly falling backwards himself.

Blake was back on his feet in an instant. "Splendid, Stanley—Amazing!" he said, his face lit with a smile. "Inspired! Very well done indeed!"

Stanley, who was still processing the fact that Blake had just attacked him—*really* attacked him—and was still a good few seconds from figuring out exactly what Blake was talking about, glanced down at his arm and was astounded by what he saw:

His forearm seemed to have spontaneously grown a curved, rounded black shell. It almost looked like

"A *shield,*" Blake said excitedly. "Now that's something I didn't expect. Hold it up, please."

Stanley complied, and Blake closely examined the smooth, shiny black shell, as well as the small nick that had been left by his sword strike.

"I'm sorry for attacking unannounced," said Blake. "But I wouldn't have tried it if I wasn't sure about the strength of your abilities. I hope I didn't scare you."

Stanley, whose heart was still racing, mumbled a slightly-audible "That's okay." He took a closer look at the shield attached to his arm, and ran his fingers over the smooth surface. It was cool to the touch, and had a texture that he couldn't quite identify—smooth and solid, but with an odd glassy feel, almost like a polished seashell.

"This is a major step," said Blake. "See if you can alter the shape—try turning it into an *actual* shield. A rounded buckler, say."

Stanley thought of a knight gearing up for battle, and focused on the image of a round shield. The black armoured shell on his arm changed almost instantly into the shape he envisioned. He couldn't believe how easy it was.

"Now you're getting it," said Blake. "Let's see if you can increase the size—turn it into a big tower shield—make it as tall as you can."

With a bit of effort, Stanley willed the shield to stretch itself vertically, until it was taller than he was. He tried to widen it, but as he did so, he suddenly felt very lightheaded. The blackness of his shadow shield seemed to wash over him and engulf him.

Next thing he knew, he was leaning back in the chair in front of Blake's desk. His head was pounding and he groaned, looking around blearily. "Ugh," was all he could manage to say.

Blake looked up from a book he was reading. "Welcome back," he said brightly. "You fainted," he added, before Stanley could ask. "Nothing to worry about—you just overexerted yourself, that's all. I think that's enough training for one night." He closed the book and sat back in his chair. "You've really accomplished quite a bit, Stanley. You should be proud."

Stanley was a bit too tired to feel very proud at the moment.

"It seems you have a real affinity for the shield," Blake went on. "Quite a surprise, really—shields can be tricky, even the weakest ones, but yours seems very strong, indeed—my sword barely left a scratch on it … er, sorry again about attacking you, by the way."

"It's okay, really," said Stanley. After all, this was a training session; Stanley thought back to the night at Mr. Taki's house, where Ryuno had done pretty much the same thing to test Nell's abilities. Granted, that had been done with a wooden practice sword …

"Now then," Blake was saying as he glanced at some papers in front of him on his desk, "Before we finish for the day, I wonder if you'd be inclined to discuss some of the research I've been doing."

Stanley, who would have preferred to go straight to bed, made a noncommittal noise and shifted in his chair.

"In the Saurian city," Blake began, clearly not waiting for Stanley's response, "you described your escape from your prison cell. Based on what you told me, I suspect that you unintentionally executed a flawless shadow meld."

"Shadow melt?" said Stanley.

"*Meld*," said Blake, "Although I suppose 'melt' is almost appropriate … you become one with the shadows, essentially. A very useful ability."

Blake closed his eyes and a heartbeat later, he was gone. There was no flash of light or puff of smoke to mark his disappearance—he just seemed to fade out of sight. Stanley focused his gaze on the chair. To the untrained eye it was empty, just another vacant furnishing in a cluttered office. He noted, though, that the red upholstery looked a bit darker than it would otherwise, as if the light cast by the lamps in the office wasn't quite hitting it properly.

"It isn't foolproof," came Blake's voice from the other side of the desk. "Especially in a well-lit area." The slightly-dark patch on the chair seemed to dissolve, and Blake reappeared. "You're essentially hiding behind your own shadow," he explained. "I'm not even sure how it works myself, but you can 'fade' into just about any surface, flatten yourself out completely. I'm certain this is exactly what happened in your cell back in the dungeon. It's not hard when you get the hang of it … but just mull it over for now—we can work on shadow melding when you've mastered the sword and shield."

CHAPTER 19

THE SOUND OF DARKNESS

Over the next week, as his training sessions with Blake continued, Stanley began to notice a marked improvement in his abilities (such as they were). The shadow shield just seemed to come naturally to him, and after only a few days of practice, he could manifest one with almost as much ease as he could his claws.

Claws, though, seemed to be the most dangerous weapon he could come up with. His endurance had improved noticeably, and he wasn't passing out nearly as often as before, but he still couldn't produce so much as a butter knife when it came to weaponry.

Secretly, Stanley felt that this wasn't such a bad thing, and that savage, rending claws were more weapon than one person should have.

By Monday night, Blake was getting visibly frustrated. Another two-hour lesson had ended with Stanley collapsing in a faint with no shadow sword in hand. When he came to, Blake was back at his desk looking depressed. He looked up when Stanley began to stir, and sighed.

"Well, I suppose we'd better stop for today," he said as Stanley picked himself up off the ground. "I just wish I could figure out why you're having so much trouble with your weapons." He began to count on his fingers. "Sword, axe, mace, spear—we've covered all the basics. You should have an affinity for at least one of them. It's a shame there aren't any books written on the subject."

Stanley just stood there silently. Blake was usually very level-headed, but right now his frustration was palpable.

"Well, off you go then," Blake said, leading Stanley towards the door. "See you tomorrow, same time." He pulled the door open, and Stanley was barely through when it closed behind him with a resounding *BOOM*.

Stanley stood there in the dark hallway listening to the echoes fade into the distance. He felt bad for disappointing Blake, and frustrated with himself. He held up his left hand and turned it into a claw. He could now perform this transformation with minimal effort, but still could not master even the barest beginning of a sword.

True, he wasn't terribly interested in *using* a sword, or axe, or mace, or spear, but he wanted to prove to Blake that he *could*.

As far back as he could remember, Stanley had wished for something to set him apart, some quality or ability that could make him different, make him stand out; something that would prove to the world (and to himself) that he wasn't just some regular, boring kid, easily overlooked and forgettable.

"And now that I have it, I can hardly *do* anything with it," he muttered bitterly, punching the wall so hard that his knuckles bled. Paying no heed to his injured hand (it healed up in seconds), he hunched up his shoulders and began the trek back to the room he shared with Alabaster. His mind focused on thoughts both dark and self-berating, he didn't notice the sound until he was almost at the end of the hallway. When he did notice it, he had to pause and listen to make sure he was actually hearing it.

At first it sounded like a breeze blowing from somewhere, but none of the windows was open, and it didn't sound 'swift' or 'breezy' enough to be a gust of wind. As he listened, the sound seemed to take on a rhythmic quality, fading out every few seconds, and then returning. The closest thing Stanley could equate it with was someone breathing, and the prospect made his heartbeat quicken and his skin crawl.

It wasn't as if someone else was here—at least, he didn't think so—the sound seemed to be coming from everywhere and nowhere, with no definite point of origin. It was almost as if the entire hallway was breathing.

Listening hard, Stanley proceeded further down the hall and turned right, towards the main staircase and the dormitories; if nothing else, he could at least head back to his room.

The sound was still there, still filling the hallways, still coming from no point in particular. He slowly made his way towards the stairs, feeling more and more uncomfortable as he went. He felt very exposed, and had the unnerving sensation of being observed.

As he reached the top of the great staircase, he glanced down into the entrance hall and nearly cried out; not because he saw anything, but because the sound had suddenly changed.

A strange tone now accompanied each 'inhale' and 'exhale'. It was almost musical, but very unpleasant, like rusty hinges or a heavy metal desk being dragged across a concrete floor.

His pulse pounding in his ears, and his legs and arms beginning to shake, Stanley briefly considered fleeing back to Blake's office, or to his room. Later he would wonder why he did neither, but instead took a deep breath, squared his shoulders, and started down the stairs.

Maybe it was a need to prove himself in the wake of his most recent training session. Maybe it was genuine bravery. Maybe it was genuine foolishness.

Whatever the reason, Stanley descended the great staircase in the late-night gloom, claws out and at the ready.

But ready for *what?* The abbey was more than a bit creepy at night, but it hardly seemed a dangerous place. Still, he felt better with his weaponry at hand.

He paused at the bottom of the stairs. The great entrance hall seemed to loom up around him, surrounding him with the dark, towering forms of pillars and balconies casting strange shadows on the walls and floor. Statues and carved faces on the walls and ceilings, perfectly innocuous during the day, now looked distinctly untrustworthy, as if they would turn to look right at him the moment he passed by.

His heart hammering in his chest, Stanley began to feel dizzy. His emotions were clearly causing his shadow powers to stir, despite the fact that his claws were already in use.

Not wanting to lose control, he focused his thoughts and willed his shadow mass into his chest. Instantly his mind cleared and he felt a cool, firm layer of something spread over his skin. Taking a quick peek under his shirt, he saw that his entire torso was now jet-black. Had he ever tried one on, he would have equated the feeling with that of wearing a wetsuit.

Pleased with this new development, and making a mental note to tell Blake that his 'second skin' idea had worked, Stanley took a steadying breath and listened for the breathing sound.

It now seemed to be coming from somewhere behind him and to the right. He turned and spied a smallish doorway towards the rear of the entrance hall, tucked almost out of sight beside the massive staircase. He crept quietly around the stairs and went through the doorway. Immediately in front of him was a stone wall, with a dark, narrow corridor extending about thirty feet to his right.

The strange sound seemed very loud here, and it was definitely coming from the end of the hall, where a stout wooden door could be seen. Although every fibre of his being screamed at him not to, he slowly approached it, his knees almost knocking together. Whatever was making the noise was right behind that door. As he came closer, he noticed that a sign had been hung on the door. It read:

ABBEY CATACOMBS

-CRYPT- -RELIQUARY-

~NO ADMITTANCE~

Stanley's hand was halfway to the door's big metal handle when he read the sign.

Crypt? Catacombs?

"Yeah, right," he muttered to himself, as he backed away from the door. Maybe there was something interesting on the other side and maybe there wasn't, but either way, he wasn't about to go traipsing around some spooky catacombs alone in the middle of the night.

He suddenly wanted to be upstairs in bed more than anything. He felt afraid and very alone, and wondered why he hadn't at least brought Alabaster along. He turned around and started back the way he'd come, and then froze.

Someone was standing there in the hallway, just inside the door.

Stanley's breath caught in his throat and his insides clenched unpleasantly. He stared wide-eyed at the figure, unable to make out any features in the gloom. Who was it? Stanley was temporarily speechless, and closed his eyes for a moment. When he reopened them, the figure was gone. Had it even been there? He hadn't heard any movement or footsteps. He managed a hoarse

"H-hello?" but there was no answer. He stood there for what felt like an hour, listening hard for any sign of another person in the area, and then, finally deciding that he'd imagined the dark figure, left the narrow corridor and began climbing the great staircase back to his room. The climb was long and lonely, and he felt like a small child, alone and afraid. He kept expecting to hear or see something, and his heart was beating so hard he thought it might pop right out of his chest.

Gaining the top of the stairs, Stanley started towards the dormitory. He squinted in the gloom of the darkened hallway; it seemed darker here than usual, even for night time, and he was finding it difficult to follow the route he'd walked dozens of times in the past week and a half.

Suddenly, he found that he could see nothing—all around him was complete darkness. On the verge of panic at the prospect of having been struck blind, Stanley froze, unable to remember the layout of the hallway, or just how far he was from the stairs. He reached out blindly and his hand met the cool, solid stone of the abbey wall. The knowledge that he hadn't been teleported to the middle of some dark and endless void was marginally comforting, but why couldn't he see? And what had happened to the moonlight that had been shining in through the windows just moments ago?

The atmosphere in the hallway became very close and oppressive, as if the air itself were tightening around him like a great fist. He tried to remember the way back to his room, and began to feel his way along the wall. Movement became more and more difficult, to the point that he felt like he was walking underwater.

Stanley's heart was racing, but his mind felt slow and sluggish. He could barely string two thoughts together, but he was very aware of an incredible menace all around him in the uncanny darkness. Something was here, that much was irrefutable; something was watching him, circling him like some predatory beast. The bizarre breathing sound returned, filling his ears with its unsettling metallic undertones, its origin impossible to pinpoint. It came from all around him, but also seemed to emanate from inside his own head. What was it?

Whatever it was, it was here, and it knew he was here, too. In a literally blind panic, Stanley stumbled sideways and slid down the wall to the cold stone floor, crawling on his hands and knees, with no idea where he was going. He knew that at any moment the thing would have him, that he would feel horrid hands grab him in their clammy grip, and drag him half-mad into the infinite dark.

He let out a whimpering moan that was almost a sob, his body racked with surge after surge of cold, undiluted fear, the kind that can only be experienced in the grip of a true nightmare.

And then a light appeared. Not far ahead of him and to the right, a thin, horizontal sliver of golden light came slicing through the darkness, seeming to form a luminous path leading out of the terrible dark.

Finally able to see his hands before him (they were claws at the moment), Stanley mustered the strength to crawl towards the light, dragging himself along the glowing mystical path before him.

The sound of bestial breathing and giant rusty hinges faded, and after what seemed an age, he reached the source of the light.

It was a door.

Not a heavenly portal with angelic choirs singing on the other side; just a regular wooden door like any other in Daruna Abbey, with a bit of light spilling out from underneath it, casting its glow across the stone floor of the hallway.

For that is where Stanley was: not in some black nightmare void, but lying face down on the cold floor of the moonlit hallway. He slowly picked himself up off the floor into a crouch. He looked to his left, then to his right: nothing unusual. He could pick out the various details of the hallway easily, thanks to the generous quantity of moonlight shining in through the tall windows. The starry sky was a radiant swatch of dark blue silk adorned with a thousand gleaming diamonds.

So where had it been for the last few minutes?

Stanley stood up and shook his head; the whole thing must have been a dream. He probably let himself get all worked up and anxious over a few shadows and night-time noises, and fainted because he'd lost control of his shadow powers.

"Gotta work on keeping it together, Stanley," he muttered to himself.

Now that he was awake and thinking clearly, he was aware of another unusual sound, this one undoubtedly real:

Someone was crying, and in the room directly in front of him. Deciding that the person probably wanted to be left alone, Stanley took a step away from the door, and promptly tripped over his own shoelaces, landing on the floor with a loud "*OOF!*" that echoed annoyingly down the hall.

The fall knocked the wind out of him, and he lay there for a moment or two, frantically struggling to inhale. Warm, golden light spilled out into the hall, and Stanley, gasping for breath on the cold stone floor, saw someone standing silhouetted in the doorway with what looked like a sword in her hand.

"Stanley?" said a familiar female voice.

"Nell?" said Stanley, suddenly feeling supremely ridiculous. He quickly picked himself up and tried to look as nonchalant as he could. "I, uh, tripped and fell," he said lamely.

There was a pause, and then Nell said, "What were you doing?"

"Me?" said Stanley, feeling his face heating up, "What was I doing? Well I, uh—I wasn't listening at your door, or anything, even though it might kind of look like … um … I mean I didn't even know it was your door—I just heard sort of a weird noise and, y'know, went to check it out, and then I thought I heard someone crying, but, er—"

Nell said nothing. Was she angry?

"Was that you?" asked Stanley. "Are you okay?"

Nell took a slightly shuddering breath and said, "I just want to be alone now, Stanley," and closed the door.

"But—" Stanley stood there, trying to decide what to do next. Nell was clearly upset about something, and he wanted to make her feel better. If only he could think of something to say—he hated the idea of leaving her all alone and sad, especially on a creepy night like this.

Maybe he could try telling her a joke—surely that would lighten things up. The only problem was that comedy wasn't really Stanley's forté. If only Alabaster were here.

"Uh, Nell," he called through the door, "Alabaster told me a funny joke the other day. These three guys are marooned on an island—"

"Stanley—go away please." Nell's voice had taken on a somewhat dangerous tone. Stanley gulped.

"Right," he said, "I will, right now. Um, I was just, y'know, hoping I could—help cheer you up a bit, so—"

"You can help by leaving me alone!" snapped Nell. "I mean it, go *away*. Now!"

Stanley couldn't believe how badly the situation had degenerated. "Idiot," he muttered, hitting himself in the forehead with his palm. He briefly considered apologizing to Nell for being so annoying, but thought better of it, preferring to slink away as silently and pathetically as possible.

He'd barely slunk ten feet, though, when Nell's door opened again.

"Stanley, wait," she said.

He obeyed.

"Come back," said Nell. "I'm sorry for yelling at you. It's probably better if I tell you now, anyway. You can come in if you want."

"In?" Stanley said stupidly, pointing towards the doorway. "In your room?"

"Yes," said Nell, clearly wondering whether he was being intentionally dense. "Er, unless you don't want to—"

"Oh, no, I don't. I mean I don't not want to. Um, I will, thanks."

What Stanley really wanted to do was crawl under a nice big rock somewhere and hide. He was feeling terribly flustered, and was painfully aware that he was making an idiot of himself. He followed Nell into her room, resolving to take deep breaths and say as little as possible.

Nell's room was small and sparsely-furnished, like most of the other rooms in the abbey. A single twin bed lay along the right hand wall, and a simple wooden desk with a mirror and reading lamp on it sat beneath the window at the end of the room.

Nell sat down on a wooden stool in front of her desk, and Stanley stood awkwardly in the doorway.

"You can sit down if you want," said Nell, sounding almost amused as she motioned towards the bed.

"Oh, right. Thanks," Stanley said lamely before sitting down.

What is the big deal? His thoughts demanded of him. *You spent at least a month in the same room on Uncle Jack's ship!*

He couldn't answer himself, of course, but somehow this small private room was a whole different matter, as far removed from the Ogopogo's cabin as a mansion is from a mud hut.

Nell sat quietly for a moment. This whole time she'd kept her head turned slightly away, and when she finally turned to look at him straight on, he saw why.

"I got my bandages off today," she said, turning to face him. She looked miles better than she did a week ago; the crescent-shaped wound around her left eye was healing nicely: gone were the angry swelling and the fiery, infected redness that had put her in the hospital for three days. Now it just looked as if someone had drawn on her face with a red marker. Stanley wasn't entirely sure why Nell was upset—frankly, he thought the crescent scar looked rather fetching—but then he noticed that her left eye was no longer green. Was it a trick of the light? No—her right iris was as green as an emerald, but the left one was as red as a ruby.

"The doctor said the acid gave me a bad infection, and that's what turned my eye red," said Nell, her voice wavering. "Either that or the treatment, but either way, she said the change is probably permanent." She sniffed loudly. "And Marie told me that I'll have this scar on my face for the rest of my life." She lowered her head, and big glistening teardrops fell into her lap as she started to cry.

Stanley was paralyzed. He had to do something, that much he knew—but what? The sight of Nell weeping softly into her hands was something he simply could not abide. He had to make her feel better.

Please, Nell, your delicate visage is far too fair to be marred by such bitter tears—how may I restore the sunny glow to your angelic features?

That might have been good—a bit wordy and archaic, but it could have served as a distraction, if nothing else. As we all know, though, it is essentially impossible to think of anything to say in a moment like this, and so Stanley chose to act, then and there, and *hang* the consequences.

He reached over and patted her gingerly on the arm.

"Oh Stanley," she managed, "I'm sorry, this is awful. I hate crying. I just—" she snorted loudly. "Do you have a kleenex?"

"Er, no, sorry," said Stanley, managing to feel even more useless and inept. "Uh, but if there's some in your bathroom, I could get it—"

"That's okay," Nell said thickly, "I'll get it." She got up, went into her bathroom, blew her nose loudly, and returned with a handful of tissues. She sat down and took a deep, steadying breath.

"Sorry for crying so much," she said, although Stanley couldn't guess why she was apologizing.

"I mean, I know it could've been worse," she went on, her voice wavering a bit more. "It's just that … I know I'm not very pretty, and I have these stupid freckles, but now I'm going to be even uglier because of this … *damned scar*—" She tried to say more, but quickly dissolved into deep, wracking, shoulder-shaking sobs.

Stanley was aghast. Was this why Nell was so upset? Because she felt her scar would make her look ugly? And what was all that about her knowing she wasn't pretty? Maybe he would think it over later, but now was the time for babbling, not for thinking.

"Not very pretty?" Stanley repeated, "But—Nell, you're not—er—*un-pretty* at all, you're like the prettiest girl I've ever seen! I mean, I thought you were super pretty right when I first met you. I think your freckles are cute, too, and you know what? I think that scar looks super-cool, and you still look beautiful with it. Uh—"

Nell was staring at him. Her eyes were still bright and swimming with tears, but she had stopped crying for the moment.

Stanley could say nothing more. The implications of what had just come out of his mouth were quickly starting to dawn on him, and his face suddenly felt extremely hot.

"Uh," he said again, "I should … um …" he was on his feet in an instant. Nell looked like she was about to say something, but before so much as a syllable could be uttered, Stanley was out the door, down the hall, and around the corner.

He was so embarrassed that he couldn't even think; he just knew that he had to get out of there, had to hide, had to *anything* but stay there and make more of a goon of himself. He was almost at a full run when he finally reached his and Alabaster's room. Alabaster was already sound asleep, which was just as well. Stanley threw himself onto his bed and buried his face in his pillow, finally regaining the ability to admonish himself.

"Idiot!" he mumbled into his pillow, "Idiot, idiot, *idiot!*" He could absolutely not believe what he'd just said to Nell. Why? Why on earth did he have to go and open his big mouth? He started to mentally catalogue exactly what he'd said, which proved to be a traumatic experience. He'd definitely said she was pretty, which was bad. He was quite sure he'd said something about her freckles being cute, which was much worse. And he'd definitely said that she was beautiful, which was the ultimate in personal mortification.

Of course, the rational part of his brain wanted to know just what was so wrong with paying a person a series of very nice compliments, especially if each one was one hundred percent true.

At the moment, though, Stanley simply wasn't thinking rationally, and was starting to believe that he would likely be found dead the next morning from pure embarrassment.

He supposed that the only blessing in this situation was that no one else had been around to hear what he'd said, but he would still have to face Nell again at some point. What could he possibly say to her? What would *she* say to *him?*

She might laugh at him. She might roll her eyes. She might tell the others what he'd said, and then *they'd* laugh and roll *their* eyes. Except for Ryuno—he'd probably just kill Stanley then and there.

He just wished he could stop thinking about it, just drift off into the blissful peace of sleep. He half hoped that his shadow powers might flare up and cause him to pass out, but they clearly weren't activated by embarrassment.

Mercifully, he did finally fall asleep, though as had been the case for the past while, his dreams were anything but restful.

Chapter 20

THE FALL OF DARUNA ABBEY

Stanley awoke early the next morning, certain that he was going to be ill. Dawn had come much too quickly, and he felt completely unprepared for the day ahead. He told Alabaster that he wasn't feeling well so that he could skip breakfast and put off seeing Nell for a few more hours. Faking sick, though, has its drawbacks. Stanley had to lie there for three and a half hours, and the whole time he was getting hungrier and hungrier. Finally, he decided that he simply wouldn't be physically able to skip lunch, and that it was time to stop acting like a coward. He would go downstairs, look Nell square in the eye and …

Well, he'd see what happened after.

Alabaster came by to check on him just before noon.

"Hey Stanley, ready for lunch? Or are you still in danger of barfing?"

"Yeah," said Stanley. "I'm not sick, Alabaster, I was just faking."

"I figured as much," said Alabaster.

"You did?" said Stanley, once more surprised by his friend's shrewdness.

"Yeah," said Alabaster. "You didn't look very sick—but you did have this sort of emotionally tortured look, so I figured it was basically the same thing."

"Huh," said Stanley thoughtfully.

"So what is it that's made you *mentally* ill?" said Alabaster, grinning annoyingly.

"Uh … Nell," said Stanley. "Last night I said she was … beautiful and now I'm—well, not sure what to do next."

"You said she was *beautiful?"* said Alabaster, sounding impressed.

"Yeah," said Stanley.

"To her face?"

"Yeah."

"Wow! Talk about smooth. What happened next?"

"Er—I, uh—"

"Did you kiss her?"

"No—"

"Did she kiss *you?"*

"No."

Alabaster scratched his chin and looked up at the ceiling. "I'm trying to think of what else could possibly happen in that situation."

Stanley sighed. "I ran back here and fell asleep," he said dejectedly.

Alabaster looked nonplussed. "Okaaaay—*that* wasn't so smooth—"

"I know, I know," said Stanley, putting his hands over his face. "I just felt so stupid, you know? I mean, who just *says* something like that? She probably thinks I'm a weirdo or something."

"Running away *was* kind of weirdo behaviour," said Alabaster.

"No, I mean because I said she was—y'know, beautiful. And that her freckles are cute. And that she's the prettiest girl I've ever seen. I'm such a loser!"

Alabaster gripped his shoulders. "Stanley, you're freaking out—calm down! *Why* would she think you're a weirdo or a loser?"

"Because—well, she—uh … I dunno. It just doesn't seem like the kind of thing you say to girls that you're friends with."

"That makes absolutely no sense," said Alabaster. "Did you mean what you said?"

"Well, yeah," said Stanley.

"Every word? Be honest!"

"Okay … yeah, I did."

"So what's the problem?" Alabaster demanded. "I wish I had the guts to say that kind of stuff to girls. Poetry! You're a poet with the soul of a—gruff, hairy little superhero. You complimented her, that's all. Who doesn't like compliments? What's the worst that could happen?"

"I dunno!" said Stanley.

"Exactly," said Alabaster. "Now look, I think I know where you're coming from here: you bared a bit of your soul to someone, and that can be a hard thing to do, right?"

"What?"

"Next time you see her—which will probably be in about ten minutes—just play it cool. Tell her you're sorry for running away, that you just sort of had a bit of a freakout moment, and that you're all better now."

"I'm not saying that!"

"But it's the truth! Okay, fine—tell her you had to go to the bathroom real bad. Either way let's go—I'm hungry!"

They went down to the dining hall, Stanley steeling himself for the confrontation with Nell. He wasn't going to make up some story. He was going to explain himself clearly, concisely, and be done with it. He and Alabaster waited a bit for her to show up, but by 12:15 they decided to start without her, and tucked in to their foot-long burritos.

"Boy, you can't complain about the food here, that's for sure," said Alabaster once they'd polished off their plates, including the sides of refried beans and rice.

"Yeah, said Stanley, belching involuntarily.

As it was now only 12:30, they decided to wait around for a bit, at least until they could move again. At about twenty minutes to one, Algernon came by with Koko close behind.

"Well, that's that," said Algernon, plunking himself down beside Stanley while Koko quietly sat down across from him.

"Er—what's what?" asked Stanley, when it became clear that nothing else was forthcoming.

"It's over," said Algernon, gesturing dramatically. "The journey, the quest, the dream, all of it. Over!"

Stanley and Alabaster exchanged a bewildered glance.

"What Algernon is trying to say," said Koko, "is that he, Mr. Temoc, Mr. Akechi, Father Blake, and myself have agreed that our expedition into the wilds of Verduria should halt here, at least for the time being."

"Halt?" said Stanley. "But—"

"And *why* weren't *we* consulted?" said Alabaster with mock indignation.

"We meant no offense," said Koko, clearly not recognizing Alabaster's attempt at humour, "But given that your inclusion in the venture was essentially accidental, we decided to hold our meeting despite your absence."

"Very sorry about that, Stanley, old bean," said Algernon, patting him on the shoulder. "And you too, Albert. I wanted to include the two of you in the meeting, but, well, here we are."

"The outcome would have been the same," said Koko. "The jungle is just too dangerous—Temoc said so himself, and he is the resident expert. We were not adequately prepared for the rigours of this journey; that much was clear before we'd spent barely a day in the wilderness. If you'll recall, Algernon, the majority of the riverboat's crew was lost in the attack, and the rest have gone on to an as yet unknown fate. Each one of those men and women had a life of their own—just because we did not *know* them, does not make their deaths any less tragic."

"I *know*," said Algernon sulkily. "But—"

"I'm sorry, Algernon," interrupted Koko, "but the subject is closed. A consensus was reached. We depart for Port Verdant before week's end. Only an armoured warship can hope to travel the Armadon in these troubled times, that much, at least, we can agree on." He turned to address Stanley and Alabaster again. "I apologize for not including the two of you in the meeting. Once we are back safely in Port Verdant and have delivered a report to the governor, we can discuss the possibility of a second, better-equipped expedition."

Koko got up from the table. "Please excuse me," he said with a slight bow.

Algernon sighed as Koko left the room. "Well, my friends, so ends our adventure in the savage jungles of Verduria. I'd be lying if I said I wasn't disappointed … but I guess I'd be a fool to keep going. It doesn't take a master explorer to see that this whole continent is a deathtrap. Oh well, maybe next time."

Algernon stood up and wandered off towards the entrance hall, muttering about not even having brought his camera.

"Huh," said Alabaster. "Well, I guess that really is that. Kind of anticlimactic, eh?"

"Yeah," Stanley said distractedly. Truth be told, he wasn't sure how to react to this new development. On one hand, he agreed with Koko's logic—he had to. The jungle was simply too dangerous, and he and his friends were all ridiculously lucky to be alive.

On the other hand, though, there was the matter of Stanley's dreams of the Lost City and the great blue crystal, the Moon Killer. He still needed to find the answer to his dreams—it was a need as sharp and immediate as the most savage hunger or the driest thirst. Would he have to live the rest of his life without the answers he was seeking? Could he learn to deal with it?

Such thoughts would occupy him for the rest of the day, pushing everything else aside. He didn't even go down for supper that evening (full as he was from his massive lunch), choosing to stay in his room and think instead.

Finally the time came to meet Blake for his training session. He briefly considered not going, since he would likely be too distracted to get anything done. Eventually, he decided that he should at least go and talk to Blake, and headed unenthusiastically towards his office.

⋆ ⋆ ⋆

Stanley paused just outside the door to Blake's office. He could hear what sounded like two people, a man and a woman, talking. Blake had told him not to worry about interrupting him, so Stanley started to open the door, but stopped when heard that the woman seemed to be crying.

"Oh, now, Marie," came Blake's voice, sounding concerned, "what's bringing this on? I had no idea you were so upset."

"I—I'm sorry Father Blake … Nigel … I—I just—" the woman's voice belonged to Sister Marie from the infirmary. She took a moment to get herself under control, then said, "I'm sorry, I must seem like such an idiot, coming in here and bawling like this."

Stanley knew full well that eavesdropping was not a polite thing to do, but he couldn't help wanting to know what had upset Sister Marie so badly.

"No, no, not at all, don't even think it," said Blake. "Something's obviously bothering you, there's no shame in that. Can you tell me?"

"A-alright," said Marie, sniffing loudly. "I … I think there's something … *wrong* with the abbey."

There was a pause. "Something wrong?" said Blake, "With the building itself, or—"

"With *everything,*" said Marie, who sounded on the verge of tears again.

"Er, can you explain it?" said Blake.

Marie sniffed again. "I'll try … but you'll probably think I've gone crazy."

"Marie … please, tell me."

"Okay. There's … something here. Some kind of—I don't know, it's like a feeling … a *presence.*"

Another pause. "What kind of presence?" Blake asked quietly.

"I don't know," said Marie, "Just … a presence, here in the abbey, but I don't know *where*. Sometimes it seems closer, other times more distant …"

"You mean—do you think that someone's here? Hiding? Er, spying, maybe?"

"N-no," said Marie, her voice shaking. "It's … it's not as if there's a p-person … watching me or following me. It's more like … I … I can't … it's like there's something playing music somewhere, and I can't tell where it's coming from. Only instead of music, it's … w-waves of something."

"Waves?"

"I … can't explain it. If my mind is on something else, I don't notice it, but when I'm alone, when I start to think about it … I feel …"

"What, Marie? What do you feel?"

Marie suppressed a sob. "It's like waves of darkness," she managed, before breaking down and weeping loudly.

"Shh, it's okay," said Blake, trying to comfort her.

"There's more," Marie said thickly.

"More?"

"I've … seen things."

"Seen—"

"Horrible th-things. At night, when I'm alone, always at night. The abbey always looks so nice during the day. Everything looks fine … almost everything. But at night … it changes."

"How—"

"Sometimes I'll be in a room or a hallway, and the lights will go out." Marie was almost whispering now. "But they don't turn off—it's not like the power suddenly shuts down. The light just seems to … fade out. It's not like when a light turns off. When a light turns off, it gets dark, but when it happens to me, it's …" She took a shuddering breath. "It's more like the darkness is turning *on.*"

Stanley felt a chill run up his spine.

"And when it happens," she continued, "I stand there in total darkness … even if there are windows nearby, even if moonlight was shining in through the window a moment before … I can't see anything, but there are … *noises* in the dark, and I stand there, not d-daring to move … and then it passes, and all the lights come back on, and the moonlight comes shining back in through the windows."

Marie and Blake were silent for a time.

"Has anything else happened?" Blake asked quietly. Marie didn't answer, but she must have nodded, because Blake said "What else?"

Marie swallowed audibly. "The graveyard."

"The graveyard?"

"I've seen …" her voice sounded strained. "I've seen dead bodies … rise from the graveyard and wa-walk around the grounds."

"Dear lord."

"I've seen them," said Marie, her voice breaking. "They get up from the ground—climb right out of their graves … the Saurians haven't been digging them up, it's … it's—they walk around. They stare in the windows at night. I've seen dead, rotting faces looking at me … oh god—"

Stanley noticed that his whole body was extremely tense. Marie's story seemed to have affected him. Waves of darkness? The dead rising from their graves? He peeked into the room. Blake got up from his desk, came around and took Sister Marie's hand. She stood up from her chair and threw her arms around him, sobbing heavily into his shoulder. Blake looked worried.

"Shh, it's alright," he said.

"You must think I'm completely insane," Marie sobbed.

"Of course I don't," said Blake. "I believe you."

Marie pulled back and looked at him with swollen eyes. "You do?"

Blake nodded. "While I haven't seen anything around here, I have seen some … frightening things elsewhere. In the jungle."

Marie gasped. "You mean it's not just here?"

"I'm afraid not," said Blake, "although yours is, I must say the most unsettling account of the strangeness in Verduria that I've heard. Why haven't you talked to the abbot about this?"

"I have!" said Marie, "But … he's become strange, Nigel. He wouldn't listen to me. He didn't even seem to know who I was, let alone understand what I was telling him. The whole time I was talking to him, he looked like … like he was trying to figure out who I was, or something! … I want to leave, Nigel."

"Leave?" said Blake, "But—don't you think we should—"

"No," said Marie. "I want out. It's too creepy here for me. I want to leave."

Blake nodded. "I understand. You can go back on the Monitor when it leaves for Port Verdant on Friday—"

"Nigel, *no*," said Marie. "I want to leave *now*. As soon as I can. With you."

Stanley raised an eyebrow. Was Blake going somewhere?

"What?" said Blake, "But—Marie, I'm not—"

"I don't want to stay here another day. Please, *please*, let me go with you. Don't make me stay here … alone."

"Marie, we … I'm—"

"At least consider it."

"…All right. I'll consider it."

"Thank you."

There was a brief silence. "You seem to be doing better now," said Blake.

"Yes," said Marie. "Talking about it seems to have helped. Thank you for listening. I should get back to the infirmary."

"Are you—will you be alright?"

"I think so. Knowing that I'll be out of here soon will help. If … if anything happens, or … if I get frightened again … can I come back and see you?"

"I—yes, yes of course you can."

"Thank you." Marie kissed Blake on the cheek. "Goodnight," she said, as she turned and headed towards the door.

Stanley, who had briefly forgotten that he probably wasn't supposed to be listening in, panicked for a moment, looking about wildly for a place to hide so that Sister Marie wouldn't see him. Then he remembered what he'd been practising for the past week, and decided it was time for a true test. He flattened himself against the wall, willing himself to become hidden. The shadows around him flickered for an instant, then covered him completely, just in time for Sister Marie to pull the door open and sweep by.

Stanley gasped with surprise at his success, causing Marie to pause for half a second before continuing on her way. The sensation of the shadow meld was a strange one—he felt as if he had stepped into the wall, tucked into a space that only he could enter.

Once Marie had passed, he let the shadows recede, and opened the door to Blake's office as nonchalantly as he could.

Blake looked up as he came in. "So," he said, folding his hands on his desk. "What did you think of all that?"

Stanley stared. "You knew I was there all along?"

"Not quite," said Blake, "but when you didn't come in at the usual time, I assumed you'd arrived, but didn't want to interrupt. And, given that you came in right after Sister Marie left, I *deduced* that you'd probably executed a flawless shadow meld to hide from her, since she didn't say anything to you on her way out."

"Oh—right," said Stanley, feeling a bit foolish.

"Well," said Blake, offering Stanley his usual chair, "Sister Marie certainly had an unsettling tale to tell."

Stanley nodded. Marie's story had indeed made him feel quite uneasy.

"I'm sure some would dismiss her experiences as nightmares or hallucinations," said Blake. "Of course, you and I have seen plenty of proof that a dark power is at work in Verduria—and we may be getting very close to it, indeed." Blake stood up and began to pace back and forth. "I'd thought something seemed a bit off from the moment we arrived here. Nothing specific or tangible, but ... just something about the *feel* of the place. No one else seemed to notice, so I kept it to myself—"

"I think something like what Marie was talking about happened to me last night," Stanley piped up. Blake looked at him sharply.

"Really? What happened?"

Stanley described the strange events of the previous night, after he'd left Blake's office. The sudden inexplicable darkness did seem to match Marie's story.

"Interesting," said Blake, once Stanley had finished. "Worrisome, but interesting. I think we may be on to something here." He returned to his seat before continuing. "Stanley, I'm wondering if you wouldn't mind taking a break from training tonight; I'd like you to accompany me on a brief fact-finding mission."

"Er … well, sure, I guess so," said Stanley, supposing that they'd be off to the library in a few minutes.

"Good," said Blake, consulting his watch. "It's a bit early yet, though, so I guess we have some time to kill. I suppose you've heard about the change of plans?"

"You mean about us going back to Port Verdant?" said Stanley.

Blake nodded. "It really is for the best, I think. The jungle is far worse than we'd predicted."

"Er, Blake," said Stanley, "Do you know anything about the big blue crystal? The Moon Killer?"

"Hmm," said Blake, "I confess I don't know much about it at all, aside from what its name implies. Is it literal? A device created specifically for destroying our planet's moons? What real purpose could such a thing serve? And more importantly, why is Governor Cromwell so interested in it?"

Stanley hadn't considered that someone might be seeking the giant blue crystal with less-than-honourable intentions.

"I haven't just been researching shadow powers while we've been here," said Blake, indicating the stacks of books and papers heaped around his office. "It's been a bit of an ordeal, to be honest. Any mention of our Lost City is pretty much the same as any other mythical locale; fanciful, pastoral, utopian … lots of flowery, poetic descriptions without any facts." He picked up the map Stanley had found. "Aside from this, of course. Although I'll concede that this little blue dot could be pointing to just about anything, I still say it's by far our best lead."

"But it's just a map," Stanley said disappointedly. "I mean, it's cool how it blinks and everything, but it doesn't say anything about the city, or—"

"On the contrary, I think it says more than you give it credit for," said Blake. "It looks like a simple piece of paper—or plastic, or—well, whatever it is. But it's clearly not. True, there are devices in the world that behave similarly—computerized maps and the like—but even *they* are *way* behind this. I don't even know what it is. Is it technology or is it magic? … A perfect blend of both, maybe, and if it is, if this simple map has magic about it, then it's very old, indeed—so old that it pre-dates the Lost City by, I don't know, fifty thousand years, a least! As does, I suspect, our Moon Killer."

Stanley's mouth had fallen open. His parents had recently bought a snazzy little GPS for the family car. You could go out and get a cellphone that could do the same thing, and a thousand other things besides (his mom refused to get him one).

But this thing, this strange map, a piece of technology (or magic) that was at least as advanced as the most modern gadgets available (in his world *or* Terra, it seemed), was at least fifty thousand years old.

Blake was still talking. "The Moon Killer and the Lost City belong to completely different civilizations, that's my theory. Their proximity is pure coincidence, I'm sure, but I intend to find out."

"What'll you do when we get back to Port Verdant?" Stanley asked.

Blake paused, not meeting his gaze. "I'm not going back to Port Verdant."

"But—"

"I agreed that the expedition that started there should be disbanded. I agreed that our party was unprepared for the sheer ferocity of the jungle and its denizens. We were almost wiped out within the first twenty-four hours of our trip, and we barely managed to reach the abbey at all. The jungle is just too dangerous for our team.

"But not for me. And not, I think, for you."

Stanley stared. He knew very well what Blake was getting at, but still could scarcely believe it. "But—how can you—we can't—"

"I have great confidence in your powers," interrupted Blake. "Your progress hasn't been as fast as I'd hoped, but your abilities are exceptionally strong—probably stronger than mine, or at least, they will be once you've mastered them. You've come a long way, Stanley, in a very short time. I think you're ready to really put your skills to the test."

Stanley was shaking his head in disbelief. "I … I *can't*. I can't just leave Alabaster and Nell—"

"Your friends will return safely to Port Verdant," said Blake reasonably. "And you will too, eventually."

"But how long would we be gone?" asked Stanley, unable to believe that he was even discussing this. He'd seen the horrors of the jungle firsthand. There was no way he was about to go back out there, especially without his friends at his side.

Was there?

"Probably not as long as you might think," said Blake, holding up the map. "*This* also tells me there may be other ways to get where we're going. Ways that are both faster and safer."

Stanley thought it over for longer than he should have, then said "I—can't, I'm sorry. I just can't. I don't think *you* should, either!"

"Not even to find the answer to your dreams?" asked Blake, his tone uncharacteristically sly.

Stanley looked up at him warily.

"I know it's important to you," said Blake. "I've heard you talk in your sleep. I have a pretty good idea of what this means to you—even if I don't fully understand it."

"I—"

"I'm only saying this because I'm like you, in a way. I need to find answers, solve mysteries, find the truth. I think we can help each other."

Stanley started to speak, but Blake held up a hand to stop him.

"I'll tell you what—don't decide yet. Take some time, give it the thought it requires—but consider this one last point:

"The three moons that orbit this world—every time I research them, the same basic idea comes up. The moons maintain an important *balance*. It may be natural, it may be mystical, but either way, it's very important to the well-being of this world. If one of the moons were to be *destroyed*, that balance would break, and I know enough about this world to know that when that sort of balance is destroyed, well … we've already had a taste of what happens when the nature of things is thrown off kilter, haven't we."

Stanley was quiet for a time. "Do you think the governor wants to destroy the balance?"

"I'm not sure," said Blake. "I doubt if he even knows what it is he's after. All he knows is that it's a *sky-jewel-weapon*. Maybe he thinks it's something you can just tack on to the side of a ship and blast the enemy navy with, maybe he just thinks it would look nice in his yard, who knows? I'm just saying that I'd rest much easier knowing that a device like this Moon Killer is safe from the likes of him—or *anyone*, for that matter."

He came around the desk and clapped Stanley on the shoulder. "Enough of that for now, eh? For the time being, I've got a bit to do to prepare for my trip, and now's as good a time as any for the mission I mentioned earlier. Frankly it would probably be better if we waited 'till later, but I'd rather just get it over with. Are you ready?"

"Er—I guess so?" said Stanley, getting up from his chair.

"Relax," said Blake, "We're not going far." He produced a small key from his pocket and unlocked a drawer in his desk, from which he withdrew a worn-looking leather satchel, which he slung over his shoulder. "Follow me," he said, leading the way out of the room.

★ ★ ★

Blake led the way down the corridor towards the main entrance hall. They descended the great staircase, and Blake took a quick look around before motioning for Stanley to follow him.

Stanley paused when he realized that Blake was headed towards the hallway that led to the catacombs.

"This way," said Blake, disappearing through the archway.

Stanley followed with some reluctance, though the narrow, dark hallway was much less creepy when one had company.

"Alright," said Blake as he reached the locked door, "step one. Let me see if I can finally get this door open. Keep an eye out, would you, Stanley? We're not technically supposed to be here."

"We're not?" said Stanley. "Not even you?"

"Definitely not me," said Blake, fiddling with the lock. "Daruna Abbey isn't exactly what it seems. Most of the residents are not actually members of the clergy—they go by *Brother*, *Sister*, and that sort of thing, but almost everyone here is an exile from Azuria."

"Really?" said Stanley. "But why?"

"Azuria is a very … isolationist country," said Blake, placing his palm against the door, and turning a section of the wood so that it rotated ninety degrees. "They rarely let anyone in or out, and once you're out, you're usually out for good."

"That seems pretty weird," said Stanley, curiously watching Blake work.

"Hm," said Blake, popping open a hidden panel to reveal a computerized numerical keypad. "They're a technologically advanced society," he went on, as he punched in a series of numbers, "and are very concerned with ensuring that their technology doesn't leave their borders—*and* with ensuring that the 'primitive' world at large doesn't contaminate them. Our friends here at the abbey fled Azuria some time ago, and made off with some cutting edge technology, too. Not sure if you noticed any of the equipment down in the infirmary, but I can promise you there's nothing like it anywhere else outside of Azuria. I doubt your friend would still have her eye were it not for their cellular regenerator. Incredible device. That armoured ship, too—the Monitor—that's another piece of advanced machinery. Terrifying in the wrong hands, that's for sure."

Blake sighed. "Then there's this door. It's got all sorts of locks and seals on it—can't see most of them, of course."

"So are you from Azuria, too?" asked Stanley.

"Me? No, but I've been there. Aha! I think I've got it."

There came a series of deep metallic *clunks* from the door, and it swung slowly open. Stanley was surprised to see that the back of it was made of solid metal. Beyond, a stone stairway led down into darkness.

"What's down there?" Stanley asked, a tad apprehensively.

"Probably quite a lot," said Blake, lifting an old-fashioned lantern off of its hook just inside the door. "We're looking for the reliquary, though." Instead of striking a match to light the lantern, he pressed a button on its base, and an extremely bright white light came streaming out of its glass enclosure.

"They don't use gas lamps in Azuria," said Blake, noting Stanley's quizzical look. "Come on—it shouldn't be too far." He started down the steps, with Stanley close behind.

The steps went straight down for a time, then turned, then turned again. At the bottom, Blake led the way through a very low archway and into a long, spooky stone corridor with a vaulted ceiling.

"We're in the catacombs now," Blake said, making Stanley jump. "Not that I expect you to, but don't wander off—it's easy to get lost down here." He unfolded a stiff, crisp piece of paper, on which seemed to be a hastily-drawn map. It looked very complicated to Stanley.

They went forward slowly, Blake checking the map frequently. Periodically, they passed by a doorway or adjoining hallway that led off into the dark interior of the catacombs.

At one point they passed a statue of an angel set into an alcove in the wall. Stanley thought it looked sad down here all alone in the dark, but it seemed to mean something to Blake, who sped up his pace and turned down the next corridor on their right.

This hallway they followed until they came to a four-way junction. To the left, the hall extended for a short distance, then ended in a huge, round metal door.

"That's the crypt," said Blake. "Best that we stay away from there."

"Why?" said Stanley, not that he particularly *wanted* to go in.

"Because I don't think Marie was kidding about the dead rising from the graveyard," said Blake.

Stanley gulped.

Blake headed off down the hallway to the right. "Here we are," he said, shining the lantern on another massive metal door. There was no doorhandle, but right smack in the middle was a keypad, not unlike the one on the door back upstairs. Blake quickly punched in a code, and with a resounding *ka-chunk,* the lock withdrew and the door swung silently open.

"Are these doors from Azuria, too?" asked Stanley.

"These ones are, yes," said Blake.

"How did you know the password?"

"The abbot told me." Blake left it at that, and stepped through the doorway.

Stanley followed, but he was feeling more and more uneasy the further they went. The reliquary consisted of yet another long, narrow stone hallway with doors on either side at regular intervals. Blake ignored these, and went straight to the end of the hall, where a second round metal door stood. It was identical to the one through which they'd just passed, except that it was open.

Blake *hmmd.* "I wonder how long *that's* been open. Careless."

Stanley peered through the doorway into the darkness beyond. There was no sound, no movement of air. Blake stepped over the threshold and shone his lantern around the room. Unlike the rest of the abbey, this room was completely lined with metal. The light fell on something near the far wall. It was the only object in the room.

And it was big.

An ancient-looking suit of plate armour was displayed there on a tall wooden stand. Whoever it belonged to must have been a certifiable giant—were the armour assembled, the suit would have been at least nine feet tall, probably more.

The helmet, dark and vacant, was not particularly ornate, but it was topped with a black iron crown with spikes that jutted out horizontally in a kind of barbaric halo. The helmet's face consisted of a horizontal slit which would have allowed the wearer to see, while a vertical slit bisected the helmet below the eyes.

The rest of the suit was fairly nondescript, but seemed to be of an almost rock-like texture; the owner clearly hadn't been interested in embellishments or decorations.

The armour was an imposing sight, but there was something very wrong about it, that much Stanley could feel just by looking at it. He had the distinct impression that something was radiating out of it, although what it might be, he couldn't tell—there was nothing to see, or hear, or touch—just an internal feeling that this armour was very, very bad.

Perhaps most unsettling of all, was the disturbing feeling that he'd seen it somewhere before.

"Is this what we came to find?" asked Stanley, hoping that they could get out of here soon.

When there came no answer from Blake, he looked around, but the priest was nowhere to be seen, and the lantern was on the floor. Had he left the room?

"Blake?" said Stanley, starting to feel more than a little alarmed, "Blake?"

But Blake was gone. He must have slipped out, but how could he have moved so silently? And more importantly, *why* would he just leave Stanley here in the catacombs?

Suddenly the lantern went out, and Stanley was plunged into total darkness. His breath caught in his throat and he froze. He was starting to get really afraid; how could he find his way out of this place alone, without a light? Just then he heard a noise. It sounded like a big marble rolling across the floor.

As soon as the sound stopped, the light came back on. Stanley breathed a sigh of relief, and went to pick up the lantern. As he did, he saw what had made the sound. A shiny, fist-sized oval made of what looked like red glass had come rolling from somewhere, and stopped at the foot of the armour stand.

Stanley found this exceptionally odd, and looked around for its source. It definitely hadn't been in the room when he and Blake had first walked in. Had it?

"Blake?" Stanley called again, "Is that you?"

Still no answer. He was about to head for the door, when he suddenly thought he remembered something. He took another look at the strange red oval. Had he seen it before, too? It reminded him of the colourful glass balls he'd seen in the secret room on Uncle Jack's treasure island, back during the summer, although the shape was different, and it was notably smaller.

Suddenly a memory from not so long ago sprang to the forefront of his consciousness. The high priest of the Xol'tec city had had a staff with a roundish, red jewel as part of its head piece. Could this be the same jewel? He tried to get a closer look, but then the lantern went out again. Immediately he could hear movement nearby.

Something was in here with him.

Then, a sound began, quiet at first, but growing louder by the second. It was the sound of thunder rolling in the distance. Another noise joined in, this one all too familiar: the mournful shrieking of rusty metal hinges.

The two sounds grew to an almost deafening cacophony, and then stopped. A second of silence passed, and then a sharp *clink* of breaking glass echoed through the darkness. There came a vague metallic *creak* from somewhere, and then the barest whisper of movement. Stanley thought he felt some kind of fabric lightly brush him, but he couldn't be sure.

The lantern came back on, then, and Stanley noted that his claws were out. He also saw that things had changed since the light had last been on.

The red glass oval was on the floor, cut cleanly in two.

And the armour stand was empty.

He had to shut his eyes and open them again to make sure he was seeing properly. He was. The stand was completely empty. He looked to his right. Nothing was there. He looked to his left and gasped.

The suit of armour was there.

And someone was wearing it. The armour stood there, still and silent, its wearer having to hunch its shoulders and bow its head, which was touching the ceiling.

His heart thundering in his chest, Stanley took a step back from the giant towering over him.

The armour didn't so much as flinch.

He sidestepped to the right, and the helmet turned ever so slightly.

It was watching him.

Stanley grabbed the lantern and quickly sidled over to the broken red oval. He picked up the two halves and put them in his pockets. For some reason, he thought it might be a good idea to bring them with him. While he did this, he never took his eyes off the suit of armour, nor did it stop looking at him.

He took a deep breath, and made a run for the door.

In an instant the armoured giant drew (seemingly from nowhere) a massive flanged mace, six feet long and as black as midnight. Stanley ducked as the mace came whistling towards his head. The armoured one recovered almost instantly, bringing the weapon crashing down in a mighty diagonal smash that missed Stanley by inches, leaving a sizeable dent in the metal floor.

His pulse pounding in his ears, Stanley sprang through the doorway, and, struck by sudden inspiration, leaned into the thick metal door with all his might, pushing it closed. He stepped back, breathing heavily, his arms and legs aquiver with adrenaline. His respite, though, was short lived. A deep, metallic *clang* rang out from the other side of the door, followed by another that shook dust and pebbles from the wall.

Stanley backed away, then turned and ran when a third blow caused the door to buckle outward. He tore down the hallway and left the reliquary, closing the first door behind him, as well. He reached the four-way junction just as a muted, stony crash from somewhere behind him split the eerie silence of the catacombs, and went right when he should have gone left. After about a dozen yards, he found a door that he hadn't seen before. It was metal as well, but seemed to be some sort of elevator: it had two halves that came together, and a button on the wall to the right, with an arrow pointing down.

Realizing that he'd gone the wrong way, Stanley turned and jogged back to the junction. He got there just in time to see the reliquary door start to buckle, and fled down the correct hallway as fast as he could. He ran until he reached the angel statue, and turned left just as he heard, some distance behind him but not nearly distant enough, the sound of the heavy metal reliquary door being smashed off its hinges and crashing to the ground. Stanley sprinted wildly down this last long hallway, eyes popping, terror gripping him like an electric fist.

He could hear nothing behind him, but he knew that the armoured giant was after him. Somehow, the silence was worse than the thunderous stomping and clanking that should have accompanied so large a pursuer.

Finally he reached the stairway, and seconds later, the door with the "no admittance" sign was behind him, and he was back in the main entrance hall. He waited just inside the archway, staring at the door, waiting for the first blow that would signal his need to vacate the area. Then he realized that he was stupidly wasting precious time here, and needed to hurry and warn everyone of what was coming.

"Hey!" he yelled as he leapt up the stairs, "HELP! WAKE UP! EVERYBODY! WE NEED TO GET OUT OF HERE!"

He reached the top of the staircase. "HELLO! HELLOOO! ANYBODY!"

"Stanley?"

Stanley's head turned so fast he almost injured himself. "Nell!" he said, "Oh, thank goodness!"

"What's going on?" asked Nell. She was eyeing him warily, which was not surprising, considering his breathlessness and manic appearance.

"We need to leave *now,*" said Stanley. "There's something down in the basement—the catacombs—something big, and it's after me, and it broke through two huge metal doors, and I think it wants to kill me, and probably everyone."

"Stanley, slow. *Down,*" said Nell. "And *calm* down. Your claws—"

Now was not the time to be calm.

"Nell!" said Stanley, making her jump. "If you never listen to anything else I say, listen to me *right now*. We need to go. I'll explain later, once we've got everybody out of here. Please trust me."

Nell looked at him for a moment. "Okay," she said. "I do."

Just then a thunderous, stony crash resounded from somewhere below them, making the whole building shake. Nell's eyes went wide.

"That's what I'm talking about," said Stanley.

Wordlessly, Nell disappeared into her room, and returned a moment later with the sword Ryuno had given her. It seemed to have a vague silvery-blue glow about it, but it was probably just a trick of the light.

"I don't think we can fight it," said Stanley.

"Last resort," said Nell. She slid the sword into its scabbard and slung it over her shoulder.

Stanley nodded.

There came no further sounds from downstairs, so they went looking for Alabaster.

"Hey guys," he said when he opened the door in answer to Stanley's frantic knocking. "How's it going? What's with the lantern, Stanley? Are the British invading by land?"

Nell snorted loudly, but Stanley, who didn't get the joke, and was in no mood for humour anyway, said, "We need to go, right now."

"'Kay," said Alabaster. "Where to?"

"I—I don't know," said Stanley. "Anywhere but here, though. We have to—"

"What is going on?" Ryuno had appeared, seemingly from nowhere, his sword drawn.

"Ryuno!" said Stanley and Nell in unison.

Another thundering crash resounded from downstairs, and the abbey shook again.

With a *click-clack* of claws on stone, Temoc rounded a nearby corner, followed by Algernon and Koko.

"Who is attacking us?" Temoc demanded.

BOOM

"What on earth *is* that?" said Algernon.

Several of the abbey's residents had also come out of their rooms, and came wandering towards the small group. Everyone was demanding to know what was going on.

"I believe Stanley knows something," said Ryuno. "Everyone, be silent while he speaks."

All eyes turned to Stanley, who cleared his throat nervously.

"There's … *something* attacking the abbey, some kind of, of *giant* in armour."

"Have you seen it?" said one of the monks.

"Yeah," said Stanley. "It's … super strong, and I don't think it's a good idea to try and fight it, so we should all get out of here as soon as we—"

"We can't just *leave,"* said another monk.

"Where's Blake?" said another. "And the abbot?"

"And Sister Marie," said a nun.

"I lost track of Blake in the basement—" Stanley began, but was interrupted by the first monk.

"The *basement?* You mean the catacombs? *You* are not permitted to be down there. Nor is Father Blake, for that matter. What were you doing down there? Speak up, boy!"

"Don't talk to him like that," snapped Nell, stepping towards the monk, "And don't call him 'boy'—he knows what's going on, so just listen to him and *shut up*."

"Yeah!" said Alabaster.

BOOM

The crash was followed by a distant but massive cacophony of crumbling stone. It sounded as if an entire wall of the abbey had collapsed.

"All I know," said Stanley, "is that whatever is making that noise was down in the catacombs, and now it's loose."

"We need to find the abbot," said one of the monks. He'll know what to make of this.

"The abbot is dead!" cried yet another monk, running up to them. "I just found him! He's dead! *Dead!"*

BOOM

"Wow," said Alabaster in an undertone, "this reminds me of that time at Uncle Jack's place."

"Huh?" said Stanley, still in shock at hearing that someone had died.

"Remember the night we left?" said Alabaster. "How that group of thugs attacked the place?"

Stanley's eyes went wide. The attack on Uncle Jack's mansion. The leader of the vandals had been massively tall …

And had worn a spiked helmet.

Nell also looked stunned. "And when we came back the place was completely trashed," she said almost dreamily.

Stanley sprang into action. "EVERYBODY OUT!" he yelled. "Just GO!"

"MOVE!" roared Nell, pointing her sword at the group of monks.

"YEAH!" said Alabaster.

"Let us go!" said Ryuno. "No more discussion—we have tarried too long already!"

They herded the abbey residents before them down the steps. They were about half way down when Ryuno tapped Stanley on the shoulder.

"Is *that* what we are fleeing from?" he asked quietly. He was pointing to one of the balconies above them, upon which stood the armoured giant. Stanley felt his insides run cold.

"Y-yeah, that's him."

Soundlessly, the giant suddenly leapt from the balcony, soaring through the air like a gigantic bird of prey, its black cloak billowing out behind it.

"LOOK OUT!" yelled Stanley, trying to push everyone in front of him out of the way.

Usually, shoving a group of people down a flight of stairs would not be considered acceptable behaviour. In this case, though, it was probably the right thing to do. Everyone managed to get out of the way as the giant landed with a strangely muted crash in the middle of the staircase. There was just one problem: Stanley, Alabaster, and Nell were above the giant, while everyone else was below.

"Are you kidding?" said Alabaster, "Seriously? We're the only ones left on this side?"

The giant straightened up and drew forth its massive mace, and turned its gaze to Stanley.

"We will help you!" yelled Ryuno. "You! Er—giant! Forget about them! Face *me* in single combat—unless you are a *coward!"*

The armoured one ignored him, and took a step towards Stanley, who yelled,

"It's after me! Get out of here, Ryuno! Make sure everyone gets outside!"

"Apologies," said Ryuno, "but honour demands that I stay and fight." He sprang back up the steps, but the giant was ready for him.

A swift (but almost casual) backhanded swing of its mace caught him in the arm and sent him flying.

Ryuno landed hard on the ground. "*Rrrgh!*" he growled, gritting his teeth in pain.

"Your arm is broken," said Koko, kneeling down beside him. "I think that was a warning."

The giant turned its mace upside-down and, clasping it with both hands, thrust it downward, burying its flanged head in the stone of the stairway with a resounding *BOOM*. The giant seemed to freeze for a time, but then its arms tensed, and began to shake. The tremors passed from is arms, to the great mace, and finally into the ground.

The stairway beneath their feet began to shake fiercely as if the entire place were gripped by an earthquake. All of a sudden, the quaking stopped, and as soon as it did, the giant hauled its weapon out of the ground with the force of a small explosion, and the entire staircase began to collapse.

"Whoa!" yelled Stanley, dropping his lantern as the ground gave way beneath his feet.

"MOVE!" cried Nell, leading the way up the crumbling staircase.

Just as the three of them reached the upper landing, the whole thing came apart behind them, collapsing into an avalanche of bricks and dust. When the dust finally cleared, the great staircase was gone, replaced by a pile of depressing rubble.

"Stanley!" came Algernon's voice from down in the wrecked hall, "Are you alright?"

"Yeah, we're fine," Stanley called back.

"For now," muttered Nell.

"Can you get back down?" said Algernon.

"They obviously cannot," said Temoc, sounding annoyed.

"We've lost sight of … our attacker," said Koko. "We need to get you out of here before he returns."

"Don't worry," said Alabaster, "we've got another way out—you guys just get to safety, and we'll see you later."

"What?" said Stanley and Nell.

"Alright," said Koko. "Good luck."

"Wait!" said Nell. "What are you talking about?"

"Well, there isn't much point in them sticking around," said Alabaster.

There came a loud cracking sound from above them, and great chunks of the roof began to fall into the entrance hall. Koko, Ryuno, Algernon, Temoc and the others ran for the doors. By the time the cave-in was over, there was a gaping hole in the roof, and the entrance hall was choked with mountains of impassable wreckage.

"Maybe we can tie some bed sheets together and climb out a window," Stanley suggested. Nell and Alabaster didn't answer. They were staring wide-eyed at something behind him. He turned slowly, already knowing what he would see.

The armoured giant was there, standing still and silent at the far end of the hall.

"I don't think we have time for that idea," whispered Nell.

"Guys," said Alabaster. "I told you, I've got it covered—I know a way out of here."

"You do? Actually?" said Nell. "How?"

"I've had a lot of time to explore while you two were off training. I found this one secret passage that should get us out of here, and I think we can make it."

"Where is it?" asked Stanley, refusing to take his eyes off the giant.

"It's on this floor," said Alabaster. "Not far—down the hall to our left. Now if I know anything about villains and monsters, he's not gonna make a move until we do, so on the count of three—"

The giant suddenly came stalking towards them with frightening speed.

"BLAAAGH!" exclaimed Alabaster, "Run! Follow me! AAAAAH!!" he bolted down the hall to their left, with Stanley and Nell close behind. He made a sharp right down another hall, and then skidded to a halt.

"Uh," he said, looking around.

"What?" hissed Nell, "Where is it?"

"That's the problem—I don't quite remember—"

"Alabaster—" Stanley began.

"Oh, wait!" said Alabaster, snapping his fingers, "It's this one!"

He pointed to a door directly in front of him. Nell instantly flung the door open, shoved Alabaster through, and grabbed Stanley's hand, pulling him in after her.

Stanley eased the door closed just as the giant rounded the corner. He kept his ear to the door, and found that if he listened hard, he could hear their pursuer's footfalls, quiet though they were.

The footsteps approached, stopped, and then faded away again. Stanley let out the breath he'd been holding, as did Nell, who also removed her hand from over Alabaster's mouth.

Looking around, Stanley saw that they were in a small room with a cross-shaped window high on the wall. Beneath the window was a statue of an angel. It looked just like the one he'd seen in the catacombs.

"Okay," whispered Alabaster, "this is it." He walked up to the statue and pulled down on one of its arms. With a stony scraping sound, the statue slid forward to reveal a dark hole beneath it.

Nell looked nervously at the hole in the floor. "I, uh … don't think I can go down there."

There came the sudden sound of splintering wood from somewhere close by.

"He's breaking into the rooms," said Stanley.

"It's a slide," said Alabaster, as if trying to convince Nell that she was about to have fun.

"It's a dark hole," said Nell, her jaw set. "I can't—"

Nearby, another door was bashed to pieces. Stanley was getting worried.

"Nell, if we stay here, he'll get us."

"I know, I know," she said despairingly. "Okay. Okay, I think I can go—if you hold on to me."

Stanley was temporarily stunned. "If I—"

"Can you hold on to me the whole way down?" Nell was looking at him intently. "I need you to do this, Stanley."

CRASH

Another door flew apart, this one very close by.

"Okay, yes, I will," said Stanley. "I mean of course I will, it's not that I don't want to—I mean, no, I don't only want to do it because you're—"

"See you guys down there," said Alabaster, lowering himself into the hole and sliding out of sight.

Stanley and Nell sat down at the edge of the hole. Nell scooted up beside him and wrapped her arms around his torso, squeezing tightly. He could feel her breath on his neck.

A wild, stupid part of him wanted to just sit here like this for a few minutes more, but then the door to their hiding spot exploded loudly into a million splinters of wood as the armoured giant burst through.

Nell screamed, as did Stanley, and the next thing they knew they were sliding down a long dark tunnel. The stone was damp, which was probably just as well—Stanley did not relish the idea of getting stuck with no way out. He could see nothing, but was very aware of Nell clinging to him, her grip almost painfully strong. He was also aware that some of her hair had gotten in his mouth, but he ignored it, and a few interminable seconds later, they came flying out of the secret slide-tunnel and landed in a heap on a cold stone floor.

"You made it!" said Alabaster delightedly, helping them to their feet.

"Yeah," said Stanley. "Er—where are we?"

"Well, we're—uh—in the basement, or something," said Alabaster unhelpfully.

The sound of scraping stone behind him made Stanley turn around, just in time to see the familiar form of the angel statue slide back into place, covering the secret tunnel.

"Alabaster!" said Stanley, rounding on his friend, "This isn't the way out! We're in the catacombs! This is where I was right before I came to find you—I only just made it out of here!"

"Oh my," said Nell, "Ohh my …"

"But look!" said Alabaster, holding up a piece of paper, "It says 'exit' right here!" The paper seemed to be a map, and Stanley quickly recognized it as the plan of the catacombs that Blake had been using. The map was a bit difficult to read, especially in the dim light, but Stanley managed to find their location. As Alabaster had said, a box with the word EXIT printed on it was right there, just at the end of the hall, past the four-way junction that led to the crypt and the reliquary.

"Oh no," said Nell, "Oh no, oh no, oh no."

"Nothing to worry about, Nell," said Alabaster. "We'll be out of here in no time."

"Hold on," said Stanley. "It should be pitch dark down here—where's the light coming from?"

"Down there," said Alabaster, pointing into the distance, where a tiny rectangle of bright white light could be seen. "The exit!"

"*Guys,*" Nell almost yelled, making them jump, "I have to get out of here." She sounded like she was going to cry.

"I hear ya," said Alabaster, "and we're on our way—just down there at the end of the hall, there's a shiny doorway to freedom."

"I can't!" said Nell. "I have to get out now!" she backed up against the wall and put her hands over her face. She was breathing erratically, as if she were gasping for air.

"Ohmanohmanohmanohmanohmanohmannnnnn," she murmured, "We're underground … oh man, we're underground and the whole place is going to collapse, it's going to collapse, we're going to suffocate."

"It's okay," said Stanley, "Nell, look at me, it's okay!"

"*Get me out!*" said Nell, almost screaming now. "*Get me out of here!*" She suddenly undid her zip-up and started to take it off. Fortunately she had a t-shirt underneath it.

"Whoa! Nell, let's *stop* disrobing," said Alabaster, "Let's all keep our clothes *on.*"

"She's panicking," said Stanley. "Claustrophobic people do this sometimes—take off their clothes 'cause they think it'll make them feel less confined, or something." He knelt down and put his hands on Nell's shoulders. She was very tense and her whole body was shaking. Stanley could also see that her skin was clammy and shiny with sweat. "Nell," he said as calmly as possible.

"No, no, no," she murmured, "Dad, help me, Dad, I'm gonna die, help me, Daddy—"

"Nell, it's me, Stanley," he said slowly and deliberately. "Stanley, remember?"

Nell let out a frightened moan that was almost a sob. She was still breathing in quick, high-pitched gasps.

"Shhh," said Stanley, "Nell, we're okay—see that light? Nell? D'you see it?"

"Y-y-yeah," she managed.

"Okay," said Stanley. "That's where we're going. That's the way out. You're not going to die, okay?"

"Uhh," said Nell, still shaking.

"We're in the foundation of the abbey, okay? It's been standing solid for—well, a long time. It's not going to collapse, okay?"

"Maybe you should hug her," suggested Alabaster.

Stanley gulped, then gently pulled Nell towards him, and she immediately buried her face in his shoulder. Her breathing slowed a bit, and she went quiet, but she was still shaking. Every so often, she would let out a moan or a whimper, but Stanley kept assuring her that she was alright. After several minutes, she finally stopped shaking altogether. Stanley was starting to wonder if she'd fallen asleep.

"That was some nice work," said Alabaster, sounding impressed. "Very professional. Dr. Brambles is in! How did you know that stuff about claustrophobic people trying to take their clothes off?"

"I, uh, looked it up during the summer, after we got back from Uncle Jack's place," said Stanley.

"Just in case this sort of thing ever happened! That is some serious foresight," said Alabaster. "Well played, sir, well played."

"I think I'm okay now," said Nell quietly, pulling back from Stanley. She looked tired and haggard, but calm.

"That's a relief," said Stanley, and he meant it. "Can you walk? Do you think you can make it to the door?"

Nell took a deep breath and let it out slowly. "I think so, yeah, as long as I keep telling myself that the ceiling isn't going to collapse, and that there's plenty of air down here. She shuddered, and closed her eyes for a moment. "It might help if you guys keep reminding me of that, too."

"The ceiling's not going to collapse and there's plenty of air," said Alabaster.

"Thanks," said Nell, smiling slightly. She quickly put her zip-up back on and slung her sword over her shoulder, then allowed Stanley to help her to her feet. She stood there a bit shakily for a moment, then looped her arm around his and said "Okay, let's go."

"The ceiling's not going to collapse!" said Alabaster.

"Right," said Stanley. "And we're almost out."

"Old buildings like this stay up forever, anyway," said Alabaster. "Castles, cathedrals, pyramids—man, they used to build stuff to *last!*"

Nell managed a weak chuckle. Stanley was grateful for his friend's endless banter.

"The arched ceilings are a nice touch, too," Alabaster went on. "They really give the place a sense of space. I guess that's why that big guy could fit down here. He'd look pretty funny crawling around on all fours … unless he went really fast, then it'd be creepy."

"Hey, we're almost there," said Stanley, trying to change the subject.

They were approaching the four-way junction. Not too far ahead, Stanley could see that the elevator-ish door that he'd seen before was wide open, letting the light within shine out to illuminate the blackness of the catacombs.

"Kind of weird that they've got fluorescent lights down here," commented Alabaster.

They reached the junction, and paused to look around.

"Wow," said Alabaster, "Check out the damage."

The heavy metal door to the reliquary lay not far to their right, bent and twisted, atop a pile of rubble and broken masonry.

"What was that?" said Nell.

Stanley had heard it, too—an odd shuffling sound off to their left. To his horror, the door to the crypt had also been torn off its hinges and flung to the ground in a crumpled heap. "Uh-oh," he muttered.

"What is it?" whispered Nell.

The shuffling sound came again, and in the darkness of the shattered doorway, something moved. Two red points of light appeared, and a figure came shambling into view.

It was long dead, that much was clear; a frail, skeletal thing with anciently-dry parchment skin clinging feebly to its bones. The wispy tatters of a burial shroud hung about its frame, and its slack-jawed, ghoulish face wore an infinitely vacant expression—except for the furious red fires that burned deep in its cavernous eye sockets.

"And of course there had to be zombies," said Alabaster.

The creature suddenly seemed to notice them, and let out a low and menacing groan.

"Okay," said Stanley, "Let's just get to the door, nice and slow—it might not be dangerous, just confused. About being dead."

Just then the zombie let out a rasping, guttural roar and came lurching towards them.

Nell let go of Stanley's arm and reached behind her, drawing her sword from the scabbard slung across her back. As the zombie tottered within grabbing distance, she took a swing at its grasping, bony arm, and with a quick, dry *crack,* severed it at the wrist. Almost instantly, the hand and arm burst into bright blue flame, and dry as it was, the undead fiend was all ablaze in seconds.

The three friends backed away and stared in fascinated horror as the azure flame burned the zombie to ash in less than a minute.

"H-how did you *do* that?" said Stanley, his voice filled with awe.

"I—don't know," said Nell, staring at her sword with wide eyes.

"Awesome," said Alabaster, "You had a Sword of Undead Slaying all along and we didn't even know it! What's the strength bonus on that thing?"

"What?" said Nell.

Several more pairs of red eyes appeared from out of the darkness of the crypt.

"Time to go," said Stanley, herding Nell and Alabaster towards the brightly-lit doorway.

They hurried down the hall, sprinting for the last several yards, and stepped into a wide room lined with metal and lit by what looked like bright fluorescent lights, which were almost blinding after the dimness of the catacombs.

"If this isn't actually an elevator, we're in big trouble," said Alabaster.

"Thank you for pointing that out, that's very helpful," said Nell.

Stanley looked around and spied a single button on the left wall. He ran up to it and pushed it several times.

"One-push-is-sufficient," said a calm, even voice that seemed to fill the room.

"A ghost!" said Alabaster, "Hurry, Nell—draw forth your Sword of Undead Slaying!"

"Shut up," said Nell, rubbing her chin nervously, "just shut up, *please.*"

Several skeletal forms rounded the corner a few dozen yards away and started stumbling towards them. Stanley pushed the button again, but the doors didn't budge.

"The-door-is-jammed," said the mysterious voice. "Please-remove-obstruction."

The zombies were getting closer, and there were a lot of them.

"Jamnation!" cried Alabaster.

"There's nothing blocking the door!" said Stanley, checking every inch of the opening. As he looked up at the top left corner of the doorway, though, he thought he saw something like a big black spider dislodge itself from the sliding door. A single yellow eye with a slitted pupil opened on its back and peered at him for a split second, then closed and vanished as the thing scuttled off into the darkness. Nell and Alabaster didn't seem to have seen it, so Stanley pushed it from his mind.

"Thank-you," said the voice, "Doors-closing."

Just as the doors began to slide closed, the first zombie lurched across the threshold.

"Additional-passengers-boarding," said the voice, "Doors-opening."

"No!" said Stanley, willing his shadow shield into existence to fend off the walking corpse, "Close them! Close the doors!"

"I'm-sorry," replied the voice, "that-would-be-un-safe."

Nell was at Stanley's side in an instant, thrusting her blade into the zombie's chest with a sound like a bag of chips being crushed. The thing quickly caught fire just like the first, and Nell booted it out into the hall before it burned up. The other zombies hesitated, seemingly not wanting to get close to the bright blue flames.

"Close!" yelled Alabaster. "Close close close!"

"Doors-closing," said the voice.

The doors finally slid together, shutting out the horrible undead monsters.

"Phew," said Stanley, collapsing against the wall. He willed his shield to dissolve, and had to sit down for a bit while his lightheadedness passed. That had easily been the largest shield he'd ever made, and he felt dizzy and a tad queasy.

The elevator began to move, and a green arrow appeared on a small screen above the door, pointing down.

"Hey, wait," said Alabaster, "We want to go up, not down—take us up, please. Ground level."

"I'm-sorry," said the voice, "This-conveyance-has-two-stops-only. Would-you-like-to-go-back-up?"

"NO!" said Stanley.

"Acknowledged. Current-course-will-continue."

Stanley looked over at Nell, who was also seated on the floor, her sword lying beside her. Her eyes were closed, and she seemed to be talking to herself.

"Elevators are helpful," she said, as if reciting something, "They get us where we want to go. Elevators are helpful. Elevators are safe and rarely break down."

"Are you okay?" Stanley asked.

Nell opened her eyes and looked over at him. "I'm fine," she said.

"There-is-no-need-to-worry," said the voice. "This-conveyance-is-operating-at-seventy-three-percent-efficiency. This-conveyance-is-magnetically-operated-and-does-not-rely-on-breakable-cables."

"Are you a computer?" asked Alabaster.

"That-is-correct," said the voice. "I-am-a-series-six-automated-vertical-conveyance-unit-capable-of-autonomous-function, serial-number-64A—"

"Yes-or-no-will-do," said Alabaster in a robot voice.

"Acknowledged. Yes," said the voice.

Stanley wanted to ask the elevator a few questions of his own (not the least of which would have been 'what is a high-tech elevator doing in the basement of a hundreds of years-old building'), but by now they had reached their destination.

"Arriving-at-Commonwealth-Building-main-floor," announced the elevator. "Doors-opening. Have-a-nice-day." The elevator doors slid open, and Stanley, Alabaster, and Nell cautiously disembarked. "Boarding-passengers-please-allow-the-elevator-to-empty-before-embarking." After a few seconds, the voice proclaimed, "Doors-closing," and the elevator doors slid shut.

"Where are we?" said Nell.

Stanley couldn't even begin to guess. They seemed to have stepped off the elevator into another world. They were currently standing in a huge, open room that looked like the lobby of some very modern office building. The place was in an advanced state of disrepair; broken furniture and rubble lay strewn about the once-shiny black marble floors, and a forest of wires and broken light fixtures hung down from the ceiling high above. Whole sections of marble paneling were missing from the numerous pillars supporting the roof, having fallen off and broken on the floor long ago.

Most of the lights were off, but a fair number were still on, or at least flickering, so there was more than enough light by which to see. Plants had somehow taken root here, too, and wrapped themselves around many of the pillars. They seemed to thrive on the artificial lighting, but where they got their water was anybody's guess.

A thick layer of dust lay over everything, and Stanley could see that a trail had been made across the floor, leading out into the wasteland of rubble and destroyed furniture. Someone had come this way recently.

Directly across from the elevator, perhaps a football field's length away, Stanley could see the far wall of the building, and a doorway leading out.

"I guess we might as well go outside and see where we are," he said with a shrug. "How are you feeling?" he asked Nell.

"Fine. Better now," she said. "It's nice and open in here—well, *open,* anyway—I can't even tell if we're still underground."

"D'you think were' back on Earth?" said Alabaster, as they started clambering over the rubble. "I mean, *our* Earth?"

"Doesn't seem like it," said Stanley. "This building looks like it's been this way for a long time."

"And it has a talking elevator that can carry on a conversation," said Nell.

"I'd be willing to bet that somewhere on Earth there's a ruined building like this," said Alabaster. "And the elevator could be the connecting point—like the tunnel under Uncle Jack's mansion."

"Guess we're about the find out," said Stanley, stepping over a last bit of wreckage and placing his hand on the doorhandle. He pushed open the door and led the way outside.

Chapter 21

THE UNDERGROUND CITY

They were now in what looked like the interior of a vast shopping mall. A flight of steps led down to a wide, open thoroughfare, on either side of which were rows of shops and businesses. High above, the barrel-vaulted ceiling seemed to be made entirely of windows through which one could see a clear blue, sunny sky, with massive, rounded skyscrapers reaching towards the heavens. Strangely, some of the windows were dark.

A sign hanging down from the roof proclaimed,

COMMONWEALTH PLAZA

in big blue letters. Like the Commonwealth *building,* this place was a depressing riot of dilapidation and ruin. Piles of rubble were strewn about here, too, although not nearly as thick as inside the building. Twisted, wrecked vehicles resembling cars and motorcycles dotted the thoroughfare, and every one of the shops and buildings alongside it was dark and vacant.

Here and there, lit signs still faithfully advertised their stores and products. 'Marcello's Pizza' was apparently 'the best', and several glowing neon circles suggested that everyone try 'Crystal-Caff Cola', as it was 'Clearly Delicious'.

The pristine skyscrapers outside did not fit at all with this dark, ruined interior of broken walls and sadly-flickering lights.

"Those can't be real windows," said Stanley, "can they?"

Alabaster picked up a chunk of what looked like concrete, and heaved it at the nearest window, which broke in a shower of sparks, flickered once, and went dark.

"Alabaster!" said Nell.

"What?" said Alabaster. "Everything's broken down here anyway. I guess this means we're not back on Earth—they'd only put in TV screens that look like windows if the building was underground. Which, I'm guessing, it is."

"Great," said Nell. "Well, at least it's open—the illusions is pretty convincing."

They still had no idea where they were, though. The place was as quiet as a tomb, aside from the buzzing and flickering of the few still-working signs and lights. Nothing moved, no sound or sign of life could be detected.

"Well, we can't really go back," Stanley reasoned, "so maybe we should look around a bit. Did you see that trail in the dust back there? Someone must've come through here a little while ago—if we find them, we might also find a way out."

"I guess anywhere's better than back upstairs with the zombies and giants," said Alabaster.

They descended the staircase to street level and started to pick their way among the rubble and wrecked cars. To their left, a large opening led off to another part of the complex, but Stanley noticed footprints in the dust ahead, and elected to follow them.

They passed stores, restaurants, apartment buildings, and just about any other type of building you might see in a big city, the light of the fake-sky video screens shining down on them all the while. At one point they rounded a gentle corner, and could see a ways into the distance.

"Wow," said Nell, "it just keeps going."

And it did. The road, which had widened out and looked more like a highway now, went on for what looked like miles, before disappearing into the subterranean darkness.

"It's a whole city, isn't it?" she went on. "Someone really built an entire city underground."

Stanley gazed down the long, decrepit tunnel, imagining what it must have looked like in its prime. A bustling street filled with people going to work, or to the store, or to the movies … gleaming storefronts emulating the architecture of the fake skyscrapers depicted in the video screens. An underground utopia.

"It must have been amazing once," he said reverently. "Back when it was new."

"For sure," said Alabaster, "but how long has it been like this? I mean, everything down here is like—super modern. Up until now, Terra's seemed … I dunno, pretty old-fashioned? Or at least steampunk-ish."

"It doesn't seem like anyone's been down here for years … maybe centuries," said Nell.

The footprint trail in the dust suddenly veered off and went into a nearby building across the street. The sign above the door read

COMMONWEALTH STATION

At some point in the distant past, a security gate had been lowered, but something had broken through it long ago, leaving a ragged hole. The footprints led through this hole, and past a row of turnstile barriers and broken ticket booths.

They hopped over the turnstile and found themselves standing on what looked like a train platform. Stanley walked to the edge and peered down. A single track ran alongside, disappearing into tunnels on the left and right. Hanging from the ceiling was a flickering screen displaying a long list of train schedules. Every entry on the list showed as *cancelled.*

"North and southbound trains," said Nell, reading a large sign on the wall beyond the track. "I wonder where a northbound train would take us—back to Port Verdant, maybe?"

"Maybe," said Stanley, "but how would we know when we got there?"

"Too bad they're all cancelled," said Alabaster.

Suddenly there came the echoing sound of squealing metal from the left-hand tunnel, and a moment later a sleek, short monorail train came roaring down the track to stop beside the platform. The train was about twenty-five feet long and was probably bright blue once, but now looked tarnished and dingy. A single, opaque black window occupied the front of the train, but the ones running down the sides were transparent, if rather dirty.

The train's hull looked completely solid and seamless, but a section of it promptly popped out and slid to the side, revealing a doorway.

"All-aboard-for-southbound-train-Patty-headed-for-Point-Argent," said a pleasant female voice. "Train-Patty-departing-for-Point-Argent-all-aboard."

"So … what do we do?" said Alabaster.

"We should see if there are any trains going north, anywhere near the coast," said Nell. "Excuse me," she said to the train, "er, can you tell us if there are any trains, er, going north?"

"I'm-sorry," said the female computer voice, "there-are-no-northbound-trains-scheduled-at-this-time." There was a brief sound of radio static, and the voice spoke again, but in a much less halting tone. "I really am sorry, sweetie. Northbound tracks have been compromised by an unanticipated seismic event. My scanners aren't strong enough to fully assess the extent of the damage, but I estimate it to be catastrophic."

"So much for that idea," said Alabaster.

"Er, ma'am," said Stanley, making Nell smile, "do you know if anyone else came through here recently?"

"You can call me Patty," said the voice. "And yes, actually, two individuals did come through here twenty-seven minutes and forty seconds ago. They boarded a southbound train. Pablo, I think."

"Do you know who they were?" asked Stanley. "I mean—can you describe them?"

There was a pause. "No, I'm sorry, I don't know. A human male and female, I think, but that's all I could get. Sorry."

"That's okay, thanks anyway," said Stanley.

"Who do you think it might be?" asked Nell. "Blake, maybe?"

"Maybe," said Stanley. "He just disappeared when that—giant armour-guy got loose. It was really weird."

"Let's hope Blake doesn't turn out to *be* that giant armour-guy," said Alabaster. Stanley gave him a look, although truthfully, the thought had briefly crossed his mind, unlikely though it seemed.

"That's a pretty ridiculous thought," said Nell.

"Just doing my job," said Alabaster.

Stanley shook his head. Shadow powers or no, Blake would never fit into such a huge suit of armour.

Why had he been looking for it, though?

Another burst of static came from Patty the monorail, and she spoke again, in her original manner:

"All-passengers-please-board-the-train. Patty-departing-for-Point-Argent-all-aboard."

If Blake was one of the people who took a train half an hour ago, Stanley wanted to track him down and get some answers. "Come on," he said, stepping into the car.

"Stanley!" said Nell.

"We can't just stay here," said Stanley, "Besides, we can always come back if we need to."

"Let's mosey," said Alabaster, planting his hands on Nell's back and pushing her slowly towards the open door.

"Okay okay, I'm coming, you don't have to shove me, get off!"

Alabaster wisely relented, and he and Nell both stepped aboard.

"Welcome-aboard," said Patty as the door slid shut. "Please-take-a-seat."

The interior of the monorail was surprisingly clean; a deep blue carpet lay under their feet, and the walls were a spotless white. A line of big padded recliner chairs (also blue) lay along each side of the cabin, facing inward. Stanley sat down in the nearest chair, and Alabaster sat across from him. Nell took the seat beside Stanley, trying to be as inconspicuous about it as possible.

"Hoo-whee!" said Alabaster, "Is this ever fancy! I didn't think we'd be going first class."

"With-Magitech-every-trip-is-first-class," said Patty enthusiastically.

"Sorry," she said immediately after, "I have to say that."

"We-are-now-departing. Estimated-time-to-next-stop, Greenfalls-Junction-twenty-one-minutes."

"Patty, why do you talk like that?" said Alabaster.

There was a pause, followed by some more static. "I don't know," said Patty. "I think there are some things that I'm programmed to say, and other things that I just learned to say on my own. The stuff I learned myself just comes out easier."

"You can learn?" said Nell, leaning forward in her seat. She sounded impressed.

"I sure can," said Patty. "I learn a lot from people—or at least, I used to. People are so interesting. They have so much to say. I haven't seen any people for a long time, though. I miss them. I'm glad people are taking the train again!"

The three friends exchanged a look.

"Er, Patty," said Stanley, "Can you tell us anything about where we are?"

"We-are-currently-on-the-Blue-Line, southbound-en-route-to-Greenfalls-Junction."

"Right," said Stanley. "Um, this might sound kind of dumb, but are we on the planet Terra, in the continent ofVerduria?"

A pause. "Sorry, hon, I'm not familiar with either of those names. Our planet is named Titania, and the continent in which we are located is Fiorus. Here is a map of the continent."

A section of wall at the front of the cabin slid open, revealing a large screen, on which was displayed a detailed map of Verduria. Stanley recognized the twisting blue line of the Armadon River, and had become fairly familiar with the overall shape of the continent itself.

"Patty," said Nell, "I think your information is incorrect—or at least out of date."

"My database has not been updated for a long time," said Patty. "It is possible."

"What's the name of the city we're in?" Alabaster enquired.

"Sub-Sphere Three," answered Patty. "The-ultimate-in-subterranean-living, brought-to-you-by-Magitech, working-for-a-better-world."

Pause. "Sub-Sphere Three is a massive underground city," said Patty. "It's more like a country, really—it spans much of the Fioran—sorry, *Verdurian* continent. Magitech built it so that the destruction of the continent's jungles and indigenous wildlife could cease, allowing them to recover and flourish, while the majority of the continent's population lived comfortably underground."

"That's ... amazing," said Nell.

It was almost unbelievable. An underground city, spanning a continent. How was it even possible?

"So what happened?" said Alabaster.

"I'm-sorry, I-don't-understand-the-question," said Patty.

"Well, we didn't see much of it," said Alabaster, "but the whole place was, y'know, deserted, and totally broken down."

Patty didn't answer.

Nell pressed the question. "It looked like no one had been there for—I dunno, centuries, Patty. Everything is ruined, or falling apart. What happened down here? How old is this place?"

"I—" Patty began, "I … don't really know." There was a silence, and it seemed that nothing else was forthcoming, but then she continued, "I don't know what date it is anymore. My calendar stopped working a long time ago."

Patty displayed what looked like a date on her screen; it read

`00/00/9999`

"9999?" said Stanley, "That's what year it is?"

"No," said Patty, "That's the year my calendar stopped working. The counter couldn't go above four digits, and it just froze."

"When was the last time you had a passenger?" asked Nell. In response, Patty displayed another date on her screen:

`22/04/2214`

Nell's jaw dropped. "But—that's over seven thousand years!"

"It's been much longer than that," said Patty. "I tried keeping track of the hours after my calendar broke, but I lost count after a hundred million."

"Oh, Patty," said Nell, "I'm so sorry, I can't imagine what that must have been like. Have you been down here all that time?"

"Yes," said Patty. "It's been … very lonely."

"Didn't you have anyone to talk to?" said Alabaster. "Like, uh, other trains?"

"No, the other trains don't talk to me," answered Patty. "We're never close to each other while operating, and they never have anything to say in storage. That's why I'm so glad to finally have new people to talk to! Can I know your names, please?"

"Of course you can," said Nell. "I'm Nell, and this is Stanley, and Alabaster."

"I'm so happy to meet you," said Patty, sounding delighted.

"So—this *Magitech* you keep mentioning," said Stanley, "It's a company? Did they make you?"

"Magitech: building-the-best-because-we-are-the-best."

"Sorry. Yes, Magitech made me. And Sub-sphere Three. And just about everything else."

"Even Crystal-Caff Cola?" said Alabaster.

"Yes. Crystal-Caff-Cola: Clarity-is-refreshing."

They sped on through the subterranean train tunnels, cozy and secure in the comfort of Patty's cabin, unmindful of the dim, ruined underworld roaring past them. In truth, it had been much, much longer than seven thousand years since the glory days of the great underground city.

Patty could tell them very little about the city, but she confirmed that Stanley, Alabaster, and Nell looked just like the original inhabitants.

"I guess that means they were human," said Nell.

"Not necessarily," said Alabaster.

It wasn't long before they reached the next station on Patty's route.

"Now-approaching-Greenfalls-Junction," she announced, in the middle of asking Nell how old she was, "Greenfalls-Junction-coming-up." There was a moment of static, and then she said, "Sorry about that. I think you should know, I'm detecting severe damage to the Greenfalls Junction station. Probable cave-in. Sensors show a 0% probability of bypassing the wreckage. I'm switching to another track."

The three friends exchanged a nervous glance.

Nell said, "Er, Patty, how many of the tunnels have caved in?"

"I don't know," said Patty. "Probably not many. Magitech-sub-spheres-are-cave-in-proof!"

"Sorry. That's obviously not the case. Don't worry, I'll keep scanning for damaged tracks as we go. If there's any more damage, I'll know about it long before we get to it."

"That's a relief," said Alabaster.

There was a brief burst of static, and then Patty said, "Nell, I've noticed that your stress levels are quite high—are you alright?"

"Oh," said Nell, her cheeks turning pink, "I—no, I'm fine. Just a bit nervous about the cave-in, I guess."

Another static burst. "They've been elevated since you first boarded, though," said Patty. "Much higher than Stanley's or Alabaster's. Sorry, I don't mean to pry—it's just that my scanners automatically monitor all of my passengers' vital functions."

"Oh," said Nell, looking a bit uncomfortable.

"It's probably just her claustrophobia," said Alabaster, trying to be helpful. "It's pretty spacious down here, but hey, who wouldn't be nervous about being in a crumbling, ruined, ancient—"

Stanley shook his head and waved his hands furiously at Alabaster, trying to get him to stop talking.

"Claustrophobia-can-be-a-real-problem-for-subterranean-citizens," said Patty. "Magitech-can-help." As soon as she finished speaking, a very low buzzing tone filled the cabin. Stanley, who could barely hear it, exchanged a curious glance with Alabaster, but Nell immediately sat up straight in her chair and went rigid, her eyes wide.

"Whoa," she said. "Ugh—*whoa!*"

"Are you okay?" said Stanley. "Nell?"

The buzzing tone stopped, and Nell flopped back into her chair, heaving a great sigh of what sounded like relief. "Hoo!" she breathed, "That … was great!"

Stanley glanced back at Alabaster, who merely shrugged. "*What* was great?" he asked.

"That—oh, that sound," said Nell. "It was like—being in a hot tub or something."

"How do you feel?" asked Patty.

"Amazing," said Nell. "What was it?"

"A-corrective-sonic-pulse, brought-to-you-by-your-friends-at-Magitech. Magitech: making-your-life-underground-a-little-brighter."

"Corrective—what?" said Stanley.

"Corrective sonic pulse," said Patty. "A small percentage of the population suffers from acute claustrophobia—a fear of enclosed spaces. This condition posed a problem for many citizens of Sub-Sphere Three, so Magitech developed a series of sonic emitters capable of generating a pulse that would alleviate the symptoms."

"Say whaaat?" said Alabaster.

"Oh, Patty," said Nell, a huge smile on her face, "thank you! Thank you so much!"

"Don't-thank-me-thank-your-friends-at-Magitech!" said Patty. "But you're very welcome, I'm sure," she added happily.

* * *

They roared on through the darkness, when after about forty minutes, Patty said,

"I just realized, I didn't ask where the three of you are going. Did you have a destination in mind?"

"Well—we'd like to get back to … you probably won't know it," said Nell.

"Try me!" said Patty.

"Okay," said Nell, "Port Verdant."

Patty paused, then said "I'm-sorry-I'm-not-familiar-with-that-name."

"Sorry," she added.

"That's okay," said Nell. "Anywhere near the northern coast would be good. Preferably near the, uh, well, the big river."

"I'm sorry, Nell," said Patty, "I've been looking for tracks leading back up north, but I haven't found any yet. I'll let you know if I do."

"We should try to catch up with the other train before we head back north," Stanley piped up. Nell looked at him.

"Why?"

"Well, because it might be Blake who's on it, and—before we left, he was talking about continuing on to the Lost City—"

"The Lost City?" echoed Nell. She seemed unable to speak for a few moments, but when she found her voice, she did not sound pleased. "Are you telling me," she began in a dangerous tone, "that the whole reason we're down here in this—*place*—is that you're still obsessing over this stupid Lost City?"

Stanley was taken aback by Nell's reaction. "Er—"

"We agreed that the expedition was over," said Nell. "We were going back to Port Verdant, and *then* we were going to get in touch with your uncle, which is what we should have done in the first place."

"Our involvement was kind of accidental," said Alabaster. "I mean, we didn't really mean to stow away on the boat, and our escape options from the abbey were pretty limited."

"*You* should've told us that tunnel led to the catacombs," Nell returned coldly.

"Hold on," said Stanley, "What do you mean, *we* agreed the expedition was over? Were you at the meeting?"

"I—" said Nell, "Well—yes, I was—"

"No fair!" said Alabaster.

"So everyone but me and Alabaster had a say, then?"

"Alabaster and *I*," said Alabaster.

"Well," said Nell, going pink, "I was only there because Ryuno insisted on it ..."

Stanley made a face. "Ryuno? *Ryuno* said you could be there? Why not us?"

"He—they, uh—they didn't—"

"Didn't *you* say anything?" Stanley demanded. "Couldn't *you* insist that we be there too? Or did you just not even think of it?"

Nell said nothing.

"You didn't, did you? ... Thanks a lot."

"Oh don't give me that," said Nell. "My being there didn't make any difference anyway, and neither would yours. Nobody wanted to keep going, *nobody*. Not even Blake, actually. I'm sorry for not trying to get you into the meeting—and I *did* think about it, so don't tell me what I did or didn't think—but Stanley, be reasonable. This isn't something we can finish. People have died. Died! And I can't even count the number of time *we've* come close—"

"I think we're up to eight, all told," said Alabaster.

Nell shook her head. "It's too much for us. It's too much to risk for—for what, really? Another pile of treasure, in some distant city that might not even exist? We're *done* with treasure hunts, Stanley. Or at least I thought we were."

"This isn't about treasure," said Stanley. "The Lost City is real, I know it is—and so do Blake and Temoc. There's something there, that crystal, remember?"

Nell sighed. "Yes, I remember. That scroll—"

"*And* my dreams," said Stanley. "There's books on it, too. It's real, I know it, and it's—a weapon, or something. It's called the Moon Killer, and Blake thinks the governor wants to use it."

Nell was staring at him.

"He wants to destroy one of the moons! Maybe all of them!"

"What happens if you destroy the moons?" asked Nell.

"The *balance* would—uh—well, okay, there's this balance, right? And if it breaks, it would … um …"

"If it breaks it would *what?*" said Nell.

"Well, I don't know exactly what would happen, but it would be bad. Blake said so."

"How do you know *Blake* isn't trying to destroy this 'balance'?" said Nell.

"What?" said Stanley.

"What if *Blake* wants to use this Moon-Killer as a weapon?"

Stanley hadn't thought about that angle. But no, Blake wasn't the type. He'd spent all that time helping Stanley with his shadow powers, and he'd been there to help them on their journey ever since Port Verdant.

"No—if he was going to do something bad, why would he tell me about it? He wanted me to come with him!"

"Seems like now we need to find out even *more,*" said Alabaster.

"Maybe we do," Nell said thoughtfully.

"Really?" said Stanley.

Nell looked squarely at him. "Just because Blake wanted you to come along doesn't mean his intentions are good. We really don't know much about him, and frankly I think it's pretty suspicious the way he took off just as that—thing started attacking the abbey. And do I have to mention that his 'powers' are an awful lot like—"

"Mine?" Stanley interrupted.

"Er—" said Nell, "I didn't mean—"

"Forget it," said Stanley.

"Stanley," said Nell, "I was talking about—"

"I said forget it," said Stanley. "You don't like my powers, I get it, okay? Well, I didn't ask for them. And neither did Blake."

Nell was silent.

"Patty," said Stanley, "can you please tell us when we get to where the other train is going?"

"Of course," said Patty. "Are you done fighting?"

"Er," said Stanley.

"I hope so," said Patty. "I don't like when people fight. It makes me sad."

"We're sorry, Patty," said Nell.

Stanley said nothing.

CHAPTER 22

THE LOST CITY

Stanley felt rotten. He wasn't confrontational by nature, and he hated the fact that he'd had an argument with Nell. And on board Patty, there was nowhere to go to escape the tense, awkward atmosphere that had descended on the scene.

Patty continued to chat pleasantly with them as they sped south beneath the continent, but any conversation between Stanley and Nell seemed to have dropped off completely.

Time wore on, and Stanley began to wonder exactly when they would reach their destination. "Er, Patty," he said, "do you know when we'll catch up to the other train?"

"I'm-sorry-I-don't-know-the-answer-to-that-question," said Patty. "Insufficient data, unfortunately. I can't estimate the timeframe without a fixed destination."

"That makes sense," said Stanley.

"How fast are we going?" asked Alabaster.

"Our-current-speed-is-750-kilometres-per-hour," said Patty. "We're in the big high-speed tunnels now."

Stanley wasn't exactly sure how fast 750 kilometres per hour was, but it sounded almost ridiculously fast. For one thing, he knew that cars on the highway usually didn't go over 100.

"Since there are no other trains in the vicinity," said Patty, "I can bring us up to my top speed, *900* kilometres per hour. Shall I do it?" She sounded excited.

"Er," said Stanley.

"Yeah!" said Alabaster. "Go go go! Pa-tty! Pa-tty!"

"Increasing speed!" said Patty gleefully.

There was a slight lurch as Patty sped up, and Stanley felt himself pressed into the side of his chair. Outside in the tunnels, the screaming roar of Patty's passing was deafening, but inside the cabin, the only noticeable change was a slight increase in the hum of her engines beneath the floor.

The lights in the cabin dimmed suddenly, and Alabaster leapt out of his seat, yelling,

"We're all gonna die!"

"Please don't be alarmed," said Patty, "I just noticed that Nell had fallen asleep, and decided to reduce the level of lighting."

Stanley looked over at Nell, who, sure enough, was fast asleep in her chair.

"Shall I play some soothing music?" asked Patty.

"Er—yeah, please, that'd be nice," said Stanley. It had been a long night already, and he realized that they hadn't yet gotten any sleep. A soft, pleasant tune filled the cabin, and Stanley sat back and closed his eyes. A nap sounded like a fine idea to him.

"Hey Patty," said Alabaster, "Can I have a Crystal-Caff Cola, please?"

"I'm sorry Alabaster," said Patty, "I'm all out."

★ ★ ★

A loud *DING* woke Stanley with a start. He'd been having another dream about the giant blue floating crystal, only this time, it had suddenly turned black before his eyes, before crumbling to pieces. The dream did not give him a good feeling.

The ding had also woken Nell and Alabaster.

"Sorry to wake you," said Patty, "but I just thought I'd let you know that I picked up Pablo's signal twenty-seven minutes ago. He's stopped, so we should be catching up to him in about thirty-three minutes."

"I thought Pablo was twenty-seven minutes ahead of us when we first got on," said Alabaster through a huge yawn.

"He must have gone to top speed before I did," said Patty.

"How long were we asleep?" asked Nell.

"You have been asleep for approximately three point two hours," said Patty. "I'll be reducing speed in exactly fifteen minutes."

About a half-hour later, Patty announced, "Now-arriving-at-Severson-air-force-base-and-research-centre. Please-have-valid-ID-ready. Unauthorized-persons-will-be-detained."

"Detained?" said Alabaster. "Air force base?"

"It's probably not there anymore," said Nell. "And after all this time I doubt there'd be anyone around to 'detain' us."

With a soft hiss and a buzzing hydraulic whine, Patty's door slid open. "Thank-you-for-using-the-Sub-Sphere-Three-rapid-transit-system, brought-to-you-by-Magitech! Magitech: here-to-get-you-there!"

"Really, though, thank you," Patty went on, "It's been so great to have passengers again."

"We should be thanking you," said Stanley. "We never would have gotten here without you."

"*And*," said Alabaster, "we should be thanking you for not going crazy and blasting us all to smithereens by crashing full-speed into the barrier at the end of the line!"

"Alabaster!" said Nell, "That's a horrible thing to say!"

"I said she *didn't* do it," said Alabaster.

"I know, but you shouldn't—oh, what's the use? Patty, don't listen to him, he's just joking."

"No I'm not," said Alabaster. "I'm sincerely grateful. That could really happen!"

Nell closed her eyes, took a deep breath, and raised her hands to her temples, as if trying to focus intensely on not harming Alabaster.

"Well, I guess you'll be going now," said Patty, a distinct note of sadness in her voice.

Stanley paused at the door. He hadn't thought about what would happen once the trip was over. "Er—well, we sort of have to," he said, turning to face Patty's screen. "I mean, we can't really take you with us …"

"I know," said Patty.

"We're really sorry, Patty," said Nell. "I wish there was something we could do—but we really do have to go."

Patty was silent for a moment. "Do you think maybe you could come back and see me some day?" she asked timidly. Nell looked helplessly at Stanley, her eyes bright and sad.

"We will if we can," said Stanley. "I don't know exactly where we're going, but if we can get back here, we will. Right?" he said, looking at Nell and Alabaster.

"Right," said Nell. "If we can, we will."

"Okay," said Patty. "I know you have your own lives and things you have to do—everyone does. You learn that when you're a passenger train." She was quiet for a few seconds, then said, "Good luck Nell, and Stanley and Alabaster. I'm very happy I met you. I'll never forget you."

They said goodbye to Patty, thanked her again, and then her door slid shut, and her cabin lights turned off. They stood there for a time, and then Nell said

"Come on," and led the way out of the train station.

* * *

They now found themselves in what looked like a large loading bay. Huge metal crates were piled around the room, and many more were scattered about haphazardly among the wreckage of ancient-looking machines and vehicles. Interestingly, a few of these machines, which resembled giant forklifts, were still in fairly good condition. Had the others been actively destroyed long ago?

Towards the back wall was an elevator door just like the one beneath Daruna Abbey. As they approached the door, Alabaster exclaimed,

"Whoa! A robot!"

Stanley looked where Alabaster was pointing. Against the wall, not far from the elevator, was the broken, battered form of what looked like a suit of futuristic armour. It was big and bulky, and probably would have stood almost seven feet tall, if it hadn't been a crumpled ruined heap. Its right arm and leg had both been severed, and its torso had been cut almost in half. Parts of the damaged areas were still sparking, and smoking slightly.

"This was done recently," said Nell. "What could have done this kind of damage ..." She trailed off and glanced at Stanley.

He knew what she was thinking, because he was thinking it, too. Could Blake have destroyed this robot? He probably *could*—Stanley didn't know what this robot was made of, but he had a pretty good idea of how sharp Blake's sword was.

"Maybe it tried to detain him," said Alabaster.

"Maybe," said Nell. "Although we don't know for sure *who* it was."

Stanley looked around and saw that the wall to the left of the elevator was full of holes. Examining the robot's right arm revealed that in place of a hand, there was what looked like some kind of large, round gun barrel, or rather, a collection of smaller barrels forming a single fearsome weapon, very much like a gatling gun. "Looks like there was a fight," he said, indicating the bullet-holes in the wall.

"Well, until we know what's going on, let's be careful," said Nell, drawing her sword and clasping it firmly as she headed towards the elevator. "Come on—I'd like to get some fresh air for a change."

They rode the elevator up from the depths of Sub-Sphere Three, each wondering what they would find on the surface. They'd travelled an incredible distance, and there was no telling what the great jungles of Verduria might throw at them next.

"Arriving-at-Severson-air-force-base," said the elevator at length, "Severson-air-force-base-ground-level. Please-watch-your-step."

The elevator came to a stop and the doors slid open.

"Doors-opening," said the elevator. "Have-a-nice-day. Boarding-passengers-please-allow-the-elevator-to-empty-before-embarking."

The three friends stepped off and the doors closed behind them. The first thing they noticed was the heavenly blast of cool, fresh night air. They were in a stone structure that seemed to have been built up around the elevator, which, on this level, looked like a simple metal box with a door in it.

Standing in front of them about ten feet away was a very surprised-looking Saurian. At first, Stanley thought it might be Temoc—he'd never seen any other Saurians with blue skin, after all—but a second look confirmed that it wasn't him. The Saurian stood there for a few moments, its jaw slack, and then said something in its hissing, growling language before turning tail and fleeing as fast as it could go.

"Hey, wait!" said Stanley, "We—uh—"

"We come in peace!" Alabaster hollered. "Hope he's not going to get his buddies," he said, half to himself.

The only exit from the building was an open doorway through which the blue Saurian had fled. Nell led the way through, and they paused outside to take in their surroundings. Before them, a great moonlit field sloped gently down to form a vast grassy bowl surrounded by forest, which was in turn ringed by tall, craggy black mountains. A wide, glassy river ran down from the mountains far to the south, and snaked its way across the basin to go cascading off a cliff to the north in a great waterfall.

Beside the river, not far from where they were standing, was a fair-sized village of round huts, some of which had lights on in their windows. Further back from the riverbanks, dark, bulky shapes could be seen, likely larger buildings or temples.

Stanley noticed none of this, for he was staring transfixed at what was floating in the sky above the mountains across the river.

"Oh, Stanley," said Nell, "It's … you were right."

The crystal was there, glowing brightly and casting its light on all the land around it. Directly beneath it, bathed in the blue glow, was a stepped pyramid, similar to the one back in the Xol'tec city.

"Wow," said Alabaster. "I guess this is it. *The Lost City,"* he said dramatically. "Is it everything you hoped it would be?"

"Er—well, I guess I expected more of a … city?" said Stanley. Not that it mattered, of course. Just looking at the crystal seemed to soothe his mind, and lift a weight from his shoulders.

"Someone's coming," Nell said suddenly.

Stanley froze. Three dark figures were coming towards them from the village. They were still a good distance away, and one was carrying a light, so they likely weren't interested in being stealthy.

"They wouldn't come up here with only three if they wanted to fight," said Nell. "We're probably okay."

"Unless they're gun-robots," said Alabaster.

Nell sighed.

It took the figures a few minutes to reach them. They were Saurians, and Stanley recognized the one who had met them at the elevator. The Saurian on the right was carrying a long wooden staff, and the one in the middle, who was clearly the leader, was dressed in robes that were probably blue, and carried some sort of flashlight, which he shone on the three newcomers.

As he approached, he asked something of his companions, who nodded solemnly.

"Your pardon," he then said in perfect English, "do you understand my words?"

"Er, yes?" said Stanley.

Immediately the three Saurians threw themselves on the ground. "The divine language," the leader said reverently. "My apprentice, Komec tells me that you came forth from the door of light. Great ones—may we look upon you?"

"Uh," said Stanley, not quite sure what to make of this reception, "Sure?"

"You are most kind, Lord," said the Saurian, getting up and raising his flashlight.

"Whoa, watch the light," said Alabaster.

"Apologies, Lord," said the Saurian, averting the beam.

"Lord?" Nell said skeptically.

"Lords and Lady," said the Saurian. "Celestial rulers, dwellers in the heavens, you have come to us through the door, the Portal of Light, gateway of the gods. We are again blessed, for the gods are truly returning!"

"What?" said Nell, "Gods? We are not—"

"Nell," hissed Alabaster, "I hate to be the one to say this, but *shut uuu-up!*"

"We can't go around telling people we're *gods*," Nell whispered back.

"That's fine," said Alabaster, "but let's wait for the right time to tell them—like when we're reasonably sure they're not going to *eat* us."

"I'm pretty sure it'll be worse if they think we've lied to them," said Nell. "I'm sorry," she said to the Saurians, "We're not gods or anything like that—we're just people, like you."

The robed Saurian considered this. "Gods or no," he said evenly, "you are the ones whose coming was foretold. You, great and mighty At'Khun," he said, addressing Stanley, "The light of the water moon is in your eyes. And you," he said to Nell, "Glorious Chimé Xoln'ec, goddess of the red eye. We are glad that you and your husband have reconciled and are once more in love."

Stanley and Nell, who were standing close together, glanced at each other, then quickly looked away. The robed Saurian beamed at them. "This is cause for an even greater celebration, I think. Ahh," he said to Alabaster, "And you have brought with you Mixtlekha, mischievous dark-maned master of the night wind."

"Are you saying I have a flatulence problem?" said Alabaster.

Stanley fought to keep a straight face.

"Er," said the robed Saurian, "well, ah, no doubt you will want to come and see your own wife--"

"Wife?" said Alabaster.

"The Lady of the Night is back at the village—along with Qu'en-Lakt, the god of death."

"Death?" Stanley echoed.

"He comes only to visit," the robed Saurian assured them. "Indeed, all the great ones are gathering. It is a time of portent and significance."

"I'm really sorry," said Stanley, "but we're not who you think we are—we really, really aren't gods."

The Saurian smiled kindly. "Well at the very least, you are kind travelers from afar, and that is more than enough reason to welcome you into our home. Please, come with us to the village. A great feast has been prepared to celebrate your arrival."

The mention of a feast did sound good to Stanley, who hadn't eaten since lunch time. So much had happened since then, that his last meal felt like a lifetime ago.

"We are a simple people," said the robed Saurian as they all descended the slope towards the village. "Once upon a time, this place, the whole valley was a great stone city of temples and fortresses. That was many thousands of years ago, though. Since that time, our numbers have dwindled, and the land has re-claimed most of our once-great city."

"So this really is Quetzal-Khan," said Stanley. "Or it used to be."

"You speak the ancient name," said the robed Saurian, sounding impressed. "You are, I think, much greater than you say you are. Such is the way of the gods."

"Er—" said Stanley.

"Yes, we still call our home by its ancient name, even though nowadays we are mere farmers and fishermen. Our cities may rise and fall, but this land is blessed, that much is known to all who live here, for we live in the light of At'Khun's heart. *Your* heart." He pointed to the crystal floating in the distance.

"What is it exactly?" asked Stanley. "What does it do?"

"When the time is right, *you* will know what to do with it," said the robed Saurian. "You will use it to dispel the darkness of the world."

"Me?" said Stanley, "But—I heard it was called the Moon Killer—"

The Saurian cleared his throat. "Ah yes, that is another name for it. Forgive me, it is rather a vulgar name in our language."

"But why would anyone want to destroy a moon?" asked Stanley.

"I cannot answer that," said the Saurian. "If it is your will, then it will happen. My people and I have no say in the matter. We are custodians of this place, nothing more."

Stanley was very confused. Blake and the ancient scroll had made the Moon Killer, or Heart of At'Khun, or whatever it was, out to be a deadly weapon to be feared. These Saurians, though, revered it as a benign and holy relic, which they for some reason associated with *him*.

At length they arrived at the village, a collection of about fifty round wooden huts nestled on the bank of the river. In the centre of town was a much larger, oval building, which, their guide informed them, was the chief's house.

"My daughter," he said proudly. "She is a wise leader, and will be glad to meet you."

The sounds of music and chattering reptilian voices filled the air as they approached the large house. Beaming, the robed Saurian waved Stanley through the door. He took a deep breath and stepped reluctantly over the threshold.

Inside was a long wooden table, around which were seated over a hundred blue-skinned Saurians, young and old. None of them wore any gold or jewelry; these Saurians seemed to prefer plain loincloths and simple robes over their cousins' elaborate finery.

At the head of the table, seated on a large chair draped in what looked like sheepskin was a tall and very muscular female Saurian, no doubt the village chief. She looked up when she noticed Stanley standing in the doorway, and the whole gathering went quiet, all eyes turning towards him.

Nell and Alabaster came in after him, followed by the robed Saurian, who scurried into the room and raised his hands above his head before announcing something to the room at large. As soon as he was done hissing and growling, the company erupted into elated shrieks and hoots. Stanley was set upon by a group of small Saurian children, who dragged him with great enthusiasm towards the head of the table. He was plunked down in a seat to the right of the chief, who smiled at him, and said "Welcome."

Stanley, slightly stunned by all the reptilian cheering, was surprised to see a familiar face seated across from him.

"Blake?" he said, although he could barely be heard over the noise in the room. Blake, who was clapping along with many of the Saurians, leaned forward and yelled,

"It's great to see you, Stanley—I'm glad you made it, I knew you would!"

"What happened to you?" hollered Stanley.

"Later," said Blake, gesturing at the noisy crowd around them. It was then that Stanley noticed the other human to Blake's left: it was Sister Marie. She looked pale and tired, with dark circles under her eyes and hair disheveled, but she smiled and waved at him, and he waved back, if a little uncertainly.

Nell was seated beside Stanley, and Alabaster, looking delighted, was placed on Marie's other side.

Stanley jumped as a huge heap of meat and vegetables was suddenly dumped in front of him.

"Eat!" suggested the chief.

Nell said something about it being two in the morning, but Stanley's hunger trumped his fatigue, and he ended up putting away a fair amount of overcooked meat, flat, leathery greens, and bland purple carrots.

The celebration wore on, with the chief making several speeches, all in the Saurian language, while Stanley, full as he was, grew tireder and tireder. Finally, Alabaster fell asleep leaning on Marie's shoulder, and the chief had the five human visitors ushered off to bed.

Stanley and Nell were brought to a small hut not far from the main building. "Sleep well, honoured ones," said the Saurian attendant, before bowing his snout and returning to the party.

Wondering when the others were going to arrive, Stanley and Nell went inside. Against the far wall was a woven straw pallet with a single blanket on it.

"We only get one bed?" said Stanley.

Nell looked confused, too, but then, realizing something, clucked her tongue and sighed. "They think we're *married*, remember?"

"Ohh," said Stanley. "Riiight." Okay, I'll, uh, just sleep outside. See you in the morning."

"Stanley, no—you don't have to do that—here, take the bed, I'll be fine on the floor. Er, ground."

"No no, it's okay, you can have the bed. It's fine," said Stanley.

They looked at each other, then at the bed, then at each other.

"It's pretty cool out tonight," said Nell. "I'd just feel bad if you were over there huddled on the ground with no blanket or anything ..."

"Yeah, me too," said Stanley. "I mean, I'd feel bad, too, if it was you. Without the blanket. Sorry for arguing with you on the train." He meant it, but why had that just come flying out of his mouth?

"Oh," said Nell, "Er, that's okay. Um, I'm sorry too—I meant to say something before but—well, anyway, I know it's not your fault that we ended up in the middle of a killer jungle, and I know it sounded like I was blaming you. And now it turns out you were right all along, so I'm *also* sorry for doubting you, and ... well, I've been giving you a hard time about your 'powers', and that wasn't fair either, so I'm just sorry for a whole bunch of stuff, I guess."

"It's okay, really," said Stanley, feeling that he didn't really deserve this outpouring of apologies. "You don't have to—it's fine, I ..."

Nell smiled and took a step towards him. "Um, I also wanted to say thanks, for cheering me up the other night," she said, leaning her head slightly to one side.

"I did? When?" Stanley said lamely.

"When I was sad, and you said all those nice things to me."

"Oh—right, yeah," said Stanley. Why was it so uncomfortably warm in this hut? And why did it feel like a fan was spinning in his stomach?

Nell placed her hand against his shoulder.

She leaned towards him.

"Hooo, I am *beat!*" said Alabaster, suddenly appearing in the doorway.

Nell leapt away from Stanley as if he'd just given her a massive electric shock. Stanley was temporarily frozen in place.

Alabaster stared at them. "Uh, are you guys okay?"

"Yeah, we're fine," said Nell, clearing her throat.

"Cool," said Alabaster. "Well, Marie said to send you over, Nell, so see you in the morning!"

"What?" said Nell, "She did? Why?"

"Apparently there was a mix-up," said Alabaster. "You were supposed to bunk with Marie, and *this* hut's for the guys."

"Oh," said Nell, glancing at Stanley. "…Okay, uh … if you're sure—"

"Yeah, Marie was pretty insistent," said Alabaster.

"Okay. Um, well, good night," said Nell, heading quickly out the door.

"Third hut on the right," Alabaster called after her. "O-kay, time for some serious snoozing. That nap before was just too long. You know when you sleep for like two or three hours and your body's like, 'oh good, we're really going to sleep, night-night!' but then you wake up and it's like 'hey, I thought we were done for the night! Let me sleep!' Short power-naps, that's the way to go. No more than half an hour, max."

By now Alabaster had clambered into bed and made himself comfortable. He looked over at Stanley, who was still standing dazedly in the middle of the room. "Stanley? You sure you're okay?"

"Uh?" said Stanley, "Er—yeah, I'm fine."

"You just looked a bit stunned, that's all," said Alabaster. "Well, g'night!" He rolled over and was asleep in seconds.

Stanley, whose legs didn't seem to be working properly, finally managed to cross the room and get under the blanket on the other side of the pallet, while Alabaster snored noisily. He laid down on his back and stared at the thatched roof, listening to the celebration going on in the chief's house. His heart was beating at a breakneck pace, and stayed that way for some time.

CHAPTER 23

OPERATION MOON-KILLER

Stanley must have fallen asleep at some point, because the next thing he knew, he was being shaken awake long before he would have woken up on his own.

"Unh? Wha?" he said groggily.

"Come on Stanley, time to go. We've got work to do."

Stanley sat up and saw Blake looking down at him. "What? What's going on?"

"Meet me outside," said Blake.

Stanley sat there for a moment in the pre-dawn gloom, blearily wondering if this was really happening, then reached over to wake Alabaster.

"Just you," said Blake from outside the hut. "We'll be back before they're up, don't worry."

Stanley lurched to his feet and went outside, where Blake and Sister Marie were waiting for him. Marie had an uncharacteristically grim look on her face, but bade Stanley good morning, just the same.

"Hi Marie," Stanley returned. "What time is it?"

"Twenty to six," said Blake, consulting his pocket watch. "Come on, let's get going." He set off through the sleeping village at a brisk pace, Marie close behind him. Stanley had to jog to catch up.

"Er, *where* are we going?" asked Stanley.

"Up to the Moon-Killer," said Blake.

"Wait," said Stanley, "Blake, before we go, what happened to you yesterday? What happened at the abbey?"

"Can we walk and talk?" said Blake, not slowing down, "I want to get there as soon as possible."

"Yeah, okay," said Stanley, hurrying after him.

They reached the edge of the village, and started across a rough wooden bridge that spanned the river. There in the distance, glinting with the first rays of the rising sun, was the great blue crystal.

"After I lost track of you in the catacombs," Blake began, "I rushed back to the entrance hall to find you. Instead, I found Sister Marie and our new ... 'friend'."

"It came after me, but he saved me," said Marie, smiling at Blake.

"Who *was* that guy?" said Stanley. "One minute it was just this suit of armour, and the next, someone was wearing it, and walking around smashing everything. He collapsed like half the abbey!"

"Damn," said Blake. "I should have stayed and fought."

"You couldn't have done anything," said Marie. "You said so yourself."

"I know, but surely I could have—"

"Stanley," said Marie, interrupting Blake, "Nigel—Father Blake discovered that he—*him*, that armoured giant—is responsible for all the strange things that were happening at the abbey—and out in the jungle, as well."

"What?" said Stanley.

"That thing is a Shadow Lord," said Blake grimly. "An ancient master of the Shadow Legion, and a terribly powerful one, at that."

"The Shadow Legion?" Stanley repeated. "But—"

"He would have been imprisoned in that vault long, long ago," Blake went on. "But this Shadow Lord was—and still is—a thing of ... immeasurable dark might, the third most powerful to have ever existed. The Silent One, I believe, was the name people gave him. A formidable fighter in his own right, but also a master necromancer, on top of his innate shadow powers. *He* is responsible for the dead returning to life (if you can call it that), and for the sudden periods of inexplicable darkness, *and,* I think, for each one of the aberrant beasts we've encountered in the wilds of Verduria."

Stanley could scarcely believe what he was hearing.

"So powerful was the Silent One, that even after his defeat ages ago, his armour still held a large portion of his power, and continued to radiate with it, down through the millennia. The vault in which his armour was held, was designed to contain that power—but it seems that recently, say, within the past year or so, someone left the door open. Without his spirit and consciousness, his power went unchecked, and seeped out into the jungle."

This was almost too much to believe—like something out of a fantasy novel.

"And now he's on the *loose?*" said Stanley, aghast.

"Yes," said Blake, "but we'll deal with him in time. Right now, we have more pressing matters to attend to."

Things were sounding very grim to Stanley. He wondered despairingly what had happened to Algernon, and Koko, and Temoc, and Ryuno, and everyone else back at the abbey. It seemed that everywhere he went, disaster struck.

They crossed the vast green fields of Quetzal'Khan, past herds of grazing animals that looked like a cross between cows and sheep, and plunged into the belt of forest that ringed the shallow valley. The air was alive with the hoots and shrieks of jungle creatures.

"Nothing to fear in these trees, I think," said Blake, "but let's be cautious, just in case."

They navigated the forest without incident, and some minutes later emerged from the trees and into a large clearing at the foot of the mountains. There, built right up against a sheer rock wall, was the pyramid, above which floated the colossal blue crystal.

"At last," said Blake, "at long last we're finally here." He half jogged to the base of the pyramid, where a large, solid-looking pair of metal doors waited. The doors were shut tight, and looked to Stanley like yet another high-tech relic of the ancient civilization far beneath them. The doors were obviously very old, and encrusted with moss and lichens.

Stanley was suddenly aware of a strange sound coming from somewhere behind them. It sounded like an approaching helicopter.

"Do you hear that?" said Marie, "It sounds like a rotorwing."

"Let's focus on the task at hand," said Blake. "Marie, the book, please."

Marie tore her eyes away from the sky and took a large leather-bound book out of her bag, then joined Blake by the door. Stanley recognized it as the very old and valuable volume from Daruna Abbey, *The Chronicles of Frederic Whipple*.

"Recite the Arcane Inscription of Saint Faraday," said Blake.

Marie turned to a page marked by a slip of coloured paper, and began to read:

"Door access code blue, alpha three-one-seven."

Stanley stared.

"Access-denied," said a mechanical voice that seemed to come from the door itself, "Genetic-signature-not-recognized."

Blake stared blankly at the door for a moment, then took the book from Marie, and tried the recitation himself.

"Access-denied," the voice said again, "Genetic-signature-not-recognized."

Blake turned to Stanley. "Stanley, read this line aloud, would you please?"

Stanley took the book, and stepped towards the door. Before he read the line, though, he wanted some questions answered.

"Er, Blake," he said, turning away from the door.

"Yes, Stanley?" said Blake, a touch if impatience in his voice.

"I was just wondering why the Moon-Killer is so bad … I mean, one of the Saurians said that I'd use it to 'dispel the darkness of the world'. Do you know what that means?"

"No, I'm afraid I don't," said Blake. "But these are a simple people, Stanley—they're not malicious or war-like. They revere this thing as a religious artifact, but they don't have the slightest idea what it does."

"But what *does* it do?" asked Stanley."

"As I told you," said Blake, a bit more impatiently, "it's a weapon designed to destroy one or more of our planet's moons."

"I know, but *why?* Who would want to do that? And what did you mean about it upsetting the balance? The balance of *what?"*

The sound of helicopters was getting louder.

"Stanley," said Blake, "listen to me. We can talk about all this later, okay? For now, we just to ensure that this thing is destroyed—"

"Destroyed?" echoed Stanley.

"Yes," said Blake. "We need to make sure that no one can ever use this device. It's not enough to just leave it locked up—it needs to be levelled."

Stanley couldn't believe what he was hearing. Had he been dreaming of the crystal all this time just so that he could help destroy it? No—that couldn't be it. It felt completely wrong.

"I—I don't think it should be destroyed," he said.

"*What?*" said Blake.

"I just have this—I dunno, this *feeling* that we're not supposed to destroy it. We should leave it alone."

"Give me the book, Stanley," said Marie, holding out her hand. "I'll try it again. It's okay," she said, smiling kindly, "There's nothing to worry about."

Stanley suddenly caught sight of something in Marie's open bag, something that shouldn't have been there—something that *couldn't* have been there. He was frozen for a moment, then dropped the book, darted forward, and snatched the thing before Marie could react.

"Hey!' she said as Stanley sprang away from her, holding the object with both hands. He looked down at it with wide, disbelieving eyes.

It was a mask, a plain, white, almost featureless mask with two stern-looking eyeholes and a row of vertical slits for a mouth. A thin crack ran from the top of the mask to the left eyehole.

"*Where did you get this?*" he demanded, suddenly feeling very cold, despite the rapidly-climbing morning temperature.

Marie started to answer, but quick as a flash, Blake grabbed her by the arm and yanked her towards him. Before Stanley knew what was happening, Blake's sword was in his hand, and resting against Marie's throat.

"Uhh!" said Marie, "Nigel, what—"

"Shut up," said Blake, although it did not sound like his voice. The words carried a slight rumble, as though thunder were rolling in the distance.

"Where-did-she-get-it," said Blake menacingly, "It's *mine*. I made it. I forged it long ago during the age of Old Night before the birth of the sun."

"You—" said Stanley.

"Me," said Blake.

Stanley was speechless for a moment as his brain tried frantically to accept what it had thought impossible. "It can't be!" he shouted, "Grey broke your neck! You were on the Titanodon when it went under! You died!" He backed away towards the tree line. This wasn't happening. It had to be a nightmare.

"Not quite," said Blake. "It takes more than that to kill me. Although, yet again, my body—and my powers—were destroyed. But I survived. I always do."

"You released that—silent—*thing!*" said Stanley. "On purpose!"

"Yes," said Blake. "That red jewel? The one you picked up? Etherium. His spirit, his essence, was trapped inside. I couldn't believe my luck when I saw it at the end of that idiot Saurian Priest's staff. I relieved him of it, and set the Silent One free."

"But he—he destroyed part of the abbey! He's out of control!"

"Yes. I think the several dozen millennia of imprisonment drove him a bit mad. Don't worry, he'll calm down once he works off all that tension."

"You're not just some sorcerer," said Stanley, pointing accusingly at Blake. "Who are you? And what do you want with me?"

"Who *am* I?" said Blake. "That's a good question. I have many names—most of them given to me by others over the long ages of this world. The Elves called me Vengg'Dem. The Dwarves called me Tharguil. The Orcs referred to me as Grosh. *Your* kind named me Nerobius. I always liked that one best. They came up with it just before I wiped out their precious little empire—above ground and *under*. Upstarts."

"You obviously didn't win," said Stanley, tossing the white mask on the ground. "Humans are still around."

"A fact that I am constantly aware of," said Blake. "And that brings me back to the reason we're here. Stanley, read that line, and read it *now.*"

"No," said Stanley. "I'm not doing anything you say."

"Okay," said Blake, "Stanley, whatever you do, don't read that line—it would ruin my carefully-laid plans!"

Stanley stared.

"Sorry," said Blake, "I thought you might be stupid enough to fall for that, since you are apparently content to ignore the woman in front of me with the sword at her throat."

Marie whimpered.

"I—" Stanley began.

"READ IT," roared Blake, "OR I'LL STRIKE HER HEAD FROM HER SHOULDERS!"

"*No!*" Marie screamed.

"Let her go!" yelled Stanley, his pulse pounding in his ears. In an instant his claws were out, and a layer of blackness spread over his chest and back.

"Don't be foolish," said Blake in a much softer tone. "You can't fight me, you know that. Your power is incredible, I'll admit—I knew it the first time I met you. I can feel your potential, it's palpable, and I've only felt that type of power once before. *Once.*

"But you've barely scratched the surface, shadow-boy. You can't hope to win against me, even though I, too am a mere shard of my former self … now read that damned line or she dies."

Stanley glared darkly at Blake, furious hatred burning strong behind his eyes. This was a horrible betrayal, the ultimate insult. All this time, wise, kindly Father Blake had been playing him—playing *everyone* for fools.

But there was nothing for it. He'd never be able to fight Blake—or Nerobius, or whoever he was—that much he agreed with. More importantly, he had to help Marie. He slowly knelt down and picked up the book with a clawed hand.

"That's it," said Blake.

"Shut up," Stanley snapped. "I'll do it, but shut. Up."

Blake smirked, but said nothing more.

Stanley found the passage and began to read. "Door access code blue, alpha three-one-seven."

"Access-granted," said the robotic voice, "Have-a-nice-day."

There came the sound of a gigantic bolt being withdrawn, and the doors slid slowly open with a painful metallic squeal.

"Thank you," said Blake. "And thank *you,* Marie," he said, releasing her and heading towards the doorway.

"Glad to help," said Marie, straightening her coat. She bent down, picked up the mask and handed it to Blake.

"What?" said Stanley, "Marie—"

"Was faking," said Blake. "I thought it might be too obvious, but I guess clichés can work sometimes."

"Sorry Stanley," said Marie, smiling slightly as she followed Blake into the pyramid.

Up to this point, Stanley had tried to keep his anger in check, but this cheesy ploy was the final straw. Something erupted inside him, and he sprang towards the doorway in a blind fury. In the two seconds it took him to close the distance, his entire body below his neck became covered in small, black bony plates that burst forth from his skin with a series of less-than-pleasant *clack-clack-clacks*.

His clothes straining under his new bulk, he bounded through the doorway, unceremoniously bowling Marie over, and leapt at Blake with a savage, grating roar. A pair of flat-bladed black swords sprouted from his hands, and he swung them wildly, intending to cleave Blake in twain then and there.

Blake easily blocked the attack with his own sword. "Well done!" he said as Stanley's blades strained against his own, "You've spawned swords! Two of them—too bad you don't know how to use them." He swung his blade upwards, throwing Stanley off balance, then thrust it into his shoulder.

"Aargh!" Stanley roared as searing pain lanced down his arm and into his chest.

"I wasn't kidding when I said you can't fight me," rumbled Blake.

His wound quickly healing, Stanley lashed out with his other arm in hopes of returning the favour. Blake lazily parried the attack, stepped to the side, and brought his sword down, slicing deep into Stanley's forearm. Stanley howled again as blood poured forth from the cut. Blake took the opportunity to boot him hard in the stomach, sending him tumbling away.

Stanley was back on his feet in an instant, but Blake was ready for him. He held up his left hand in a partially-clenched fist, and the next thing Stanley knew, he was enveloped in a black mist. He was temporarily immobilized, but with a mighty strain and savage growl, he broke free and charged.

Momentarily surprised, Blake brought both hands up in a sweeping motion, and the mist solidified into a black tarry blob. The blob cast long strings of itself around Stanley, ensnaring him in dozens of powerful tendrils.

"An admirable effort," said Blake, as Stanley fought against the dark strands, "but you need to calm down—you're not in your right frame of mind. Keep it away from *here,* remember?" he said, tapping Stanley's forehead annoyingly.

Realizing that he had once again lost control, Stanley closed his eyes and felt his anger subside. His claws and armoured plates started to disappear, and he felt sure that he would pass out.

"Stay with me," said Blake, snapping his fingers. "Focus! No time to sleep now."

Stanley blinked several times and shook his head.

"I'm sorry for injuring you," said Blake, "but you didn't leave me much choice. Just look at it as another phase of your ongoing training."

"You're not training me anymore," growled Stanley.

"You've made stunning progress in the past few minutes," said Blake. "It won't be long before you have total command of your abilities. No more outbursts. And you might even be able to give *me* a run for my money. I bet you'd like that, eh?"

"I don't want *anything* from you," said Stanley bitterly. "I never would have gone anywhere near you if I knew who you were."

"I know," said Blake. "Because you're an idiot. You're young, inexperienced, ignorant, I *know.* But you'll learn. Eventually.

"Now then," he said, turning and continuing down the hallway, "let's finish up here so we can get out of this lunatic jungle."

Stanley, still tied up and floating in mid-air, was pulled along behind Blake on an invisible tether. Marie walked up beside him, giving him a furtive sideways glance.

"So are you part of *the Shadow Legion*, too?" Stanley asked.

"No," said Marie, "What makes you think that?"

"Well you're working for *him,*" said Stanley. "Do you even know who he is? He almost killed me last summer, did you know that? He took over Rhedland, and he wanted to steal my uncle's treasure."

"Yes, he told me all about that," said Marie. "He also told me that his plan to kill you was a mistake, and he's glad he didn't go through with it. He says you're very special, Stanley. He has great plans for you."

"I don't *want* to be part of his plans," Stanley shot back. "He's totally bonkers—and if he's part of this Shadow Legion, then he's just as responsible for all the scary stuff that's been happening, as that Silent Guy is."

"I realize that now," said Marie. "Like I said, he explained everything to me, and now that I know I'm not *crazy*, like I thought I was, I'm seeing things much more clearly."

"But *that's* crazy all on its own!" said Stanley.

"He saved my life, and as far as I'm concerned he's still the Nigel Blake I met back in June."

"That'll do, you two," said Blake. He was standing outside a second metal door, arms folded. He nonchalantly pushed a button on the wall, and the door slid open with a smooth hiss.

The room beyond was vast, and had clearly been built by the civilization responsible for Sub-Sphere Three. Unlike the desiccated underground empire, though, this building, concealed inside a pyramid, seemed to be at least in a reasonable state of repair. Most of the lights were on, and a number of computer terminals spaced around the room still seemed to be working.

In the centre of the chamber was what looked like a slightly smaller metal version of the stone pyramid outside. The pyramid-shaped machine was covered in blinking lights and computer monitors, with several work stations at floor-level, and a huge transparent screen directly across from the door. The massive machine reached almost to the ceiling, where a large blue sphere was affixed to its peak.

Blake walked up to the big screen and stood examining it for a time. It displayed a 3-D image of a planet, clearly Terra, surrounded by its three moons. Lines of complicated figures and calculations were running up and down the screen as the planet rotated and the moons revolved around it.

"Marie, pass me that datapage, would you please?" said Blake. "I'd like to keep a copy of this for later—it might prove useful. Or at least interesting."

Marie handed him the laminated page with the map of Verduria on it. The yellow arrow was now right on top of the blue dot. Blake took the page and placed it on the transparent screen, where it stayed in place as if he'd glued it there.

"Computer," he said, "copy all files to this datapage."

"`Authorization-required,`" responded the voice that had spoken to them outside.

"Wonderful," said Blake.

"Er—" said Marie, flipping through the book, "Ah, data archive transfer, code blue nine-nine-eight epsilon.

"`Access-denied,`" said the voice. "`Genetic-signature-not-recognized.`"

Blake sighed. "Stanley, you know what to do."

"Why me?" said Stanley. "Why does it work when I do it?"

"Obviously you have the right genetic signature," said Blake, "whatever that entails. Hurry up."

"Forget it," said Stanley. "You can't trick me again. I'm not gonna do it."

Blake rubbed his eyes with his thumb and forefinger. "My time and patience are running thin," he said, stalking towards him. He reached out and took hold of Stanley's right hand. "Accelerated regeneration is a useful trait. Usually." He gripped Stanley's middle finger and wrenched it sideways with a sickening, crackling pop.

Stanley cried out and tears filled his eyes. The pain in his finger was epic. He'd never had so much as a sprain in his life, and now his finger was sticking out at a nauseating right angle. After a few seconds, the finger began to twitch, and with a sound like cereal recently endowed with milk, returned to its original position. It was very painful.

Teeth gritted, breathing raggedly, Stanley looked from his finger to Blake. His prospects didn't look good.

"That can be repeated any number of times," Blake threatened. "I can break every bone in your body a hundred times over. Every time you'll heal, and every time you'll feel the pain, just as sharp, just as immediate." Stanley blanched, and Blake started to circle him, not unlike a shark.

"But maybe that won't be enough. You're a heroic individual, Stanley, and it can be difficult to entice heroic individuals through pain." He paused. "How about your friends, then? What if *their* lives were in jeopardy? What would you say then?"

"*No,*" Stanley seethed.

"Really?" said Blake. "What about the pretty little female—Nell? At least—I *assume* you think she's pretty, the way you look at her—I don't understand what you apes see in each other. What if I were to break *her*, hm? Fingers … arms … legs … ribs."

Stanley felt his claws come back out. "*You leave her alone,*" he snarled, spit flying from his mouth. "LEAVE HER ALONE!"

"I will. If you read that access code."

Stanley stayed silent.

"Fine," said Blake. "Marie, please go back down to the village and get Nell, will you? Tell her I'm hurt and that Stanley needs her help. Let the loudmouth come too, if he wants. He could stand to be silenced."

"*Give me the book!*" Stanley yelled hoarsely.

Marie walked over and held it up in front of him.

"Data archive transfer code blue, nine-nine-eight epsilon."

"Access-granted. Data-transfer-commencing." A few seconds later, the computer announced, "Transfer-complete."

Blake picked up the datapage and handed it back to Marie. "And now, the demolition. Stanley, one final line for you to read." Marie held the book back up and indicated another code. Stanley looked at it, then at Blake, who said,

"I tortured the Abbot to death to get the passcodes for the reliquary. It was much worse than a few broken fingers. I'll do the same to her—I'll make sure she doesn't die for days."

Tears were running freely down Stanley's cheeks.

"Just read it," said Blake. "The world's not going to end just because this building gets blown up. You said yourself you don't really know what it's for, what it's all about. Leave things like that to the people who *do* know. You'll be much happier that way."

Stanley glared at him with all the malice he could muster. "I'll stop you," he hissed. "Somehow I'll stop you. Self-destruct code blue nine-six-three omega."

"Self-destruct-sequence-activated," the computer announced. "This-facility-will-self-destruct-in-ten-minutes. Please-vacate-the-premises-in-an-orderly-manner."

"Well done," said Blake. "I knew you'd do the right thing."

"Just go away," Stanley muttered. "You got what you wanted—get out of here and leave us alone."

"True, I did get what I wanted," said Blake, "but we're far from finished. Our next stop is Azuria, and you're coming with us."

"What?" said Stanly, "No! Let me go! I did everything you said!"

"You've got a long road ahead of you before I let you wander free," said Blake. "In time you'll start to see things my way. Until then, your training continues."

"*FREEZE!*"

Stanley, Blake, and Marie looked up in surprise. Standing in the doorway were four armoured figures. They looked like soldiers, and their gear was very advanced. They wore black-and-grey camouflage fatigues, with thick armour plates on their legs, arms, and torsos. Their heads were covered by helmets, glowing blue goggles, and black balaclavas.

"What in the world—" said Blake.

"Azuria Security Commission," said one of the soldiers, stepping forward and pointing her gun at Blake, "You are hereby ordered to vacate this facility and relinquish any and all findings you may have obtained."

"I'll be glad to comply with your first order, *ma'am*," said Blake, "but I'm not relinquishing anything. Now get out of my way if you want to live. This is your only warning."

"No, this is *your* only warning," said a voice that Stanley hadn't heard for some time. A fifth soldier came striding into the room, dressed in a manner similar to his companions. He wore no helmet, though, and Stanley recognized his stony, severe features despite the absence of his big curly wig.

"Governor Cromwell," said Blake. "Well this is unexpected." He and Marie backed away from the door, Stanley in tow.

"Stanley," said the governor, "I have to admit that I'm surprised to find you here. This may come as a shock to you, but this is not Nigel Blake."

"I know!" said Stanley. "He's a Shadow Lord! He set that armoured giant loose! His name's Nerobius!"

"No more talking," said Blake, clenching his fist so that the tendrils entrapping Stanley clamped down, squeezing the breath out of him.

"Release the boy," said the soldier who had spoken first. "Miss," she said to Marie, "I advise you to step away from him, as well."

Blake drew his sword and made a move towards Marie, but the solider opened fire, knocking him off his feet. The black tendrils evapourated and Stanley fell to the floor, gasping for air. The soldier came forward in a crouch-walk and helped him to his feet.

"Up you get," she said, guiding him over to the door.

"She's—she's with him!" Stanley managed through coughs and gasps. Another soldier, though, was already putting handcuffs on Marie.

"Marie Laflamme, you're under arrest for your role in the theft and trafficking of Azurian technology to the world at large." The soldier glanced over at Stanley, then at Blake's prone form, and continued. "You're also under suspicion of assisting in terrorist activity, with intent to destroy valuable old-world tech."

Stanley was furious with Marie for helping Blake, but he knew that she and the other residents of Daruna Abbey had taken the advanced equipment to help others, and not for nefarious purposes. After all, she'd helped save Nell's life, not to mention her eye.

"Wait," he said, finally able to stand up on his own, "there's something you guys don't realize. Marie and the others—they only took the—uh, stuff—"

"The tech?" offered the soldier.

"Yeah, the tech," said Stanley. "They only took it so they could help people—they used it to help my friends, *and* me, and they didn't ask for any money or anything. They just did it out of the goodness of their hearts, so—"

"We'll be sure to take your testimony into account," said the soldier. "If what you say is true, their punishment will be light."

"Thank you, Stanley," said Marie, as the soldier guided her outside.

"Stanley!"

Nell suddenly came charging into the room, followed closely by Alabaster.

"Nell!" Stanley exclaimed, as she threw her arms around him.

"Hey!" said one of the soldiers, "Who let *them* in here?"

"That'd be me," said a familiar, if completely unexpected voice. The owner of the voice came striding into the room, clad in a dashing blue naval uniform. His hair and beard were a bit more kempt than the last time Stanley had seen him, but there was no mistaking that face.

"Uncle Jack!" said Stanley, smiling hugely. "What are *you* doing here?"

"I was about to ask you the same thing," said Uncle Jack, "Names reversed, o'course. Are ye alright, lad?"

"Someone mind telling me who this *old guy* is?" said the soldier.

"Hey!" said Alabaster, "He may be old, but he's a heck of a lot older than *you!*"

There was a brief moment of silence as all eyes turned to him. "Uh—hold on, that sounded better in my head—"

"This is Jackson Warrington Lee," said Cromwell, "Current Regent Lord of the Rheddish Empire."

Stanley's jaw dropped.

"Yeah, well, with all due respect, sir, this is an ASC operation—"

"Which is takin' place in Imperial territory," Uncle Jack finished. "Don't forget *I'm* the one lettin' *you* lads come in here an' do yer thing, not th'other way 'round."

"We're the ASC," said the solder, "We don't *need* your permission to—"

"Stand down, mister!" barked Cromwell. "Azurian state policy works both ways—they don't interfere with us, we don't interfere with them. Jack—ah, that is, the *regent* here is doing us a big favour letting us come in fully-armed. Even so, we're still looking at about a year's worth of paperwork thanks to this operation."

"My word! Look at this place! It's—it's everything I'd hoped it would be!" Algernon had come wandering into the room, followed by Koko.

"Stanley! Cousin! You're alive! What a relief! How 'bout Uncle Jack, eh? Regent! Who knew?"

"How did you all get here?" asked Stanley.

"We came by rotorwing," answered Cromwell.

"Helicopters," added Uncle Jack.

"We flew all night to get here once we saw the state of the abbey," said Cromwell. "Completely leveled."

"No!" said Stanley.

"I'm afraid so," said Cromwell. "Salvage crews are working to remove anything worth saving, but the damage has been done. Fortunately, everyone managed to escape—aside from the abbot."

"He killed him," said Stanley, nodding with disgust at Blake's prone form.

"Indeed," said Cromwell. "And just who *is* this person? I did some digging, and Nigel Blake was reported missing in action—he was assigned to the Maelstrom sometime last year, and was never a resident of Daruna Abbey."

"It's him!" said Stanley to Uncle Jack, "The Masked Man, remember? It's the same guy!"

"That nutty sorcerer?" said Uncle Jack, "Really? As I live an' breathe—"

"He seemed to be using some sort of magic on the young man," said the first soldier.

"That wasn't magic," said Stanley. "Not quite—he's a Shadow Lord, and that was part of his power."

They all stared blankly at him.

"A … er, a lord of the Shadow Legion?" Stanley offered. "Said his name was Nerobius?"

"We'll get the particulars later, when you're debriefed," said Cromwell. "For now—"

He stopped mid-sentence, as the whole building had begun to shake. The lights suddenly turned red, and an alarm started to sound.

"The self-destruct sequence!" cried Stanley. He'd become so distracted that he'd forgotten all about it.

"Self-destruct sequence?" said Alabaster, "This adventure has everything!"

"Everybody out!" yelled one of the soldiers.

"Wait!" hollered Cromwell. "We're here to save this facility! We can*not* let it go critical! Computer—ah—disengage self-destruct!"

"Authorization-required," said the computer.

"I—this isn't Azurian tech," said Cromwell, "I don't have the access codes!"

"I think I do," said Stanley, looking around wildly for *The Chronicles of Frederic Whipple*. Spying the book on the floor nearby, he seized it and flipped madly through it 'till he found the page Marie had marked.

"It's got to be here somewhere," he said, running a finger down the page.

"You can do it, Stanley," said Nell, putting her hands on his shoulders. "Just stay calm."

"How much time?" said Cromwell.

"Unknown sir," said the first soldier. "Recommend we evacuate immediately."

The building's shaking grew worse, and a steadily-rising hum began to emanate from the huge machine. The alarm's pitch increased to an almost ear-splitting screech.

"Damn it—I'm ordering a general evacuation," yelled Cromwell. "Everybody outside, on the double. That includes you three," he said to Stanley, Alabaster, and Nell.

"Wait!" said Stanley as his finger fell on a line of text near the bottom of the page. He stood up, and in his loudest, clearest voice, yelled,

"Disengage self-destruct sequence, code blue seven-seven-seven-alpha!"

The building stopped shaking immediately, and the alarm ceased in mid-screech. The humming noise from the great metal pyramid died down and the lights returned to normal.

"Genetic-sequence-recognized," said the computer, "Self-destruct-sequence-cancelled. All-systems-returning-to-normal. Have-a-nice-day."

Everyone was frozen in place for a second or two, and then the room erupted with cheers and applause.

"Awesome!" roared Alabaster. "You're a super-hero! An action hero! You've covered all the bases!"

Nell hugged him tightly "That was amazing," she said, before kissing him on the cheek.

Stanley was more than a bit dazed as the solders came over to clap him on the back.

"That was some quick thinking," said Cromwell, shaking his hand. "You've just saved an important piece of old-world technology. The ASC won't forget that. Incidentally, I'd be interested to know why it recognized your 'genetic signature'."

"Me too," Stanley said truthfully. Cromwell saluted him, then gave a quick thumbs up.

"AACK!"

Stanley snapped his head around to see Alabaster struggling in the grip of

"Blake!" said Cromwell, "Or whoever you are—let him go!"

Blake, looking none the worse for having recently been shot, had his arm locked around Alabaster's neck, using him as a human shield. "Right," he said, backing away from the group, "I'll make sure to do that. Stanley, I know this must be getting a bit old, but I'm going to need you to start the self-destruct sequence again." The black shadow sword materialized in his hand and he held it up in front of Alabaster's face.

"Unhand me, you sinister fiend!" said Alabaster.

"No way," said the first soldier, "I plugged that guy!"

"An' we'll plug 'im again," said Uncle Jack, drawing a pistol form inside his coat, "'Less he releases that lad right *now*."

"Those feeble pea-shooters can't keep me down for long," sneered Blake.

"How about *swords?"* Nell demanded, thrusting her silvery-blue blade into Blake's side. She'd managed to sneak up beside him while he was distracted.

"EEEYYAAAAHH!" Blake shrieked, releasing Alabaster. "What in the world—"

He tried to say more, but his body went suddenly rigid, and his face went slack. He groaned, and seemed to deflate until, a few seconds later, all that was left of him was a dry, mummified skeleton.

"Gross!" said Alabaster, "He's a zombie!"

They all recoiled in horror as Blake swayed drunkenly for a few moments, then burst into bright blue flames, burning to ash in seconds.

"Revolting," Cromwell commented, "a reanimated corpse? The very idea! ... At least that poor man has finally been returned to his eternal rest."

"So—what was animating him?" asked one of the soldiers.

As if in answer to the question, an inky black cloud rose up from the pile of ashes and sooty clothes, taking on a vaguely humanoid form. The cracked mask floated up from out of Blake's coat pocket and hovered there in the cloud at head level.

"Hm," said the cloud's rumbling voice, "Stellarite sword. Never thought I'd see one of those again." The mask turned slowly from left to right. "Miserable interlopers—couldn't have shown up five minutes later, could you?" The voice sighed. "I know when I'm beaten—but this isn't over. My greatest servant has been unleashed on your world, and the others will be free, too, before long. I'll be seeing you all again. Soon."

The mask faded from view, and with a sudden high-pitched, almost metallic scream, the cloud surged forward and roiled tenebrously out of the room and down the hall as if propelled by a violent wind.

They all ducked reflexively, and then Cromwell bellowed,

"AFTER IT! DON'T LET IT GET AWAY!"

The soldiers sprang into action and tore off down the hall after the departing apparition. Stanley was a half-step behind them. The masked man, Blake, Nerobius—whatever the Shadow Lord was called, he wasn't going to let it escape.

He overtook the solders and flew out the door into the bright morning sunshine. He cast around wildly for any sign of the black cloud, and for an instant thought he saw a dark shape just inside the tree line, but then it was gone, one more shadow in the forest.

"He's gone," said Marie, who was seated on the ground under guard by the soldier who'd arrested her. "You'll never find him."

"We'll see about that," said Cromwell, walking up and scowling at her. "If he's here, we'll get him."

"He said he was going to Azuria," said Stanley.

"That's about the *stupidest* thing he could do," said Cromwell. "He does that, he's as good as ours. Even so, I'll be leaving a garrison here, too, just in case."

The rest of the company came filing out of the pyramid, the great metal doors closing behind them with weary finality. Stanley looked up at the towering blue crystal high above them, glinting in the sun. They'd saved it. But *what* had they saved, exactly, and why? What was it all for?

"What is it, really?" he asked Cromwell.

The governor followed his gaze. "To be honest, we don't have a clue—but if that *freak* wanted it destroyed, it's a pretty safe bet we should do what we can to protect it." He looked down at Stanley. "Part of our job is to secure and retrieve technology that's been illegally removed from Azuria. But that mandate also extends to any other advanced tech we find. I've been working on this case for years."

"So you're not really the governor?" said Stanley.

"Oh, I'm the governor," said Cromwell. "I came by that post all on my own. But I'm originally from Azuria. I left, oh, years and years ago over a … disagreement with my superiors at the ASC. I'm sort of an absentee agent, you might say. I worked with your uncle for a while, actually. I had no love for the old Rheddish Empire, that's for sure. If I'd known you were his nephew … well, you might not have had to be involved in this."

Cromwell's soldiers returned from their search of the area. "No sign of the—ah—Shadow Lord, sir," said one, saluting.

"Fair enough," said Cromwell. He turned to Stanley and the others. "We'll have the garrison conduct a proper sweep over the next few days, but I'm sure he's long gone. We're heading back to the L.Z. See you there."

He and his soldiers disappeared into the trees, Marie in tow.

"Well that was … um … something," said Alabaster as he and Nell came over to join Stanley.

Nell was looking pale and shaken.

"Are you okay?" said Stanley.

She nodded. "I'll be fine. Just a bit … freaked out. I've never done that before. Attacked someone like that. I threw up."

"I saw it!" said Alabaster.

"He wasn't a person," said Stanley. "He was just another zombie. Uh—with a Shadow Lord inside …"

"You can take solace in the fact that your heroic act saved me from certain doom," said Alabaster. "And now, like the noble Wookiees of Kashyyyk, I owe you my life, and will forever more be your devoted companion and protector!"

Nell ignored him.

"Ahem," said Alabaster, "Well, I'll just, ah, shut up and go over here."

"Can I have a hug?" Nell asked Stanley.

"Uh, yeah, sure," said Stanley, and she wrapped her arms around him, resting her head on his shoulder.

"What happened in there?" she asked after a moment. "Why did you go off all by yourself?"

Stanley thought about it. "I—I dunno, I just thought I could trust Blake, I guess. But then he tried to get me to help destroy the—well, the whole building."

"I wish I'd come with you. I wish I could have been here sooner."

"It's probably better that you weren't," said Stanley, remembering the Shadow Lord's threats. "You showed up at just the right time."

Nell's arms tightened around him.

"Alright you two, break it up, break it up!" said Algernon. "Heh! There's a time and a place, and all that!"

"Algernon," said Koko, "shut up."

Chapter 24

THE END ... OR THE BEGINNING?

They made their way through the belt of forest and back across the sloping fields towards the Saurian village. Parked across the river from the small settlement were three long, grey vehicles. As they drew closer, Stanley could see that they were aircraft. Each was about thirty feet long and resembled a helicopter with a pair of rotors, one on either side of its wide hull. A large, sectioned glass canopy occupied the front of each craft, and the letters A.S.C. were emblazoned on the side.

"So you *flew* all the way here?" Stanley asked Cromwell.

"Yes," said the governor. "When the wreckage of the Empress Hildegarde was discovered, I deemed it necessary to take action."

"If we'd flown here to begin with, the boat would never have been wrecked," Nell said darkly.

"That's a fair assessment," said Cromwell, "but you have to understand the politics and bureaucracy of Azuria. The top brass don't allow us to just fly around in rotorwings wherever we please. Much as I'd want to. I tried to get them to authorize the use of air travel from the beginning, but they wouldn't hear of it. It wasn't until the expedition was nearly wiped out that command agreed to intervene, damned fools, and by then you were completely off the radar. It's a terrible tragedy, the losses sustained on this mission. For what it's worth, I'm glad we found you."

"So are we, believe me," said Stanley. "You got here just in time."

"There's a word for this sort of thing," said Alabaster.

"Yeah," said Nell. "Deus ex machina."

"No," said Alabaster. "*Awesome.*"

It turned out that the surviving crew members of the Empress Hildegarde had, against all odds, made it back to Port Verdant after many harrowing adventures of their own. It was thanks in part to their report that Cromwell had managed to leverage the use of rotorwings to search for the rest of the expedition party.

Back at the village, a small crowd had gathered by the three vehicles. Temoc was there, talking to the village chief, and Ryuno was sitting in the open hatch of one of the aircraft, looking morose. He looked up when he saw Stanley and the others approaching, and hopped out, jogging over to meet them.

The young Marusai's left arm was in a sling and dressed with a wooden splint, a souvenir of his encounter with the Silent One. His nose was also still bandaged, but he made no complaint as he waved at them with his good hand.

"I was beginning to worry. Are you all safe? I saw Sister Marie from the abbey brought back here in shackles. What happened?"

"She was working for some bad people," said Cromwell. "Or rather, a bad *person*."

Ryuno looked thoughtful for a moment. "Father Blake—"

"He was a Shadow Lord," said Stanley.

"Shadow Lord," said Ryuno, tasting the words. "A *demon?"*

"We haven't written out the possibility," said Cromwell. "He wasn't human, that's for sure. We never knew the real Nigel Blake."

"I should have come with you," said Ryuno.

"It's okay," said Stanley. "Nell defeated him all by herself."

Nell went bright pink at this. "I didn't do it by myself. *You* helped," she said nudging Stanley, "and so did Alabaster, in his own way."

"*Sto-op!"* said Alabaster, "You're embarrassing me, it's too much!"

"And … this helped, too," said Nell, holding up the sword Ryuno had given her. "He called it something—Stellarite? Do you know what that means?"

"No, I've never heard that word before," said Ryuno, taking the sword back from her. "These swords have been in my family for … well, longer than anyone can remember, I'm sure."

"It shines when there are enemies about," said Alabaster, hunching his shoulders and wriggling his fingers.

"Alright people, listen up," said Cromwell. "This operation is officially over, but our work here is not. I'm going to need at least one squad of volunteers to stay here as a garrison until we can come back and properly fortify this area. We've seen firsthand today that there's a new terrorist faction in play. Our knowledge of them is essentially nil, but you all saw what one of them did to Daruna Abbey. *One* of them. Both it, and the one we met here today are still at large, and could be anywhere by now. For all we know they might be on their way back here with a bunch of their buddies, so I want us to be ready.

"Now, I need to head back to H.Q. to deliver my report, so Lieutenant Breaker's in charge—while I'm gone, her word is *law*, boys and girls." He indicated a soldier standing to his right, who took off her helmet and saluted smartly. Though she was dressed differently, Stanley recognized her as the leader of the soldiers who'd escorted them to Cromwell's mansion back in Port Verdant; her blonde ponytail and the scar across her nose were unmistakable.

Cromwell was still speaking. "Temoc, here, will be staying, too, to act as a liaison between our organization and the Saurian population. The rest of us will be returning to Port Verdant for the time being. I'm going to need to ask some of you some questions concerning the past couple of weeks, so I'll ask our civilian companions to board the Falcon with me when we ship out in a few minutes. You all know what you have to do, so get it done. I've got a long flight ahead of me, and I want to get under way."

Cromwell marched up to the closest rotorwing and barked a series of orders at the pilots, who scrambled aboard to start their pre-flight checks.

"Hass Stanley."

Stanley turned around to see Temoc standing before him. He hadn't seen much of the Saurian during their stay at Daruna Abbey. He seemed to have recovered nicely from his injuries.

He reached out and shook Stanley's hand. "I wanted to bid you farewell before you took to the skies," he said. "You have proven yourself a capable warrior, and I thank you for your assistance in the Xol'tec city, and against the Shio-Kahn. I owe you my life, and my great claws, and I will not forget this debt of honour."

"Oh," said Stanley, a bit taken aback, "Well—you're welcome, definitely. I mean, you'd have done the same for me. We wouldn't have made it far on this trip without you."

Temoc grinned in his frighteningly Saurian way. "You are a man of humble temperament and great honour, I think. It is my hope that you will always act nobly, and with honour, and use your abilities for the betterment of all—unlike Blake, the betrayer."

"I will," said Stanley, though he felt a slight hitch in his chest at the mention of his 'abilities'.

"Noble lady," said Temoc, giving Nell a small bow, "May your hatchlings be great warriors, and may you always fight with your mate at your side."

"Uh," said Nell, "Er—thank you, Temoc, that's—very kind of you."

"The people here will be grieved to see you depart," said Temoc, "but I will explain to them the way of things. In turn I hope they will teach *me*—it appears that I may not be Oltonnac, after all. Farewell, my friends." He turned and rejoined the crowd of Saurians gathered by the bridge.

"What was that all about?" said Alabaster.

"Oltonnac Saurians typically have green skin," said Koko, who had been standing with Algernon nearby.

"No, I mean why didn't he acknowledge *me* as a humble and honourable warrior? I was standing right here!"

"He must have been looking the other way all those times you fought monsters singlehandedly and without thought for your own safety," said Nell.

"Oh," said Alabaster. "Well, I guess that makes—*hey!*"

"Don't feel bad, Albert," said Algernon. "He wasn't trying to be rude—it's just that most Saurian warriors don't speak directly to those who haven't proven themselves in battle. It's an older cultural norm among the Saurians, and is falling out of favour as the tribes have more and more contact with foreigners. It's unusual that Temoc spoke to any of us at all, actually. All things considered, he's probably the most progressive Saurian you could ever hope to meet!"

"That's … actually quite interesting," said Koko, sounding mildly impressed.

"I thought so too," said Algernon, "and that's why I'll be staying here. At least for the time being."

"What?" said Stanley.

"I think archaeology might be a tad out of my league," said Algernon. "Now, *anthropology*, that's where the action is! Exotic locales, fascinating people, travel, adventure—that's the life for me!"

"You said the same thing about archaeology," said Koko.

"Ahem," said Algernon, "Yes, well, at least now I can be sure that my work won't lead me into situations where I'm liable to be brutally sacrificed by the people I'm studying. I'm sure my findings will be groundbreaking back home!"

"Can you still technically be an anthropologist if you're studying Saurians?" said Alabaster.

"Probably," said Algernon. "If not, I'll be the world's first *xeno*-anthropologist! Cheerio, Cousin Stanley, and Nell, and you too, Albert. Next time you see me, maybe I'll be on the cover of National Geographic!" he doffed his pith helmet and meandered over to butt into a conversation between Temoc and the Saurian chief.

"Are you staying too, Koko?" asked Stanley.

Koko sighed. "Yes—as one who saved Algernon's life, I need to remain with him until I am convinced that he can safely survive on his own. It's the way of my people."

"Really?" said Alabaster, "*That's* why you're always hanging out with him?"

Koko nodded. "Perhaps we could part company if he were to return home … maybe even if he stays here. Either way, I'll have to leave him at some point—I've been asked to return to my homeland in Angoria to act as an emissary. Er, excuse me—Algernon seems to have fallen in the river. I wish you a safe journey."

"Bye, Koko," said Nell, as he ambled off to help Algernon.

Uncle Jack, who had been talking with Cromwell, approached them and said, "Alright mates, Charlie tells me he's rarin' to go, so whatt'ya say we all hop aboard? We've got a long flight ahead of us."

"Omigosh!" said Nell, "Patty!"

"Everyone mount up," said Cromwell. "Pilots! Get those engines going!"

"Mr. Cromwell—er—Governor?" said Nell.

Cromwell glared down at her. "Damn fine work there, dealing with that—well, whatever it was. I know it can't have been easy. What can I do for you?"

"Er," said Nell, "Uh, thank you. There's—someone we need to see before we leave—"

"How long?" said Cromwell.

"Maybe half an hour?" said Nell, looking over her shoulder at the small stone building in the distance.

"No. We're leaving now—anyone not on board in the next five minutes is staying behind."

"But—"

"This isn't some weekend trip to Grandma's," said Cromwell. "I've got a schedule to keep. Make your choice."

Nell's face fell. "We said we'd go back to see her."

"If we could," said Alabaster.

Seeing the downcast look on Nell's face made Stanley feel terrible, and the idea of leaving Patty all alone in the underworld didn't help, either, even if she *was* a computer.

A computer?

"Wait!" said Stanley, "You said your mission was to look for technology, right? Well we know where there's some really—uh—*good* technology."

Cromwell raised an eyebrow. "Where?"

"It's best if we show you," said Stanley.

Cromwell rolled his eyes. "Alright, alright, I guess a half-hour delay won't kill us. Lieutenant Breaker!" he called. "You're with me. Let's go."

A short time later, Stanley, Nell, Alabaster, Cromwell, and Lieutenant Breaker stepped off the elevator and back into Sub-Sphere Three. The governor and lieutenant walked along in a sort of trance, gaping at even this small corner of the vast underground city.

They approached the train platform, where Patty was still waiting patiently, just as they'd left her.

"Nell!" Patty exclaimed as they drew closer, "Stanley! Alabaster! You're back! I'm so glad. Do you want to go for a ride?"

"My god," said Cromwell.

"Oh, I'm sorry, Patty—no," said Nell. "I mean, it's not that we don't want to, but—we have to go. We came to say goodbye."

"Oh," said Patty, "Well—that's okay. You came back just like you said you would. So I'm happy. Goodbye, Nell. And Stanley, and Alabaster. I'll miss you."

Nell turned away. She looked like she was going to cry.

"This is unbelievable," said Cromwell. "This machine—it's sentient. How old is this place?"

"It's not Azurian, that's for sure," said Lieutenant Breaker. "It's beyond anything we've got, I can tell just by looking at it."

"Can you do anything for her?" asked Stanley.

"She's so lonely," said Nell, her voice wavering, "and she's been down here for so long. Just … come and talk to her sometimes, okay?"

"I think I can do better than that," said Lieutenant Breaker. "Patty?"

"Hello," said Patty, "What's your name?"

"Er … Jenna—Jenna Breaker."

"It's very nice to meet you," said Patty. "You're so pretty! You remind me of Nell."

"Thank you, it's nice to meet you, too," said Lieutenant Breaker, suppressing a smile. "Patty—how would you like to go outside?"

"Outside?" echoed Patty, "You mean *really* outside? Up to the surface?"

"Yeah."

"That would be … I'd love to!" said Patty. "I've never been outside."

"Can you really do that?" asked Nell.

"An old-world sentient computer?" said Breaker, "One that still runs? Oh yeah. We'll dig her out of here if that's what it takes. Although I don't think it'll come to that. Patty?"

"Yes?"

"I've got to head back up now, but I'll be back later on this afternoon, okay? Maybe we can have a little talk then?"

"I can't wait!" said Patty.

"Please be nice to her," Nell said quietly to Lieutenant Breaker. "I know you see her as just another piece of—technology, but—"

"You have my word," said Breaker. "And don't worry—I can tell she's more than just some simple machine. Here—"

She pulled a small white card out of her pocket and handed it to Nell. On it were three capital letters:

R.E.M.

Beneath the letters was a simple drawing of two hands clasped in friendship: one human, the other, robotic.

"That stands for the Robot Equality Movement," explained Breaker. "It's an organization advocating the rights of sentient A.I.s everywhere. If you ever come to Azuria, you'll have a friend in the R.E.M."

"Wow," said Nell, "Uh—thanks."

"It's dumb, I know," said Breaker a bit embarrassedly. "I came up with that as sort of a slogan, but it doesn't even really rhyme."

"Lieutenant," barked Cromwell, who was waiting by the elevator, "Save the extracurricular activities 'till you're off duty. We gotta move."

"Sir," said Breaker.

"Goodbye again, Nell," called Patty. "And Stanley, and Alabaster!"

"Bye Patty," said Stanley, waving at the ancient monorail train.

"Bye bye!" said Alabaster.

"Goodbye, Patty," said Nell. "Thank you so much for helping us. I'll never forget you."

"I'll never forget you, either," said Patty.

The monorail car's lights flashed twice, and then turned off.

★ ★ ★

The rotorwing's engines roared to life, its propellers spinning faster and faster until they were a barely-visible blur.

"Mount up," Cromwell yelled over the din of the engines. "Next stop is Port Verdant."

Stanley, Alabaster, and Nell clambered up the short ladder to the left of the rotorwing's hatch. Cromwell followed, pulled the hatch closed, and stuck his head into the cockpit.

"*Lift off!"* he barked at the pilots. The engines began to roar louder.

The rotorwing's cabin wasn't exactly spacious, but there was room for ten passengers, five on either side. Uncle Jack and Ryuno were already buckled into their seats, as were two of Cromwell's soldiers.

"Take your seats and strap in," said Cromwell.

Stanley, Alabaster, and Nell sat down in a line beside Uncle Jack.

"All set?" the old man asked.

"Yeah, I think so," said Stanley. He looked out the window, across the valley, and saw the great blue crystal floating there in the distance. Gone was the sense of urgency that it once invoked in him; now he just felt a sense of peace and completion.

"What are you looking at?" asked Nell.

"The crystal," said Stanley.

Nell followed his gaze. "D'you think you'll keep dreaming about it?"

Stanley *hmmd.* "Probably not—it just, I dunno … kind of feels like we've done what we needed to do, y'know?"

"Prepare for liftoff," said one of the pilots. Half a second later, the rotorwing gave a sudden and jarring lurch as it took off with improbable speed.

"Gaah!" said Alabaster. "AHHGAGAHHHH!!!!"

Stanley felt himself being squashed back into his seat, while his stomach seemed to have been left back on the ground.

Within seconds, the ground was far below them; the valley of Quetzal'Khan, now a small disc of green surrounded by its ring of mountains, was in turn encircled by a great dark chasm. There was no way anyone could ever make it in or out on foot. Stanley looked for Patty's monorail track, but couldn't see it. To the north was the mighty Armadon River, now a massive, raging torrent thirty miles wide, emptying into the chasm in a towering, furious waterfall.

Stanley's mind boggled at what would have happened had they succeeded in making it this far by boat. "Wow," he said half under his breath, "we had no idea what we were getting into."

"No indeed," said Cromwell. "Hopefully this will help convince the government of Azuria that some serious changes in policy are needed. On that note," he said, looking squarely at Stanley, "I'd like to ask you all some questions about the past couple of weeks."

⋆ ⋆ ⋆

The flight north from the Lost City was exceptionally long. Cromwell's 'question' session quickly evolved into an epic retelling of the ill-fated expedition into the heart of the Green Continent. Stanley, Alabaster, Nell, and Ryuno took turns describing each harrowing phase of their adventures, while Cromwell and Uncle Jack listened with stunned looks on their faces, and Cromwell's soldiers took page after page of notes.

Stanley left out the parts detailing his shadow powers.

When the tale finally came to an end (just before the confrontation at the Moon-Killer), they were all silent for a time, and then Cromwell cleared his throat.

"I think we may have the beginnings of a very serious problem here."

"Aye," said Uncle Jack.

"No!" said Alabaster, "We're out of fuel, aren't we? We're gonna crash, *aren't we?* We're gonna CRAAAASH!"

Cromwell's eyes narrowed, as if he were seriously considering flinging open the hatch and heaving Alabaster out into the wild blue yonder. "Please don't interrupt me, son. I mean '*we*' as in humanity, the world at large. This—faction—this *'Shadow Legion'* ... sounds like some kind of covert ops unit. We really don't know anything about it. That's the first thing that worries me. The second is that word—*legion*. One of these things singlehandedly leveled a very big and very solid stone building. I'd hate to see what an entire legion could do."

"We've met that scurvy dog with the mask before," said Uncle Jack. "I thought he was just some nutty magician, but—Charlie, he had control o' Rhedland for a while, there."

Cromwell nodded. "So that was the same one then? You're sure?"

"Definitely," said Stanley. "He said his name's Nerobius ... he never told us his name before, but I know it's him. He—" Stanley paused. "He said he had 'many names' and he talked about ... well, Elves, Dwarves, and Orcs ..."

"What about Balrogs?" said Alabaster.

"Uh, no," said Stanley.

"Whewf!"

"Maybe he was just kidding," said Cromwell.

"There's magic in this world, no doubt about it," said Uncle Jack, "but I've never heard of Elves an' all that stuff—'least, not outside o' stories an' fairy tales."

"Yeah, but you'd never heard of shadow—er, legion ... *things*, either," Alabaster pointed out.

"That creep said something about freeing 'the others'—which I also don't like," said Cromwell. "If there's more of these things imprisoned somewhere, we need to make sure they stay that way."

"In that case, I'd say we've got our work cut out fer us," said Uncle Jack. "When I get back to Ethelia, I'll get the ball rollin' an' see what we can come up with. 'E was in control o' the whole Empire for a while there, 'e must've left some clues behind. What about you, Charlie? Think ye can convince those stubborn ol' coots runnin' Azuria that they need to take some real action here?"

"Let's hope so," said Cromwell. "Blake—er, Nerobius said that that's his next stop. And I seriously doubt we've seen the last of him."

⋆ ⋆ ⋆

The hours wore on as the Falcon soared north over the Verdurian jungle, following the winding blue ribbon that was the Armadon far below. The talk eventually turned to what was next for Stanley and his friends.

"I figure it's best if we get the three of yeh home as soon as possible," said Uncle Jack.

"Home?" said Stanley, "but—I thought we could … I dunno, stay and help you."

"I don't think so," said Cromwell. "I know you've been through a lot, but you're not quite the type of troops we're looking for. Not yet, anyway."

"This ain't yer fight, lad," said Uncle Jack, "if it's a fight at all. I'm gonna get yeh home, and that's fer the best. Trust me."

Stanley flopped back in his seat. Uncle Jack did have a point. It was purely by accident that they'd even come back to Terra at all—and it hadn't been a safe trip, not by a long shot.

He wanted to do something—*anything* to stop whatever nefarious plans the Masked Man—or rather, *Nerobius*—was hatching.

But he also wanted to go home. It felt like months since he'd had a good night's sleep in his own bed. Now that the adventure, the search for the Lost City was done, he found that he just felt … tired.

Uncle Jack was right. Whatever wickedness was afoot, Stanley really had no part in fighting it. Even if this *were* his world, which it wasn't, what could he do?

"When we get to Port Verdant, we'll take the Ogopogo all the way back, just like we did in June," said Uncle Jack. "Might take a bit've explainin', what with the lot've ya suddenly showin' up in Westport, but—"

"Why don't we just go back the way we got here?" said Alabaster. Nell and Stanley looked at him.

"Er," said Uncle Jack, "Huh. That there's a good point, Alabaster. How *did* ya get here?"

Stanley wondered if this was the best time to be discussing this, but Cromwell didn't seem the slightest bit fazed by the increasingly odd nature of the conversation.

"Same way as before, pretty much," said Alabaster. "A weird tunnel. This one was through the jungle, though—we came out in this clearing with a bunch of big red crystal chunks—"

"We flew over that on our way to the abbey," remarked Cromwell. "We can drop you there, if you want."

"But the tunnel was gone after we came through," Stanley pointed out.

"Well, we'll just take a look-see anyway," said Uncle Jack.

★ ★ ★

The hours rolled past, and the sun began to sink towards the distant, endless expanse of verdant jungle to the west. At some point Stanley had fallen asleep, and woke with a start as one of the pilots announced,

"Approaching destination. Brace for landing."

"Take us down nice and easy," Cromwell ordered.

The Falcon's descent was neither nice nor easy, as the aircraft made a series of lurching, gut-wrenching drops, before finally touching down with a jarring *thud*.

"Hoo," breathed Uncle Jack, who was looking very green, "Ya spend yer whole life at sea, facin' storms, monsters, an' worse—but then they toss ya into an airship an' next thing ya know yer a lubber all over again! No offense, Charlie, but I'll take a fifty-foot wave over *this* ride any day."

"You just need to get used to it," said Cromwell, gracing them all with a rare half-smile. "Flight is the only way to travel. Alright—all out who's getting out. Pilots—keep those engines hot."

They all unbuckled their harnesses and followed Cromwell out the hatch, and into a familiar clearing littered with large chunks of bright red crystal. The crystals seemed to glow in the light of the late afternoon sun.

"Ah, the place where it all began," said Alabaster.

Stanley looked around at the crystals, and at the large stone building rising out of the trees on the eastern side of the clearing. It seemed like an age had passed since they'd found their way here from the museum—almost as if it had been another life.

"I can't believe we're back here," said Nell. She looked up at the blazing orange sky, which was already fading to purple in the east. Stanley glanced sideways at her, so she wouldn't think he was staring. The crescent-shaped scar around her left eye was still very vivid—it was already difficult to remember what she'd looked like without it. Her eyes, one green, one as red as the crystals here in the clearing, suddenly met his, and he quickly looked away, missing her smile by milliseconds.

"What a waste," said Cromwell, scowling down at the chunks of crystal. "Would've been nice to see this thing back before it got wrecked."

"Do you know what it was?" asked Stanley.

"I can make a pretty good guess. It was clearly another Moon-Killer—probably the inside of this pyramid here was just like the one down south, once. We checked it out, though—nothing of value left in there anymore. This thing fell a long, long time ago, and the Saurians've had plenty of time to trash the site."

"Odd that they would not take the crystals," said Ryuno.

"They're probably sacred," said Cromwell, "or cursed, or some such lunacy."

Uncle Jack suddenly piped up, "'Ere—what's this?" They all watched him cross the clearing and hunker down by the base of the pyramid. He was looking intently into a dark patch of foliage. The group gathered around to see what had caught his attention. "Anybody lose a necklace?"

He held up a small heart-shaped pendant on a fine gold chain.

"Oh!" exclaimed Nell, "Omigosh! That's mine!"

Uncle Jack handed her the pendant. Aside from a bit of grime, it didn't look the worse for its time sitting on the jungle floor.

"I'd forgotten all about it," she said, wiping the heart clean. "It must have fallen off right when we came through—"

"Meanin' that the three of yeh must've come through right here," said Uncle Jack, pushing aside a few large, wide leaves, to reveal what looked like a dark hole.

Stanley's jaw dropped. He sprang forward and almost flung himself to the ground beside Uncle Jack to get a better look. The hole opened up onto a dark, faintly green tunnel that extended off into the distance. It was the same tunnel through which they'd come from the museum—it had to be.

"But how?" said Alabaster. "We tore this place apart looking for the way back! And now it's here? What's the deal?"

"Maybe it's not always open," said Stanley, trying in vain to catch a glimpse of the tunnel's end.

"If it isn't, we should probably get through while we still can," said Nell.

"Aye, ye could be right, lassie," said Uncle Jack. He stood up and turned to Cromwell, who didn't seem at all surprised to be looking at a mysterious tunnel to another world. "Charlie," he said, reaching out to shake the governor's hand, "looks like this is where we part ways—fer now."

Cromwell returned the handshake and nodded. "It's been good to see you, old friend, if only briefly. You'll be back before long, I assume?"

"Aye," said Uncle Jack. "We got a lotta work to do. Good luck in Azuria, mate. I'll spread the word to the old crew, see if we can get the ball rollin' back in Rhedland."

From somewhere off in the distance, a high-pitched howling shriek rang out through the jungle.

"Saurians," muttered Cromwell. "The Xol'tecs probably know we're here. If we're done, I'd suggest we go our separate ways—*before* they get here, preferably."

"Wait," said Ryuno, who had been hovering patiently close by. "I—Nell, I wanted to ask you something."

Stanley made a face.

"You had a ten-hour flight to ask anything you wanted," snapped Cromwell.

"Forgive me," said Ryuno. "Nell, I—I've been asked to return to my home—to Narrone, to see if anyone there can help us in the times to come. It will not be an easy journey, but … I have to ask, will you come with me?"

Stanley was aghast. How could Ryuno honestly be asking this, especially *now*. Later, given some time to think and reflect, Stanley would come up with all sorts of perfect, indignant responses to Ryuno's question … but that would be later.

Nell, though, *did* have an answer. "No, Ryuno," she said flatly. "I'm sorry. I don't know exactly who it is you want me to be, but I'm not her. You've taught me a lot and I'm thankful for that, but I have to go now. I need to go home."

Ryuno nodded. "I thought that would be your decision, and I understand. Please—I would like you to have this." He presented the short sword that she'd recently returned to him. Nell looked down at the weapon.

"Oh—Ryuno, I can't. That's a family heirloom—"

"—of which you are now the master," Ryuno finished. "I know of your victory back at the temple. This sword is not just a gift—you've earned it."

Nell glanced at Stanley for a split second, then accepted the sword. "Thank you," she said, "I'll take good care of it."

Ryuno nodded, then stood there dumbly for a few seconds, as if there was something more he wanted to say.

"Let's go, Marusai," barked Cromwell, "We take off in one minute, whether you're on board or not."

Ryuno suddenly took hold of Nell's hand, leaned forward, and lightly kissed it before anyone knew what was happening. "I hope we will meet again someday," he said, locking eyes with her for a moment. He then released her hand and backed away towards the Falcon. "Farewell, all of you," he said, raising his good hand. "Ours was a difficult journey at times, but I feel honoured and fortunate to have met you. I hope we, too can meet again—under calmer circumstances."

He climbed back aboard the Falcon, followed by Cromwell, who saluted briskly, and then slammed the hatch shut behind him. Over the din of the rotorwing's engines, another shrieking howl rang out, this time much closer than before.

The Xol'tecs were closing in.

"That's our cue, mates," said Uncle Jack. "C'mon, if this tunnel's our ticket outta here, let's take it. Can't expect Charlie and his crew to wait forever, eh?"

"Sounds good to me," said Alabaster, dropping onto all fours and disappearing into the underbrush.

Nell took a few deep breaths, then followed Alabaster.

Stanley looked up at Uncle Jack.

"In ya go, lad," said the old man. "I'll be right behind ya."

Stanley nodded, then plunged into the green, leafy tunnel.

It was dark in here, and soundless, which was a bit odd, considering that they were in the middle of a jungle. Stanley reflected, though, that maybe they were already 'out'.

After a few minutes of crawling, he saw a small point of light ahead, which grew bigger and bigger, until he could see the jungle again. This jungle, of course, was very different from the one he'd just left. For one thing, it was indoors.

Stanley came scrambling out of the foliage and into the early afternoon sunlight, which was pouring in through the skylights in the roof of the East Stodgerton Museum of Natural History. He was back.

"Upsy-daisy," said Alabaster, as he and Nell swooped in on either side and helped him to his feet.

He stood there, gaping at their surroundings, at the walls, the ceiling, the fake jungle all around them, and the boardwalk pathway that led through it. All was just as it had been the day they'd left.

There was a rustling in the bushes, and Uncle Jack's white-haired head came into view. "Ah," he said, picking himself up and dusting himself off. "Well, looks like we've made it, eh? Er—where are we, exactly?"

"My dad's museum," said Stanley.

"Huh!" said Uncle Jack. "Well, that's a surprise." He turned around and peered back into the bushes. "Looks like I'll need to head back home if I want to get back to Rhedland."

Since no one seemed to be around in this part of the building, they made their way back to the main lobby. The lobby was also deserted, but presently there came the sound of approaching voices from a pair of double doors at the back of the room. The doors burst open, and Stanley's classmates poured through, chattering happily about all they'd seen in the museum that day.

At the head of the procession, walking backwards, was Mr. Brambles, who was in the middle of wrapping up the tour. Beside him trudged a sullen-looking Mrs. Drabdale, and Mr. Steele, who was hanging on Mr. Brambles' every word.

"—And we can all agree that in a few million years, apes will rule the Earth," he finished. There was a brief pause, and then the entire class burst into thunderous applause.

"Sounds like the tour went pretty well," Stanley commented. He felt vaguely sorry he'd missed it.

"Not much point in mentioning that we've been gone for like, three weeks, eh?" said Alabaster.

"I think we know the drill by now," said Nell with a sigh.

Uncle Jack just smiled.

Just then, a sound like the shrill cry of a bird of prey tore through the lobby.

"YOU!"

Mrs. Drabdale had noticed them, and was pointing accusingly in their direction.

"Body snatcher!" cried Alabaster, pretending to flee.

"WHERE-HAVE-YOU-BEEN?" shrieked Mrs. Drabdale, "I've been combing this place looking for you since this morning, after expressly telling you *not* to wander off! I should have *known* you two would be up to some shenanigans the minute I turned my back," she seethed at Stanley and Alabaster, "And you," she moaned, "Prunella! To say that I am absolutely *shocked* at your … why, I never—there just aren't any *words* for how utterly flabbergasted I am! Imagine, trying to make off with museum property!"

Nell looked down at the sword she was holding. "What, this?" she said, holding the weapon up, "Er, no, this is actually—"

"I don't want to *hear* it!" Mrs. Drabdale bawled. "You'll be expelled for this, mark my words—all three of you! Expelled! And the police will be involved, oh yes—"

"Begging your pardon," Mr. Brambles interrupted, "but that's not ours."

"Uh?" said Mrs. Drabdale, "It's not?"

"This is the Museum of Natural History," said Mr. Brambles. "Swords don't exactly grow on trees, do they? Heh!"

While Mr. Brambles chuckled merrily at his own joke, Uncle Jack took a step forward.

"My apologies, ma'am," he said, doffing his hat to Mrs. Drabdale, "That's actually *my* sword." Nell looked at him, then handed it to him wordlessly. "I carry it around for—ah—religious reasons."

"Oh!" said Mrs. Drabdale, "I had no idea, Mr.—?"

"Lee," said Uncle Jack. "Jackson Lee. You can call me Jack, of course."

"Well—it's a pleasure to meet you, Mr. Lee—er, Jack," said Mrs. Drabdale, with what was probably her version of a coy smile.

Stanley exchanged a horrified glance with Nell and Alabaster. This wasn't really happening, was it?

"Jack!" cried Mr. Brambles, "What on *earth* are you doing here? What a surprise! What a treat!"

"You two know each other?" said Mrs. Drabdale.

"Jack is my uncle-in-law," said Mr. Brambles proudly.

"And Stanley's my great-nephew," said Uncle Jack, patting Stanley on the shoulder. Stanley's face was a mask of revulsion as Mrs. Drabdale batted her eyelashes at Uncle Jack.

"I had no idea Stanley had such a charming relative," she said.

Alabaster gagged audibly.

Mr. Steele, who was looking more and more uncomfortable, quietly led the rest of the class outside to the waiting school bus. Some of Stanley's classmates were suddenly looking ill.

"Oh," said Mrs. Drabdale, "I guess I'd better be going now. Er, if you're in town for a few days, Jack, I wonder if you wouldn't mind joining me for coffee some evening?"

Stanley was paralyzed with horror. This had to be a nightmare.

"He'll be staying at Casa Brambles!" said Stanley's father, throwing a chummy arm around Uncle Jack.

"Guess that answers that," said Uncle Jack. "I do believe I'll take you up on your offer, Mrs.--?"

"Drabdale," said Mrs. Drabdale, "Rowena Drabdale. I'll be in touch!"

She turned and almost skipped over to the big double doors at the front of the museum. She then looked over her shoulder, giving Uncle Jack a little wave with her fingertips before floating out the door.

"That went well," said Mr. Brambles.

Stanley could do little more than stare ahead blankly, a stunned look on his face.

"She seems pretty nice," said Uncle Jack. "Little high-strung, but nice. I thought you lads'd said she was some rampaging devil-woman!"

Stanley simply could not speak. Neither could Nell or Alabaster, it seemed.

"Come on," said Mr. Brambles, "What say we call it a day? I'll give you all a ride home. Er, as soon as Rose comes to pick me up."

★ ★ ★

Stanley was quiet all the way home, and when they finally arrived back at the red brick house on Bubbletree Lane (after dropping off Nell and Alabaster), the first thing he did was give his mother and father the biggest hug he could muster.

"I'm really glad to see you guys," he said.

"Aww, well we're glad to see you too, son," said Mr. Brambles, hugging him back. "Why wouldn't we be?"

"Don't tell me you missed your dear old mom and dad this much after one day," said Mrs. Brambles, sounding amused.

"It seems like a lot longer than that," said Stanley.

Uncle Jack clapped him on the shoulder, and Stanley released his parents before following the old man up the steps to the front door.

"Such a sensitive little guy," said Mrs. Brambles fondly, brushing a tear from her eye.

★ ★ ★

That night, Stanley slept in great peace and contentment, delighted at being back in his own bed, in his own house, with his family close by. For the first time in what felt like years, he did not dream of the great blue crystal floating above the jungle a world away.

He did have another dream, though, just before dawn; a terrible nightmare that he wouldn't remember in the morning. A terrible nightmare that he'd had many times before.

You and I are one ...

The End

Printed in the United States
By Bookmasters